THINE ENEMY

Last autumn Philip Gibbs went to six German cities, wandered among the ruins, saw how many people were living in basements, cellars, air-raid shelters, and over-crowded lodgings, went into the Russian sector of Berlin, and talked with refugees who had fled in terror from the Russians, and met all manner of folk now living under American occupation in Bavaria.

Out of this experience and the stories he heard and the life he saw he has written this novel which is revealing in its dramatic narrative of what happened, and is now happening, in the troubled soul of the German people. At the present time of history in Western Europe with its constant menace to peace it is important that we should know and understand.

Utterly fair as usual Sir Philip does not gloss over German cruelties—the horror of the concentration camps—but shows how, as always in war, the innocent suffer for the guilty—the peasants evicted from their homesteads, the children, the young mothers, the very old people, the secret rebels against Hitlerism, of whom there were many, and the men in high position, like von Hassell and his confederates, who tried to kill Hitler and were executed by him or forced, like Rommel, to commit suicide.

All this comes out in the theme of this powerful and remarkable novel. In it also are the qualities of compassion, pity for human agony, hatred of cruelty, and sympathy for young people of all nations which readers have observed in the work of Philip Gibbs.

It is a courageous novel and a tragic one, and it should be read by all who realize that if Western Germany were to go the way of Soviet Russia then Europe would be lost, and that our own future depends not a little upon our wise handling of the German problem. But there is no word of propaganda here. It is a novel with a tragic human story about those who were our enemies, suffering terrible punishment for the wickedness of their leaders and the crimes of many brutal men debauched by a ruthless and pagan creed.

THINE ENEMY

"If thine enemy be hungry, give him to eat; if he thirst give him to drink. For doing this thou shalt heap coals of fire upon his head."

BRITISH RED CROSS LIBRARY

Members of the Red Cross Library Service visit the wards each week for the distribution, also the return of books by patients.

This book has been obtained for your entertainment and interest. You are expected to take good care of it, and return it to a member of the Red Cross Library Service, or to the Sister-in-Charge of the ward before you leave hospital.

As this book is given to you on loan, you must not pass it on to anyone as you are held responsible for its return; the book is hospital property and under no condition must it be taken away by the patient or others.

Your help and co-operation are asked for and expected, and other patients who will wish to read this book will appreciate your consideration of their interest.

CHAPTER I

HILDE MENZEL felt very cold in her flat in Königsberg. It was cold inside these rooms because the electricity had been cut off and it was difficult to get wood for the stove. If she hadn't had two small children and a six-months-old baby she might have gone out between the air raids and picked up a bit from the heaps of charred timber in the ruins. Her father-in-law had promised to bring in some logs this afternoon but he was very late.

She was hungry and that made her body cold. She had divided a few biscuits—all she dared to spare—between Hans and Trudel, only eating two herself. Trudel had screamed because she wanted more. The children's bodies had lost their plumpness. The skin was tight over their ribs.

Outside it was freezing hard. The snow lay white on the broken roofs of skeleton houses which she could see through the windows. The castle walls above them were blotted out by the falling flakes.

But it was not the coldness of her body which mattered. It was the coldness of the fear inside her. The Russians were smashing their way through East Prussia. The Horror was coming close. Her father-in-law had been talking to some of the officers in the garrison. They were preparing for a siege. All the younger women had been ordered to dig trenches, but that was only a proof that the city was doomed. A high officer who had ordered the shooting of any civilian who tried to escape from Königsberg—several had been shot—had committed suicide. Everybody now was panic-stricken. Hilde had seen this fear creeping into the eyes of her friends—once laughing girls exulting in the news of Hitler's victories, wearing frocks from Paris after the surrender of France, dancing in night clubs with officers from Poland. She had seen this fear even in the eyes of elderly women like her aunt, Frau von Grottenbach, who had always said that Hitler was a madman who would drag Germany down to ruin and had remained cold and cynical however good the news had been. Now they were all terror-stricken like Hilde herself who once had been brave and fond of laughter, hiding her tears when Peter went back to the front after his last leave before the baby was born.

She was frozen with this fear which was terribly infectious, though she tried to hide it from the children. But this afternoon Hans, who noticed everything with his big blue eyes, asked her why she looked at him in such a funny way. "You look frightened," he told her. "Is it because of the air raids? Do you think we're going to be killed?"

That was before she had taken the children into the shelter for the night. The baby was sleeping in the cradle after she had fed him from her breast. Now she had come up to this room again in case her father-in-law came with the wood and might bring the latest news about the Russian advance.

The wireless didn't work any more because of the cut in electricity. In any case the wireless news had always been a pack of lies. Her father-in-law had refused to listen to it. But even from that the frightful truth had crept through lately by the casual mention of place names which made people's hair rise in horror. Had they got as far as that? Good God, that meant . . . It was covered up by the false heroics of Dr. Goebbels and his liars deceiving no one in Königsberg who knew now that the horror was closing upon them. "Our glorious armies stand firm, joyfully carrying out the Führer's orders never to yield a foot of ground. . . ." "They hold a line of impregnable strength. . . ." "Yesterday there was heavy fighting in the neighbourhood of . . ." Great God! Had the Russians got as far as that?

From the wounded streaming back, and from stragglers cut off from their units, and from officers sent back to Königsberg with urgent orders, it was possible to know what was happening or to get a glimpse of what was happening through a mist of blood and fury and chaos on what was called the Front.

It was no longer a front according to Hilde's father-in-law, Karl Menzel, Professor of Philosophy at Königsberg University until dismissed for criticizing the writings of Alfred Rosenberg. He had been an Intelligence officer during the First World War until taken prisoner by the English in Flanders. He still knew the meaning of war and defeat. The Russians, he said, were thrusting wedges into the German line by well-timed hammer-strokes and their overwhelming man-power reckless of life. They were surrounding masses of demoralized and exhausted men who by Hitler's orders were forbidden to retreat to shorter and straighter lines. They were being 'liquidated' in groups.

Hilde's husband, Peter Menzel, was out there somewhere. Probably he was dead. In a kind of dream one night she had seen him dead on the frozen snow staring up to the stars. She had screamed out at this vision or dream, waking Hans. She had told her children that their father was coming back, but he would never come back. He was dead. His long thin hands which had caressed her body, the hands of an artist etcher who had made himself a little fame before the war, were still and frozen. He was dead, she thought, like most of her boy friends who had danced with her in days of victory and climbed the Bavarian Alps with her when she had been a girl near Munich, and had made love to her sometimes before she met Peter.

Now the Russians had made another break through. She had heard about that in the morning from a girl whose lover was a despatch rider. He had been badly wounded but had ridden on his motor-cycle forty miles to Königsberg until he crashed. In hospital he had whispered ghastly things to Rosa Schultz who had repeated them to Hilde with terror in her eyes—always that look of terror now in women's eyes in Königsberg.

"They'll be here in less than a week," he had said. "The Russians swarm like vermin and they're mad beasts when they're drunk. There'll be a massacre in Königsberg, and no mercy for women. You must get away."

Rosa's face had been as white as the snow beneath her feet in the market-place when she repeated her lover's words.

"How can we get away?" she asked. "They forbid us to leave. They want to keep the roads for the retreating troops. But I'd rather die than stay. The Russians have no pity for girls like me. They do horrible things to women, and I'm young and pretty. I'd rather die."

They'll be here in less than a week. Hilde Menzel spoke those words aloud to herself in her ice-cold room. She also was young and pretty. Peter had always thought her pretty. She gave a shudder which shook her body. The Horror took hold of her like a bear's hug but she tried to thrust it back from her body and brain.

'I must keep my nerve,' she thought. 'I must keep my courage for the children's sake. I mustn't go mad like Clara who cut her throat yesterday. It's wicked to do that if one has three children. Somehow I must save them. O God, help me to save them!'

Suddenly she fell on to her knees and flung her head and arms on to a chintz-covered sofa in this drawing-room in Königsberg where, in hundreds of other rooms, women like herself were alone with terror. A little enamelled clock on the mantelshelf—it was a wedding present from her sister Christel in Bavaria—ticked rapidly like a fast-beating pulse. It seemed very quiet and peaceful in this room in a city awaiting inescapable doom, like Danzig and other cities in East Prussia. The pale light of a winter afternoon with snow falling gleamed on the panels of a rosewood piano. Peter Menzel's photograph in a silver frame smiled down upon a kneeling wife who had seen his dead face staring up at the stars. Here in Königsberg was a quiet and elegant apartment with some precious porcelain in the cabinet and some flower pictures on the walls. Not yet had Russian soldiers—Mongols and savages—trampled into it, mad drunk after the sack of a city, smashing everything, with blood running in the streets outside and the shrieks of women rising to these windows. That was happening, while the little clock ticked, in towns and villages of East Prussia not far away from Königsberg.

A siren howled. There was to be another air raid. For a month past the Russians had been bombing the docks, setting on fire ships, railyards, factories and storehouses, and breaking all lines of communication by train. At night the sky was hotly red above these raging fires and the snow on the broken roofs and ruins was crimsoned like frozen blood.

A frightful thing had happened outside the port of Königsberg. A ship called the *Wilhelm Gustlof* had sailed for Hamburg with four thousand women and children on board. It was the first open acknowledgement by the High Command that the city was about to be besieged. Hilde had gone down to the port through an air raid, leaving her aunt to look after the children. She was desperate to get them on to this ship after hearing about it from her father-in-law, too late perhaps. Oh God, if she were too late! . . .

On the way she had to take shelter from heavy bombing. Down

in the shelter under one of the Banks were other women who were frantic to get on to the *Wilhelm Gustlof* with their children. One of them was her friend Lotte Folz. After the raid they had gone together to the docks but were barred out. The ship was already overcrowded. No more passengers could be taken on board. Cries and wailings rose from a long line of mothers waiting with their children. Lotte Folz became hysterical, clinging to the belt of a young officer in command of the dock guards, beseeching him to save her little ones. He answered sternly, though there was a look of pity in his eyes for all these stricken women.

"I can't do anything about it. I'm sorry. Let go of my belt, please. There will be another ship soon. *Um Gottes Willen*. . . ."

Hilde herself had wept. She had come too late to save Hans and Trudel and the six-months-old baby. . . .

They wouldn't have been saved. The *Wilhelm Gustlof* was torpedoed. There were few if any survivors. God had not stretched out His hand to save the innocents. They were all drowned, those innocent ones. For five years the seas had been littered with the wreckage of ships sunk by German U-boats and later by Japanese torpedoes and dive-bombers. The bodies of English women and children had been washed on to many shores. It was a war without mercy for the innocent ones. God may have wept at all this wickedness but did not stretch out His hand to alter the range of high explosives. Men were allowed to work out their own destiny and pursue their own evil.

Hilde Menzel rose to her feet.

'I must go down to the shelter,' she thought. 'I must look after the children.'

She heard a knock at the door of the outer room leading into the corridor. It was a heavy thud and then something fell against the door.

'It must be Papa,' she thought. 'He's carrying some heavy logs.'

She went to the door and opened it, and a girl fell upon her in a drunken way.

"Hilde!" the girl cried. "Hold me!"

Hilde held her up. It was Lotte Folz who had gone with her to the docks. She had been a pretty girl until the terror had caught hold of her when she had become sharp-featured, with sunken eyes and a pallid face. Now she looked like a drunken woman with unkempt hair and dirty hands. There was snow on her boots and the wind had swept it against her face and breast.

"Lotte!" cried Hilde. "What has happened? You're trembling. You're as cold as ice."

She put the girl into a chair and knelt down and chafed her hands. She seemed almost lifeless.

"The Russians!" she said in a faint voice. "They're coming."

She fell a little sideways over the arm of the chair.

"You look so ill, Lotte," said Hilde. "Have you been drinking? Why don't you sit up?"

"I drank something," answered the girl. "I think I did."

Her hands seemed to stiffen. A whiteness crept up to the knuckles.

"It was the only way," she said. "I had to do it."

"What have you done?" asked Hilde.

She was very frightened now. It was a different kind of fear from her own attack of terror. It was more immediate. Lotte was dying in front of her eyes.

"For God's sake tell me!" she cried. "What have you done, Lotte?"

"I drank something," answered the girl. "My two little ones are dead already."

Hilde gave a cry.

"Lotte! What are you telling me?"

"I think they're dead," said Lotte; "but they just looked asleep when I left them. Oh, Hilde, they looked so pretty in their sleep of death!"

"You're dreaming it," said Hilde in a harsh voice. "You haven't done it. You're only ill."

"I think I'm dying," said Lotte, in a whisper.

Her eyes were glazing. She spoke only in that whisper

"I can't see you, Hilde. Where have you gone? Hold me."

Her hand fluttered out and Hilde held it, and felt the tightness of the girl's grip, very tight until the cold hand became limp. Lotte's body drooped forward so that Hilde had to press her back with both hands or she would have fallen from the chair.

Lotte Folz had died and Hilde gave a sharp cry. Lotte was dead, like her two little ones.

"What is happening?" asked a man's voice, sharply.

It was Dr. Karl Menzel, her father-in-law, who had come into the room—a tall, thin, elderly, white-haired man stooping under the burden of a heavy rucksack.

"It's Lotte Folz," said Hilde. "She has killed herself. She has killed her two children. She's dead."

"God in heaven!" said the elderly man, in a low trembling voice. Slowly he undid his rucksack and slid it from his shoulders and let it drop to the floor.

"I can't hold her," said Hilde. "She's heavy. Help me."

Between them they slid the body on to the floor and Menzel took a rug and covered the dead girl. He seemed to be panting and breathed noisily.

"The children mustn't see this," he said. "They mustn't see it before we go."

His hands were trembling but he spoke calmly.

"Go where?" asked Hilde.

She stared at her father-in-law, this man who had been a professor of philosophy at Königsberg University and now picked up sticks from the ruins of the city and starved himself so that Hans and Trudel could have more food. Twice a week he had managed to get potatoes for them by some secret barter.

"We must get away," he said. "Königsberg is doomed."

"How can we get away?" asked Hilde. "We're caught in a death trap."

She looked down at the rug which hid the sight of death and shuddered.

"We must take to the roads," said Karl Menzel. "There are no orders against it now. They were withdrawn tonight. Many people are going. We must join them. Listen. Do you hear?"

Through the closed windows came the sound of some tumult in the streets of Königsberg, like the surging of a tide on a rocky shore, or like a great wind beating through a German forest. It was the dull murmur of a moving multitude in flight, and through it came sharp sounds of creaking wheels, the beat of horses' hoofs on ice-bound roads, the lash of whips, the cries and shouts of men and women.

"They've heard the news," said Karl Menzel. "The Russians are closing in. They'll be here soon."

"How soon?" asked Hilde, faintly. Her hands went up to her throat. Her face was whiter.

"Who can tell?" asked her father-in-law uncertainly. "Our troops are forming a line around the city to hold them back for a time. You must get the children ready. We must start at daybreak."

"Start walking?" asked Hilde. "How can the children walk? We should all die in the snow. It's better to stay here."

"I've planned it out," answered her father-in-law. "I have a cart and two strong horses. I knew this was coming. We must keep the children warm. I've been hoarding food for the journey. There's just a chance, by God's grace. . . ."

His voice trembled with emotion and excitement. He was a philosopher. Always he had been vague and absent-minded about the affairs of life. Until his wife had died he had always been waited on and mothered and made tidy before he went to his lectures. Now he had become a man of action, driven to it by desperate conditions.

Hilde gave a cry of anguish.

"Why do you talk of God? There are only devils in this world. If there's a God He turns his face away because our leaders have done devilish things. You've told me that a thousand times. But it's unjust. Why should the children die? Why should I die? Do you call that the grace of God?"

She was hysterical. Her face was distorted by pain. She spoke in a shrill voice and then, suddenly, mastered herself.

"If you have a cart and two horses—that is something."

"We must start at dawn," said Karl Menzel. "Try to keep your courage. We must think of the children."

As he spoke there was a heavy crash of high explosives which shook the block of flats as though they had been struck by a giant hand. It was followed by the sound of an avalanche as some building near by collapsed into ruin. From the streets rose the screaming of women.

"We had better go down to the shelter," said Dr. Menzel, taking her arm. "We can't stay here with this dead girl."

"No," said Hilde.

She shuddered again at the sight of that bundle on the floor.

"We must come back later and pack a few things," said her father-in-law. "Clothes and blankets for ourselves and the children. The wagon will be here at dawn."

Down in the street carts with creaking axles were moving again. It was the beginning of the flight from Königsberg.

CHAPTER II

FORTY miles away from Königsberg delaying actions were being fought by a thin screen of rearguards left to cover the main German army falling back to defend the city. They were holding scattered villages, woods, and isolated farmhouses. For three days now the roads had been choked with transport, troops, guns, tanks, armoured cars, field kitchens, ambulances, staff cars, and horse-drawn carts. Horses had fallen dead on the frozen surface of the roads. Wagons with broken axles had lurched into ditches. Across the snow-covered plain were black blotches of tanks abandoned for lack of fuel and worn-out guns and burnt-out lorries, set on fire by low-flying bombers.

Some of the villages were deserted except for a few old men and women who clung to their homesteads whatever the risk. From others the farmers had driven their horses and cattle with their womenfolk into Königsberg, or were trekking southwards and westwards in slow crawling columns, causing much cursing and shouting from German officers as they pulled on one side to let the army transport pass. In other villages the inhabitants still stayed, ignorant of their extreme peril or too late to get away. God in heaven—too late! The Russians were all around them, and closing in.

A young sergeant named Franz Reber was in the neighbourhood of one of these villages, Mühlheim—about two kilometres from where he stood. It was still defended by the remnants of a Saxon division. He could hear the tattoo of their machine-guns firing in spasms. Russian artillery was thundering from a good half a kilometre from the village. Sergeant Reber stood with his back to a black barn in a big farmstead with many barns and outhouses. He was with one of the rearguards left behind to delay the Russian advance. They had just pulled into this place from a wood now occupied by the enemy a few kilometres farther back, east of Mühlheim. They had lost a lot of men under concentrated fire. Now perhaps there would be an hour or two before Ivan attacked again. Sergeant Reber, leaning against the barn, sheltered from the wind, watched the scene around him in a curiously aloof way as though he had nothing to do with it, as though it were a stage play, very boring, of which he was a spectator, or as though he were dead but still able to see all this. His body was numbed by the cold.

Some of the men were straggling towards the farmhouse for a few minutes' shelter from the icy wind. The frozen snow which had drifted heavily into the farmyard scrunched under their heavy boots. One man fell, his rifle crashing, and lay sprawled out until two of his comrades picked him up with hoarse laughter. It might be their last laugh, thought Sergeant Reber in his detached way. They were tough-looking fellows as hard as baked clay. Men had to be tough who had fought all the way to Stalingrad and all the way back, as some of them had with Reber himself. Most of them had tied bits of cloth round their heads under their steel helmets. They were unshaven and bearded. Their uniforms and heavy coats were torn and plastered with the slush of snow and mud. Only the boys sent up from the last reserves—straight from the training camps—had smooth faces—boys of sixteen and seventeen sent up to the shambles. No one spoke. Some of the boys had frightened eyes. The men moving towards the farmhouse were as silent, except for that laugh, as the dead they had left behind an hour ago in a wood slashed by Russian gunfire. Only God knew what was happening in their minds, if anything. They knew that the German armies were in retreat everywhere. They knew that their own chance of life for another hour or two was slim. Very soon some more of them would be dead. Apart from the youngsters—one was blubbing—they weren't worrying about that. They were too used to it, too cold, and drunk for lack of sleep.

Outside the farmyard other men were lying in the ditches with rifles and machine-guns. A battery of field-guns had unlimbered in the yard. Sergeant Reber watched all this in his disembodied way. He had seen it all a thousand times before. A motor-cyclist dashed into the farmyard and brought his machine to a standstill within three inches of a pigsty. He was bleeding from a wound in the head. His steel helmet was capped with snow. A corporal took his message scrawled on a bit of paper and handed it to Colonel Trautwein, a youngish, steel-eyed man, who came down the steps from the farmhouse. He took the message, read it and scrunched it up in his hand.

A car with a radio mast pulled into the farmyard. It kept in touch with the other rearguards and picked up messages from Königsberg. The man in charge of it, Holzapfel, came out of the car and stamped his feet and blew on his frozen hands.

Stretcher bearers with Red Cross armlets were dealing with the walking wounded who had gone into one of the barns and were now being helped into ambulances lined up outside the barn. Sergeant Reber's eyes saw, without interest, the soles of their heavy boots turned towards him as they lay in their bunks. For months and years—it seemed like a lifetime—he had seen the soles of men's boots in endless columns of ambulances lurching slowly down Russian roads and mudtracks. Above the boots were men's bodies, lying under army blankets if there were enough to go round, and inside each body a human brain, capable of pain, even of thought, an individual mind, the soul of a man, but speechless and ticketed as a number like a leg of mutton. That was very odd, thought Sergeant Reber in his vague way as though standing outside his own body. Each man, each individual soul, had followed his own destiny unerringly. He had followed its thread of Fate. The bullet, or the bit of shell, had hit him at the ordained moment. It had been waiting for him a long time, even when he was in his mother's womb. There was no escape from Destiny, thought Sergeant Reber, who was a fatalist. Germany was following its preordained Destiny—Hitler was only its blind instrument. The doom of Germany had been ordained when the first tribes gathered in the German forests; the pattern of history, the rise and fall of civilizations, just made visible the blue print of an inevitable sequence of events, one leading to another.

The eyes of this fatalist leaning against a barn in East Prussia wandered for a moment from the farmyard over its low wall to the snow-covered plain beyond. Above the whiteness, cutting the skyline were black woods here and there. Half a dozen villages were burning. Heavy smoke rose up from them and red tongues of flame writhed below the smoke. Russian guns were firing on a wide arc with heavy rumbling. For two years now—or was it two thousand?—Sergeant Reber, one ant in an army of soldier ants, had marched, eaten, slept and sometimes dreamed with that thunder of guns in his ears, sometimes distant, sometimes close. Close, very close now, was the sharp hammering of machine-gun fire, like the hammering of coffin nails.

Sergeant Reber felt outside time. He had had that feeling many times before in hours of exhaustion, as though he were looking at all this from another star. Eternity must be like this, timeless. Past, Present and Future would be the same—all one picture. One picture. Reber used to paint pictures, or try to, as an art-student in Munich. As a drowning man who sees all his life like the quick moving reel of a film picture, he saw himself back in Munich. He was not seeing the snow and the black woods and the burning villages. He saw very vividly a scene in the Oktober Fest in Munich with a lot of young people—his fellow students—dancing to an open-air orchestra. He was dancing with a girl called Christel. She was laughing up at him. She always laughed when he said he was in love with her. . . .

Back to his body again. Somebody was coming towards him. It was a fellow sergeant named Folz. He liked Folz. He was a bit of a humorist and a bit of a philosopher. They had talked for hours together in dugouts and trenches and Russian billets and the basements of bomb-wrecked houses. Folz had been anti-Hitler and anti-war. He had thought the Russian campaign an act of monstrous insanity ordered by a raving maniac. Dangerous talk with S.S. men quick of hearing. He had been damned ironical sometimes, very savage in his humour and only now and then sentimental when they were alone together. He was sentimental about his wife, Lotte, and his two children. He carried their photographs in his wallet.

Folz came up to him now and spoke in his North-German accent.

"Hullo! I thought you were dead."

"Perhaps I am," answered Sergeant Reber. "I'm frozen, anyhow."

Folz stood next to Reber with his back to the barn, sheltered from the wind. Then he spoke again.

"Lotte is in Königsberg with the two children. Only forty kilometres."

"You'll be seeing them soon," said Reber.

Folz gave a quick sigh.

"Shall we get there?"

"Why not?"

Folz did not answer for a moment. He stared over the low wall surrounding the farmyard. The sun was sinking now, a red ball in a leaden sky touching the snow fields with a rosy light. Sharp stabs of flame shot through the black wood nearest to them. The enemy was ranging on the farm buildings. Several shells burst in the fields beyond, exploding in the soft earth. Bad shooting.

"They've brought their guns closer," said Folz. "They're moving up."

"Folz!" shouted a voice. It was Trautwein, that youngish Colonel who was in command of the rearguard. The men were coming back now from the farmhouse to take up their positions. The gunners with the field battery were getting ready for action. A sergeant was giving them the range. Two stretcher bearers staggered into the yard carrying a wounded man.

Folz walked towards the Colonel who was shouting some orders. Sergeant Reber looked after him. Folz was his closest friend. They had been through hell together, the hell of that winter in Russia when they had been in their summer uniforms because Hitler believed it would be a parade march to Moscow. Thousands of men had been frozen. Their arms and legs had gone black. They had screamed in agony if they were touched. Their limbs had gone rotten. The surgeons had done butchers' work. Folz had received parcels of clothing from his wife Lotte. He had shared them with Reber, saving his life. Besides, Folz was a humorist. He had made Reber laugh even in this hell on earth.

Reber followed him with his eyes as he walked towards the Colonel in a slow, tired way. The whine of a shell overhead ended suddenly. A dung-heap was tossed up in the middle of the farmyard. A jagged bit of steel caught Folz. He staggered, fell, and lay dead there, crumpled up almost at the Colonel's feet.

Sergeant Reber ran towards him and then stopped. It was no use running.

"I'm sorry," said Colonel Trautwein. "A good soldier."

He spoke to two of the men.

"Bury him in that loose earth. Look sharp about it. Not much time left."

He spoke to Reber.

"Holzapfel has been wounded. Take over, will you?"

Holzapfel had been wounded by a shell which had burst close by the radio-car, smashing the windscreen. They were carrying him away.

Sergeant Reber walked towards the car. He was thinking of Folz. Somehow he had known that Folz would never see his wife Lotte again or the two kids. Reber had lied to him when he said that he would see them again. It was a lie of comradeship. Often he knew when men would be killed. It was something in their eyes.

He went into the radio-car and put on the ear-phones. No contact. Only a buzzing and crackling. . . .

Folz had hated the war from the beginning. He had been a student of philosophy at Bonn. That was where he had met Lotte. He had married her two years before the war. Then she had joined her parents in Königsberg where her father had some administrative post. Now Folz was dead . . . Folz was dead . . . Reber was alive, for a few more ticks of time. He might join Folz before the sun went down.

A voice was speaking into the radio telephone.

"Sergeant Richter speaking. Are you there? . . . Sergeant Richter speaking from Mühlheim. Can you hear me?"

It wasn't easy to hear. Strange confused noises were coming through with the voice. It was as though this Sergeant Richter were speaking through some tumult of shouting and rifle-shots and stamping feet and heavy crashes.

"Speak a bit louder," said Reber. "What's happening? What's the situation?"

The situation in Mühlheim was not good. Mühlheim was the village two kilometres away from this farmstead.

"What's that?"

"They're here," said the voice. "They've swarmed in. Mongols. Mad beasts, killing everyone. The women—— Oh, my God! . . ."

The voice trailed away. Through the ear-phones Reber heard horrible noises, blood-curdling noises. There was the yelling of madmen or demons. They were cheering in the Russian way like the howling of wolves.

"*Ooorayee . . . Ooorayee. . . .*"

Reber felt his blood freeze. He had heard those yells before when the Russians had attacked across the open with fixed bayonets.

The voice spoke again.

"They're killing us all. . . . The women. . . . They're all round us . . . I'm——"

There was a sudden crash. Then a woman's shriek. Then silence.

The hair had risen on Sergeant Reber's scalp. An icy finger touched his spine.

"Get away, Richter!" he shouted. "Get away, man!"

There was no answer except another of those demoniacal yells.

"*Ooorayee!*"

Reber took off the ear-phones and came out of the car. He was shaken and trembling. Could anything of war's horror shake him now? He had been an eye-witness of frightful scenes in Russia. Terrible reprisals had been taken for the shooting and stabbing of German soldiers by civilians. He had taken part in hand-to-hand fighting in cellars and houses when men saw red and there was no quarter. German soldiers had not been angels. They had done terrible things. But these Russians, these Mongols, were worse than beasts. They were demons. They spared neither woman nor child when they were mad with blood-lust or drink. They gloried in killing. They laughed when blood ran from their bayonets They were oriental hordes like those of Ghengis Khan.

"Did you pick up anything?" asked a voice near to him.

It was his young-looking Colonel wearing the Ritter cross, still smart in his long grey overcoat though he had been in dirty places with them, cool and unflurried, even in the heat of battle, one of those men without nerves, fanatical in his courage and in his loyalty to Hitler, refusing to believe that Germany was doomed and that the war was lost.

"Mühlheim," said Sergeant Reber. "It's in their hands."

The Colonel stared at him.

"That's bad. We're outflanked. We shall have to pull out."

"They're killing everyone," said Sergeant Reber. "The women . . ."

"Fortunately we have a good field of fire," said the Colonel. "When they attack from the wood over there we shall mow them down. But we shall have to pull out now that they're in Mühlheim."

"I heard the screams of the women," said Reber in a low voice.

The Colonel nodded.

"We must get out before they attack seriously. The other rearguards are withdrawing. It's a general order."

He was silent for a moment and glanced towards one of the barns into which a shell crashed. Shells were rushing overhead like screaming birds. They had the range of the farmhouse and were tearing holes into its roofs and walls. It was beginning to catch fire. Smoke was coming through the slated roof. Flames leapt out from one of the windows.

Colonel Trautwein spoke a few more words which were orders.

"You will take over the radio-car, Reber. Report our situation to the other rearguards."

He strode away towards an armoured car which had just pulled in.

Reber stood motionless for a moment. His eyes wandered to the spot where they had buried Folz. He saw the mound of loose earth hastily shovelled above the body. By the side of the grave lay Folz's steel helmet, pierced by a bit of shell. Reber went across and picked it up. His eyes searched for two bits of stick, easy to find within a yard of where he stood. They were bits of birchwood lopped from a tree by shell-fire. He tied them together in the shape of a cross then stuck it into the grave and hung the steel helmet on it.

"*Auf Wiedersehen*," said Sergeant Reber in a low voice.

How many graves had he seen like this, how many birchwood crosses and steel helmets in that flat field of Russia? Most of his friends lay under the earth like this—fellow students at the Academy in Munich where he had studied art in another kind of dream. Now Folz had joined this crowded company. Perhaps before the sun went down. . . .

He got into the car again and put on the ear-phones. The sun was sinking lower. The snowfields over the wide plain were flushed by its rose-coloured light. The woods became blacker. Before darkness came a line of men appeared out of the near wood followed by another line, and then another. Sergeant Reber through his broken windscreen could see them like black dots on the hard frozen snowfield, like black ants on the march. He could hear these ants shouting, cheering:

"*Ooorayee! . . . Ooorayee! . . .*"

They were met by a sweep of machine-gun fire. The first line of ants seemed to crumble away. The second line moved on ten yards, twenty yards, and fell, and was still. The third line moved over them and met the scythe of machine-gun bullets and were laid low. The fourth line. . . . The fifth line. . . .

The Russians were attacking on a wide front. Sergeant Reber was getting messages from units on the left and right. Through the broken windscreen he could see the flash of gun-fire as far as forty kilometres away. The leaden sky was flickering above the horizon. It was getting dark now. Snow was beginning to fall. It was blowing through the broken windscreen. He could see nothing more. He continued to receive messages.

"Russian attack broken. . . . They're only testing our defences. . . . They've gained ground north of Mühlheim. . . . We're pulling out. . . . What's happening with you?"

A runner stood by his car to carry these messages to the Colonel, but they failed to reach him. He was killed after giving orders to pull out when the Russian attack was called off. It was just a probing attack to find out the weak spots.

Snow was falling heavily now and darkness came. Presently it was a fierce blinding snowstorm. Under cover of it German rearguards were pulling out but keeping up a desultory fire to conceal this retreat nearer to Königsberg where the main German army was screening the city.

The deserted farmhouse was a blazing torch. Its red glare glowed through the heavy veil of snow. Through this storm men with snow-capped helmets and long overcoats heavy with snow, and big boots splodging through its soft whiteness passed like a ghost army with guns, armoured cars, ambulances and horse-drawn wagons.

Sergeant Reber was in trouble with his car. He couldn't get it out of a snowdrift. Cursing didn't seem to help. He stopped cursing and spoke a word to himself.

"Desti ny!"

He was alone for a time in this world of whiteness.

From the Baltic to the Black Sea the German armies were being broken by the spearhead thrusts of the Russians in pincer movements encircling masses of men—the remnants of divisions forbidden to retreat by the direct orders of a mad-eyed man in Berlin who had believed himself infallible and invincible.

CHAPTER III

THE refugees from Königsberg choked the roads south-westwards in long, crawling columns. Their pace was no faster than that of farm horses plodding in the shafts of heavy wagons in which women and children and old people were packed up with mattresses, pots and pans, bits of furniture and stores of food; no faster than the herds of cattle mixed up among them, and hand-carts pushed by women; no faster than the walking pace of those who trudged behind the carts and wagons. Here and there a motor-car had been caught in this tide of human beings and dumb beasts and had to crawl with them along the snow-bound roads.

For five years the stars had looked down upon such tides of people in flight. It had happened in Belgium and France, in Finland, Poland and Russia. It had been a flight, panic-stricken and futile, from the swift advance of German armies. Now the Germans were in flight from the Russians who were smashing their way westwards in overwhelming numbers, reckless of death, drunk with the joy of revenge, relentless in their fury. As always in war the helpless victims were those who had had no hand in making it but were caught between the fires.

The farmers had tilled their fields peacefully and tended their cattle. The womenfolk had taken care of the children and homesteads, weeping for sons sent into the shambles. They hadn't asked for this war though they had not revolted against it. They were the dupes of false gods calling them to sacrifice on pagan altars in the name of the Fatherland.

For days now the refugees had been on the roads moving south-westwards. Nearly always from the start it had been snowing heavily. Farm-carts had lurched into deep snowdrifts and there were halts while other horses were brought up to haul them out, Some of them, overloaded, lost their wheels. Snow lay on the covered wagons and blinded the horses as they stumbled on and beat into the faces of the walkers. It put white cloaks on to their shoulders, crept into their boots, and made their clothes sodden. Overhead, three times, black birds of death swooped low over this column of refugees who were bombed and machine-gunned. The screams of women and children rose above the creaking of axles, the scrunching of wheels, the lowing of cattle, the wild neighing of frightened horses. After each of these raids the carcasses of mutilated horses and cattle had to be shovelled away or cut up for meat before another move could be made. A man and woman had been killed and were buried hurriedly below the snow.

One of the covered wagons belonged to Dr. Karl Menzel, ex-professor of philosophy. Inside it, huddled in blankets among wooden packing-cases, were his daughter-in-law, Hilde, and her two children Hans and Trudel, and Peter the six-months-old baby which Hilde tried to keep warm against her body. With them also were two of the professor's nieces named Ursel and Hildegard and their mother Frau von Grottenbach whom Hilde called Aunt Tessa. There was one other girl named Rosa who came from a farm and sat shy and silent among her companions. It was she who really owned the cart and horses which by a fantastic stroke of luck—a miracle it seemed—had come into the hands of Karl Menzel.

For a month his mind had been running around like a rat in a trap for some way of escape from Königsberg, not for his own sake but for the rescue of Hilde and the little ones. All that time he had been in the grip of a hidden and gnawing fear for their sake. How could he get them away? How could he save them from the Russian hordes who were pressing nearer and nearer to Königsberg? All roads had been reserved for military transport. Lately the railway lines had been smashed in the air raids. After the tragedy of the *Wilhelm Gustlof* he dared not think of a sea passage. Two horses and a covered wagon haunted his imagination and drove through his nightmare of anxiety and fear. How could he get two horses and a covered wagon, except by a miracle of God in whom he had ceased to believe but to whom now, The First Cause, the Architect of Destiny, he cried out in agony of soul during sleepless nights?

A covered wagon and two horses would cost a fortune if any farmer near Königsberg would part with them at such a time when he might need them to save the lives of his own family. An ex-professor of philosophy had no such fortune. All he could scrape together was a few thousand marks which he spent in hoarding food for the coming siege if they had to stay. Königsberg was already getting short of food. The farmers were hoarding their own stocks. Prices were soaring up. He dared not raise false hopes in Hilde's mind or his own. Hilde's face frightened him. He saw the terror in her eyes. Like a rat in a trap his mind ran about searching for a way of escape.

Was it a mere coincidence, or was it some thread of fate, or was it some guidance of a Power beyond the ken of all Philosophy, which led him at last to a farmstead outside Königsberg where he hoped to barter his dead wife's jewels—poor little trinkets really—for a few potatoes?

The farmer took him into his kitchen and hardly looked at the trinkets.

"Those things are useless," he said. "Everything is useless now. In a few days we shall be overrun by the Russians. Germany is *kaput*."

"If you would let me have a few potatoes," said Menzel in a pleading voice.

The farmer stared at him.

"Aren't you Karl Menzel?" he asked.

"Yes, that's my name. I'm a doctor of philosophy."

"I'm Fritz Gottlieb," said the farmer. "We were together in the First World War."

Yes, thirty years ago they had lain together in the straw of Flemish barns. They had crouched together in the trenches on Vimy Ridge. They had been under the British drum fire at Loos and on the Somme. They had marched across the Somme bridge-heads to the outskirts of Amiens before the tide of war turned. They had sung German *Lieder* in French *estaminets*. They had made love to the same little slut in Lille. They had been very young then. Now Gottlieb was an elderly, grizzled man with a weather-beaten face under hair almost as white as Menzel's.

He had lost three sons in the present war. There was nothing now for which he wanted to live except his daughter Rosa. She mustn't fall into the hands of the Russians, poor girl.

"If you'll take Rosa," he said, "you can have my best pair of horses and the covered wagon."

"Did I hear you say that?" asked Menzel in a trembling voice. "You will come with us, of course?"

Gottlieb looked into his eyes and answered gravely as a man whose mind is made up beyond all argument.

"My wife and I will stay and look after the farm. It's possible that the Russians won't kill us. They're farmers, too. In any case what does it matter? Now that our sons have gone. . . ."

So the miracle had happened, or the great coincidence, or the working out of destiny in human lives for some mysterious and unknown purpose. . . .

Now the girl Rosa was sitting at the back of the covered wagon staring through the flap at the long column of refugees within her range of vision. With fair hair, straw-coloured, looped over her ears, she looked like the Blessed Virgin in an old German painting by Grünewald or Pacher. She stared at her fellow-refugees, men, women and beasts battling against the heavy snow which came in sudden gusts and flurries every few hours with a blessed respite now and then. Her eyes were unblinking. They were like the mild eyes of her father's cows. Now and then big tears fell down her cheeks but she did not raise a hand to wipe them away.

Dr. Menzel drove the sturdy farm horses but more often led them on foot. They never went at more than a walking pace. For a man of sixty, a scholar and professor, never very robust, always taking quack medicines when he lived in Königsberg, this was a hard ordeal. But some tremendous will-power had taken possession of his frail body—a desperate *idèe fixe*—an impulse which seemed to give him an unnatural endurance. To get out of East Prussia, to drive this wagon beyond pursuing distance of the Russian hordes, to save Hilde and her little ones held him and drove him on. But he could not silence the cough which tore at his lungs. That was nothing, he thought. He had often had a cough.

Hilde worried about him. She heard his constant coughing. Once when he came into the wagon during a halt to have a meal with them she spoke to him anxiously.

"You mustn't walk so much with the horses. You're exhausting yourself."

"No, no!" he assured her. "I had a worse time in the first war. This is child's play—a picnic."

Aunt Tessa, his sister—Frau von Grottenbach—felt his overcoat, a thin black coat with an astrakhan collar.

"You're sopping wet, Karl. For goodness' sake let one of us lead those blessed horses."

"I will lead them," said Rosa. "Allow me."

They were almost the first words she had spoken beyond *Bitte schön* and *Danke schön.*

"You see, Fritz!" said his sister. "Rosa comes off a farm. She's used to horses and she's young and strong."

"Later on perhaps," said Menzel. "When I get tired."

He was harsh in his refusal to give up driving or leading the horses. There was a kind of daemon in him which drove him on. It was his job to save these people. If he could lead them into safe places he would have fulfilled the call of the Power outside himself. Plato had believed in some such Power. Aristotle had given reasons for a Universal Consciousness whom the Christians called God.

"Your teeth are chattering, Fritz," said Aunt Tessa. "For goodness' sake swallow some of this hot tea."

She had made tea on a spirit-stove which she had brought with her few packages. She was wearing her best clothes and a fur coat, but they were beneath a blanket in which she had wrapped herself, putting it over her head like a gypsy. Her hands were dirty—it was difficult to wash in this covered wagon—but they sparkled with the light of several rings which she wore for safety's sake. For days during the first part of the journey she had talked a good deal. Hilde had often said that nothing would stop Aunt Tessa from talking—and even sang nursery rhymes to the children and kept Hans and Trudel amused by telling them fairy tales.

One of her daughters—Ursel—cried out once in a querulous way.

"Mother! Can't you stop talking? You make my head ache. And I'm freezing to death."

"I shall go on talking until I die," answered Aunt Tessa. "In any case this isn't a funeral. Let's keep gay, or pretend to, for the children's sake. Don't indulge in self-pity, my dear. It's a weakness in our German character."

"Shut up, Mother," said Ursel, rudely.

"Do you think the Russians will catch us?" asked Hans, who was sitting on Aunt Tessa's lap.

"Good gracious no!" cried Aunt Tessa brightly. "They're miles away now, and there's a strong German army guarding the roads. They'll all be killed like rats."

"I'd like to kill a lot of them," said Hans. "I'd like to cut their heads off with a sharp knife."

"Our Führer would be glad to hear you say so," answered Aunt Tessa. "Heil Hitler and the spirit of German youth!"

She winked at Dr. Menzel who was drinking a cup of hot tea and trying to unfreeze himself. He knew his sister's opinion about Adolf Hitler. It was more violent than his own. She regarded him as a man possessed by seven devils. A homicidal maniac. His niece Hildegard sat crouched on the floor of the wagon wrapped in a blanket like her mother but every now and then she fumbled in a handbag for a little mirror and lipstick which she used repeatedly.

Once Dr. Menzel lost his temper with her because of this habit.

"Why do you keep using that lipstick?" he asked. "There are no young men here. It won't make any difference to the Russians if they overtake us."

"I find it comforting," said Hildegard. "It amuses me."

"It's disgusting," said her uncle.

Presently he touched her hand and said: "I'm sorry. It doesn't matter. . . . The column is moving again. I must go out and lead the horses."

At every halt he came into the wagon with the same question. "How are the children? Are they keeping warm?"

They were not keeping warm in spite of the blankets in which they were wrapped. Snow came into the covered wagons and icy draughts defied the canvas. Hans snuggled deeper into Aunt Tessa's lap as she crooned to him, or played a game of cat's cradle, or tried to interest him in a toy motor-car which he had brought with him. Trudel cried because she was cold. Hilde felt her baby's body under its wrappings and was frightened. It was like touching a toad. She held her face against its cheek to give it some of her own warmth, but she had little warmth in her own body and her feet felt like blocks of ice.

"This is terrible," she said to her aunt. "We shall all die of cold."

"If only one could keep out the draughts," answered her aunt. "But I dare say it's worse at the North Pole."

Aunt Tessa's face had become blue under its make-up which left a dab of red on each cheek. When the children were sleeping, Hans still on her lap with his face tightly pressed to her body, she whispered a few words to Hilde.

"So long as we get away from those devils nothing else matters."

"Little Peter is stiff with cold," answered Hilde. "I'm frightened."

"Don't be frightened, my dear. Put another blanket round him."

Rosa Gottlieb pushed over her own blanket.

"Take this. I don't feel the cold."

It was one cartload of human creatures in an interminable tide of refugees who belonged to many types and classes from the city of Königsberg and its neighbouring farmsteads—shop-keepers, peasants, smartly-dressed women, men from the docks, a troupe of girls who had danced in the night clubs of Königsberg and then had fled from the *danse macabre* which would follow soon. They had fled in thin shoes in which they had walked through the snow until some of the peasant women had taken pity on them and packed tighter for them in their carts.

At the tail end of Menzel's wagon was a group of French prisoners of war who had been working as labourers in Königsberg and now for some inexplicable reason had joined the refugees, perhaps with some idea of escape from barbed wire and serfdom or Russian air raids over the wooden huts of their camp. Perhaps they had been sent away to lessen the number of mouths in a besieged city. One of them was a sergeant-gunner with black eyes and a little black moustache and a week's growth of beard on his chin.

'He's like d'Artagnan,' thought Hilde, who saw him through the flap of the covered wagon.

He spoke to one of his companions during a respite from the snow which he beat from his chest.

"This is not amusing, unless one has a sense of humour in a cold hell."

The man at his side answered gruffly.

"We were imbeciles. The Russians would have liberated us."

"They might have cut our throats in the enthusiasm of the moment," answered the sergeant-gunner. "In any case we're free men. *Vive la Liberté!*"

He laughed at his own jest. This liberty of the road in East Prussia might end in the liberty of death. One day he would lie down in the snow and go to sleep and never wake up again. It was very tempting.

"I know a little *bistro* in Montmartre," he said presently. "Behind the zinc is a plump girl whose lips I used to kiss."

"Shut your beak," said his companion.

This companion of his was without a sense of humour and he didn't love the Germans.

"These *sales Boches*," he said, "are getting it in the neck. May they all freeze in hell."

The sergeant-gunner did not answer that remark until he had walked another mile holding on to the tail of Menzel's cart. Then he had something to say. As a Parisian he needed a little conversation from time to time.

"I am a humanist," he said to a man who did not understand that word. "I have a sense of comradeship with these people. We are comrades in misery."

"Shut your beak!"

"They're innocent of this war," said the sergeant-gunner. "It was made for them by the lunatics on top. War is always made by the lunatics on top. The question is how can we get rid of our lunatics? The answer, my friend, is very difficult. In Paris there are also many lunatics."

"Shut your beak, Saligaud."

Hilde Menzel liked the look of the French sergeant. She had heard some of his words and understood them.

She spoke to her father-in-law.

"Those French prisoners look starving. We must give them some of our food."

"No, no!" said Dr. Menzel, who was in the wagon munching some bread and cheese which Fritz Gottlieb had packed for them.

"We have to be careful. We haven't too much, and the children come first. We can't feed everybody."

Hilde stretched out her hand to a wooden box without a lid.

"I'll give them this tin of meat and one of these loaves."

"It's folly," protested Menzel. "We're like shipwrecked people. We have to be selfish to save our own lives."

"I agree," said Hildegard; "we don't want to starve."

Hilde leaned out of the wagon and spoke in French.

"*M'sieur! Voici quelquechose à manger.*"

The French sergeant's black eyes lighted up.

"*Très aimable, mademoiselle. Je vous remercie infiniment.*"

He shared this *ravitaillement* with his companions by the roadside.

It was during a halt. The whole column, many miles long, was stationary. For some hours now it had stopped snowing. From far along the road came the pitiful lowing of tired cattle. Children were crying in the covered wagons. Men were stamping their feet or beating their chests to bring warmth into frozen bodies. Women came down from the carts to stretch their limbs. Young boys were collecting sticks from a neighbouring wood to make fires on which to boil the kettles. Food was being handed down by old men and women in charge of the stores. It was a respite from the battle with the snow.

Away back in the column were some English prisoners of war. Perhaps they had been sent out of Königsberg to lessen the number of mouths, like the French prisoners. They were with their guards—elderly men who had fought against the British in the First World War on the Somme and at Passchendaele. The younger men who had once guarded the prisoners had been called up to the fighting front. These veterans sat in the snow with their rifles over their knees looking exhausted by the long march. The English prisoners were munching black bread and talking among themselves.

"These old birds," said one of them, glancing at the German guards, "look done brown already. I can't help feeling sorry for 'em. They ought to have been in their coffins years ago."

"Soon will be, thank God," said one of his companions.

A third man spoke.

"Past a joke, I call it. I never thought I should be walking through East Prussia with a crowd of dirty refugees. My Ma won't believe it when I tell her."

"You'll never tell her, my child," said the first one who had spoken; "you'll be a frozen corpse lying in the beautiful soft snow like a dead sparrow."

"That's right. We'll all be frozen meat before long. Dead as mutton and not so good to eat. Cheerful prospect, ain't it? Like Captain Oates in the Arctic. But nobody will make a song and dance about us."

"Why the hell should they?" asked another man. "Who do you think we are? Field-Marshals? Knights in shining armour?"

He turned to one of his guards sitting there with his rifle across his knees.

"Cheer up, Grandpa! *Wie gehts mit Ihnen? Nicht besonders gut?* Not feeling so blinkin' well, eh? And no wonder, you old Rip van Winkle. Serve you right. You'll soon be dead anyway. All you Jerries are going to die. Wait till the Russkis come. They'll make mincemeat of you. Well, you asked for it, didn't you? *Sie haben für Alles gefragt.* Now for God's sake don't look so down in the mouth or I'll burst into tears."

When the march was resumed after an hour's halt it began to snow again. The English prisoners of war carried the rifles of their guards.

"Poor old barstards!" said the man who had spoken a bit of German. "Give 'em a hand, chaps."

Farther up the column was Schirach von Holzendorff, once in the German Embassy in London which he knew better than Berlin and liked better. He was with his wife and two daughters, in one of the few motor-cars among the farm-carts. He sat at the wheel with his younger daughter Erike. Mile after mile he drove at a snail's pace between two herds of cattle driven by farmers. For miles he was utterly silent and every now and then had to get down to brush the snow off his windscreen. Once only he spoke aloud unconsciously.

"Will no one kill that man? Even now it's not too late."

Erike turned her head and glanced at him. She knew what was in her father's mind.

"Why didn't you do it, Father?" she asked. "You had the chance more than once."

He looked at her sideways as though astonished that she had read his thoughts.

"I hadn't the courage," he answered. "Besides when things were going well I believed in his genius, as we all did. We were all his dupes and therefore his accomplices. History will condemn us for that."

"I had nothing to do with it," said Erike. "History can't condemn me and I don't care if it does. I shan't be there to know."

"Don't talk nonsense," said her father irritably.

He had to get out again to wipe the snow from his windscreen. When he sat by the wheel again he saw that his daughter was shivering.

"Better sit behind with your mother," he said.

"Father," said Erike presently, "I wanted to poison myself in Königsberg. I still have three little pills. Wouldn't it have been better if I had taken them? We shall all die in the snow."

Herr von Holzendorff shuddered at his daughter's words.

"Don't talk like that," he said harshly. "Don't talk so loudly. Your mother might hear."

"She knows," said Erike. "She also has the little pills. So has Theresia."

So had Herr von Holzendorff in his waistcoat pocket, though he kept that a secret.

"If the Russians overtake us," said Erike, "I shall take the little pills, Father."

"They won't overtake us," he said harshly again.

In the car his wife sat with her arms round Theresia.

"Keep close to me, Theresia," she said. "This is a terrible journey."

"There was a quicker way of escape, Mother," said Theresia.

"Hush!" whispered her mother. "Your father might hear."

"It's queer," said Theresia presently, "I keep thinking back to those years in London. I keep seeing pictures of St. James's Park in Springtime with all the flowers out, and the Changing of the Guard, and tea in Kensington Gardens. I was very happy then. I had some nice English friends. Do you remember Shirley Gascoigne and Elizabeth Underhill?"

"England has always been our enemy," said her mother. "England hates Germany. They have made war on us twice."

Frau von Holzendorff had been a hundred per cent Nazi, unlike her husband, who had been critical of Hitler. They had quarrelled violently about that.

"I remember a day at Hampton Court with Elizabeth Underhill," said Theresia. "We couldn't get out of the maze and nearly died of laughter."

She laughed then in a strange way.

"Theresia!" exclaimed her mother, anxiously. "You're feverish."

"I think I'm a little mad, Mother," said Theresia. "I keep seeing pictures in the snow." Her face was flushed and presently she began to weep in an hysterical way.

There was another car caught in this tide of refugees. It was the radio-car which had broken down outside the farmhouse near Mühlheim. Sergeant Reber had got it going again but had lost his way in the snowstorm and then had become jammed at a cross-roads in this crawling column. There was nothing to do but crawl with it until he could escape by a side road farther south, and find his way back to his own unit now close to Königsberg. It was no wonder that the high command had forbidden the flight of civilians from the city until the last moment. They made the roads impassable to troops and army transport. How the devil could he disengage himself from this tangle of men and beasts?

Not that he was going to worry about it unduly. It was all preordained, he thought. Everything happened—the breakdown of his car, this snowstorm, the flight of these people, according to a logical sequence of events laid down from the beginning. It was Folz who had first put these ideas into his head. Folz had studied philosophy and quoted Spinoza who maintained that everything was ruled by an absolute logical necessity. It is logically impossible, he said, that events should be other than as they are. Reber had found some kind of comfort in this fatalism. It explained a lot of things otherwise mysterious in his war experience and in this impending doom of Germany. It had all been written down beforehand in the Book of Fate. If Folz hadn't walked towards the Colonel at that precise moment when the shell arrived he wouldn't have been killed. But he had to walk that way at that precise moment. So it was in a thousand cases, as he had seen. Now he was here, jammed in among a horde of refugees because some grits of muck in his carburettor had cut him off from his comrades. It was the will of Destiny, that is to say the absolute logic of events over which he had no control.

These thoughts passed through his brain as he drove slowly, slithering and side-slipping on the ice-bound road. But with other parts of his brain he thought of other things and his body reacted to his thoughts. He felt hungry and remembered that he had some stale bread in his overcoat pocket to which his left hand fumbled. He had picked up four of the walking refugees. Three of them were sitting huddled up behind. They were young peasant women with woollen shawls over their heads. They were clinging to one another for warmth. None of them spoke a word. Next to him as he sat at the wheel was a young woman of higher class. She was so silent and motionless that he was almost unconscious of her because one part of his brain was on another line of thought, but once he spoke to her.

"What's happening in Königsberg?"

"Everybody's in a state of terror," answered the young woman. "The girls are digging trenches outside."

She spoke good German, he noticed, without a dialect.

"Are most of the civilians getting out?"

"Many are staying. Perhaps they're right. Shall we ever get out of East Prussia?"

"It's a long way. I shall have to turn off the road presently. You'll have to get into one of the wagons."

"Dear God!" said the young woman by his side.

They were silent for a long time after that. The silence was broken by the young woman.

"Did you ever meet a gunner named Otto Hessell?"

Reber nodded. It was queer that she asked that question.

"Yes. He was killed near Stalingrad. I knew him well. Why?"

"He was my husband. He was notified as missing. I thought he might be a prisoner."

"He was killed. Within a yard of where I stood."

"Perhaps it's better to be dead."

"Some of us have to go on living," said Reber.

"Fear makes us women go on living," she said. "The Russians do awful things to women."

"Some of them are decent," said Reber. "Some of them are good-natured."

He remembered the sounds he had heard from Mühlheim.

"Some of them are savages," he added. "They go mad if they have drink in them. There are many different types. War gives a chance to the worst types. Ape men and cave men. Subhuman brutes."

It was some time later when he spoke to her again.

"You're Magda, aren't you?"

"Did Otto tell you?"

"Yes, I remember now. He loved you very much."

He glanced sideways at her for a moment. It was the first time he had seen her with observing eyes. Like all the peasant women she had a shawl wrapped round her head and shoulders but had a delicate, intelligent-looking face, very white and thin.

"We were happy," she told him.

It was ten minutes before he asked another question.

"Where are you trying to get to?"

"Berlin. My parents are there."

"The English are bombing it to hell," said Reber.

He had to keep his eyes on the road and a farm-cart a yard ahead. He had to put on his brakes. The column halted again. It had stopped snowing. A peasant woman got down from the wagon ahead. She had a bundle in her arms. She was moaning like a wounded animal. An old farmer helped her down and spoke some words to her. She carried the bundle to the side of the road and laid it down in the snow and fell face forward over it.

Reber had seen this happen before. Some of the babies were dying of cold. They were left in the snow like dead birds when the column moved on.

Reber saw all this as a black-and-white etching.

'If I stay alive,' he thought, 'I must do some drawings of this—those women black against the snow, kneeling or lying over their dead babies—the farm-carts with the people huddled in them—those dark woods with snow heavy on their branches—those English prisoners carrying the rifles of their guards—that farmer with his arm round his old mother—a hundred years old she looks—and that girl in a fur jacket with high-heeled shoes, and that French sergeant talking to a girl in a covered wagon twenty yards down the road."

Reber's eyes were fixed on the girl talking to the French sergeant. Her face reminded him of another girl called Christel whom he had known in Munich before the war. He used to be in love with her.

'It can't be Christel,' he thought. 'I see everything in a kind of dream, a kind of unreality. I suppose it's because I have no food in my belly. That makes one lightheaded."

Magda Hessell spoke to him.

"I have some food in my rucksack."

He had pitched her rucksack into the back of the car with the three peasant girls and their bundles.

"Do you want it?"

This mention of food did not excite him. He felt past hunger.

"I suppose we had better eat something," she said indifferently.

Reber's stomach sent a message to his brain.

"Can you spare me a bit?"

"Of course."

He wasn't past hunger, he found. In the back of the car the peasant girls were rummaging in their bundles and sharing their food. For the first time they talked to each other in the East Prussian dialect.

During another halt, Hilde Menzel was preparing a meal for her children and the others when suddenly she stopped scooping out some cheese from a tin and listened intently.

"Why do you stop, Mother?" asked Hans. "And why do you serve Trudel first?"

"Because I'm a lady," said Trudel. "Ladies are always served nrst."

"Listen!" said Hilde in a low voice to her aunt. Her face had gone white. She was listening to a droning in the sky, coming closer, coming lower. She knew that sound. It was the heavy droning of Russian bombers—the Yaks.

She called to her father-in-law, who was standing by the horses which he had just fed. He was getting worried about them. The offside horse had been limping before they halted. He did not hear Hilde's voice calling to him.

"What is it?" asked Aunt Tessa, who was fumbling in one of the cases for a tin of sardines.

The farmer's daughter, Rosa, seized Trudel and put her arms round her in a protective way.

Some way down the road there was a heavy crash as a bomb burst in a field nearby. It was followed by the shrieks of women.

The two girls, Ursel and Hildegard, buried their heads in their shawls. Hilde seized her baby from its cot and it set up a loud wailing.

The French sergeant stood on the step of the wagon and spoke a few words urgently.

"*Donnez moi les enfants. Vîte, madame!*"

Hilde hesitated for a moment and then handed him her baby. He gave it to one of his comrades—the one who had cursed the *sales Boches*—and shouted to him to run with it to the wood beyond the road.

"*La petite fille*," said the French sergeant.

He took Trudel who began to shriek and then Hans whom he flung into the arms of one of his comrades.

Hilde leaning out of the wagon saw her children being carried off by these French prisoners of war who were running hard with them.

There was another crash of high explosives. Earth and snow vomited up from the field very close. From the line of refugees in this part of the column rose cries of terror. Many of them were running towards the woods.

Professor Menzel had shouted out to his womenfolk after the first bomb had burst.

"Hilde! . . . Tessa! . . . Take cover . . . *Um Gottes Willen.*"

His two young nieces climbed out of the wagon and crawled under another farm-cart, but Hilde did not move. She seemed to be frozen and speechless. She had lost her children. Perhaps they would never come back. It was that terror which paralysed her.

Suddenly she moved, and sprang out of the wagon, nearly falling to the ground.

"I must go to the children," she said to herself. "I must be with them."

She started running but fell on the frozen snow and then

scrambled up and ran towards the wood as another bomb exploded within a few yards.

Professor Menzel followed her, calling her name. When she fell again he stumbled down at her side and lay there clutching her arm.

Frau von Grottenbach was left alone with Rosa.

"I shall stay here," she said. "You run, my dear."

The blue-eyed girl who looked like a Madonna in an old painting did not answer but seized her in strong peasant arms and dragged her out of the wagon and then beneath it as though she were a sack of potatoes. They lay there in the snow and filth as other bombs crashed and a low-flying fighter plane flew up and down the line like a black vampire splashing the carts and cattle with machine-gun bullets. Up to the leaden sky rose the shrieks of women and children and the curses of men and the screams of wounded animals.

Farther along the line Sergeant Reber in his radio-car had heard the droning of the Yaks. He spoke to the wife of Otto Hessell.

"Those swine are going to bomb us. Better run for it!"

Without a word she flung herself out of the car and ran towards the wood.

Sergeant Reber turned to the girls at the back of the car.

"Run like hell!" he shouted.

He ran with them. Twice Magda Hessell fell and he dragged her up and ran on to the shelter of the wood.

Down the road Herr von Holzendorff had heard the drone of the Russian bombers.

"Something unpleasant is going to happen," he said in a low voice to his younger daughter.

He spoke in English as he often did to his family.

"We had better take cover," he said.

She answered in English.

"What's the good, Father?"

"Get out!" he said sternly.

He sprang down, tore open the door of his car and shouted to his wife and his other daughter.

"We must run for the woods. Those devils are overhead."

Frau von Holzendorff answered him fretfully. There was a look of terror on her face.

"You know I can't run. You know my heart is bad."

"We must crawl under a cart," said Holzendorff.

He tried to drag her out but she was a heavy woman and seemed paralysed by fear.

Suddenly Holzendorff let go of his wife and put his arms round his younger daughter who stood close to him. It was when a Russian bomber flew low above them with a rush of wings which seemed to tear the sky above their heads.

The little pills which this family had carried secretly were no longer needed. A bomb had fallen very close. For them it was journey's end. . . .

It was only three minutes when all this had happened. Then suddenly there was silence except for moaning and a noise of crackling wood and canvas where some of the farm-carts had been set on fire. Many horses had been killed and lay in pools of blood. The farm-carts burned down to their iron axles.

There was a motor-car on fire between two wagons not yet caught by its flames. It was Sergeant Reber's car. He saw it burning when he came back from the wood with Magda Hessell and the peasant girls.

This fatalist and dreamer whose mind wandered away from his body sometimes when he was very tired or very cold, became active and resolute. He ran stumbling across the snowfield. Was it free will or destiny which impelled him to get to his burning car and drive it off the road so that its flames would not touch the nearby wagons? Perhaps he had the right of choice at that moment to watch his car burn out and set other wagons alight or to risk his own life in getting it away. But in that moment he did not argue in his mind about free will or the logical and inevitable sequence of events.

It was only the back part of the car which was burning fiercely. He sprang into the seat and set the engine going. It throbbed with life after a few seconds.

One of the farmers shouted to him.

"Leap for it, you fool!"

Sergeant Reber wrenched at his wheel and drove the car off the road on to the snowfield. The flames were licking round him now. He flung himself out with his clothes burning. Big hands of Prussian farmers beat them out and rolled his body in the snow and carried him to one of the wagons into which he was hoisted, horribly burnt.

Sergeant Reber was still alive but he would never get back to his rearguard for the defence of Königsberg. The radio-car was burnt to a cinder and he was in a flame of agony. Now he was one of the refugees.

The Frenchmen brought back the children. They were unhurt. Rosa Gottlieb crawled from underneath the wagon and dragged out Aunt Tessa, her fur coat bespattered with filth and her face smeared with it. Hilde, who had come back, thanked the French sergeant when he put the baby in her arms and when his comrades returned with Hans and Trudel.

"*Je vous remercie infiniment, m'sieur.*"

He answered with a friendly smile.

"*Enchanté. Je suis humaniste, vous savez.*"

Something had happened in Professor Menzel's wagon since they had left it for those few minutes. Something had gone. Two of the wooden cases of food had disappeared.

"Somebody has stolen them!" cried Aunt Tessa, who had first discovered the loss.

"Impossible!" answered Professor Menzel, still searching for them. "It's beyond belief. Robbery during an air raid? No! No!"

"Nothing is beyond belief," said Aunt Tessa. "All the scum of life has come to the top in this war—all the thieves and bandits and murderers. The devil himself has been let loose."

In those few minutes of terror from the air someone from a nearby wagon, impelled by hunger, perhaps, had risked life to steal part of Menzel's precious stores which he had been hoarding secretly for Hilde and the children. It was like the loss of stores to an Arctic explorer. It might mean death in the snow.

Two mornings later when the first pale light was creeping over the landscape of East Prussia and gleaming on the tops of covered wagons with their canopies of snow, Hilde gave a piercing cry. Menzel started up from his sleep beneath a thin blanket which did not keep him warm. Aunt Tessa and her two daughters and Rosa were all awakened by this cry.

"What is it, Hilde?"

"Little Peter! He's cold. He's stone cold. He's dead."

She was one of the women who carried a little bundle from the wagon and went across the road and laid it in the snow and fell face forward across it.

Snow fell again. For miles the walking refugees stumbled on, blinded by the falling flakes. An icy wind caught the top of the snow and made it rise like smoke and blew it up from the road swirling it about. Only half the bodies of those who trudged and stumbled forward, holding on to ropes and chains, were visible through the white swirling veil. The axles creaked and whined. The horses' hoofs plodded silently. Everything was hushed by this soft whiteness, falling, falling. Even the distant guns were quiet.

CHAPTER IV

SERGEANT REBER had been hoisted into Professor Menzel's wagon not because there was plenty of space in it but because it was no more packed than all the others and was close at hand. He was unconscious at first but awakened to what was an ordeal by fire, a tortured agony. He was terribly burnt about the body, face and hands, and for a time horribly disfigured. Seeing women and children about him he restrained his impulse to scream. It was only by shuddering spasms and his mask of pain that they knew how frightfully he was suffering. It was twenty-four hours before he spoke from the mattress on which he had been laid, the others crowding together to make this place for him. His body was almost naked but for the blanket put over him.

He spoke to Hilde who was leaning over him with some ointment which she had brought in a little medicine chest.

"Your face reminds me of someone I knew before the war."

"How are you feeling?" she asked.

"It was a girl named Christel. I knew her in Munich."

Hilde stared at him without recognition because of his burns.

"I have a sister named Christel. She lives in Munich."

"*Ach, Gott in Himmel!*" He clenched his teeth to suppress a scream.

It was a week before he had some respite from pain and was able to look about him at these new companions. A deterioration had taken place among these people since they had set out in their flight. The pretty Hildegard had given up using her lipstick. She and her sister Ursel were dirty and dishevelled like two drabs in a dosshouse. Since the loss of her baby Hilde had wept in sleepless nights when the children could not see her tears, and her face was white and unwashed. Aunt Tessa alone still dabbed her face with rouge but the skin beneath looked leathery and grey and her dress was stained with food and filth inescapable in this crowded wagon which reeked with the smell of unwashed bodies, stale food, cheese and the vomiting of the boy Hans who had been ill.

A week later something happened to Professor Menzel. He was leading the horses when suddenly he stumbled and fell and did not get up again. He lay there on the road in a crumpled, twisted way. It was the French sergeant-gunner who picked him up when the wagons behind halted because of this body lying ahead of them.

He shouted to the others.

"*Votre Papa! Très malade. Il faut faire quelquechose.*"

A young farmer jumped down from his wagon and helped to carry Professor Menzel.

"It's a stroke," he said. "He looks bad."

Aunt Tessa gave a scream when her brother was hoisted up. He was paralysed down one side and for a time was speechless.

"Our wagon becomes a hospital," said Aunt Tessa. "Fate is against us."

Another blow befell them three days later when Rosa Gottlieb was leading the horses. One of them dropped dead in the shafts. The other had been limping for some days.

Rosa fell on her knees beside the dead horse and big tears rolled down her cheeks.

"What has happened?" asked Hilde, putting her head out of the covered wagon.

"Rudi is dead!" cried Rosa. "Our poor Rudi!"

They managed to get the wagon on to the side of the road. They all got down from it. Sergeant Reber stood among these women and the two children. He had covered his nakedness by wearing an old pair of trousers lent to him by Professor Menzel and a short fur coat which belonged to Ursel.

The dead horse was being removed. Rosa Gottlieb was weeping over it until dragged off by a young farmer, not urgently but with rough speech.

"No use crying over dead meat, young woman."

"What shall we do now?" asked Hilde, terribly distressed.

"One thing is certain," said her aunt. "We can't go on. We must get shelter somewhere."

One of the farmers spoke to Sergeant Reber.

"Over there is Quakenbrück. It's a fair-sized town. You may get help."

Reber nodded and spoke to Hilde.

"It's the only thing to do. I'll go into the town and find some place for you."

"Can you walk?" she asked. "Are you well enough?"

He nodded.

"My burns are healing. The pain has gone. I will come back and let you know."

He walked towards the town of Quakenbrück not far from the road. He could see the spire of its church and its cluster of roofs and its big farmsteads on the outskirts. It was in a district called the Artland redeemed from swamps and marshes made by the seven branches of the Hase river. Cattle were grazing in the flat fields which were hedged round like those in England. It was a Sunday morning when Franz Reber walked that way. He had told Hilde that he was free from pain but he limped badly and could feel the blisters smarting under Ursel's fur jacket and Professor Menzel's old trousers, twelve inches too short for his long legs. On one side of his face was a large scab disfiguring him.

There were no people about as he walked down the winding high street. The shops were shuttered and the town seemed deserted, because of the early hour not long after dawn.

Not quite deserted. Sergeant Reber saw an old man coming towards him. It was a priest in his black gown and biretta. He was on his way to early Mass.

Reber stopped in front of him.

"Excuse me, sir. May I speak to you?"

The old priest started violently. He had been walking with his head bent, muttering a prayer. He raised his head and stared at Franz Reber with a look of apprehension because of this strange apparition burnt and scarred about the face, strangely garbed.

"Who are you, my son?" he asked.

"I come from those refugees on the road. I'm one of them, for a time."

"Poor people!" said the priest. "My heart bleeds for them. It bleeds for our poor Fatherland in this time of dreadful peril."

"I ask for your help, sir," said Reber.

The old priest raised his hands a little.

"In what way? I am very helpless. I'm an old man with nothing but my prayers to offer."

Franz Reber appealed to his pity.

"A wagon has broken down. One of the horses has died. Inside the wagon is a young mother whose baby was buried in the snow. There are other women and two children and a paralysed man, and two young girls who are fleeing from the Russian advance."

"They are right to flee," said the old priest. "I shudder at the thought of any young girls in the hands of the Russians."

"They can go no farther," said Reber. "They need shelter. Can you help me to find decent lodgings for them in this town?"

The old priest raised his hands again—thin transparent hands—with a gesture of despair.

"Quakenbrück is crowded with refugees. Hundreds of them have arrived, almost thousands. Every room is taken. Many of them are camped behind the church and in other fields. I pity them all. I pray for them all."

Sergeant Reber looked into his eyes, the blue watery eyes of old-age.

"I ask your pity and your help for one cartload of human beings. I seem to remember a story about a good Samaritan. Pardon me for reminding you of it."

The old priest made a gesture of helplessness.

"What can I do?" he asked. "I cannot help all these refugees who have been pouring along these roads for weeks past. I have no food. I have no money. Tell me what I can do, my dear sir. I am a servant of our Lord Jesus Christ, but alas I cannot perform miracles like that of the loaves and fishes."

"Perhaps there is a farmhouse or a lodging-house to which I can take my friends for rest and shelter. One of them is ill. The others are exhausted. They need rest and a roof over their heads."

The priest shook his head.

"The farmhouses are overcrowded. The houses in the town have put whole families into their small rooms, not asking for payment and for pity's sake. Quakenbrück is on the high road from East Prussia you understand."

He bent his head and seemed to be thinking deeply. Then he raised his head and spoke again.

"There is one house which may be empty today. I have an idea that the refugees are moving on."

"That's wonderful," said Reber. "Who owns the house . . . and where may I find it?"

The priest hesitated as though doubtful about his answer.

"It's the house of a Jewess. Her husband——"

He checked himself and added a few words.

"It's three houses away from my church yonder. It has a green door. The woman's name, poor soul, is Goldstein."

"A thousand thanks," said Reber.

"May God go with you," said the priest.

A church bell began to ring with single strokes on one monotonous note. A few people came out of the houses staring at Sergeant Reber as he walked towards the church—a human scarecrow and a disfigured man. He found the house with the green door and knocked upon it. It had a brass plate beneath the knocker. On it was the name of Dr. Rachel Goldstein. He had to knock three times before the door was opened by a middle-aged woman. She had black hair and eyes and a dead white face with Jewish features. Down one cheek from her right eye to her chin was a scarlet line. She looked frightened at the sight of this strange man.

"Frau Goldstein?" he asked.

She answered in a low voice and he saw fright in her eyes.

"Who are you? What do you want with me?"

"I've been sent here by an old priest," said Reber. "He gave me your name. I'm looking for shelter for some refugees whose wagon has broken down."

The fright left her eyes at his explanation of his visit. Her voice altered its tone.

"More refugees? Until last night this house was filled with them. They're coming in a tide."

She looked at Reber's scarred face and strange attire.

"Have you had an accident?" she asked.

"It's nothing. Let me tell you about my friends. If you could give them house-room for a time."

"I'm a Jewess," she told him as though she might have been a leper.

"That makes no difference to me," said Reber.

She looked into his eyes as though wondering whether he spoke with sincerity and for a moment veiled her own eyes and answered with a kind of bitterness and irony.

"It makes quite a difference sometimes, even here in Quakenbrück, and more in Belsen."

That name of Belsen meant nothing to Sergeant Reber. He had never heard of it.

"My people will be grateful for shelter here," he said. "If you would be so very kind. . . ."

"Come in," she said.

She led him into a room on the left side of a little square hall. It was well furnished and spotlessly clean and polished. There were some oil-paintings on the walls, one a striking portrait of a young woman with black hair and eyes. He looked at this for a moment with an artist's eyes and said, "That's good. Very strong."

"My husband painted it," she answered.

"He knows how to paint," said Reber.

"He's dead," she told him in a quiet voice. "He died in Belsen."

Again she mentioned that name of Belsen, which meant nothing to him.

"Tell me about your friends," she said, before he could express sympathy for the death of an artist.

He told her about Hilde and Frau von Grottenbach and the two children and the two nieces and Rosa the farm girl and Professor Menzel who had had a stroke.

"There is also myself. I'm a refugee until I become a soldier again—if I become a soldier again."

"No soldiering for a little while," she told him. "You ought to be in hospital."

"You will take us in then?" asked Reber.

She nodded.

"Of course. If it weren't you it would be others. The mayor of Quakenbrück knows every empty room."

"Ten thousand thanks," said Reber. "I'll bring them along. They will be deeply grateful."

He paused for a moment before leaving her room and his look went to the portrait again.

"You?" he asked a little doubtfully because this was the portrait of a young Jewess.

"Before the War and before Belsen," she answered.

It had no scarlet line from the right eyebrow to the chin.

He went back to the road and told his news to Hilde and the others. Two farmers from one of the wagons helped to carry Professor Menzel who was unable to walk. Hilde held the hands of her two children who were excited at leaving the wagon and going to a house again. Ursel and Hildegard were ashamed of their dirtiness and dishevelled look and were timid of entering Quakenbrück as though they were cave-dwellers entering civilization. Aunt Tessa walked by the side of Sergeant Reber and once asked him a question in a low voice.

"What's going to be the end of this adventure? Shall we be safe here?"

"For a little while perhaps," he answered.

So they came to the house of Dr. Rachel Goldstein.

CHAPTER V

It was a temporary return to civilized life in this small stone house in the town of Quakenbrück on the road to Berlin. To wash again, to sleep in clean, white beds, to sit in little rooms with polished floors and furniture was a blessed state after weeks in a covered wagon. Some of the refugees, kind-hearted folk on the whole, had carried up the bags and cases from the wagon, and Hilde, Aunt Tessa, and the two girls had put on decent frocks again after being huddled in blankets and shawls. Hildegard and Ursel had tidied their hair and used lipstick again as Sergeant Reber noticed with observing eyes. Hilde's face remained white because of the wounds in her heart, but Reber who had known her sister Christel before the war, was struck by the beauty of her face made more striking because there was such a tragic look in her eyes, unless sometimes she smiled at Hans and Trudel, now delighted with life, able to stretch their limbs, to run from room to room and seek an adventure in the little garden behind the house. Frau von Grottenbach was no longer looking like an old gypsy. In the evenings she wore a dress brought from Paris by one of her relatives and seemed years younger than when she had sat on a packing-case singing nursery rhymes to the little ones. Even Rosa Gottlieb had put on a neat black frock and brushed her straw-coloured hair.

Sergeant Reber had a sense of unreality. 'This is all an illusion,' he thought. 'It has no reality in any permanent sense. It is only a stopping-place for a tick of time on a tide of terror, flowing towards a dark Unknown. There's no safety here for these women and children."

He said nothing like that to Hilde or the others until one evening when they were sitting alone Hilde questioned him. He had been sketching her in pen and ink on a piece of writing-paper which he had found on the desk in the room.

"May I see?" she asked, noticing what he was doing.

He pushed over the drawing.

"I would like to do your head in oils," he said. "You have a good head for a painter."

She looked at his drawing with grave eyes.

"I was never so pretty as Christel," she said.

Franz Reber smiled for a moment remembering Christel.

"I only knew her as a young girl. I used to flirt with her."

"I long to see her again," said Hilde. "I long to see my father and mother. I've been separated from them for six years. It seems like a lifetime."

"It is a lifetime," said Reber. "We've gone from one life to another in that time. At least I have. That art student in Munich who was myself is now a ghost. I was a fresh young fellow then, a child, high-spirited and gullible. I believed in Hitler, the Nazi creed, all the muck of Alfred Rosenberg, the pagan altars, the Wagnerian myth."

He laughed and then became grave again.

"I was just typical of the Hitler Youth. Now I'm one of the untouchables. I've waded through blood. I reek with the smell of death. I've seen abominable things, the hanging of civilians, the rape of women, the slaughter of men in the mass. I've lost all illusions, or rather everything seems to me an illusion. I'm really dead inside. I only just walk about and eat and sleep and talk. But inside I'm really dead. My mind is outside my body and I see everything as a kind of dream, or as a kind of pattern woven by the Fates. It's a very queer feeling. It makes everything seem futile and objectless. Shall I come alive again?"

Hilde answered him gravely.

"I can understand what you mean. I feel a little dead, too, because of my dead baby, and my lost man."

She caught her breath for a moment as though a sob had risen to her throat but then spoke again quietly.

"You've been through worse things. They've been an outrage to your former sensibilities. You love beauty as an artist and you have seen only ugliness and beastliness. One day you will get back again. All that will fade out of your mind. They were not your fault. You were the helpless instrument of evil powers.

"I wish I could think so," said Reber. "Sometimes I dare to think so."

"After this war," said Hilde, "we may find beauty again and faith in God."

She checked herself and looked at him across the table.

"Franz," she said, "will there be any after the war for any of us? What is going to happen? Is Germany going to be utterly defeated?"

Franz Reber was silent for a time. His pen was making patterns on another slip of paper.

"The German people can't be destroyed utterly," he said. "But those who live will walk through a valley of darkness. Our enemies will want revenge. We have made many enemies."

"Yes," said Hilde. "The Führer hasn't been merciful."

"Nor the Generals," said Reber. "We didn't make war with bouquets in our hands."

"I'm afraid," said Hilde. "I'm afraid for Hans and Trudel. When little Peter died I wept, but now I'm almost glad he died though it's like a knife in my heart."

Reber reached out his hand and touched hers.

"I understand. But what can I say except that I'm a fatalist? All that happens is ordained by Destiny. We're all moved by Destiny. I seem to see that. We can't escape from Destiny or alter its course."

Hilde shook her head.

"That's the worst pessimism. It denies all freedom of the human spirit. It gets rid of God. It makes us slaves without free will. We've no choice in that case."

"I've had no choice," he answered bitterly. "I've been a driven man, like all my comrades, under an inescapable compulsion."

They talked gravely of life's mystery with a sense of enormous tragedy bearing down upon them. This was only an interlude—a few hours of sanctuary from pursuing demons.

"I can't see any hope for us," said Reber. "On the Eastern Front we can't hold out against Russian man-power. Our armies are being cut to bits. The front is too long and we've lost too many men. The Americans and English are on the Rhine."

"The West Wall didn't hold," said Hilde. "We believed it was impregnable."

Reber laughed harshly.

"Everything we've been told is a lie. We've been fed on lies. Choked with lies. My friend Folz was right. He always said so."

"Folz!" exclaimed Hilde. "Lotte's husband?"

Reber nodded.

"His wife is Lotte. He has two children. He was desperate to see them again. Now he's dead."

Hilde looked into his eyes and her face whitened.

"Lotte is dead. The two children are dead. Lotte killed them in Königsberg and then killed herself. She died in my room."

Reber put his hands over his face and groaned heavily.

"Many women in Königsberg killed themselves," said Hilde.

Upstairs Professor Menzel lay stricken. The will-power which had kept him up on the first stages of the journey had broken down. He was like a sick child, frightened and querulous if left alone. Hilde and Aunt Tessa took turns in sitting by his bedside. He found difficulty with his speech and his right arm lay limp and twisted above the bed-clothes. But his eyes brightened when Hans or Trudel came into his room and he raised himself in bed a little and tried to hide his weakness.

"I shall soon be well," he told Hans one morning, speaking quite clearly. "I'm thinking out some good stories for you."

"About soldiers?" asked Hans.

"About the olden times," said Professor Menzel, "when there was no war and the German people were happy and made beautiful things and the best music."

"That sounds dull," said Hans. "If you could put in a few dragons it might be all right, Grandpa. Or knights with battle-axes dripping with blood."

"You bloodthirsty little wretch!" cried Aunt Tessa, laughing at this fair-haired boy of six with eyes like cornflowers and the face of an angel.

One evening Dr. Rachel Goldstein came into the sitting-room. She had held aloof from these refugees who had taken shelter in her house. She was polite to them when they met on the stairs or in the kitchen, but very cold and rather ghostlike.

"She's like a ghost in the house," said Hildegard. one evening. "She goes about silently. She hardly ever speaks. I think she hates us."

"I'm not surprised if she hates us," said Aunt Tessa. "She's a Jewess. We haven't been very kind to the Jews. Even before the War the Führer would not allow them any rights and our young hooligans smashed their shops. I saw it in Berlin. I was disgusted."

"They're dreadful people," said Hildegard. "I detest them all."

"They're human beings," said Aunt Tessa tolerantly. "I used to know some very nice Jews. Now I suppose they're all in concentration camps, poor creatures."

"Well, that won't do them any harm," said Hildegard. "They're the best place for them."

It was after that conversation that Dr. Rachel Goldstein came into the sitting-room one night when Franz Reber was alone with Hilde, the others having gone to bed.

Reber rose from his chair and said, "Sit down with us, won't you? We hardly ever see you, Dr. Goldstein."

He had no prejudice now against this Jewess. He found her kind. She had examined his burns one morning and had dressed them with some soothing stuff. Her tragic face and that scar down it made him curious about her, and he agreed with Hildegard that she was ghost-like and mysterious.

When he gave her this invitation her face flushed for a moment and she shook her head.

"Thank you, no. I came in only to draw the curtains."

She moved towards the door, but Hilde spoke to her.

"Do come and sit with us. We're very grateful for being in your house. It's like paradise after the covered wagon. Have you lived here long?"

Dr. Rachel Goldstein looked at Hilde and for a moment her eyes softened, perhaps because she remembered what Franz Reber had told her about the baby buried in the snow.

"You want to be kind to me," she said, "and I don't want to be impolite to kind people. But it's dangerous for Germans to talk to Jews. They keep away from me in Quakenbrück where I had a good practice. Most of them are afraid to come to a Jewish doctor. Now I've lost my practice and people who used to be my friends. I helped to bring many children into the world in Quakenbrück. Now their mothers turn their heads away if they see me in the street. I'm a pariah. I'm one of the untouchables. I'm a Jewess in Hitler's Germany."

She spoke with a kind of suppressed passion and bitterness. There was silence in the room until it was broken by Franz Reber.

"I'm against all that. Once as a young Nazi I was stuffed with anti-Semitism. I believed it. I believed in a creed which I know now was false and inhuman and unbeautiful. I've come to loathe cruelty."

Dr. Rachel Goldstein looked at him and laughed. It was not a pleasant laugh. Her face became like a Greek mask of tragedy.

"You're a German," she said. "You're one of Hitler's soldiers. If you're ordered to shoot Jews, to torture them, to push them into gas-ovens—thousands of them—you will obey because you're a German and a soldier of the German army. Heil Hitler! . . . Excuse me. I will go. Pardon me for saying these things. I've been very foolish."

She was going towards the door again but Reber strode towards her and took her arm.

"What do you mean by all that?" he asked. "You can't go away having said these things. What has happened to you? . . . Why do you talk about torture and gas-ovens? What madness is in your mind?"

He spoke angrily. She had accused the whole German army and the German people as though they were all torturers and murderers. He let go of her arm but stood between her and the door

She repeated his last words, that question of his.

"What madness is in my mind? Look at my face. Can't you see that scar on it? It was done by the slash of a Nazi whip. If I stood naked before you you would see how they flayed my body. I was in Ausschwitz and in Belsen. Have you never heard of Ausschwitz? Have you never heard of Belsen?"

"They mean nothing to me," answered Franz Reber.

Hilde was silent. Several times in Königsberg she had heard some of her friends talking about Ausschwitz and Belsen and Dachau and Buchenwald in lowered voices, looking over their shoulders before whispering. They were concentration camps. Thousands of Germans had been put in them for criticizing Hitler or speaking against the War. They were crowded with Jews who had been taken there in cattle-trucks from many parts of Germany. What happened to them no-one knew.

Dr. Rachel Goldstein began to speak again and her face was a mask of pain and there was a horror in her eyes.

"You are young people. You are innocent of all this. How can I dare tell you of the things that happen in those places?"

"Tell us," said Reber. "We must know."

Dr. Rachel Goldstein stared at him but as though not seeing him and looking through him to some dreadful vision beyond.

"They stripped the Jews naked. Men, women and children. They drove them into the gas-ovens. I heard their screams, and then their silence. My husband was one of them. They stripped him naked and drove him to the gas-ovens, but he didn't scream. He looked at me and smiled. I was kept back for other uses. It was all well organized. Nothing was wasted. The hair of these Jews was used to stuff mattresses. Their dentures were taken out and the gold extracted."

Franz Reber cried out in indignation and disbelief.

"I can't believe it. You're lying to us. You're mad."

She ignored his words. Perhaps she did not hear them. She was staring at that dreadful vision of Ausschwitz and Belsen.

"They did worse things than that. In the gas-oven one dies quickly. It's better than slow torture. It's less wicked than using living bodies and human souls for foul experiment. There were doctors—men of science—who were devils in white clothes. They infected many prisoners, many young men and women, with foul diseases. They destroyed their sex organs by horrible means. They made them idiots."

"No!" cried Reber. "It's unbelievable!"

Dr. Rachel Goldstein looked at him sombrely.

"These things are going on now all over Germany. In the concentration camps it's a living death for thousands and tens of thousands. If they are lucky they die. They die of dysentery, typhoid and hunger. They're starved. I've seen them crawling about on their hands and knees. Babies are born there. Little children see the corpses of those who die day by day and lie rotting until they are shovelled away. They go mad with hunger, these prisoners. Women scream for food to give their little ones and fierce dogs are turned on to them to keep them quiet. Even the guards are frightened of them. The women guards go round with whips. I am a Jewess and they tortured me, but I have pity for the Germans who are there for the crime of free speech or because they were falsely denounced by informers trying to save themselves or curry favour with the S.S. I have seen all this. I have suffered all this. I saw my husband, an artist and a gentle soul, led off to the gas-ovens. You ask what madness is in my mind! I wonder only that I am not a raving lunatic . . ."

Suddenly she flung herself against the door with both hands clasped above her head, moaning like a stricken animal.

Franz Reber took hold of her and held her in a strong grip.

"You tell us these horrors," he said. "I can't believe them. I daren't believe them. There's not such wickedness in Germany. There aren't such devils in Germany. How dare you tell us such things?"

Hilde spoke to him quietly.

"Franz, they're true. I've heard them whispered about. These things are happening. My father-in-law has heard them. My friends have heard them. For a long time I refused to believe them. Now I believe."

Franz Reber let go of Rachel Goldstein who stumbled towards a chair like a blind woman and held on to it.

"You believe it?" he asked incredulously.

Hilde looked him in the eyes.

"The human beast has come out of its lairs," she said. "Men—some men—have become devils. Or they were devils kept in chains by civilization and Christian tradition. Their chains have been broken and they've been let loose."

Franz Reber gave a loud groan which seemed to be torn from his heart and throat.

"O Christ!" he cried. "O Christ! Are we as bad as that? Torturers and homicidal maniacs. If this woman's story is true——"

He turned to Rachel Goldstein.

"You are a Jewess," he said. "You tell us that all the Jews were driven into gas-ovens. Then how are you here? Why are you in Quakenbrück alive and left in peace?"

Rachel Goldstein was still holding on to the back of a chair. This ghost-like woman with a scar down her cheek had become cold and quiet again.

"I am a doctor," she said. "They wanted to use me in their laboratories and tortured me when I refused. I was marked down for the gas-ovens and I would have gone with courage, I think. But the commandant's wife was in labour. The commandant came and asked my help. Something had gone wrong, he said.

The camp doctor was a fool. His wife was dying. I saved her. This man who had murdered thousands of my own folk wept and asked my help and promised me release if I would save the mother and child. . . .. That is how I was set free. That is why I am in Quakenbrück shunned by most of its inhabitants who are afraid of coming to a Jewish doctor, though once they knew my skill and were glad to pay for it."

Franz Reber was silent. Somehow it was necessary to believe this woman. Hilde believed. There was a terrible truth in Rachel Goldstein's voice and in her eyes. Suddenly he felt he was bound to believe.

"Ghastly!" he said in a low voice. "I'm filled with horror. We deserve to be defeated. If there's a God He will punish us."

He stood there with bent head staring at the floor.

Dr. Rachel Goldstein glanced at him—this young man with scars of burning on his face. It was curious that her voice had a note of pity in it when she answered.

"I'm sorry to have told you these things," she said. "I'm a Jewess, but I'm also a German. The German people are not guilty of these things. Many Germans are in the concentration camps—my comrades in suffering. I don't want the innocent to suffer for the guilty. I only want that when a terrible hatred and madness take hold of me and I too become evil."

Hilde went towards her with deep emotion and put her arms about her and kissed her cheek. "I want to go down on my knees to you. What you have suffered tears at my heart."

Dr. Rachel's white face flushed again and she pushed Hilde away almost roughly.

"I'm a lucky one," she said. "Pity those who are still there."

She hesitated in a nervous way and then spoke again.

"Forgive me, and thank you. I used to have good manners but I lost them in Ausschwitz. Good night. If you will excuse me . . ."

She left the room closing the door quietly behind her.

"I feel disembowelled," said Franz Reber in a low voice.

CHAPTER VI

THEY stayed in Quakenbrück while weeks passed and the first warmth of Spring melted all the snow and presently reawakened the earth after its Winter's sleep. That was because Professor Menzel was too ill to be moved and the Russians from whom they were fleeing seemed to be held up for a time or paused before another advance. Königsberg had fallen and the silence of death surrounded it.

But Franz Reber was still a sergeant in the German army. The War had not yet ended. His burns had healed.

"Why am I staying here?" he asked. "Why don't I report to the first officer who passes this way?"

He asked those questions to himself in the loneliness of a small bedroom barely furnished in this house of Dr. Rachel Goldstein. The bed and one chair took up most of the room which in the old days had been used by a maidservant. On one of the walls was a German lithograph of Moses striking the rock. She must have been a Jewess like her mistress. On the mantelshelf was a cuckoo clock which no longer worked.

Generally he sat on the bed when he wanted to think and he was thinking night after night over this question of rejoining the army. If he failed to do so he laid himself open to arrest as a deserter.

He was not quite honest with himself in these secret thoughts. He was held back, he believed, from reporting to the nearest officer or military unit by a spiritual revulsion from the War itself—a War which ought never to have been fought, as his friend Folz had convinced him after a year of argument.

"I shan't go back," he said to himself, "because I don't believe in the War and hate its senselessness. I shan't go back because in any case we shall be defeated and have already lost. I shan't go back because it's only dragging out the agony and the death and it would be best to surrender now instead of going on to the last hour of Germany's utter destruction."

Those reasons for living like a civilian, like a man in hiding, seemed honest and adequate. There was no insincerity in them. As a soldier he was finished, without heart or hope in the cause of fighting. Dr. Rachel Goldstein's narrative of torture and mass murder had profoundly affected him. How could he go on fighting to defend men like Hitler and Himmler who had thought out these atrocities in cold blood, who knew every detail of what was happening in the concentration camps and prisons, who gloated over the 'liquidation', as they called it, of the Jewish race, and whose secret police seized upon any man or woman or young girl who dared to whisper a word of criticism or horror against their bloody tyranny? 'If I go on fighting,' he thought, 'if I put on a uniform again having heard what this Jewess has told me, I am an accomplice of evil, one of the instruments of their maniacal hatreds and foul perversities. By moral cowardice, my fear of arrest and imprisonment in one of those camps I should be guilty of these crimes, I should share the guilt which will disgrace Germany and our German people for ever in history. I wish to God Folz were here to talk things over. Folz would tell me whether I'm thinking honestly and whether I'm justified in deserting.'

Franz Reber was thinking honestly up to a point. But one thought he shirked. There was another reason which made him stay in this house week after week. Perhaps he was unconscious of it. He found the life in this house, this sanctuary amidst the storm of war, sweet and pleasant because of Hilde Menzel. Not that he had fallen in love with her in any coarse or primitive way. He wouldn't dare to fall in love with her in that way. She was the mother of Hans and Trudel. Her husband might not be dead. In any case his love for her was reverential. It was, he thought, no more than a beautiful comradeship in this time of tragedy. They had been together in the covered wagon, and lying there with his wounds burning he had watched her face and listened to her voice when she was trying to keep the children happy while she bled at the heart for the baby she had laid in the snow. At first she had reminded him of Christel, the young girl who had gone skiing with him in Bavaria when he was a boy of eighteen. Then he had seen a different kind of beauty in Hilde's face, a more spiritual courage, a wonderful unselfishness, a kind of saintliness. Now in this house when the others had gone to bed, when Hilde and he were alone together in the little room downstairs while she sat sewing and mending the children's clothes, they had long talks in quiet voices or just long silences together. As a soldier in Russia he had been starved of women's companionship. He had never, all that time, sat in a civilized room with a woman of intelligence and culture. He had been cut off from home life and from all that meant civilization. He had lived in ruins, in trenches, in mud-holes, in filth, in the stench of death. Here in the house of this Jewess in Quakenbrück, on the road to Berlin, he had come back to decency, to cleanliness, and to a woman's understanding and intelligence. She understood his perplexities, his disillusionment, the grim fatalism with which he had steeled himself in a kind of stoicism. She understood even if she disagreed. In her silences she was good company. He liked to glance at her as she sat mending the children's clothes, looking almost too young to be a mother. She had fine thin hands with long fingers. She was not blonde like a German Mädchen, like her sister Christel, but had dark hair and eyes and high cheek-bones and curved, thin eyebrows.

"You look Italian," he told her once.

One night he spoke to her about his position as a soldier and his inward struggle on that subject.

"If I don't report soon I shall be arrested as a deserter."

She was startled.

"Then you had better report, Franz. That would be horrible. You've stayed too long with us."

Franz Reber nodded gloomily.

"I'm perfectly well again, barring scars. Perfectly well in my body."

"Not in your mind?"

"I revolt against this war. It's only dragging out the agony of Germany. My stomach turns at the idea of going back into that hell on earth and the stench of the battlefield and the heaps of dead bodies, and the mutilated and the blinded. To what purpose is all that? From the beginning what purpose was there in it except to increase the megalomania of Adolf Hitler and the lust for power of those who surrounded him?"

Hilde Menzel dropped her needlework.

It was a moment or two before she answered him.

"Did you talk like that at the beginning?" she asked, "when Hitler was winning great victories and seemed invincible?"

"I was one of the deluded fools," he admitted. "I was a hundred per cent Nazi. I quarrelled with my father because he mocked at them. It was Folz who made me see things in a different way. And I've grown up since then. I have learned to think."

Hilde answered him after a pause.

"Yes, we're all different now. But is it quite fair to desert in the hour of defeat? Is it right to go into hiding when the Fatherland is doomed? One doesn't think of Hitler now. One thinks of Germany. Would you be happy in your mind if you became a deserter?"

She was not reproaching him. She was asking questions which reached down deep into his consciousness.

He shifted in his seat uneasily and his face flushed slightly.

"I shouldnt go into hiding for cowardice," he said. "It would be for conscience' sake. After hearing Rachel Goldstein's story I can't bring myself to fight for leaders who have ordered and connived at such foul cruelties, disgracing our German name for ever."

They stared into each other's eyes thinking of Rachel Goldstein's tale of torture and mass murder.

"The German people aren't guilty of that," said Hilde, in a low voice.

"They came out of German minds," he answered bitterly. "We called ourselves civilized."

Hilde's face had gone white.

"We only heard fearful rumours," she said. "We were powerless anyhow. What could I do? What could Ursel and Hildegard have done even if they knew? Hans and Trudel aren't guilty of these things, poor mites."

Franz Reber groaned heavily and sat with his elbows on the table and his head hunched over his arms.

"We shall have to pay for those crimes," he said. "All of us will have to pay somehow—even Hans and Trudel. The gods will demand vengeance on us as a nation, as a people. I seem to see that. It's part of the pattern of Fate."

"How do you mean?" asked Hilde, frightened by his words which seemed to be wrenched out of him.

"I believe in Destiny," he said, "without understanding it.

A man has his own private destiny. It was begun for him by his ancestors in the forests. He does what he does because of heredity, the logical steps of historical development, and some pre-ordained plot which he has to follow."

"That's a terrible creed!" cried Hilde. "That excuses Hitler and Himmler—if they were blind instruments of Fate."

Hilde's words shook him a little.

"It's all very mysterious," he admitted. "Perhaps I'm wrong, but I feel that I personally have no control over my own fate. I'm just a blind sheep driven on to whatever end is waiting for me."

"You have a free choice," said Hilde. "It's in your own will-power to decide which way you are going at this moment—to be a deserter in the hour of defeat, or to fight on for the Fatherland until the last."

"Fight on for Hitler?" he asked. "Fight on for Himmler? Fight on for more concentration camps, more medical experiments on human beings, more abominations?"

"Fight on to prevent the Russians making slaves of us, ill-treating our young girls, and me, the mother of Hans and Trudel."

A shudder passed through her body. Was she not in this house at Quakenbrück because she had fled from Königsberg to avoid the fate which caused that shudder?

Franz Reber rose from the table and strode up and down the room torn by the conflict of his thoughts. One thought was that if he decided one way at this crossroad of life he would never see this woman again, this young mother for whom he had a kind of love and a kind of worship.

He stopped and spoke quietly.

"So you advise me to report?"

Hilde shook her head. He saw that her eyes were wet.

"You mustn't ask for my advice, or for anybody's. You must obey what's in your own mind and what you think is best. Which-ever way you choose I shan't blame you, Franz. I think I under-stand you after our talks together and this comradeship. You're struggling to find truth and the absolute ideal, and in your heart you love beauty as an artist and hate cruelty and all its ugliness. You've been hurt and damaged, Franz. Your soul has been wounded. I wish I could comfort you."

"You're of great comfort to me," he said. "This wayside halt has been like an oasis in the desert. I hate to leave it."

He left the next morning. All through the night he had sat on his narrow bed in the little room thinking things out. But he had no freedom of choice really, or no sense of freedom. Hilde had decided for him. That shudder she had given at the thought of what would happen in Germany if the Russians came in had forced his decision. He must be one of the defenders.

Hildegard and Ursel wept when he told them he was leaving them and the two children cried a little until they became excited about a frog in the garden. Hilde did not weep but said, "I shall pray for you."

"Yes, pray for me," he answered. "That's one way of thinking of me."

She held out her hands and he clasped them and kissed her cheek.

He went upstairs for a few minutes to say good-bye to Professor Menzel, that white-haired scholar and teacher who had led his family out of Königsberg. He lay there stricken in his bed but with his eyes alive.

"You must go?" he asked.

"Yes, I must go, sir."

"I'm dying," said the Professor. "I'm afraid for the women-folk and the two children. They need a man to help them. Tell them they ought to leave me here."

"They won't leave you," said Reber.

"The Russians may come quite soon now. They must get away."

"That would be wise," said Reber.

"They must get some transport. I can do nothing while I lie here like a log."

"Perhaps the Russians won't come to Quakenbrück," said Reber.

"I'm afraid," said Professor Menzel.

"I must go now, sir. *Auf Wiedersehen.*"

The old man clung on to his hand.

"Don't leave me! I'm afraid."

"Of death?" asked Reber.

"No, no! That's a release. I'm afraid because of what is going to happen."

"What is going to happen?"

"Germany is doomed. The vengeance of our enemies will be terrible. I pity the young people—Hans and Trudel."

Tears oozed out of his eyes and fell down his wax-like face. Reber waited with him until he fell into a sleep, the beginning of the long sleep. Then he removed his hand from the old man's clasp and crept out of the room.

Sergeant Reber returned to duty.

CHAPTER VII

HILDE MENZEL felt a loss and a loneliness without Franz Reber. Now that her father-in-law was so stricken there was no man to whom she could turn or upon whose strength and service she could depend in these dangerous days. Besides she had been glad of Reber's company and conversation. She felt curiously older than Franz though they were about the same age and he had gone through all the horrors in Russia. He was like a bewildered boy when he talked of Destiny. There was no logic, she thought, in what he said. There was no sense in it according to her own faith but she had seen how he was struggling in his mind to find some philosophy which would reconcile him to the things that were happening and to the things he had had to do and suffer. Was she not equally bewildered and as deep in despair? Was she not terrified of the future and the present peril? Yet she felt more mature, older and wiser in a way than this young soldier who had come into her life through the flap in the covered wagon, covered with frightful burns. She was glad he had chosen to go back rather than slink about as a deserter, glad for his sake and sorry for her own. What now? How long could they stay safe in Quakenbrück? Their store of food was nearly exhausted. None of them had any money beyond a few hundred marks. Would it be their fate to go into a refugee camp, to live on potato soup and black bread, to become dirty and verminous, to catch every kind of infectious disease?

"We must get to Berlin at all costs," said her Aunt Tessa with whom she discussed these things after Reber had left that day. "If we can get to Berlin there'll be a roof over our heads and food for the children. Your Uncle Fritz and his wife will be there to welcome us. Their house in the Grünewald is very comfortable."

"How are we going to get to Berlin?" asked Hilde.

Her aunt did not answer that question. The door opened at that moment and Rachel Goldstein came into the room.

"You had better go up," she said. "The Herr Professor hasn't long to live. I've been into his room."

Hilde and her aunt ran upstairs followed by this woman doctor.

"Papa!" cried Hilde.

His eyes were open but he did not see her. Nor did they move to show his awareness of their presence.

"Dearest Karl!" cried his sister.

Dr. Rachel Goldstein felt his pulse and then put her hand over his heart.

"The end has come," she said. "He's dead. I will leave you."

Hilde and her aunt fell on to their knees by the bedside, crossing themselves, and presently Ursel and Hildegard came into the room and wept bitterly and noisily.

Hilde stood up and then stooped a little to kiss her father-in-law's forehead. She felt almost glad that he had gone. She almost envied him but for the thought of her children. No more terror. No need of flight. No tearing anxieties for other people—the little ones. No more anguish because Germany was defeated. How lucky were the dead! she thought.

She spoke to Ursel and Hildegard who were making such a noise of weeping.

"Be quiet. He's at peace. You and I haven't found peace yet."

They wept even more noisily, giving way to emotion.

Outside the door she found Rosa Gottlieb waiting with her hands clasped in prayer like Pacher's Madonna, a blonde Madonna.

"Go in, Rosa," said Hilde. "Keep those girls quiet."

"The poor gentleman is dead? Something told me when I was in the kitchen."

"For him it's the end of the journey," said Hilde. "But not for us, Rosa. We still have far to go."

Suddenly she too wept but quietly, not making a sound lest the children should hear. Papa Menzel was the father of Peter who had disappeared behind the veil. He was dead too. And Franz Reber had gone. Now everything was on her shoulders. She would have to be leader and guide in this valley of darkness. The first duty was to go to an undertaker. Papa Menzel would have to be buried. The priest would help her about that—the old priest who had directed Franz to this house.

She waited until Rosa came down to look after the children and then walked out into the High Street of Quakenbrück. Some people were about. They were refugees—peasant women from East Prussia, sturdy and neatly dressed but with anxious, worried faces.

"Is that Hilde Menzel?" asked a man's voice which startled her because she had been walking very deep in thought.

It was a young officer named Paul Schäfer. She had danced with him in Königsberg. He had known Peter. She had thought him good-looking and good-natured.

"What are you doing here?" he asked.

"I'm one of the refugees. We fled from Königsberg."

"How horrible!" he exclaimed. "How terrible! Those refugee columns make me shudder. They go on and on."

"No, it's not pleasant being a refugee," said Hilde. "But it's worse to be caught by the Russians."

"Yes. And the news isn't good. They still advance. God alone knows. . . ."

Hilde caught hold of the young officer's arm.

"Paul, how can I get to Berlin?"

"Why to Berlin?" he asked. "Berlin isn't very beautiful just now. American Fortresses and the R.A.F. are making it their target for the night. Every night."

It was on the way to Munich she told him. "I could get a train to Munich from Berlin."

"Munich is being bombed, too," he said gloomily. "All our cities are under fire. Those American swine and the damned English. . . ."

"We must get to Berlin," said Hilde desperately. "I have my children with me. I have others to look after. We have no money left. The life in a refugee camp. . . ."

"Too frightful," agreed Paul Schäfer. "Thank God my wife is in Bavaria. It seems pretty safe there outside the towns."

"From Berlin I could get to Bavaria with the children," said Hilde. "But we can't walk to Berlin, Paul. What shall I do? Help me. I need help."

The young officer pondered for a moment.

"I might get you on to a goods train. I'm transport officer in Quakenbrück. There's just a chance . . . but you mustn't count on it."

She counted on it. She prayed for this chance, but day after day passed and no message came from Paul Schäfer.

Karl Menzel was buried in Quakenbrück. Hans and Trudel were kept away from the graveyard but had to be told.

"Where is Grandpa?" asked Hans several times. It was Aunt Tessa who told him.

"God has taken him away."

"Then God is very unkind," said Hans fiercely. "Why should God take my Grandpa away?"

"He is now happy in Heaven," said Aunt Tessa.

Hans puckered his forehead.

"Does that mean he's dead? If so, why don't you say he's dead?"

"It must be funny being dead," said Trudel, who was playing with a kitten under the kitchen table. "When you're dead you can't move. You're like a broken toy. It doesn't work any more."

"I don't want my Grandpa to be dead," said Hans. "He's a friend of mine. He told me very good stories. I hate him being dead."

He gave a loud howl and then wept bitterly to the surprise ot Trudel who took things—even death—in a matter-of-fact way.

"Cry baby!" she said scornfully. "My kitten isn't dead anyhow."

Her kitten was very lively indeed.

Ursel and Hildegard walked about Quakenbrück looking into shop windows and once or twice to say a few prayers in church. Often they met friends from Königsberg and talked with them excitedly after embraces and laughter. They were young enough to laugh now that they had escaped from the covered wagon and now that the winter was over and the sun was shining and the terror of the Russians seemed so remote in this country town. It was better than digging trenches outside Königsberg as they had done for a week before their flight. It was better than being in a Labour camp as they had been for six months like all German girls. It almost seemed like a holiday, this stay in Quakenbrück.

"If there were only a few nice-looking boys about it wouldn't be too bad," said Hildegard one morning.

Ursel looked at her sideways.

"You think of nothing but boys and your own pretty face which isn't so pretty as you think. The shape of your nose leaves much to be desired."

"It's quite a nice nose," said Hildegard, glancing at herself in a shop window.

It was only a week since they had wept noisily by the bedside of Karl Menzel their uncle. Now they could laugh again, though terror lay behind them and perhaps ahead of them.

Then a message came one evening from Paul Schäfer. It was a note to say that he had found room for them in a covered truck of a goods train bound for Berlin.

It will be very uncomfortable [he wrote] *but it's the best I can do for you. Tomorrow at 7 a.m.*

"Thank God for that!" cried Aunt Tessa. "We shall be safe in Berlin. The Russians will never get as far as that."

"Fate drives us there," said Hilde, in a low voice. "I can see no other way. But there are many air raids. It may be very dangerous for the children. Sometimes I wonder if we ought to go to Berlin. Even now I'm not sure . . ."

"The air-raid shelters in Berlin are wonderful," said her aunt. "Your Uncle Fritz has told me that in many of his letters and he has a strong, well-built house. What else can we do, Hilde? Starve to death in a refugee camp?"

"We must go," said Hilde.

She said good-bye that night to Rachel Goldstein.

"Thank you. I hope we haven't been too much trouble."

"When you go," said Dr. Rachel Goldstein, "I shall have another crowd of refugees. They won't be so nice, I think. They won't be so polite to a filthy Jewess who escaped from the gas-ovens."

Hilde went forward and held out her arms but Dr. Goldstein shrank back.

"God forgive us all," said Hilde. "For all your tortures. For all your agony."

Rachel Goldstein looked at her with hard eyes and then suddenly wept.

"You have been kind to me," she said. "I'm not used to kindness. It hurts."

She did not shrink again when Hilde kissed her cheek.

An hour later Hilde and her family were in a closed truck on the way to Berlin.

CHAPTER VIII

It was not a good journey. The train was shunted into sidings to let troop-trains pass. The closed truck was packed with other refugees, mostly mothers and children, sitting on their baggage and bundles. The air became fusty. Some of the children were sick and wailing. The mothers were agitated and one became hysterical.

"This is worse than the covered wagon," said Ursel. "I feel very ill."

Hildegard was busy with her lipstick and the little mirror in her handbag but after several hours tired of this entertainment and tried to get forgetfulness in sleep crouched in the corner of the truck. Hans and Trudel played and quarrelled with the other children until, to Hilde's relief, they became tired and sleepy.

Close to her was a young woman of her own class who had come from Königsberg. They talked to each other from time to time. During one of these conversations the young woman mentioned the name of Sergeant Reber.

"He drove me in his radio-car until it caught on fire."

"He was carried into our wagon," said Hilde. "He was terribly burnt."

"He knew my husband," said the young woman. "Otto Hessell. He was with him when Otto was killed."

"I think my husband is dead," said Hilde. "Peter Menzel. "I had a dream or a vision. . . . I'm sure he's dead."

"It's better to be dead than a prisoner in Russia. Do you think the Russians will get to Berlin?"

Hilde stared at her with a look of horror.

"To Berlin? No, that's impossible. That's a terrible thing to say."

Magda Hessell raised her hands slightly.

"If we lose the War. . . ."

"You frighten me," said Hilde. "The Russians in Berlin? . . ."

Her forebodings had never gone as far as that. Franz Reber had told her the War was lost but she had never followed up that awful possibility as far as Berlin being ever in the hands of the Russians.

"I'm sorry I frightened you," said Magda Hessell. "But I'm a pessimist. I've lost all hope and all faith. It's better to be dead. I would like to be dead with Otto."

She spoke in a low voice. Nobody but Hilde could hear her on a train which clattered and chugged over hard worn lines. Hilde touched this girl's hand. She looked very young to be the wife of a dead soldier.

"Isn't that a surrender?" she asked.

"A surrender? How do you mean? We shall all have to surrender. Germany is lost. We're all lost."

"We mustn't lose our German soul," said Hilde. "Even if we're utterly defeated——"

"Our German soul?"

Magda Hessell raised her eyebrows and her eyes looked into those of Hilde.

"We've already lost our German soul. It has been debauched, violated and raped by devils and maniacs who have led us into this abomination."

"Those are terrible words," said Hilde.

"The truth is terrible," said Magda.

She was a young woman, rather beautiful except for the pallor of her skin and a haunted look in her eyes. They were both silent after that for a long time while children wailed and the noise of the train shunting again made talk impossible.

It was Magda Hessell who spoke again later.

"Franz Reber was kind to me. What's happened to him?"

"He has gone back to duty," said Hilde.

"He'll be killed, of course," said Magda. "All those boys will be killed before the end comes."

After being shunted into sidings for several hours at a time the train reached a station outside Berlin. It was nine o'clock in the evening and darkness had fallen over the capital but while some of the refugees stood on the platform collecting their bits of baggage the night sky was suddenly lit up vividly by a white light intensely brilliant, silvering the trees in the park and revealing the spires, domes and roofs of Berlin. Out of the silence sirens howled demoniacally.

A railway official spoke to Hilde Menzel standing there with her relatives and children.

"They come over at this time every night. They're dropping flares for the English bombers who will follow on. You must get down to the shelter over there, and pretty quick too."

They could see the flares suspended like balloons and touching the clouds with their spreading light.

"Isn't it pretty?" shouted Hans, who was holding his mother's hand. "Like fireworks!"

Hilde felt paralysed with fear. Perhaps she had been mad in bringing the children to Berlin.

Her Aunt Tessa spoke to her sharply.

"Hilde, are you dreaming? For God's sake . . ."

The air-raid shelter was only a few yards away. Rosa carried Trudel who was fast asleep. Ursel and Hildegard had grabbed their handbags and were running along the platform to the shelter entrance.

"Get down!" shouted a harsh voice.

There was an earth-shaking explosion. The first bomb had fallen. Black and sharp-cut in the white illumination over Berlin were the bird-like shapes of the British bombers, coming over like migrating swallows. The German anti-aircraft guns opened fire. Shells burst into a hundred thousand stars reaching up to the black birds who were weaving in and out as though in some mystical dance, until some of them were hit and fell like flaming torches. The white light changed to red—a furious throbbing red spreading over the whole sky as fires burnt fiercely in the ruins of Berlin where palaces, churches, government offices, banks, hotels and railway-stations were hurled into piles of rubble and twisted steel.

One great building like an Egyptian palace stood untouched except for some broken columns. It was the Chancellery of the German Reich where the man who had caused all this ruin and death still refused to admit defeat and issued mad orders to his Generals. All this death and all this ruin had come from his vainglory and megalomania—the death of millions of men defending their own soil, the death of hundreds of thousands of civilians in cities over which German aircraft had flown in England and many countries. In these ruins of London, Coventry, Portsmouth,

Liverpool, Leningrad, Warsaw, lay the bodies of old men and women, young mothers and children. Not enough! Not enough yet! On the coast of France strange new weapons had been in position to destroy more life and pile up more death—the innocent dead, the non-combatants. "This war will be won by technology," said the Man of Destiny before his exhausted armies staggered back in retreat, while British and American bombers were raining death upon German cities, tenfold in terror and destruction, with overwhelming vengeance in this murder of European civilization.

Now among the victims were German refugees. They were crowded round the railway-stations. Thousands were unable to get into over-crowded shelters. The moon and the stars looked down upon these huddled forms among their bundles and baggage. Women with children at the breast, old grannies, young girls. When the raid was over there were no pleasant scenes round the railway-stations in Berlin. . . . All was very quiet afterwards when the moon and the stars looked down to the wreckage and the ruin.

In the British Lancasters, young airmen—nice young fellows without blood-lust or cruelty—chatted with each other over the 'intercom'.

"Jolly good show!"

"We got the target all right."

"The flak was pretty hot."

"Pathfinder made it easy for us."

"A lucky kite, this. Some of the others——"

"Shut up. It's unlucky to talk of luck."

What had happened beneath them was outside their range of knowledge and interest. They had done the job and were getting back again.

Some of the refugees from Königsberg sat huddled in the air-raid shelter in the Grünewald. The children slept. Ursel and Hildegard listened white-faced to the muffled thunder above them and the earth-shaking crashes until their heads drooped and they went into their own dream world. Hilde Menzel stayed awake with troubled thoughts and many fears. Was there any escape from terror? They had fled from the Russians, but there was no safety in Berlin. They had come from one hell to another.

CHAPTER IX

BARON FRITZ VON MEISSNER was in his study after breakfast when his son Hermann tapped at his door and hardly waiting for a *Herein* entered the room.

"Father, cousin Hilde is here with her children and Aunt Tessa and the two girls! All the way from Königsberg."

"*Gott in Himmel!*" exclaimed his father. He put away some notes he had been writing, slipping them between the covers of a well-thumbed Shakespeare in one of his bookcases.

"Where are they?" he asked, quietly, after those first words of astonishment.

They were in the drawing-room with his wife Elizabeth who was embracing the children.

"This is a miracle!" said Herr von Meissner.

His cousin Tessa burst into tears at the joy of seeing him. She flung her arms about him and kissed him on both cheeks.

"Fritz! I never thought I should see you again."

When he had liberated himself he looked at Hilde with a grave smile.

"Can that be the pretty niece I knew as a little girl?"

He stooped to caress the two children who looked up at this tall silver-haired man with a white moustache.

"I've forgotten their names," he said. "Forgive me."

"Hans and Trudel," said Hilde.

"And the little one—Peter, wasn't it? I had a letter from you when he was born into this wicked world, poor child!"

It was Hans who answered.

"We left him in the snow. He was quite dead."

Herr von Meissner looked at Hilde who was weeping now and put his arms round her.

"Poor little mother! How tragic! But perhaps the little one has been spared many things. This is a terrible time for all of us."

Presently he asked a question after a moment's hesitation.

"Your husband, Peter, that nice fellow? What news?"

"No news," said Hilde, mournfully.

"He has not been reported as a prisoner of war?"

"No, Uncle. I'm afraid . . ."

Herr von Meissner nodded.

"It's the same with my son Wolf. We get no news of him. He may be a prisoner in Russia. That would not be too pleasant, God knows."

Hildegard and Ursel were talking and laughing with their cousin Hermann, a young man in one of the Government departments. He had uneasy eyes and every now and then looked at his father with a kind of apprehension or anxiety.

"After that cattle-truck this is Heaven!" cried Hildegard.

She glanced round the drawing-room in this house in the Grünewald with its chintz-covered chairs and mahogany tables and Persian rugs on the polished floor. On the walls were portraits of her uncle's ancestors and one of himself as a young officer in the Guards.

Hermann von Meissner smiled at this enthusiasm of Hildegard. "It's a very unsafe heaven! Half the houses in Berlin are destroyed. Every night we have to go into the cellars. My nerve has gone to pieces."

To Hilde Menzel this coming to her uncle's house on the outskirts of Berlin was an extraordinary experience. It was the next best thing to getting home to her own father and mother in Bavaria, but she knew that the heavy comfort of this house was only an illusion of safety and well-being. It was like being inside a ship hunted by submarines and dive-bombers, with everything orderly and even luxurious until the moment when it might be a wreck and a shambles.

More than half the houses were already destroyed in Berlin and the raids went on with increasing fury but here in this house which still escaped, a gong was sounded at meal-times—there was not much to eat—by an old manservant with deferential manners. The children had a nursery in which was a wonderful doll's-house and many toys. As a child Hilde and her sister Christel and her brother Paul had played with them. It was a house belonging to a period when there was great wealth in Germany in the hands of the old aristocracy and the new rich, full of solid furniture and frightful oil paintings of Bismarckian times, but with a heavy dignity. The people who built it felt secure in their wealth and social power. Now, Berlin lay in ruins around them and there was no security for life itself. Every night at dusk, as Hermann had said, the family went down to the cellar in which some camp-beds and chairs had been put. The two children were already asleep there, having been put to bed earlier and they hardly stirred when the strong walls of the cellar were shaken by the heavy crash of bombs not far away and the thunder of German anti-aircraft guns rose to a fury.

"We are fairly safe down here," said Herr von Meissner seeing the pallor of Hilde's face as one enormous explosion seemed to upheave the stone floor.

He sat in a camp-chair reading a book by the light of an oil-lamp on a small table, or writing—sometimes for several hours—with great concentration and detachment.

"Try to get some sleep, Fritz," said his wife Elizabeth.

He smiled at her and shook his head.

"I must get on with these notes, my treasure."

"They're so dangerous," said his wife in a low voice. "If they were found——"

"Everything is dangerous," he answered calmly. "But one day they may prove to the world that there were people in Germany who believed in liberty and decency and civilized ideas."

"I'm afraid, dear heart," answered his wife in a kind of whisper.

"No, no, Elizabeth! You are very brave. Whatever happens I shall thank God for your help and courage."

She was sitting close to him in a garden-chair and he took her hand and raised it to his lips. Then he turned to his writing again, not noticing that his wife's eyes were wet with tears.

Hilde watched and listened. One night she asked Hermann about his father's writing.

"Why is Uncle always writing, Hermann? He pays no attention to the air raids."

Hermann answered her in a low voice.

"It's a kind of document he wants to leave to the world. It's in bits and pieces. We have to hide them in the strangest places. The house has already been searched three times by the S.S., but they found nothing."

"Is he under suspicion?"

Hermann glanced round the cellar. Hildegard and Ursel were fast asleep after playing cards with Hermann. They had come down to the cellar in pyjamas and dressing-gowns and Ursel with her tousled hair looked like a pretty boy with one arm falling over the camp-bed and her mouth slightly open. Hildegard was made up with too much lipstick and in the dim light away from the oil-lamps looked like a doll with dabs of colour on the cheeks. In the corner where the children slept, Rosa lay on a mattress by their side sleeping with her face turned sideways on a silk cushion. Aunt Tessa was hunched forward in an old arm-chair, snoring faintly. Hermann's mother was also sleeping and the light from one of the oil-lamps touched her fair hair revealing silver threads. Herr von Meissner was reading his document and once gave a heavy sigh which came across the crypt-like cellar which had a damp smell and a faint reek of wine which once had been kept there.

Hermann spoke very quietly to Hilde.

"My father is always watched, but I daren't tell you. He's an old knight, *sans peur et sans reproche*. I wish I had his idealism or half his courage."

There was a heavy explosion and Hilde's face whitened.

"Hermann," she said, "I live in terror because of the children. How long is this going on?"

"We ought to make peace," answered Hermann. "The longer this goes on the more Germany will be destroyed. But that man has vowed to drag Germany down with him—and all Europe. In his madness he's the enemy of the German people and of civilization itself."

"Why doesn't someone kill him?" asked Hilde.

Hermann stared at her with sombre eyes. His voice sank to a whisper.

"There are men in high positions who think that is the only way. Some have already paid the penalty. Perhaps now it's too late. I keep telling my father it's too late."

He looked round nervously as though afraid that his whispering might be heard.

"It's not safe to talk like this, Hilde, even in a cellar I ought not to have told you so much. My father——"

"You can trust me," said Hilde, looking into his eyes.

Herr von Meissner looked over to them as he put his papers together and turned down the oil-lamp.

"Go to sleep you two young people," he said quietly.

It was not easy to go to sleep though some slept. Anti-aircraft fire was in full blast. Even in the deep cellar came the noise of vast explosions.

"There will be more ruins in Berlin tomorrow," said Herr von Meissner.

Next morning he walked with Hilde through the ruins of Berlin. They walked through the Tiergarten. Huge craters pitted the lawns and pathways. Many of the trees were lopped of their branches. Some of the statues in the Siegesallee, the statues of German heroes, had been knocked off their pedestals.

"That reminds me of Passchendaele," said Herr von Meissner.

They walked through the Brandenburger Tor into Unter den Linden and presently after passing the Wilhelmplatz stood outside the Adlon Hotel. It was only a pile of rubble. Some of the bedrooms had lost their front walls and were exposed nakedly with charred curtains and bits of furniture flung about.

"My wife and I used to have happy times in the Adlon," said Hilde's uncle. "I used to give pleasant little dinner parties there. Herr Adlon used to present my wife with a bouquet when we left."

He gave a deep sigh.

"That was before Germany was led into this hell by a lunatic who mesmerized the people and debauched the mind of youth."

Hilde was silent. Her mind went back to the early days of Hitler's power. She was old enough to remember them, old enough to remember the despair of Germany before he came, when young men could not find employment nor any hope. Hitler had given them hope. By some magic he found work for them and lifted up the spirit of German youth. As a young girl she had cried, "Heil Hitler!" when he passed down Unter den Linden, this very street in which they stood, which had been draped in banners with the blood-red swastika. She had heard the tramp of ten thousand feet, the young Nazis marching proudly with their flags flying. She had been caught up in the exaltation of a young Germany reborn, marching, singing, shouting, filled with a new consciousness of pride and self-fulfilment, fanatical in loyalty to the Führer who had led them out of the Slough of Despond. *Mein Kampf* was their Bible. They had accepted his racial theories without question. National Socialism was their new religion, displacing Christianity which was, they said, a slave religion. In her Labour camp where she had served six months like every other German girl and boy she had listened to lectures on all this and had believed every word of them. She had been distressed by her father's scepticism and hostility. Once at her father's dinner table she had raged at him for disloyalty and treachery and then had burst into tears and left the room. That was when she was sixteen years of age. Now she was twenty-six, the wife of Peter who had been killed by the Russians—surely he had been killed—and the daughter-in-law of Professor Menzel who had hated Hitler even when he was winning great victories. Now she walked in the ruins of Berlin.

Herr von Meissner looked down the Wilhelmstrasse. Hardly a building was intact.

"That was the British Embassy," said her uncle. "I used to have lunch there with Lord D'Abernon when I was in the Embassy in Rome. He was a giant of a man and a good friend of Germany. It was he who organized the Locarno Pact which for a time seemed a promise of peace in a new era of good will."

"The English hate us," said Hilde. "Haven't they always hated us?"

Herr von Meissner looked sideways at her and smiled.

"They were afraid of us. Fear is the mother of hate. But I had many English friends, some of them in high places. We forced them to be enemies by demanding military and naval supremacy on land and at sea. In this War they believed with good reason that Hitler desired the mastery of Europe and then the conquest of the world. Who can deny that now? And who is blind to the ruin he has caused by this insane ambition? Here it is round us and Berlin is a great graveyard, one great ruin. That is because of one man's lust for power and because of the false loyalty of his lickspittles, and because of the sacrificial loyalty of our young German manhood who believed in him and obeyed his orders to the death as still they are doing, poor lads."

"Uncle!" said Hilde touching his arm, "you risk your life in speaking like this in a public place. People passing might hear you."

"They would agree with me now," he answered carelessly. "The people passing are the victims of this maniac. All they want now is a cessation of bombing, and peace before the Russians sack this city."

The people passing looked miserable and tragic. But there were only a few in Unter den Linden which was silent and deserted except for an occasional passer-by.

One of them who seemed to come up from a hole below a hill of rubble which had once been a tall five-storied house looked at Herr von Meissner and then greeted him.

"My dear Fritz. Is your house still above ground?"

"So far, my dear Erhard," said Herr von Meissner. "How are you carrying on under that mountain of débris?"

"Not too well! It's difficult to keep clean and sanitary arrangements have to be improvized. But my wife and daughters are wonderful."

"Let me present my niece Hilde Menzel. She's a refugee from Königsberg. Hilde, my dear, this is General Jaeger of whom you must have heard."

General Jaeger, elderly, tall, lean, gave a wintry smile.

"Nobody has heard of me since I was dismissed by a certain gentleman who lives near here." He glanced towards the Wilhelmstrasse.

"Come round this evening before the air raid," said Herr von Meissner.

General Jaeger shook his head.

"A death-trap, my dear fellow! You know your house is being watched."

Herr von Meissner shrugged his shoulders.

"It's too late for all that nonsense. If they had wanted me—if they had found evidence against me—I should have been among the martyrs of July 20th."

Hilde Menzel heard those words with fear in her eyes as she looked at her uncle—that tall, thin, mild-eyed man who had been so kind to her in her childhood and young girlhood. There had been a plot against Hitler's life. Count Stauffenberg, Chief of Staff of the Home Army, had put a bomb in the Führer's headquarters at

Rastenburg in East Prussia. The bomb had exploded but the Führer had shifted from his place a few seconds before. Hilde had known Count Stauffenberg who had come to coffee with them in Königsberg and her father-in-law had been a friend of Ulrich von Hassell whose tragic face with melancholy eyes she remembered now. There had been many other high people in the plot and all but a few had now been executed. Those still alive were waiting in prison for the firing-squad.

All this had been whispered about in Königsberg. All this had been told in low voices by her father-in-law and others in her own flat—Peter's flat—when the door was shut and the children were asleep and she was serving coffee to these friends of Dr. Karl Menzel. Never once had her uncle's name been mentioned in connection with the plot but now he made no secret that he had been one of the conspirators, no secret to this General Jaeger who had come out of a cellar below the ruins.

Herr von Meissner was silent until two people had passed. They looked like man and wife and were carrying an iron bedstead rescued from the ruins. Then he spoke again.

"Is there any news of poor Goerdeler?"

General Jaeger raised his hands.

"They tortured him in prison. They've taken him to Plötzen See. I haven't heard whether they've shot him yet."

"God give him courage to the end," said Herr von Meissner.

Two military policemen strode by with hard, grim faces under their steel helmets. General Jaeger and Hilde's uncle stopped talking until they had gone by. It was the General who spoke again.

"The Russians have forced the Oder south-east of Breslau. The end is in sight."

Herr von Meissner nodded.

"The Americans are attacking from Aachen. But that madman refuses to surrender, and every day our beautiful cities get blasted off the earth and our women and children lie in heaps under the ruins. God himself must weep for them, the innocent victims of all this evil, sacrificed by those gangsters and gunmen who have made a hell on earth and a graveyard of Germany, for the sake of power and vainglory. Homicidal maniacs. Sadists and torturers. Devils incarnate."

His voice rose harshly. His face was twisted into a mask of rage. It was the first time Hilde had seen her uncle—generally so quiet and grave and gentle—torn by an inward passion and transfigured by a fire of wrath.

General Jaeger tapped him on the shoulder.

"Not so loud, my friend! We don't shout out these things!"

Herr von Meissner was silent for a moment and then laughed.

"Free speech is possible now even in Berlin. These rubble heaps have no ears. It's like talking in the ruins of Pompeii."

He turned to Hilde with a smile.

"I'm sorry, my dear. We must have bored you."

He raised his hand to General Jaeger.

"*Auf Wiedersehen.*"

He took Hilde's hand and tucked her arm under his own and walked farther along Unter den Linden turning into the Friedrichstrasse until held up by a mountain of rubble.

On the way back to the Grünewald Hilde spoke to her uncle in an anxious voice.

"Uncle, are you in danger?"

He hesitated for a moment and then answered quietly.

"I think the danger has passed. They're hardly likely to arrest me now. Soon they will all be arrested themselves by the English or Americans as war criminals. It will be their turn for trial and execution."

"Have they any evidence against you?" asked Hilde, anxiously.

Herr von Meissner laughed again quietly.

"Nothing but a vague suspicion. Stauffenberg and the others —my dear friend Ulrich von Hassell—did not give me away. They've been torturing Goerdeler who was the real leader of our underground movement but my name hasn't been dragged out of him or they would have seized me before now. I shouldn't be walking with a pretty niece today."

He waited until they had passed a group of Berliners coming through the Brandenburg Tor which was guarded by steel-helmeted sentries. All these people looked haggard and sunken-eyed. Night after night for months they had been going down into the air-raid shelters overcrowded and comfortless while above them their city was being pounded into dust and broken masonry.

The shelters, however deep, were not proof against ten-ton bombs now being dropped by the British airmen. Great numbers of people had been killed in them. Now refugees from East Prussia and from across the Oder were streaming into Berlin, sleeping in the open and unprotected by any cover from the nightly visit of Lancasters and American Fortresses with their terrifying loads of high-explosives.

"I'm writing the story of July 20th," said Herr von Meissner. "I've been writing it for months. I want to let the world know that there are men in Germany who stood for civilized ideals and risked death and torture—and endured death and torture—to rid the world and their own people of that madman and his gang of criminals who were the enemies of the Christian tradition and the instruments of Evil. We also have our resistance movement and our martyrs for liberty. I've had the honour to be in their company and their counsels, though so far I've escaped their martyrdom. I will be the historian of their heroism. That's why I keep on scribbling when you young people are asleep."

Hilde put her hand on his arm.

"But, Uncle, if they found your writings! . . ."

Herr von Meissner laughed and a cunning look came into his eyes.

"They would have to be very clever to find them. They're all in bits and pieces concealed in different places, very ingenious places. Only Elizabeth and my son have the clues to their whereabouts."

They walked on in silence through the Tiergarten which was almost destroyed.

Suddenly Hilde stopped and began to weep.

Her uncle stared at her and his eyes softened.

"Why are you crying, my child? God knows there's much to weep about."

She was weeping because of the death of her baby, Peter. She was weeping because Peter, her husband, had disappeared into the unknown. She was weeping because of the hideous ruins of Berlin which once to her, as a young girl, had been an enchanted city with picture galleries and palaces and open-air cafés in Unter den Linden, and theatres where she had listened in rapture to many plays, and private houses in quiet streets where she had danced and flirted a little and laughed with boys, all destroyed now, all flung into this chaos of ruin. She wept because British and American armies were invading Germany from the West and Russian armies from the East. She wept because of a great terror in her heart and a sense of misery all around her and in her soul. What had been the use of fleeing from Königsberg to save her little ones? There was no place in Germany where they could be safe. Was there any safety in this flaming volcano called Berlin?

CHAPTER X

SERGEANT REBER was in Berlin—one of the suburbs of Berlin. He had arrived some weeks after Hilde Menzel and his fellow-travellers in the covered wagon, and he had come in an ambulance with the soles of his muddy boots exposed beyond the bunk where he lay with sixteen other wounded. He was one of the thousands of wounded men who streamed back from the River Oder where they had tried to hold the Russians near Breslau. A bit of shell hit him within twenty-four hours of his arrival in a trench on the river's bank. He had been talking to a boy of sixteen lying next to him in the muddy ditch behind his machine-gun. Russian artillery was firing all along the line and the soft black earth was vomited up by the shell bursts. There was an incessant rattle of machine-gun fire from both sides. The boy was crying as Reber noticed.

"Don't be scared," said Reber. "Death is nothing and that's the worst that can happen to you, my child."

Franz Reber didn't hear the boy's answer if he answered. Something hit his left arm like the kick of a horse and he was knocked senseless. When he came to consciousness again he was lying in the ambulance with sixteen other men. One of the field-ambulance men must have given him a shot of morphia for he felt doped and dazed but with a dull nagging ache almost intolerable in his left arm. At every bump in the road one of his fellow-travellers cried out in agony with a long whimpering groan.

Franz Reber's brain began to work. Thoughts and even words took shape in his consciousness. He asked himself questions.

'What's happened to me? Where am I? I must be alive because I feel pain. Why wasn't I killed by that bit of shell? Why do I always stay alive when the other fellows are killed? It's very odd that! It's happened to me a lot of times. I can't get killed. I wonder if that boy was hit. He was crying. I said something to him. Yes, I remember speaking to the poor kid just arrived from a training camp, just a child. I feel very silly in my head. I feel . . .'

He groaned heavily. A frightful pain shot through his left arm. He began to talk aloud in a kind of delirium of which he was half-conscious.

"This war ought to end. I said so to a girl somewhere. What was her name? Hilde. Hilde. It's no use going on. Someone ought to kill Hitler. He wants it to go on for ever. He wants Germany drowned in rivers of blood, fresh red blood, very scarlet blood, boys' blood like crimson madder or Venetian red mixed with flake white—a very good colour. I used to use it in Munich when I painted in oils. Messy things, oils. I remember treading on a tube of cadmium yellow and walking about the carpet in the drawing-room—a most awful mess everywhere, but a very good colour. One has to use a lot of flake white . . . flake white . . . snow. Millions of flakes falling. . . . The covered wagons are capped with snow. . . . Dead babies buried in the snow. Hilde's baby. . . . Folz was buried in the snow. . . . Old Folz. A good chap. . . . Hell!"

He groaned again as the ambulance, in a long column of ambulances from the battle of the Oder, brought a tide of wounded back to Berlin.

He lay in a bed in a temporary hospital which had been a school. Many of Berlin's hospitals had been gutted by bombs. There were sixty of his fellow-wounded in this long room with broken windows. Nurses moved about quietly in felt-soled shoes. Franz Reber's nurse was a hard-faced wench who changed his dressings roughly.

"No use squealing," she said when he cried out. "You men are all babies. You can't bear the least bit of pain. Women have far more courage than men."

"You're a she-devil," he told her. "I expect you've been a warder in a concentration camp."

"Take care I don't report you for that," she answered angrily. "You may become an inhabitant of a concentration camp, if you don't take care."

"Wait till the Russians come to Berlin," said Reber. "They'll treat you rough, my beautiful one."

He grinned at her. She was not beautiful. But he had frightened her and she stared at him with sombre eyes.

"They'll never reach Berlin. The Führer is going to win the

War. They're just being lured on to destruction. He has many new weapons."

"He'll keep the last one for himself," said Reber. "He ought to have used it a long time ago."

"I shall report you," said the nurse. "You ought to be shot."

"I have been shot," answered Reber. "This arm is giving me hell. What more do you want?"

He was not serious. It amused him to anger this hard-faced wench who still believed with hero-worship that her beloved Führer was going to win a war already lost. The Russians were over the Oder. Americans and British were on the Rhine. His comrades were fighting in the last ditches against overwhelming odds. They were closing in upon Berlin. Berlin? What would be left of Berlin when they entered its ruins over the German dead? Every night now the air raids became more intense and frightful. It was better to be in the trenches than lying here in a room with broken windows quaking under that infernal racket overhead, listening to the crash of heavy bombs, watching the red glare of fires throbbing on the white-washed walls through slits in the black-out curtains. That hard-faced nurse was right when she said that the women were braver than men. Some of these wounded men were terrified. Several of them had shell-shock and trembled with ague and became gibbering madmen who had to be tied into their beds. Some of them, doped with drugs, cried out horribly in their sleep. Reber had believed himself past all sensations of fear, steeled or deadened by a fatalistic philosophy and completely indifferent to death. But under the fury of these air raids over Berlin he had a kind of animal fear. His flesh shrank from the likelihood of being torn to ribbons between one explosion and another. Only his mind fought for mastery over this fear of extinction and disintegration.

'What does it matter?' he asked himself. 'There's some kind of life after death. I feel almost certain about that. I've seen a look of surprise on dead men's faces as though they were astonished by some vision at the moment of death. Not always, of course, but I have seen it a number of times. Perhaps when the mind is liberated from the body it sees a vision of perfection, a beauty beyond that of the world in which we live, though that is hard to beat. Or they may be astonished to see themselves dead. Perhaps they don't know it all at once. Or perhaps they see everything from a new perspective, stepping out of time into eternity which is timeless, and seeing all life and all history, and all the past and all the future, in a bird's-eye view. Of course I don't know a thing about all that. I'm only quoting Folz who had studied philosophy and metaphysics. In any case why should I flinch at the idea of sudden death? My destiny must be fulfilled. I ought to have been dead a thousand times before on the law of averages. Most of the other fellows were killed. Why should my beastly little ego go on in this life longer than theirs? I'm not very keen for it to go on. I don't want it to go on. A defeated Germany won't be amusing. Our enemies will take their revenge all right, and we've asked for it, haven't we?'

So Franz Reber quaked with his body under the fury of another night's air raid while his mind struggled for mastery over fear.

The nurses brought in frightful stories of death and destruction. A ten-ton bomb had smashed through an underground shelter killing everybody. A crowd of refugees from East Prussia had been caught in the open and many women and children had been blown to bits. These words worried Sergeant Reber. He thought of Hilde Menzel and the two children Hans and Trudel, and Aunt Tessa, and those two pretty girls, Ursel and Hildegard, who had tried to flirt with him. He had no idea what had become of them. Perhaps they had never reached Berlin. Perhaps they were still in Quakenbrück. Perhaps Quakenbrück was already in the hands of the Russians. Hilde Menzel was often in his thoughts. In a way he had fallen in love with her, in a spiritual way free from any sex impulse, as he believed. He had been smitten by her tragedy when she had laid her baby in the snow. Afterwards, in Quakenbrück, they had been almost like brother and sister, able to talk without reserve comforted by each other's presence, in a kind of intellectual comradeship. She had a clear candid mind. She was pitiful and understanding. There was no hardness in her like the hardness in so many German girls who had been brought up under Hitler's creed and discipline becoming rough and boyish by service in Labour camps and stuffed with the propaganda in which he himself had once believed, until he had met Folz and had gone through the Russian campaign and had thought things out for himself when standing in the midst of death which strips men's souls of falsity.

There was a man lying in the next bed to his with whom he talked when the agony of his wound had passed. He was a pilot in the German Air Force by name of Reinhard Haushofer, a young man of Reber's age, twenty-five or so.

"We've lost this War because we were beaten in the air," he said. "Hermann Goering let us down."

He spoke the last words in a low voice.

"You think so?" asked Reber for politeness' sake. He was not much interested in the technical reasons for defeat.

"He underestimated the English power of recovery. We ought to have thrown all in during the Battle of Britain but he funked it and called it off. That gave them time to build up a new air force with all the heavy bombers which are now pounding us into dust."

"Very unfortunate," said Reber, who was thinking of Hilde Menzel.

"We didn't bomb England half enough," said Haushofer. "We ought to have blasted it off the map. It's a small target compared with Germany."

"Haven't we given it hell?" asked Reber, carelessly. He was thinking that luck had smashed his left arm instead of the right. He still had his painting hand.

"Not really," said Haushofer. "Coventry was a good show I helped to make it so."

"What about London?" asked Reber. "Isn't it flat?"

He had no personal grudge against London. His mind had got beyond all this competition in destruction. It seemed to him all senseless. It was civilization that was being destroyed.

"Too much of it still stands up," answered Haushofer. "We flattened it out round St. Paul's Cathedral and blasted the London Docks, but on the whole we didn't finish the job. I must say the English anti-aircraft fire became formidable. It was difficult to break through. We had heavy losses to our bomber squadrons."

"Well, we can't complain that they're hitting back at us now," said Reber. "Tenfold perhaps, judging from what's happening here. It's just black murder on both sides."

"We ought to have wiped out the English on Dunkirk sands," said Haushofer. "The Führer held us back."

"Not for love of the English," said Reber. "Doubtless he had other reasons. But it doesn't matter now. What's done is done Destiny has to be fulfilled."

Haushofer, who had been wounded in the leg by a bit of shrapnel when reconnoitring the American positions across the Rhine, raised himself in his bed and glared at Reber.

"Destiny be damned!" he said. "Life is what one makes it. After this war we must get ready for the next. Germany has lost two wars but we shall win the third."

"On which side?" asked Reber, with a deep irony lost upon this young airman. "On the side of the Russians or against them. On the side of the Anglo-Saxons, now our enemies but presently perhaps our friends?"

That was too difficult for Haushofer. He lay back in bed again with a curse on his lips.

"Ten thousand devils!"

"I agree," said Reber. "And all let loose from hell's kitchen."

On the other side of him was a young gunner named Georg Gürtner. He had been wounded in the stomach and was in a bad way it seemed, but now and then he talked to Reber in a low voice between spells of exhaustion due to loss of blood. One night he talked after the nightly air raid, which had been more than usually terrifying because of heavy bombs exploding close to this school-house, shaking its walls with violent concussion.

"Are you awake, Sergeant Reber?"

"Yes, Gürtner."

"Are you badly wounded?"

"Nothing but a broken arm."

"I think I'm dying."

"Do you mind much?" asked Reber.

"Yes, I don't want to die."

"Why not?"

"I wanted to see a girl again. I love her."

"Does she love you?"

"Yes, she loves me."

"Is she a nice girl?" asked Reber. "Some of our girls are little sluts not worth living for . . . I'm trying to comfort you."

"She's a very sweet girl. I'm unworthy of her. If I die I want you to go and see her. Will you promise that?"

"Certainly," said Reber. "But I hope you won't die, my dear fellow—I mean if you want to live. Perhaps if you want to live badly enough you won't die. Life is like that sometimes. Will-power seems to have something to do with it. A surgeon I knew in Russia told me you can't kill some men. They just refuse to die."

"I'm a Catholic," said the young man. "I believe in a future life."

"I'm not a Catholic," said Reber, "but I believe in some kind of a future life. I think we go on after death, somewhere, somehow, in a spiritual way."

"I want you to tell Gita that if I die I shall wait for her in heaven."

"Are you sure you're going to heaven?" asked Reber. "I wish I could be sure of that."

"God will forgive my sins," said Gürtner. "Our Lady will pray for me."

"Which lady?" asked Reber.

"Holy Mary, Mother of God," said Georg Gürtner.

"I envy you," said Reber. "I wish I had your faith, my dear fellow."

"Some of my comrades jeered at it," said the young gunner. "They were taught to become pagans. Germany under Hitler has become pagan by propaganda against Christianity. We Catholics——"

He began to cough and some blood oozed out of his mouth.

"I don't think you ought to talk so much," said Reber.

"I must give you her name and address," said Gürtner after this spasm of coughing. "You'll promise to call on her?"

"Yes, I promise."

"Tell her that I loved her to the last from the depths of my heart. Can you remember that?"

"You loved her to the last from the depths of your heart."

"Yes, that's it. And tell her that with my last breath I kissed the little crucifix she gave me. Can you remember that?"

"I'll remember," said Reber.

"I must give you her name and address."

"Yes, I must have that."

"A thousand thanks. You're very kind, Reber."

"Not at all, my dear fellow. Only I hope you will tell her yourself one day."

"Her name is . . ."

He had another spasm of coughing and vomited blood.

"You ought not to talk so much," said Reber again.

Georg Gürtner lay still for a few minutes and then raised himself in bed.

"Her name and address . . ."

"Tell me."

"Her name . . ."

"Yes?"

He began to cough again and then fell back in bed as though exhausted.

"Nurse!" shouted Reber.

One of the nurses came quickly to the bed.

"You'll wake the other men," she said crossly. "They're just settling down to sleep."

"Gürtner is in a bad way," said Reber.

The nurse turned to Gürtner's bed and seemed to be busy with him for a moment.

"He's dead," she said.

Another wounded man took Gürtner's place. He wore a bandage over his eyes, having been blinded by a bomb explosion.

'War is a very unpleasant business,' thought Reber. 'Why are human beings who call themselves civilized tearing one another to pieces with high explosives, blinding one another, disembowelling one another, dropping death upon women and children, blasting fine cities off the map, gutting the miracles of architecture, destroying the treasure of old crafts and arts, smudging out the proofs of civilized life, thrusting us back to the cave-men way of life? By what madness are we forced to do these things? That fellow Haushofer who is snoring a foot away from my head is talking already about a third war which Germany will win. What devil is there in the human brain to produce such thoughts? Or am I mad myself because I see in all this not heroic courage, not glorious patriotism, not a noble loyalty, but a degradation of the soul and a return to barbarism. I must think it all out. Perhaps if my body is blotted out in one of these air raids my mind or my soul, or some remaining consciousness of me, may find the meaning of all this—if it has any meaning. I wonder if Hilde Menzel . . .'

He lay back on to a hard pillow and fell asleep.

One morning he saw in the ward a woman he knew. He was almost sure he knew her. She was standing by the bed of one of the wounded and he saw her profile—a finely cut profile with a straight nose and sensitive mouth and a high forehead and a sharp cheekbone. He had seen her in profile when she was sitting next to him at the wheel of his radio-car. She was the wife of Otto Hessell, who had been killed by his side in Russia. What was her name? Magda.

He called her name and she turned and saw him and moved over to his bed.

"How astonishing to find you here!" she exclaimed.

"Equally astonishing to see you," he answered with a smile. "What happened to you after I was burnt?"

"Some dear souls found room for me in a covered wagon. Then an armoured car gave me a lift as far as Breslau. After that a cattle-truck in which I nearly died."

She sat on the side of his bed and asked after his wound. How had he had time to get wounded? She thought he was in hospital for his burns. It was a cousin of hers in the other bed. He was dying, so the nurse had whispered to her.

"Everybody's dying," she said. "Or everybody's dead, or everybody is going to die. For Germany it's like the end of the world."

Reber nodded.

"The end must come soon," he said. "Where are the Russians?"

"Across the Oder. They've surrounded Breslau."

"And the Americans and English?"

"Across the Rhine."

"And still that maniac refuses to surrender."

Magda Hessell put a finger to her lips and glanced across his bed nervously.

"Heil Hitler!" said Reber, stretching out his right hand above the bed-clothes. "God bless our noble Führer who has led us to this glorious finale, so worthy of his genius."

Magda Hessell saw no humour in this bitter sarcasm.

"Berlin is a doomed city," she said. "It's a graveyard. My parents lie under its ruins. That was my homecoming."

Suddenly she wept with her hands up to her face, but quite silently because of all the wounded men about her. Some of the lightly wounded were watching her, but there was nothing unusual in a woman weeping.

Reber did not speak to her until she took her hands down and dabbed her eyes with a little handkerchief. He was not without a sense of pity. But they were all in the same misery.

"Where are you living now?" he asked. "Have you found shelter?"

"An air-raid shelter—a Bunker—crowded with refugees."

Berlin was like a plague-stricken city filled with the dying and the dead. Pity was no good. The living, he thought, would soon be the dead.

"Can't you get to some other place?" he asked. "Haven't you any other relatives? You can't go on living in a Bunker."

"Otto had some cousins in Dresden," she told him, "but Dresden exists no more. The Americans have made dust of it. The Americans have destroyed all our cities. They spare nothing."

"Dresden was beautiful." Reber gave a groan of anguish. "I lived there once. I studied art there for a time. It had an elegance . . ."

'Art has been killed,' he thought, 'with other fine things. Art is dead because civilization is dead.'

"I must go back to my dying man," said Magda.

He held her back for a moment.

"There's a lady I want to find. She was one of the refugees from Königsberg. She may have reached Berlin."

"Did I know her?" asked Magda.

"You may have seen her in one of the covered wagons. She was Hilde Menzel. She had two children and left a baby in the snow."

Magda nodded.

"Yes, I came with her from Quakenbrück. She has a beautiful face."

"I worship her," said Franz Reber. "She's one of the saints of life."

"You are in love with her?" asked Magda.

"No," answered Reber. "Not that kind of love. Not the beastly kind of love."

A faint smile touched the lips of Magda Hessell and crept into her tragic eyes.

"Love needn't be beastly. I loved my Otto without beastliness, though with all the passion of my heart."

"I mean I am worshipful in her presence," said Reber. "She was the wife of my friend Peter. But that doesn't matter. If you see her in Berlin tell her that I'm in this morgue. Say that I would give my right arm to see her again."

"If I see her I'll tell her that," said Magda. "But the odds are against seeing her. Most people are living underground."

She raised her hand slightly and went back to the bed where the cousin of hers lay dying. Presently Reber saw her move away from the bedside and go out of the ward.

CHAPTER XI

THREE hours before the next air raid over Berlin Herr von Meissner was in the drawing-room with some of his family. The two children were in the nursery riding a rocking-horse with Rosa, who, in return for food and shelter, was acting as their nurse. Hildegard was playing chess with Hermann who was absent-minded and had already been check-mated once. Ursel was deep in an arm-chair reading a book by an English writer named John Galsworthy. Aunt Tessa was playing a game of Patience. Elizabeth von Meissner was seated at a mahogany desk writing a letter. Herr von Meissner himself was talking in a quiet voice to Hilde. They were talking about skiing on the mountains above Garmisch. Here was a peaceful scene on the outskirts of Berlin. In this heavily-furnished room there was no stench of death under the ruins of the German capital, no sign of impending doom except on the faces and in the eyes of this family group. Hermann was nervous and fidgety over the chessboard as Hilde noticed. Her own face revealed an experience of anguish and terror by little lines about the eyes and mouth—the terror of Königsberg, the anguish in the covered wagon. But she smiled at her uncle who was recounting some of his adventures in the Bavarian Alps as a young man.

"Your mother and I took risks without a thought. One false step and we should have been killed. It was the sense of danger perhaps which thrilled us so that nothing would keep us away from the highest peaks. Your mother was very sure-footed and found an inexpressible joy in climbing. I remember . . ."

As he spoke those last words there was a heavy knocking at the front door and the clanging of a bell in the hall.

Hermann knocked over the black Queen and sprang up white-faced.

"Father!" he said in a low voice.

Frau von Meissner left her writing-desk and went towards her husband.

"Fritz!" she said in alarm. "Who can that be? Are your writings safe? Have you hidden them all?"

Herr von Meissner had risen from his chair.

"Everything is hidden," he said. "But it may be nothing to cause alarm, my dear. Some refugees begging for food, perhaps."

"Beggars don't knock like that," said Hermann in a low, agitated voice.

There was another heavy knock and another clanging of the bell.

"Open the door, my son," said Herr von Meissner. "Let us all keep calm."

He spoke very calmly but the skin of his face had gone a little grey and his fingers fumbled as he buttoned his black jacket.

They listened.

There was a harsh voice in the hall answered by Hermann in a low tone.

He had left the drawing-room door open. There were several footsteps on the stone floor. Three men came into the room. They were S.S. men in their black uniforms. One was an officer, whose hand was on the holster of his pistol.

"Herr von Meissner?"

"I am Herr von Meissner. What is the purpose of this visit, gentlemen?"

The S.S. officer watched him closely with steely eyes. His hand closed over the butt of his pistol.

"I have to arrest you for high treason in connection with the plot of July 20th. You will come with me, please."

"The plot of July 20th!" exclaimed Herr von Meissner. "That is many months ago. Most of those who were implicated have been executed. Why do you arrest me now?"

"Some of them are not yet executed," answered the black-uniformed officer. "One of them has given evidence against you."

"Under torture?" asked Herr von Meissner.

The S.S. officer shrugged his shoulders.

"Under examination. But I don't propose to answer further questions. You will come with me. My men will search this house."

Hermann rushed forward towards the officer, but two of the S.S. men grasped his arms.

"I protest!" he shouted in a loud but trembling voice. "My

father is the noblest man in Germany. You have no right to arrest him. I won't let you take him away."

"We shall have to take you away also if you don't keep silent," said the S.S. officer.

"Hermann," said Herr von Meissner, "your protest will be of no avail. Control yourself, my son. I have to go through with this. God bless you all if I don't see you again. You know how much I've loved you."

"Fritz!" cried his wife Elizabeth. "My dearest husband!" She flung her arms about him, weeping.

He kissed her forehead and then her hands.

"I owe everything in life to you," he said. "If they kill me your name will be on my lips when I die and I shall wait for you on the other side."

"I must ask you to come," said the S.S. officer, "otherwise——"

"I come," said Herr von Meissner.

He looked round the room which had been his home since boyhood. His eyes rested on Hilde for a moment and he smiled at her and said, "Good-bye, my dear. Give my love to Hans and Trudel."

Aunt Tessa gave a piercing cry.

"Hush!" said Herr von Meissner. "Tessa! Hush, all will be well."

In a moment he had gone from the room and the house seemed empty without him—the head of the house, the head of the family, Herr von Meissner, Ambassador of Germany in many capitals.

They heard a car drive away. Two of the S.S. men remained searching for hidden papers in the study, turning out all the drawers and cupboards.

In the room in which the family had been sitting Aunt Tessa was hysterical. Hermann paced up and down like a demon-haunted man, white-faced and sunken-eyed, with a lock of hair falling over his forehead, until he stopped to comfort his mother.

"There's no evidence against him," he said. "There's no evidence, Mother."

Elizabeth von Meissner took his hand.

"We must try to be as brave as he is," she said. "We must try to be worthy of his love. He has always been a knight. No-one has loved Germany more than he does. If he has to die he will die as a martyr for Germany and for civilization."

She seemed to be sure that her husband would have to die. She seemed to have resigned herself. Hermann went down on his knees and put his head on her lap. He was the weak one, the broken-hearted.

CHAPTER XII

FRANZ REBER came out of hospital with his left arm in plaster. He had had no opportunity to get into touch with his parents who lived in the Fasanenstrasse, or perhaps not sufficient urge to do so. He almost shirked going to see them. Something had changed in him since he had last been home—almost everything. If they could see into his mind his father and mother would not recognize him. His face and body might be the same apart from that smashed arm, but his soul or his intelligence had changed utterly, making a different being of him. There had never been much sympathy between Franz Reber and his father. The latter had not encouraged the boy's artistic impulses and had tried to persuade him to abandon art as a career. Only his mother had given him encouragement in that direction and some of the family discussions on the subject had been heated and painful because of this conflict.

There had also been political differences. His father had been hostile to the Hitler Youth Movement when young Franz had been one of its standard-bearers with fanatical enthusiasm. Then the War had come interfering with all academic studies and the dreams of youth. Now he felt a stranger to the author of his being. So he thought as he walked through the ruins of Berlin.

'I seem to be coming back to my father and mother after a life on a different planet,' he thought, 'or a sojourn in hell. In any case how do I know that they're alive? They may be dead under the ruins of our house.'

It was a strange and tragic experience for this soldier of the campaign in Russia to be coming home again not knowing whether there was still a home, not caring very much. Death and destruction had become familiar in his mind. Not caring very much, that was the tragic thing. He wouldn't weep if he found that his father and mother had been killed. He wouldn't be shocked or surprised. He would remain with a sense of deadness inside himself or at least with a complete lack of natural grief or human emotion. Germany was defeated but he felt no grief. The enemies were at the gates but he didn't care. It would be a relief and not a cause for tears when they entered Berlin and ended the War. It would put a stop to air raids. It would merely be the fulfilment of the expected and the inevitable.

'I have no sense of humiliation because Germany is defeated,' thought Franz Reber, climbing over a pile of rubble which barred his way. 'I'm no longer a nationalist. I'm no longer a patriotic soldier of the German Reich. I'm no longer capable of being stirred by old heroic slogans or Hitlerian screamings. I'm a hater of war's filth and murder, a detached observer of human abomination. I should feel like this if I had been dead and buried and came back as a ghost to walk through the ruins of Berlin. I have the mind of a ghost. I'm just a ghost in the body of a man with a broken arm walking over this damned rubble.'

So he talked to himself in the secret chamber of his mind as he picked his way through ruin in a city where many other men and women were climbing over fallen masonry and twisted girders, or groping in the ruins as though for lost treasures of a former life.

Franz Reber stood outside the skeleton of a house in Fasanenstrasse, to which he had come by way of the Uhlandstrasse. He was not quite sure of it at first and had to look at other houses to get his bearings. Was this where he had passed some years of his boyhood? The whole front of the house had fallen, leaving some of the rooms open to the sky. The one on the third storey to the right had been his bedroom where he had done his drawings and raced through exciting books, and dreamed queer things. A charred curtain flapped in the wind. Behind it there was still one picture hanging on a broken wall naked to the sky. It was a portrait of his mother done in oils. A big hole had been plugged through it by a bomb fragment.

Somehow he had expected this. He was not stunned or shocked. Only by a freak of luck could it have been otherwise.

A young man came out of the cellar underneath this house. He glanced at Reber and scowled.

"No more room down there," he said gloomily. "We can't take in any more lodgers."

"This is my old home," said Franz.

The young man stared at him and answered more civilly.

"Oh! Well I suppose that makes a difference. Or doesn't it?"

"Who are you?" asked Franz. "Why are you here?"

The young man shrugged his shoulders.

"I'm a refugee from Breslau. There are two women down there and another man—an escaped prisoner of war like myself. It's a nice cellar. We're keeping it private as far as possible."

"That's all right," said Franz Reber. "But I propose to join you. I've nowhere else to go. I'm just out of hospital."

"Well, we shall have to shove up a bit," said the young man. "We can hardly refuse admittance to the ancient inhabitant of the ruins above us. What's your name, by the way? Mine is Ernst Winkelnkempler."

"Mine is Franz Reber."

"Come down then. Take care of the top steps. They're a bit smashed."

Franz Reber followed him down. He knew this cellar. He had used it as a boy for developing photographs. It had a damp deathly smell but it seemed warm down there and a rush of warm air swept his face.

"We fixed up the stove," said his guide. "And we've got an oil-lamp going. After being a prisoner of war it's quite luxurious."

He pulled an old curtain on one side and spoke in a clear voice to a group of people in the cellar.

"Someone else to join us!"

"Ten thousand devils!" answered a voice.

One electric bulb gave a poor light to a big cellar, but in the faint illumination Franz Reber saw some people seated round a stove on kitchen chairs and one big arm-chair. There was a tattered carpet on the stone floor and a deal table against the wall at the far end. The place had evidently been used as an air-raid shelter—perhaps by his father and mother.

"This is Franz Reber," said Ernst Winkelnkempler. "He says his family lived here."

"Well, we're living here now," said another voice.

The speaker was a young man with a shaggy, straw-coloured beard. Reber saw pale blue eyes staring at him out of a haggard hairy face. He was in uniform with the badges of the Tank Corps. He was a sergeant.

"Come and sit down," said a girl's voice. "I'll squat on the floor."

She slipped off one of the kitchen chairs, rubbing against Reber's left arm as she passed him, and sat on the dirty bit of carpet with her hands clasped round her knees. She was in a pair of blue slacks with a yellow pullover.

"I don't want to disturb anybody," said Franz. "Only don't knock against my left arm. It's in plaster."

"Wounded in one of the air raids?" asked Ernst Winkelnkempler.

"On the Oder."

"That hairy savage—Baümer—escaped from the English in Italy," said Winkelnkempler. "The Italian girls fell in love with his blue eyes."

"The Italian peasants were damned good to me," said the blue-eyed sergeant. "Now I wish they hadn't been."

"Why?" asked Reber.

The bearded young man laughed bitterly.

"What's the good of being in this cellar waiting for the Russians to come into Berlin on one side and the Americans on the other? I'd rather be a prisoner of war with the English."

"Then why escape?" asked Winkelnkempler.

"Why did any of us escape to this stinking graveyard?" asked the straw-bearded man.

He turned to Reber, the newcomer, and spoke with a kind of savage emotion.

"I had a wife and two children in Berlin. I went through incredible adventures to get here."

"And what then?"

Reber knew the answer.

"They lie buried in the ruins. A pretty homecoming!"

Reber nodded.

"It's like that in Berlin."

The girl in blue slacks and a yellow jumper who had given up her chair to Reber gave a tragic laugh.

"Don't let's talk about death and all that. We're alive, aren't we? Heil Hitler and to hell with the Russians. I'm going out to do a bit of looting. Coming, Erike?"

She looked over to a thin dark-haired girl who was smartly

dressed in a tailor-made costume. She was touching her mouth with a lipstick and looking at herself in a tiny mirror in a handbag.

"Yes, I'll come. But you look very disreputable, Elsa."

"Who cares, my pretty one? Berlin is not a fashion parade."

The two girls went out. Winkelnkempler came to sit by the stove leaning forward with hunched shoulders.

"Who are they?" asked Reber.

Winkelnkempler shrugged his shoulders.

"They used to be in a cabaret down the Friedrichstrasse. The one called Elsa has a lot of spirit. She hasn't forgotten how to laugh."

"A miracle!" said Reber. "Some women have more courage than men."

"They'll need a lot when the Russians arrive," said Winkelnkempler gloomily.

"Perhaps the Americans will get here first," said Reber.

Winkelnkempler made an ugly grimace.

"Are they more civilized? It's they who are destroying Germany city by city. In the next war I hope their skyscrapers will be knocked down like ninepins."

Reber stared at him and raised his eyebrows.

"The next war? Do you like this kind of thing?"

"I like revenge," said Winkelnkempler. "Hitler hasn't pulled it off this time. He has made many mistakes. Next time we'll wipe out all our enemies."

"Perhaps they'll be our friends," suggested Reber half ironically.

"We shall have to join with the Russians," said Winkelnkempler. "That combination would be invincible."

The straw-bearded man raised his hands.

"You're talking like a madman. I suppose you're as mad as I am. We've all gone mad in this madhouse which was Germany."

He gave a deep groan.

"I'd like something to eat. Failing that I shall sleep."

He lay down on the floor and presently slept with one arm over his head.

"He's a sentimentalist," said Winkelnkempler in a low voice. "He weeps at night and cries out like an hysterical woman."

"Poor devil!" said Reber.

"I don't believe in getting soft," said Winkelnkempler. "I believe in keeping tough. Isn't that the German spirit? I shan't lie down under this defeat. Every day will increase my hatred. I shall feed on it and sleep with it. We Germans must go on hating and living for revenge."

Reber glanced at him sideways. There was a red light in his eyes as he leaned forward to the stove warming his thin hands.

'This man,' thought Reber, 'has the instincts of a wild beast at bay and yet I suppose he thinks he is inspired by a noble patriotism. If I told him that I've become a war-hater he would think I had gone soft and was a white-livered coward. Shall I argue with him? What's the good. Does one argue with a chimpanzee?'

"How does one get food?" asked Reber.

Winkelnkempler gave a harsh laugh.

"One doesn't. There's a mile-long queue outside the shops—those that exist. The markets are not worth the walk to them. Those English and American swine have smashed all the railways. Now and then a few goods trains get through. The Berliners walk out with rucksacks and get a bit of cheese or a few pounds of potatoes now and then. Those girls may bring something back for a meal. Otherwise we have to line up at the canteens for refugees. Potato soup and black bread. Not so bad as being a prisoner of war in Russia. I lost four stone before I escaped after only three months."

"How did you escape?"

"On the march. I flung myself into a snow-drift. It was dark and the Russian guards were blinded by snow. I hid in the woods, in farmhouses, under dung-heaps, in hay-lofts, in ditches. For seven days and nights I had nothing to eat. I killed a Russian sentry outside a village."

"How did you kill him?"

"Crept up on him and strangled him. He was as strong as an ox but I choked him all right."

"And then?"

"I swam across a tributary of the Oder. Ice was floating down stream. I wasn't warm."

"You must be a strong man," said Reber.

"I am strong. I used to be an athlete. I won the swimming championship at the Olympic Games in '34. Hitler handed me the cup. It was my day of glory."

He gave a harsh laugh.

"I was a kid then. Now I'm as old as death."

"How old?"

"Twenty-four."

He looked thirty-four or more, with deep sunken eyes and grey leathery skin tightly drawn over his skull and cheekbones.

Presently he stood up and stretched his arms.

"I must go out and breathe the air. This cellar is suffocating."

He raised his hand and strode through the curtain to the broken steps.

Franz Reber stepped over the sleeping body of Baümer and explored the cellar. The girls had curtained off one corner. Behind the curtain were two mattresses on the stone floor and a wash-basin and jug on a small table. On one of the mattresses was a small pile of feminine garments neatly folded. There was a shelf on the back wall and on it stood a bottle of scent, a hair brush, and some books.

Reber looked at the books and took one down. It was Goethe's *Faust*. It was his own copy with his name on it and a pencil sketch of his mother's head on the title page. He stared at it and suddenly his eyes became wet. This small dog-eared book and that pencil drawing wiped out the years of war and took him back to his boyhood and to a room upstairs in a house now gutted. He remembered doing this sketch of his mother. He remembered telling her that she was beautiful, and she had laughed and blushed. They had read many books together when he was a boy. She was a good reader and more than once he had wept secretly because she put so much emotion into her reading.

But later home life had been difficult because of his father's sternness and his mother's fright of him. He had been glad to get away to Munich to study art. Then the War had come and the old home life had seemed only a dream of another existence thrust out of his mind, almost deliberately, because of its contrast with this new phase of life and experience at the front in Russia with its frightful hardships and abominations. Now suddenly his remembrance of youth rushed back at him—the loving kindness of his mother, his own dreams and laughter as a boy, the recollection of former happiness. Something broke inside him—the hard crust of his bitterness, the sense of deadness inside himself. He found himself weeping with salt tears running down his face.

"Great God!" he said to himself. "My father and mother! I didn't care whether they were alive or dead."

He was overcome and stricken by a sense of enormous guilt because he had suffered no anguish on their account until now when he remembered them with tears.

He strode through the cellar stepping again over the body of Baümer the sleeper, and went up the broken steps. There must be neighbours and friends, he thought, who could tell him about his father and mother. For some minutes—perhaps half an hour—he stumbled over blocks of masonry and rubble heaps which had been his house. He shifted some of the débris and found bits and pieces of furniture and household things. He picked up unbroken the bronze figure of a Mercury which his mother had brought back from Florence. They had had a holiday in Italy when he was twelve or thirteen. He remembered the antique shop in which she had bought this little figure.

Presently he was aware of someone watching hin. It was the straw-bearded Baümer who had finished his sleep and now stood outside the cellar.

"Everybody's doing that!" he said with a queer laugh. "All the Berliners are searching in the ruins of their old homes."

"It's not amusing," said Reber.

He put the Mercury into his side pocket.

"It's like the end of the world," said Baümer. "Everything smashed. Everything gone."

Franz Reber stopped, seeing a glint of metal between two blocks of stone. It was a gold ring with a little pearl. It had belonged to his mother. He put it in his waistcoat pocket.

He remembered that Baümer had come home after escape from Italy to find his wife and children dead in the ruins.

'Poor devil!' he thought in his heart. 'Poor devil!'

"The man who caused this is still alive," said Baümer. "They say he's gone mad."

"He was always mad," said Reber.

Baümer laughed quietly.

"We didn't think so until defeat came. I was one of the young fanatics. I carried the lighted torch at the Olympic Games. We thought him marvellous then—the reincarnation of Siegfried. We worshipped him, *Unser Führer! Heil Hitler! Heil Dir im Siegerkranz*. Now he hides in a cellar, raving mad they say, and he has dragged down everything with his own ruin. He'll have a fine tomb when he kills himself, greater than an Egyptian pyramid. All these ruins above the bodies of women and children who were sacrificed to his gods and devils—my wife and my children among them."

A spasm of pain shook him and his face became a tragic mask.

He moved towards Reber, climbing over some blocks of masonry.

"Can I help you?" he asked. "Are you looking for anything special—dead bodies for example! Pardon me for suggesting it, but I did the same thing—without success."

"I don't know," said Franz Reber. "I don't know what's happened to my father and mother. I must find out."

He felt a little faint for a moment, probably for lack of food.

Baümer noticed it and gripped his arm.

"Steady!"

Franz sat down on one of the blocks of stone. He felt drawn to this man Baümer. He seemed a little mad but kind and comradely in a queer way.

"Why did you choose my cellar?" he asked presently when he felt less faint. "Why did Winkelnkempler and those two girls come here?"

"Blind chance," answered Baümer. "An air raid. People running like rabbits. I was talking to Winkelnkempler at the corner of Fasanenstrasse. He stared up at the sky cursing the English. The two girls were running, bare-headed. A shell fell pretty close and I grabbed Elsa and picked her up. She had fallen with a basket full of cabbages. 'Better get underground', I told her. I saw this cellar gaping under the ruins. We dashed into it and fell in a heap, Winkelnkempler on top of us. The steps are broken. 'Quite a nice cellar', said the girl Elsa when things were calmer. 'We had better stay here. Home from home and all modern conveniences'. That's what she said, as gay as a lark with hell all round. Now and again she makes me laugh, and that takes a bit of doing. . . . How are you feeling? Is that arm hurting you?"

"It's nothing," said Reber.

Baümer was sitting on one of the blocks of masonry.

He seemed inclined to talk.

"That man Winkelnkempler is a queer bird. He's looking forward to a third World War, before this one is ended. More corpses. More ruins, the end of civilization."

He looked at Reber with a ghastly smile in his pale blue eyes. Reber had an idea that Baümer was intellectually close to him and stripped of all falsity of Hitlerian heroics and the sham philosophy of the Goebbels propaganda machine in which as boys they had both believed.

"We must get back to the Christian tradition," said Franz. "Or we must find some other religion to kill the beast in us and reassert some higher morality than mass murder."

"I was a Catholic," said Baümer. "I used to sing in the choir. I used to serve Mass on the altars. I was a holy little boy and a serious-minded young man, faithful to my wife, devoted to my children. Now I've lost my faith. Perhaps I've lost my soul. Everything has gone to hell including the souls of men. Hitler let loose the Devil, or became his slave and servant. Now the Devil laughs. It's his world. He's having a fine time. *Heil Herr Teufel!*"

He gave Reber that ghastly pallid grin and then raised himself from his seat on the block of masonry.

"I must forage for some food."

He raised his hand in salute and jumped into the roadway across a pile of débris.

Reber knocked at several doors in houses which still stood in the Fasanenstrasse. One was opened by an elderly lady with white hair.

"It's no use, young man," she said. "My house is already filled with refugees and homeless friends."

"I haven't come for that," he answered. "I'm the son of Herr Reber. Did you happen to know him?"

The lady looked at him sharply.

"You don't look like his son—or like his beautiful wife."

Franz Reber assured her that he was their son. Did she know what had happened to them.

She knew but hesitated to tell him.

"My poor young man!" she exclaimed.

Franz Reber's heart gave a lurch.

"Dead, do you mean? In the air raids?"

She glanced nervously up and down the street.

"It's dangerous to talk here. Come inside."

He went into a little sitting-room to the right of the hall.

"Sit down," she said. "I'll shut the door."

He sat down heavily on a stiff-backed chair. The old lady studied his face with her sharp, piercing eyes.

"How do I know you're not an S.S. man?" she asked. "One has to be very careful."

"I was in Russia," he told her. "Afterwards in East Prussia. Here are my papers."

He pulled out his wallet from his pocket and the old lady looked through them.

"Do you remember," she asked, "what was on your mother's writing-desk?"

He fumbled in his pocket with his right hand and pulled out the little bronze Mercury.

"I've just found it in the ruins."

"That's right," she told him.

"Tell me for God's sake," he said impatiently. "What has happened to my father and mother?"

She lowered her voice to a whisper.

"He was executed on the same day as Ulrich von Hassell. They became great friends. He lived in this street."

Franz Reber's face went white. If he could believe this old woman his father had been in the plot of July 20th. Suddenly he remembered some of the last letters he had received from his father. They had been handed to him during the retreat in some Russian village whose name he could not remember. "Letters from home," said one of his comrades. His father's letter had been gloomy and tragic. The retreat in Russia had filled him with foreboding.

I am afraid Germany is doomed [he had written]. *We are now fighting on two fronts. That is fatal. We have been led into this death-trap by the powers of Evil and we must slay this Satan of Evil or be destroyed.*

Franz sat there silently with his head drooping in deep thought.

"I daren't tell you any more," said the old lady. "Perhaps I ought not to have told you so much. How do I know you won't denounce me? The S.S. have already questioned me because I knew your father and mother."

"My mother!" said Franz. "You've told me nothing about her."

The old lady looked at him with pity.

"My poor boy!" she cried. "My poor boy!"

"Tell me," he said.

She took his right hand and patted it.

"It's a very dreadful world," she said. "Germany is condemned to death. I'm an old woman now. Thank God I can't live much longer to see all that we shall have to suffer as a defeated nation. I'm sorry for the younger folk like yourself, my dear young man."

"My mother," said Franz. "Tell me."

"She took something," said the old lady. "She died in her sleep, I hope. She was heart-broken."

"Did she ever speak of me?" asked Franz in a voice of anguish. "I didn't write much. I feel guilty now."

"She grieved at not hearing from you," said the old lady. "In the end she made up her mind that you were dead or a prisoner in Russian hands. 'My Franz', she called you, and now I meet you and tell you these dreadful things. Have you the courage to bear them, my poor boy?"

Yes, he had the courage to bear them. He could bear them too well. His emotions were still very deadened. His mind was swamped with tragedy, death, mutilation, ruin and all misery. In the Black Death of the Middle Ages men and women must have been like this, unweeping for the unburied dead, too familiar with death to regard it with horror, wondering only who would be the next victims among their families and friends. A new Black Death had come to Germany in these days of destruction and defeat. Before then it had come to Poland and Russia, perhaps even to England when German bombers had gone droning through the skies triumphantly, smashing cities and homesteads beneath their wings. It had been a competition in murder and the enemy had won. *Vae Victis!*

"Are you one of our wounded heroes?" asked the old lady looking at his left arm.

"One of the wounded," he answered. "On the Oder. I'm just out of hospital."

She patted his right hand again and then raised it to her lips and kissed it so that he was embarrassed.

"I wish I could put you up here," she said, "but I can't. This house is crowded to suffocation by my homeless friends, poor dears. Of course we go down to the cellars every night. When your father's house went down I thought we had all been buried alive."

She gave a little cackling laugh.

"How absurd we are to be afraid of death! At my age too! It's ridiculous."

"I must go," said Franz. "Thank you for what you have told me."

She went with him to the door and before opening it whispered to him with her lips very close to his ear.

"Is Hitler still alive?"

"I believe so."

"Too bad," she whispered. "He ought to be dead. Don't tell anybody I said so!"

She opened the door and spoke above a whisper.

"I'm so sorry. I had to tell you, didn't I?"

She looked down the street where many houses had been wrecked.

"Oh, dear, what a mess," she exclaimed. "I daren't poke my nose out nowadays. Our poor Berlin!"

She waved a little old hand to him as he walked slowly away deep in tragic thought.

One thought came to him as a question.

"What is there to live for now—for any of us Germans? What kind of future can we make? Can we ever get back to sanity and peace, and perhaps laughter and life's beauty?"

Suddenly something was released inside his emotional being, which had seemed so cold and dead. He leaned up against a broken wall and wept. He had never guessed that his father was a man of heroic courage, ready to risk martyrdom for Germany's sake. It needed heroic courage to take part in a plot against Hitler.

He had despised his father once. He had almost hated him for thwarting his ambition to become an artist. Somehow, like so many fathers and sons Franz and his father had been reserved with each other without sympathy and understanding on either side. Now Franz was overwhelmed by this revelation of courage and self-sacrifice. He would have given his right arm, and more than that, to have embraced his father for the last time, to have wept in his arms, to have expressed his devotion and love so long withheld.

CHAPTER XIII

FRANZ came face to face with Hilde Menzel in the Tiergarten. He was first aware of the two children who came running towards him when he was walking with his gaze on the ground regardless of the few people passing.

"Sergeant Reber! Sergeant Reber!"

It was young Hans who shouted to him. He and Trudel seemed delighted to see their fellow-traveller in the covered wagon and the soldier who had stayed with them in Quakenbrück.

Franz lifted the boy as high as his chest and kissed him.

"Me too!" said Trudel.

They had run ahead of Hilde who now came up.

"Franz!" she exclaimed. "What has happened to you?"

She looked at his arm which was still in plaster.

"It's nothing. A smashed arm from a bit of shell on the Oder."

"Does it hurt?" asked Hans, staring at it.

"Not now."

The little boy and girl ran off to dig in a shell-crater with bits of broken wood which they found near to it.

"The children are happy, even in Berlin!" said Franz. "How good to see you, Hilde. Even in this ruin and desolation!"

He raised her hand and put it to his lips.

"Quakenbrück seems a dream," she said. "Berlin is a nightmare. But thank God you're alive, Franz."

He looked at her with reverential eyes.

"Magda Hessell told me about you," he said.

"We were foolish to come," said Hilde. "I find Berlin terrible and we shan't escape the Russians. They'll be here soon. I still live in terror. There's no escape."

Franz raised both hands in a gesture of despair.

"I'm sorry for all women," he said in a low voice.

He looked at her with worshipful eyes, not hiding his pity.

"Tell me everything since I left you," he said. "Where are you living, and how? Have you any shelter from these appalling air raids?"

"We live in comfort," said Hilde, "but there's a dreadful tragedy in the house. I weep all night."

She told him of her uncle Fritz von Meissner. They had heard nothing of him since his arrest. He might already be dead. They were not allowed to know the name of his prison though Hermann had been to the police headquarters.

"On what charge did they arrest him?" asked Franz.

Hilde spoke in a whisper as though there might be listening ears even in this desert of the Tiergarten.

"The plot of July 20th. He was a friend of the others."

Franz stared at her. His own father had been executed for the plot of July 20th when Count Claus von Stauffenberg, Chief of Staff of the Home Army in 1944, had set off the bomb at Hitler's headquarters in East Prussia. He too had been a friend of the others.

"After all this time?" he asked.

"One of them may have given his name away. There are some not yet executed. Perhaps under torture."

Franz Reber went pale.

"So we've come to torture in Germany," he said with anguish. "We deserve to be blotted off the face of the earth."

He stared sombrely into Hilde's eyes.

"What has happened to us?" he asked. "Mass murder of Jews. Horrible experiments on human beings. Thousands of us in concentration camps. Torture. Haven't we been a civilized people? Haven't we boasted of our blood and race?"

"There are men like devils," said Hilde. "In Germany they gained power. It's the power of Evil."

Franz struck his chest with his right fist.

"Once we shouted 'Heil Hitler!' Were we all mad?"

"We didn't know," said Hilde. "How could we know?"

Reber raised his head.

"These things go on," he said. "They haven't finished. May defeat come quick and make an end of it. We must get cleansed—by defeat."

"Defeat will be terrible," said Hilde. "The Russians . . ."

She shuddered as she stood there in the Tiergarten. Twenty yards away her two children were shouting and laughing in a shell-crater.

"Germany must find her soul again," said Reber in a low voice. "Somehow I must find my own soul. I must get cleansed, too. I have filthy and frightful memories and my soul is besmirched."

Hilde touched his hand.

"You believe in beauty," she said. "You'll come back to it."

They sat on a block of stone silently for some time. A few people passed them. A thin dark vapour hung over Berlin like a low-lying cloud. Buildings were still smouldering and smoking after the last air raid two nights ago.

"Franz," said Hilde presently, "I daren't stay here any more. Berlin terrifies me. Those air raids. . . . This waiting."

"Where can you go?" asked Reber.

"I must get to Munich."

"They're bombing Munich," he said.

"Not so much and we should live in a village ten miles away. I should feel happier with the children in Bavaria. My father and mother are there with Christel."

"Trains can't get through," said Reber. "Only by round-about ways, and with the risk of being bombed. They're smashing up the lines everywhere."

"I must try to get through," said Hilde, desperately. "If I stay in Berlin I shall go mad."

Franz looked at her in a startled way.

"Don't go mad," he said. "For God's sake, don't go mad, Hilde. To me—since I've known you—you live in my mind as the heroic woman, the brave mother, with a spiritual courage beyond my range. Don't let me down."

Hilde's eyes filled with tears.

"I'm nothing like that, I'm filled with terror. It's the thought of the children that makes me a coward."

Trudel set up a loud scream. She had cut her knee in the shell-crater. Hilde ran towards her and Franz followed.

"Girls are awful cry-babies," said young Hans. "It's only men that are brave. I'm glad I'm not a girl. When I grow up I shall get a machine-gun and kill the English and the Russians—lots of them."

"Hans!" cried Hilde. "If you say things like that I'll spank you. When you grow up there will be no more war and no more killing, thank God."

"No more war!" exclaimed Hans. "I can't believe that, Mother. Then what shall we all do?"

All his young life he had heard about war. From his nursery window in Königsberg he had watched marching soldiers, guns, tanks, aeroplanes, armed lorries. Life was unimaginable to him without war and killing.

Franz Reber glanced at Hilde.

"German youth!" he said with dark irony.

He lifted Trudel to his shoulders and walked with them to the big house in the Grünewald.

CHAPTER XIV

FRANZ returned to the cellar underneath the ruins of his old home. The other inhabitants seemed to have settled down there as though they proposed to go on living there for ever. Winkelnkempler brought in an iron bedstead which he found amidst the débris of a house farther down the street.

"One may as well be comfortable," he said.

Elsa the dancing-girl had found an oleograph of the Madonna and Child by Raphael which she nailed up to one of the walls, using the heel of a shoe as a hammer.

"That will keep the bombs away," she said. "Hail Mary full of Grace. . . ."

She smiled at Winkelnkempler who scowled at this and uttered scornful words.

"Silly superstition!"

"It's the only thing left," Elsa said. "Once I was a good Catholic."

The other girl, Erike, contributed to the decoration of the cellar by bringing in two brass candlesticks.

"What's the use of those?" asked Winkelnkempler.

"Very decorative—and useful if we could get some candles."

"This plate would be useful if we could get some food," said Winkelnkempler.

Now and again they got some food. The girls dragged back a sack of potatoes from the market to which they had gone at dawn. Baümer by some miracle had found a case of tinned meat and vegetables which obviously had been packed up for a flight from Berlin by people who had not escaped in time. Baümer had gone into the cellar of another ruined house to look after a dog with a broken leg which had limped into it. There on the floor, tied up with string, was this priceless treasure-chest, which he had opened and examined. He had brought it back on his shoulder followed by the limping dog, a black spaniel with whom he had made friends, and who now became his devoted slave, always sitting by his side and looking up at him with adoring eyes.

Baümer was touched by this devotion.

"Animals are so much better than human beings," he said one night.

"Not very flattering to us," remarked Elsa, with a light laugh.

"We humans ought to be smudged off the face of the earth," said Baümer. "We've invented every diabolical weapon for destroying one another. We've become more cruel than the devils of hell. What do you think, Reber?"

"I've said the same thing," said Franz. "But I'd like to save the innocents."

"The innocents will become the guilty," said Baümer. "When they're old enough they'll start killing one another, torturing one another, struggling for power over one another."

"Why not?" asked Winkelnkempler. "That's the law of life. It's the law of the jungle where your beautiful animals live. It was through struggle and killing that man became what he is."

"An intelligent ape," said Baümer bitterly. "Or perhaps I should say an unintelligent ape."

Elsa looked over at Baümer with smiling eyes. It was astonishing that this girl could still be gay in this cellar under air raids.

"You depreciate your own qualities as a human being," she said. "You don't look like an ape. You don't think like an ape. You had pity in your heart for a dog with a broken leg. You're kind to two little sluts who must be a nuisance in this cellar. You've shared your food with us and stinted yourself so that we should have more. Shall I tell you what you are?"

"I should like to know," said Baümer carelessly.

"You're a good Christian."

Baümer shook his head.

"I've no faith and no hope."

Winkelnkempler laughed harshly.

"We Germans have abandoned the Christian myth. It was a slave religion. It preached pity and turning the other cheek and forgiving one's enemy. Are we to forgive the English and the Americans and the Russians? I'll see myself in hell first. I hope to live to kill a few. I believe in hatred. I believe in revenge. I believe in our German Destiny."

Franz looked over to him through the semi-darkness of this cellar lit only by a tiny oil-lamp. He could see Winkelnkempler's lean, haggard face and sunken eyes and sharp cheekbones like a Rembrandt etching.

'This man,' thought Franz, 'is a killer. He belongs to the cave-man age. Perhaps there's only a minority which has got beyond the cave-man age.'

"I believe in Destiny, too," he said. "But I don't think it's going to work out in the same way as your idea of it."

"How then?" asked Winkelnkempler, warming his thin hands at the stove.

"So far Destiny has led Germany to defeat," said Franz. "Perhaps through defeat and all this suffering humanity may advance to some higher stage of wisdom, doing away with war and mass murder. I'm not talking only of Germans."

"An illusion!" said Winkelnkempler, impatiently. "A miserable defeatist idea! How can we Germans attain our rightful place in the world without another war?"

"What is our rightful place in the world?" asked Franz, ironically. "Sitting in cellars like this under the ruins of our cities?"

Winkelnkempler glared at him through the semi-darkness.

"Our rightful place is that of the Master Race. We must co-ordinate Europe. We need *Lebensraum* as Hitler has said. We must discipline the inferior peoples. That's our Destiny."

"*Mein Gott*!" exclaimed Franz. "I used to hear that kind of stuff when I was in a Labour Camp. Must you drag it out again? It makes me want to be sick."

Winkelnkempler stood up from the iron bedstead on which he had been sitting near the stove. There was a menacing tone in his voice, and his right fist was clenched.

"I believe you're a white-livered traitor. If you hadn't some right to this cellar I'd kick you out of it. You ought to be in a concentration camp with other traitors."

Franz answered calmly.

"I'm a traitor to all that clap-trap, Winkelnkempler. We were stuffed and choked with it through loud-speakers and by Hitler's screaming voice. I used to believe it. Now I know it was not even believed by those who preached it, not even by Goebbels and his propaganda slaves and lick-spittles. It was frozen out of me in the Russian campaign. The blood of my comrades washed it out of me. I've got beyond all that filthy nonsense, though where I am now I don't know. If I stay alive I shall have to reshape myself. I shall have to find some other philosophy of life."

"You're a deserter," said Winkelnkempler fiercely.

"We're all deserters," said Baümer. "Why are we in this cellar hiding like rats?"

"We must get back to religion," said Elsa. "I've a good mind to become a nun and give up naughtiness."

The other girl, Erike, gave a shrill laugh.

"What nonsense you're all talking!" she cried. "We may all be dead before morning comes. I'm a fatalist. I take things as they come. What's the use of worrying about humanity and German Destiny? We're just stray dogs and cats in a dirty cellar. . . . Listen!"

It was the first crash of bombs in that night's air raid—one of the most terrible raids over Berlin. The ground under the cellar heaved and quaked. The walls trembled. Above them heavy bits of masonry were dislodged from the ruins already made and came thumping down like loose boulders in an avalanche. Into the dimly-lighted cellar came the red glare of fire and the scarlet fury of the sky above the doomed city.

The two girls sat crouched on the floor. Winkelnkempler lay down on his iron bedstead, motionless like a dead man with his eyes open. Baümer moved about now and then restlessly and then lay down with his face to the wall. The black spaniel nuzzled against him trembling in every limb. Franz sat on a kitchen chair with his head drooping on his chest. The little oil-lamp burned with its tiny dim light touching the oleograph of Raphael's Madonna and Child, and the two brass candlesticks on a deal table.

In Berlin that night thousands of other people sat in cellars and shelters feeling the earthquake shocks of falling bombs and crashing buildings, but the refugees from East Prussia encamped round the railway-stations were caught in the open and there were scenes of terror and dreadful death.

CHAPTER XV

HERMANN VON MEISSNER brought news of his father's execution. When he came into the room after he had been away all day Hilde Menzel knew by his face that this had happened, and the others knew. He was white to the lips and crossed the floor to his mother like a drunken man and fell on his knees before her, burying his face in her lap, his body shaken by sobs.

Frau von Meissner did not weep. Hilde, watching her with pity, marvelled at her courage and calmness.

"He died for the Fatherland," she said. "He died for Germany as a knight-errant against the powers of Darkness. Don't weep for him, my poor Hermann. Be as brave as he was."

"I'm not brave," said her son. "I've no courage. And I weep for you, Mother."

Perhaps—who knows?—this news was a relief to Frau von Meissner. For more than six months she had trembled at every knock at the door. The arrest of so many of her husband's friends—Stauffenberg, Ulrich von Hassell, Alexander von Falkenhausen, Carl Friedrich Goerdeler, Hans Haeften, Albrecht Haushofer, Oster, Chief of Staff of Military Intelligence—had fastened suspicion on her husband. She had known that all his sympathy was with these men who were conspiring against Hitler whom they believed to be the arch enemy of Germany and the author of its inevitable defeat. They had come to this house separately for long conversations at which she had been present. Her husband had met them separately again in other cities and at friends' houses. The plot itself against Hitler's life had never been mentioned. But Elizabeth von Meissner knew what was the ultimate purpose of those meetings and of her husband's secret activities. Hitler must be killed to save Germany from destruction. Hitler must be killed to save German honour from the stain of atrocious cruelties against the Jews and the horror of the concentration camps crowded with Germans of liberal minds. When the plot failed on July 20th by Hitler's hair's-breadth escape from Stauffenberg's bomb she felt as though her blood had frozen inside her body. How could he husband escape when so many of his friends were taken? Every day for seven months she had expected his arrest. His courage, his calmness, his nobility, had been unshaken, and he had risked his life by writing the history of the plot and the underground movement as a proof to the world hereafter that not all Germans had failed in resistance to Hitler's evil power.

She had helped to hide those papers. She had gone out at night into the garden to bury them in tin boxes, empty sugar tins, under trees and bushes. She had tried to be brave but as a devoted wife she had lived with terror. Now he was dead, a martyr's death, and a kind of serenity came to her as though her husband had died after a long and lingering illness. She had been released from her rack of torture and terrifying anxiety. All her pity now was for Hermann who was broken by his father's fate. She was a little impatient with Aunt Tessa who wept and moaned and with the two girls who became hysterical.

"It's no good giving way to grief," she told Hilde one night when they were down in the air-raid shelter. "I admire you, my dear. You keep quiet even if you weep."

"Aunt Elizabeth," said Hilde. "I must get away from Berlin. Do you mind if I leave you? The children——"

"I know," said her aunt. "Those poor babes! Berlin is no place for them. This house is like a pack of cards when those frightful bombs are dropping. At any moment——"

She did not end that sentence. At any moment all of them might be buried alive or dead like whole families she had known.

"It's safer in Bavaria," said Hilde.

Frau von Meissner raised her hands slightly.

"Does your father think so? Is any German city safe?"

"We should be ten miles outside Munich," said Hilde. "Our village has not been touched yet. It would be paradise after Berlin."

A letter from her father and her mother had arrived that morning by some kind of miracle. He had had three letters from Hilde. The description of her journey from Königsberg had moved them deeply. Her mother had wept because Hilde had had to leave little Peter in the snow. They thanked God that Hans and Trudel were alive and well.

My friend Heisenberg hopes to get through to Berlin by car to rescue his daughter who is going to have a child. She is still well enough to be moved. He offers to bring you back to us and needless to say we are deeply grateful to him and are filled with joy, in spite of all this tragedy, at the thought of seeing you again with your dear children.

He had added a postscript.

We expect to be occupied by the Americans. Their entry cannot be long delayed.

Hilde looked round the cellar where her children and companions were sleeping. Aunt Tessa who had been a good comrade on the journey from Königsberg was breathing heavily with her mouth open. Ursel and Hildegard lay very quiet under their blankets. Rosa Gottlieb to whom the two children were devoted lay on her back with her hands clasped in an attitude of prayer. Even Hermann, so restless and so nervous, lay still and sleeping with one arm flung outside his coverlet.

"If it weren't for the children," said Hilde, "I should feel like a deserter leaving you all in Berlin. Can't you all come, Aunt Elizabeth? Why should you stay here in this city of death?"

Her aunt raised Hilde's left hand and kissed it.

"We must resign ourselves to what comes next. There are no trains running now. All the lines are broken. If Herr Heisenberg gets through with a car we shall rejoice for your sake, my dear."

"Ursel and Hildegard!" said Hilde "I should hate to leave them. They're so young and so pretty. If the Russians come . . ."

A cold shudder passed through her body.

"Don't think of horrors," said her aunt. "Go to sleep, my dear. You're always so wakeful at night."

Hilde saw Franz Reber once more before Herr Heisenberg's car arrived in Berlin. He came round one morning and heard the news that she might be going with the children.

"It's time," he said gravely. "The war is reaching its climax. It's a race between the Americans and the Russians. Berlin must fall before many days are out."

"What will you do, Franz?" asked Hilde.

He gave a quiet laugh.

"I shall go on living like a cave-man in my father's cellar where I have strange bed-fellows."

He begged the chance of a bath and a shave. His left arm was out of plaster now after a visit to the hospital, and when he came downstairs again he looked ten years younger though his uniform was loose on his body which had become very thin.

Hilde smiled at him. She was in the sitting-room, mending the children's clothes.

"Very debonair!" she said. "It's the first time I've seen you so clean and spruce. In the covered wagon you were a mass of burns. Even at Quakenbrück you were badly scarred. Now a mask has fallen from you—the mask of pain."

"The mask of filth," he answered.

"If Herr Heisenberg's car comes for me I shall be seeing Christel," she told him. "Shall I give her your love?"

A smile touched his lips.

"She may remember a boy called Franz Reber who went skiing with her and tried to kiss her more than once. But that boy is dead. The Franz Reber who lives, who is still alive by some miracle, is an old man haunted by abominable memories and trying to find his lost soul. Tell her that."

"I shall tell her," said Hilde, "that the Franz Reber I know has not very far to look to find his soul. It looks out of his eyes with pity and pain for women and children. I'll tell her that."

He was abashed by those words and his face flushed.

"Thank you," he said. "Those are kind words if they are true."

"I think they're true, Franz. And I have to thank you for so many things. I shall never forget our talks in Quakenbrück and the games you had with the children, and your comradeship."

He was silent for a little while standing in front of her.

"We talk as though we were being parted by death," he said.

"In Germany now," said Hilde, "we have to talk like that."

He nodded.

"One never knows from one day to another."

Presently he spoke of Bavaria.

"You'll be seeing the mountains again. Perhaps you will be climbing them. You'll breathe the clean air up there above the

War and all the dirtiness. I'd give a lot to be there with you on a high peak with the world below us and only beauty round us. A dream!"

"When this War is over," said Hilde, "that dream will be waiting for you. Beauty will still be there. I shall look out for you, Franz."

He took her hand and raised it to his lips.

"I have a very great love for you," he said. "I mean that with reverence and comradeship."

"Thank you, Franz, my dear. If we don't meet again before I go, I want you to know that I shall think of you always as a friend. I met you in days of misery, a friend who helped me."

He kissed her cheek and held her in his arms for a moment before saying good-bye.

CHAPTER XVI

THE Americans arrived in the Bavarian village of Kaulbach towards the end of April. Wolf von Arnheim who had the big house in Kaulbach heard the news that they had reached Munich ten miles away. It was brought to him by his friend Dr. Schwarzwald, one of the directors of the Alte Pinakothek which had been destroyed in the air raids like the Opera House and so many other buildings.

Strong and wiry at the age of sixty-five, Dr. Schwarzwald had cycled over from Munich to see his daughter who was staying with an aunt in Kaulbach to get away from the bombing, now for some days at an end by the grace of God and the American Air Force.

Wolf von Arnheim heard his voice in the hall and answered it.

"Come in, Schwarzwald. I'm in the study."

He had been sitting in his study—a big square room lined with books which once he had read. Now it was no use reading books. He had been sitting in a swing chair, hunched up at his desk with his head between his hands. He straightened himself up as Schwarzwald came in like a little old terrier, white haired with blue eyes under shaggy eyebrows. Before the War they had gone mountain climbing together.

"What's the latest?" asked the Baron von Arnheim. "What horror are you going to tell me?"

His friend's voice was shaky with excitement and emotion. "The Americans are in Munich. I was in bed when I heard them first. The noise of their tanks was deafening. They're still roaring in like ten thousand devils. The vibration is shaking the ruins. A wall fell down in the Opernplatz. My wife is terribly frightened because of our pretty Gita."

Wolf von Arnheim, two years younger than his friend, gave a short gruff laugh. He had felt his heart give a kind of lurch, missing a beat perhaps, because of this new episode, this new and inescapable sign of Germany's downfall.

"They're more civilized than the Russians," he answered heavily. "We're lucky about that."

Dr. Schwarzwald flung up his hands with a gesture of despair and rage. He uttered a shrill, goblin-like laugh.

"More civilized? Those demons who have destroyed all our cities, beneath which millions of our dead lie rotting. Millions of our women and children. Open cities without any military objective, like Dresden, Nürnberg, Wurzburg. Blind vengeance! Mass murder of mothers and babes. More civilized, you say?"

Wolf von Arnheim sitting in his swing chair again answered gloomily.

"If Hitler had sued for peace a year ago we might have been saved all that. It was that madman's fault. His megalomania—his refusal to listen to our Generals."

He checked himself by a heavy groan.

"But, my dear Schwarzwald, don't let's discuss civilization or Adolf Hitler. Both are dead. Both have committed suicide."

"I must go," said Schwarzwald, presently. "My wife will be anxious about me. I just looked in to tell you the news."

He stared at Baron von Arnheim with those blue eyes under shaggy eyebrows.

"You look ill, Wolf. I'm not surprised. How can any of us keep our nerve or even our sanity? These piled up horrors! This sentence of doom!"

Wolf von Arnheim shrugged his shoulders, his broad Bavarian shoulders, and answered with a harsh laugh.

"I keep my sanity—so far. But many of my friends have thought me mad for a long time. Among them you, Schwarzwald, when I told you what was going to happen to Germany."

"I must go," said Dr. Schwarzwald again. "*Auf Wiedersehen.* Our dear old Munich is in the hands of the Americans. God help us!"

He raised a thin, hairy hand and went quickly out of the room. The latch of the front door clicked. There was a scrunch of gravel as he mounted his bicycle.

The Baron von Arnheim, brother-in-law of Herr von Meissner, executed for a plot against the Führer's life, stood up from his chair. He was a tall, keavily-built man wearing the leather shorts, white stockings and embroidered jacket of the Bavarian folk. The events of the past years, especially of the past months, had whitened his hair which previously had been grey, and put dark pouches below his eyes. The skin of his face had turned mud-coloured at the news of Hitler's suicide and Himmler's call for surrender before he too killed himself.

Not for any love of Hitler had his face turned muddy, like a dead man's, nor had defeat come to him with any surprise. He had seen its inevitability for a long time, ever since the retreat from Stalingrad. But it was all very shaking to a man of his age and to a man who had hated this war from the beginning. The future of Germany, he thought, would be a long agony. They would have to pay the price of defeat and it would be a fearful price. Already Germany lay in ruins, most of its cities utterly destroyed as Schwarzwald had reminded him needlessly, as though he didn't know it—as though the horror of it all, the state of Munich itself with so much of its beauty lying in rubble, was not burning in his soul like those smouldering fires.

He held on to the back of his chair and stared down at his hands, big farmer-looking hands, as though interested in the pattern of his veins but without seeing them. A shudder passed through his body for a moment and a deep sigh came up from his stomach. He had been a prophet of defeat when Hitler attacked Russia. He had loathed this war, so unnecessary even to Hitler who had vowed that he was a man of peace. He had been five years in England as a younger man, three of them as a prisoner in the First World War, and had liked its people and their way of life. He had been all for Chamberlain when he flew to Munich—the Man with the Umbrella, as they called him, the man who had made every concession on behalf of peace and then was betrayed. He had hidden his secret hatred of Hitler and his gang of ruffians. It would have been better if he had been shot, he thought, like his brother-in-law, Meissner, a braver and nobler man than himself. He had chosen the martyr's crown, had Meissner, like Ulrich von Hassell and many others, whereas he had funked it and compromised with evil, and stretched out his right arm with a *Heil Hitler* for the sake of his wife and children.

He went to the door of his room and called his wife.

"Lili! . . . Mother! . . ."

"Yes, Wolf."

"I have something to tell you."

His wife came from the kitchen where she had been cooking some cabbage soup. Apart from French prisoners of war who helped with the garden and brought in wood for fuel there were no servants in this big house. Frau von Arnheim was ten years younger than her husband but the lines of her face had become sharp lately and her hair had greyed as his had whitened. He had been frightened sometimes by the look in her eyes, a look of anguish. She had been a worshipper of Hitler in the beginning. They had quarrelled about that almost to breaking-point. Now defeat had broken her pride.

"Has anything horrible happened?" she asked. "Has anything happened to Hilde and the children?"

"No, no," answered her husband soothingly. "They must be on their way. Perhaps the car broke down. In a way it's good news. The Americans are in Munich. We shall be safe with them."

His wife put her hands to her bosom.

"Christel!" she said. "Will she be safe from American soldiers?"

Wolf von Arnheim hid his own anxiety because of Christel his pretty daughter. Pretty girls might not be safe in an army of occupation. Thousands of women had been maltreated by the Russians according to stories coming from the refugees now in flight from them. The Americans would be different.

"They'll behave decently," he told his wife. "Christel knows how to look after herself. Where is she now?"

"She cycled over to Munich again. Nothing will keep her away from the University. During the air raids I worried myself to death about her."

"She has a very high spirit," said Wolf von Arnheim, "and I admire her for that. I like her courage. I like her gaiety which somehow she has kept amidst all this terror."

"I wish Hilde and the children would come," said his wife, anxiously. "I can't help thinking that something terrible has happened to them. It must be a month since they left Berlin. Oh, Wolf!"

She began to weep and he went over to her and put his arms round her.

"Things will be better now," he told her. "The War is over. No more blood. Peace, at last!"

"Where are our sons?" she cried. "Where is Carl? Where is my laughing Paul? . . . If they're dead I don't want to live."

"Courage!" he said. "Courage! We must go on living for Christel. We must live for Hilde and the two children."

"They may never come," said his wife. "We've been waiting a month. They may be dead like Carl and Paul."

"We should have heard," said Wolf von Arnheim. "No news is good news. I've not given up hope about our dear Paul. One day we shall see him again."

"Do you believe that?" asked Frau von Arnheim, looking into his eyes. "Wolf, don't lie to me, my dear."

"I believe it," he said, lying to her. "I'm certain of it, as I am of Hilde and her children. And here is Christel."

He had heard the scrape of her cycle wheels on the gravel-path and saw her riding past his study window.

Presently she came into his room. She was wearing a yellow jumper and blue slacks. She had gold spun hair combed back from a broad forehead and her mother's delicate features with sharp cheekbones and rather deep-set blue eyes.

"Our conquerers arrive!" she cried, with a kind of excited amusement.

"How are they behaving?" asked her father. "Do they seem a decent crowd?"

Christel laughed.

"You never saw such sham ferocity, a lot of fat boys trying to look fierce, swarming on to tanks and jeeps as thick as flies on a jam-pot and armed to the teeth with rifles and Tommy-guns as though the peasants of Kaulbach were going to attack them with pitchforks! Some of the farmers just laughed at them. It was like an American movie at the cinema in Munich. They scowled horribly when they heard this laughter but I noticed one or two of them couldn't resist a secret smile. They saw the absurdity of this armed occupation of a peaceful Bavarian village."

"I don't see the absurdity," said her father, harshly. "I see only the humiliation."

"They look so ridiculous!" said Christel. "I dare say they're quite good-natured really. Just a lot of boys dressed up as soldiers.

I wonder if we shall learn to speak English with an American accent."

"Christel," said her father sternly. "They're our conquerors, as you say. We must behave with dignity. Even the vanquished have a right to their pride."

"Oh, I'm not going to throw myself into their arms, Father," said Christel, lightly. "As a matter of fact they won't speak to us. They've had strict orders not to fraternize."

"How do you know?" asked her father.

Christel laughed again.

"One of them told me."

"You've been speaking to them?"

"To one. A fresh-faced youth. I spoke to him in English. I said 'Welcome to Bavaria'."

"Most indiscreet, Christel," said her father. "You're incorrigible. What did he answer?"

"He blushed like a schoolboy and spoke real American. 'Say, Missy, you're a nice looking gal, but we ain't allowed to talk to Germans. There's a strict order against fraternization. Thanks a lot all the same'."

She gave a caricatured imitation of the American accent.

"Christel," exclaimed her father, "don't make yourself cheap, my dear. You'll have to be very careful. These Americans are decent fellows, I dare say, but they're in a foreign country and come as victors. You're old enough to know the facts of life and the bestiality of men, especially when they're away from their own women."

Christel smiled at him in a superior way.

"My dear Father, I'm not an innocent child. I'm a third-year student in Philosophy. I've read many books which reveal human nature as it is and as it ought not to be, and I've been in a Labour camp with girls who were not very prudish in their speech. You needn't be alarmed. I'm not one of the cheap women, being the daughter of Wolf von Arnheim."

The Baron von Arnheim looked relieved.

"Forgive me," he said. "There was no need for me to speak like that. As you say you are Christel von Arnheim. It still means something."

Christel had laughing eyes.

"Those Americans," she exclaimed, "I can't think of them as our enemies."

Christel went to her own room upstairs and changed out of her yellow jumper and slacks which she flung on the floor in a heap when she put on a blue frock and an overall. She sat at a table by the window with her elbows on it and her face cupped in her hands. Almost from habit there was an open book in front of her. Reading was a kind of drug to her. It was Kierkegaard's book on Existentionalism which had been discussed by her fellow-students in Munich, discussed during air raids and while German cities were burning and the ruins of Munich littered the streets above the shelters into which they dived when bombs were crashing. Her eyes read some of the words on the printed page but not her mind. She was thinking of the scene in Munich when the Americans had arrived. They had brought with them a battalion—or was it a company—of little brown, smiling men. They were, she was told, Hawaiians.

Suddenly she saw through her window a big Army car pull into the drive. She sprang up and ran to the head of the stairs, calling out.

"Father! . . . Mother! Americans are coming!"

Her mother appeared white-faced at the bedroom door.

"What is it?" she asked in a frightened voice.

"American officers," said Christel. "They're knocking. Shall I open the door?"

"I will answer the door," said her father who appeared in the hall downstairs. "Go into the drawing-room, my dears. Keep very calm."

Presently he brought into the drawing-room three American officers and Ludwig Dorten, the mayor of Kaulbach, who looked nervous and embarrassed.

He bowed to Frau von Arnheim and Christel while beads of sweat glistened on his round head as bald as a billiard ball.

"These officers wish to see over your house," he said. "It is of course necessary to carry out their orders."

"For what purpose do they wish to see over the house?" asked Frau von Arnheim, very coldly.

"They may wish to commandeer it, madam."

Christel was watching the American officers. One who wore

the badges of a major was a tall, lean-faced young man with a hard mouth and hard eyes, she thought, but good-looking in a severe way. He might even be intelligent, she thought. The two others were fresh-faced young men with plump bodies and tight uniforms.

"We speak English here, gentlemen," said the Baron von Arnheim. "I was several years in England. This is my wife and daughter."

The American major nodded slightly and his mouth remained hard. Christel saw his eyes rest upon her for a moment searchingly.

He spoke politely but coldly.

"In that case I shan't need an interpreter. You will understand me when I say that I propose to requisition this house."

Christel looked at her father and saw that his face had paled. She was standing next to him and caught hold of his hand.

"We have no other house," he said. "I have no doubt you will take that into consideration."

The American major answered politely again but in the same cold tone.

"I have to find billets for our officers and men. I guess you understand, sir."

Wolf von Arnheim's face flushed slightly after its pallor.

"As the vanquished we have few rights," he said. "I understand that."

"Fine," said the major. "Maybe you'll be good enough to let us go round the house."

"I will accompany you," said the Baron von Arnheim in his perfectly correct English.

Christel spoke hurriedly in German.

"Don't take them into my bedroom, Father."

But he had to take them into her bedroom.

"What room is that?" asked the American major when he approached the door.

"My daughter's room. She wishes to keep it private."

"Open it, please."

The three American officers stood in Christel's room and for a moment a ghost of a smile softened the hard lips of the major when he glanced at the blue slacks and yellow jumper lying on the floor and other garments tossed about the bed and chairs.

"My daughter is rather untidy," said Wolf von Arnheim. "She prefers her books. She is a great student."

For some reason the major was attracted to the book on the table by the window.

"Kierkegaard," he said, after a glance. "I read an English translation of it at Harvard."

The other young officers were looking at some photographs on the walls. They were enlargements of snapshots taken on the Bavarian Alps, showing snow-covered peaks. One was a photograph of Christel up the face of a precipitous rock.

"My daughter is fond of climbing," said Wolf von Arnheim.

"Looks darned dangerous to me," said one of the young officers.

"Very dangerous," said Arnheim. "But my daughter has great courage."

"I think we have seen all we want," said the American major curtly, as though regretting this conversation which had become human and friendly. "I must ask you to have the house empty by six o'clock this evening. You will only be allowed to carry out a few personal possessions. No furniture of any kind must be removed."

Wolf von Arnheim stared at him with incredulity.

"By six o'clock? That's impossible. My wife and daughter——"

"You have my orders, sir," said the American major sharply.

"It's outrageous," said the Baron von Arnheim angrily. "I'm expecting another daughter with her children."

"I repeat my order," said the American major. "Do you understand, sir?"

The Baron von Arnheim understood. Germany was defeated. Germany was occupied. There could be no argument.

Christel and her mother heard the order to leave their house at six o'clock that evening with consternation and anger.

"Why should they push us out of our own house?" cried Christel after the three Americans had left. "It's abominable."

The Baron von Arnheim had cooled down after his own anger. "It's the law of War," he said. "Occupying troops have the right of billeting in civilian houses. In any case we're the defeated. *Vae Victis*."

"I don't believe it, Father," cried Christel, hotly. "Our occupying troops live in tents and hutments! We didn't seize people's houses."

Her father shook his head.

"That's not true, Christel. In the First World War I was in Army Divisional Staff in France. We were always billeted in French châteaux. One I remember at Cambrai."

"But what are we going to do?" asked his wife, tearfully. "We can't live in a ditch or an open field."

"We shall have to use the stables," said her husband.

"They're filthy and full of rats," cried Christel. "They haven't been cleaned out for years. I utterly refuse to have my toes nibbled by rats, Father."

The Baron von Arnheim breathed heavily. He was much distressed but knew there was no appeal against the order of occupying forces.

"We must resign ourselves," he said. "We must bear all this with courage and dignity. Christel, my dear, go and pack a few clothes in your small grips. We've just an hour. I'll help your mother and take a few things of my own."

"That American major is a beast," said Christel. "He must have been born on an iceberg. The other two looked more human. One of them had a sense of humour in his eyes."

"Go and pack, Christel," said her father, sharply.

Christel went to her own room and gave a fleeting smile at the disorder therein. Those Americans must have been scandalized at this untidiness. It was the greatest impudence, she thought, that they should dare to turn them out of their house and out of this room which was her private sanctuary and study and the secret chamber of her dreams.

She seized two grips and stuffed some clothes inside and her hair brushes and a few ornaments from her dressing-table. Then she gave a wild look at her bookshelves. She couldn't leave her books behind. It would be like abandoning her soul—the works of Kant and Hegel, her German Shakespeare, the plays of Bernard Shaw in English.

She stuffed about twenty of these books into the second grip. They were heavy but no great burden to her being a mountain-climber and as strong as a young colt.

Suddenly she looked round the room with angry eyes. All her little treasures were here. The drawers of a cabinet were stuffed with letters and photographs, pressed flowers which she had brought back from the mountains, trinkets given to her as a child by her family. In a corner of the room were her skis and snowboots. This little room was part of herself. Why should she have to leave it for some unknown American who would paw over her private things and even read her letters? Some of them were love-letters from boys who were now dead or prisoners of war. The American army had been ordered not to speak to Germans. Perhaps they were afraid of being contaminated. What impertinence! Did they think Germans wanted to make friends with them and fawn upon their victors? A lot of dough-faced ignoramuses!

"Are you ready, Christel?" her father called out.

"No, Father!"

"We must go. Your mother and I are ready."

"I'm not ready. I'll follow you later."

It was twenty minutes later when she humped her bags downstairs and dragged them to the front door.

Two sentries were outside and American soldiers were unpacking stores from an Army lorry.

One of the sentries barred her way with his rifle.

"I'll have to look in your grips, lady," he said sternly. "Open 'em up. *Verstehen Sie?*"

He was surprised when she answered in English very haughtily. "They're my private things. Kindly let me pass."

The soldier grabbed one of the bags—the one stuffed with books.

"Gee! What's all this? Gold nuggets?"

"Books."

He opened the bag and pulled out a book. He opened it and looked at some woodcuts of Greek gods and goddesses. It was a history of Greek philosophy.

"Do you read stuff like this?" he asked with a grin. "It don't look amusing to me."

He put it back into her bag and said "O.K."

She dragged the bags over to the stables at the other end of the garden. Her father and mother were there standing by their suit-cases. Her mother was white-faced and distressed.

"This is terrible!" she cried. "We shall have to live like gypsies."

Christel's father was trying to make the best of a bad business. "It won't be too uncomfortable when we've cleaned up a bit. I'll get the French prisoners to give us a hand. They're very decent fellows."

"Where are we going to sleep, Father?" asked Christel. "On the straw like pigs?"

"The rooms upstairs are decent enough—where the Polish prisoners used to sleep. The bedsteads are still there."

"And still verminous!" said Christel.

Christel's mother began to weep and the Baron von Arnheim put his arms about her. Presently when she had recovered a little he went over to Christel and spoke to her in a low voice.

"For your mother's sake make a joke of this. Make it seem like a picnic on the mountains when we used to sleep in wooden huts and enjoy being primitive. I rely upon your courage and your spirit, Christel. Don't make it worse than it is."

"I'll make it better than it is," said Christel. "I'll make a bonfire of this dirty straw."

"Wait for the Frenchmen," said her father. "I've sent a message to Sergeant Meunier. He's a friend of mine. A good fellow."

Sergeant Meunier came with two of his men. They had been prisoners of war in Germany since the summer of 1940 working on a farm where they had learnt to speak German. Sergeant Meunier had taken up with a German girl in the village of Kaulbach and she had had a child by him, now a small boy of two. He came up now wearing bits of his old uniform supplemented by German field-boots and a knitted pullover made for him by his girl.

"*Nom d'un chien!*" he exclaimed. "*Quel charivari! Les Americains sont des drôles garçons.*"

He spoke in a mixture of French and German to the Baron von Arnheim.

"You are turned out of your house, M'sieur le Baron? *C'est formidable ça!* It's not amusing for you or for Madame la Baronne. *Mais après tout c'est la guerre.*"

"My dear Meunier," said the Baron. "I shall be greatly

obliged if you and your comrades will clean out these stables. You are now free men but I hope I may count upon your friendly feelings towards my family and myself."

Sergeant Meunier gave a good-natured laugh. He was a typical French peasant of good-class having worked on his father's farm in Normandy before the War. He was a young man of about twenty-five but looked older because of a reddish beard.

"We have no grudge, M'sieur le Baron. Speaking for myself I may say that I've been happy in Kaulbach. German earth is very much like French earth. *La terre!* The sky above is the same sky. A German girl has been kind to me and is the mother of my son. In the beginning I called the Germans *sales Boches*. Certainly they made war upon us, not for the first time. But they are the leaders who make war. We who are not the leaders do not wish to kill each other. We wish to live in peace with our women. It's the same in all nations. The people are duped by their leaders. When war is declared they fight for their own side. That is natural. They destroy each other with the latest weapons. It is all the idiocy of our present system."

"You will clean out these stables?" asked the Baron von Arnheim.

Sergeant Meunier was a good fellow, but he was a great talker.

"Certainly we will clean out the stables. But they won't be magnificent when they're cleaned out. The Americans have perhaps been too severe in turning you out of your fine house. On the other hand Germany is now defeated. As a Frenchman I don't regret Germany's defeat. Herr Hitler was not a good type. He was surrounded by ruffians. It is possible that ten million, twenty million, people have died because of his ambitions. It's very certain in my mind that he and his comrade Himmler are now roasting in hell. That's the justice of God. But because I have a German girl who is the mother of my son I am not without pity for the German people who will have to pay the price of defeat."

"Perhaps it will be well to begin cleaning out the stables," said the Baron von Arnheim.

They cleaned out the stables. They cleaned out four little rooms upstairs divided by wooden partitions. In each room was an iron bedstead with a mattress which Christel regarded with suspicion. The ex-prisoners of war—free men now since the American liberation—lit a fire in the harness-room downstairs.

"You will need it for the *pot-au-feu*," said Sergeant Meunier. "In any case the evenings are still cold."

"We've brought no saucepan," cried Christel. "How can we cook without a saucepan?"

Her father had brought over some food in a rucksack which many a time he had used for expeditions to the mountains. He had got the food from the farm where the French sergeant was working, but how could they cook it without a saucepan?

"I'll go and get one," said Christel.

"No, no!" cried her mother. "You mustn't go among those Americans. For heaven's sake, my dear——"

"They won't bite me," said Christel. She had recovered her spirit. She had made up her mind to be very haughty with any American who might cross her path.

"I'll show them I'm not afraid of them," she said to herself.

But it was, she found, an ordeal when she entered the kitchen of her father's house by the back door. It was an immense kitchen with a stone floor and it was crowded with American soldiers standing about with their backs to the walls or sitting on wooden boxes containing their stores. Some of them were lying on the stone floor with their packs under their heads. Four of them, squatting on their haunches, were gambling with dice. They were talking in their American drawl, humming songs, whistling between their teeth or moving their jaws in a rhythmic way, chewing gum.

As she walked into the kitchen among them a silence fell upon them. They stopped talking, singing and whistling but went on moving their jaws. She was conscious that they were all staring at her. She felt a stiffness about her knees and a flush creeping up from her neck. She had to step over one of the men lying on the floor. He didn't budge to get out of her way. It needed all her courage and will-power to walk as far as the kitchen stove among these staring and silent soldiers. She grabbed a saucepan and a kettle and made her way to the door again. No-one challenged her. Holding her head high with the kettle in one hand and the saucepan in the other she passed through the ordeal again.

Unfortunately her eyes caught those of an American soldier

leaning up against the wall. He grinned at her slowly with his mouth twisted as he chewed his gum. The grin lighted up his bold staring eyes. His left eyelid winked at her. Her face hardened. She raised her head a little higher. She looked very haughty indeed. Two seconds after getting beyond the kitchen door she heard a burst of hoarse laughter and a flame of colour rushed to her face.

'Beasts!' she thought to herself. 'Our American conquerors. I hate the sight of them.'

Suddenly her anger gave way to pity for her father and mother. She was young enough to put up with anything. In the mountains she had accustomed herself to hardship and the primitive way of life. Often she had slept under the stars on the bare rocks alone in the world. But she was sorry for her father and mother used to comfort and getting old. How shameful, she thought, that her father, the Baron von Arnheim, should be thrust out of his home into his own stables, like a dog. Not yet had she learnt the price of defeat.

CHAPTER XVII

HILDE had been a long time on the roads between Berlin and Munich. It had been a painful and distressing journey, mainly because Herr Heisenberg's daughter had been terribly ill. The jolting of the car—an ancient Benz—had caused her torture and she had fainted several times. Twice they had been machine-gunned by low-flying American aircraft mistaking them perhaps for a German Staff car. In any case they were Germans. Several times the car had broken down because of punctures in worn-out tyres and some internal trouble which had baffled the diagnosis of Herr Heisenberg. They had to make long détours because of American armoured cars and transport surging along the road to Munich. Then one evening Herr Heisenberg spoke to Hilde anxiously.

"This is too much for Elfa. We must put up somewhere. It shakes her to pieces. I'm afraid——"

He did not end that sentence but Hilde knew the end of it. He was afraid his daughter was dying.

They found a place of rest in a farmhouse just off the road to Munich about a hundred kilometres away. At first the farmer had refused to receive them. His house, he said, was filled with refugees. He could take no more. His wife was going to have a baby and was in no state to fetch and carry. But it was the farmer's wife who overruled her husband's refusal after seeing Elfa Heisenberg who had been helped out of the car and was lying on the grass outside the gate.

"She looks at death's door," said the woman in a low voice, "and she's as beautiful as Our Lady in Heaven. I couldn't turn her away from our gate like they turned away the mother of God when there was no room in the inn."

"We could sleep in one of your barns," said Hilde.

"Yes," said Hans. "I wouldn't mind sleeping in the straw like a pig."

"Me too!" said Trudel. "I'd like to sleep in straw like a bunny rabbit."

The farmer's wife put both hands to her bosom and laughed but her eyes suddenly filled with tears.

"What is going to happen to our little ones?" she asked. "I have two younger than these poor mites and one coming. It's a bad time to bring a new life into this terrible world. Now that we're defeated——"

"What does defeat matter," said the young farmer who was standing next to his wife. "It's better than war. We've had enough of blood and bombing."

"I'll make a room ready for the young lady," said his wife. "My man and I will have to sleep in the kitchen. The rest of you will have to pack in with the other refugees."

"One can't call one's house one's own," said the farmer, sulkily.

"You're lucky to be alive with a roof over your head," said his wife. "You might have been dead or sitting in the ruins of your old home like so many friends of ours in Munich."

"True enough!" admitted the young farmer with a good-natured laugh after his moment of sulkiness.

Elfa Heisenberg was laid on a bed in a little room at the top of the farmhouse and Hilde and her children were given straw mattresses on the floor of another room, long and low under the rafters where three families of refugees were already in occupation. They were mothers and children who had fled from the Russians across the Oder. Among them were some young girls of fifteen and sixteen whose mothers were terrified of them being caught by the Russian troops. The children were verminous and Hilde tried to keep Hans and Trudel away from them at least during the day when they could play out-of-doors. At night the long low room was not a place of peace. A baby cried incessantly. The atmosphere was foul. The mattresses were alive with fleas. Hans and Trudel picked up some pestilential microbe and were very feverish.

Herr Heisenberg was anxious and perturbed. He was an elderly man of considerable scholarship and kindly nature but nervous and indecisive. The journey from Berlin had already exhausted him because of the mental tension and the state of his daughter's health. Hilde thought he was on the edge of a nervous breakdown. He was suffering from insomnia and sharing a bedroom with six other men who were the fathers or husbands of the women refugees.

"I feel distraught," he told Hilde. "What's the best thing to do? Shall we push on to Munich before the child is born?"

Hilde answered firmly. She was in no doubt about the right thing to do although she was longing to get home to her father's house after exile and terror.

"We must stay here until Elfa has had her child. It would be madness to move her now. And Hans and Trudel are still very feverish."

"Of course you are right," he admitted. "You understand these things better than I do. How is my poor Elfa today?"

Hilde was frightened about his daughter with whom she sat as much as possible while the children were kept in bed. Elfa looked very ill and very weak. The shaking on the journey had been bad for her. Lying there in the little attic room with its low beams she was restless and distressed. Several times she wept silently and sometimes moaned as though in pain. When she slept, Hilde, watching her, was struck by the beauty of this girl who was about to be a mother. She was as beautiful, thought Hilde, as St. Cecilia in her tomb and as white as that. One evening she seemed calmer and spoke quietly to Hilde.

"I'm sorry to be such a trouble."

Hilde held her hand.

"You're no trouble. We only want to look after you. Are you feeling stronger?"

Elfa shook her head and smiled.

"I feel very weak. I'm afraid my baby will never be born. It's rather silly having a baby, don't you think?"

"Silly?"

"It's such a terrible world. There's no hope for people like us."

"Things will get better," said Hilde. "And children make the best of life, because it's life. Hans and Trudel are very happy when they're well."

"If my baby is born it will be without a father," said Elfa. "My Carl is dead, you know. He was killed when the English broke through the West Wall."

"Yes," said Hilde. "In a way it's best to know that he's dead. I shall never know for certain about my own Peter."

"It's my birthday tomorrow," said Elfa. "I shall be twenty-one. It will be funny if the baby is born on my birthday."

The child was born on her birthday after a terrible night of suffering and anguish. Hilde and the farmer's wife did their best for Elfa but at dawn this child-mother lay still and white, as still and white as her new-born babe who never gave a cry of life. Herr Heisenberg fell on his knees, weeping by the bedside, and the farmer's wife who had wept before he came lit two candles at the head and foot of the iron bedstead, and crossed herself and said a 'Hail Mary' with clasped hands.

The refugees in the farmhouse followed the coffin in which mother and child were laid, and during the burial when they stood with bent heads around the open grave, they were frightened by a rushing sound of wings above them and then the heavy droning of engines as a squadron of American Fortresses roared through the sky towards Munich, a hundred kilometres away. But no bombs were dropped. The Americans had finished with their bombing. Germany lay in ruins beneath their wings. They had made a good job of it. That is to say by orders from Bomber Command they had abandoned pinpoint bombing of military targets and had flung their high-explosives on to crowded cities, residential areas, destroying old houses and palaces, picture galleries, the architectural glories of mediaeval towns and the uncounted lives of women and children. A bit overdone, perhaps, thought some of the American pilots afterwards. A new phase of human warfare.

Mass murder. It had been done on both sides, of course, but more completely by the Americans and English—by ten times as much.

It was a week later, when the children's temperatures had come down again, that Hilde was driven by a broken-hearted man to her father's house in the village of Kaulbach. As they neared the village in which she had spent her childhood her heart gave a lurch and her eyes became wet. She knew these roads and farmsteads and meadows. She knew the old cottages with their colour-washed walls with garlands of flowers painted on them. She knew the sweet scent of this countryside. She had picked wild flowers in the fields and had made daisy-chains down by the brook there with her little sister Christel. Far away she could see the faint blueness of the mountains beyond Garmisch. As a young girl she had climbed them with Peter who was now dead. She had gone North with him to Königsberg with always a nostalgia in her heart for Bavaria, her homeland, with its softer climate and its softer speech. Now she had come home again without Peter and without a baby she had left in the snow on the flight from Königsberg.

There were American soldiers in the villages near Kaulbach. She stared at them with curiosity and a sudden rush of tears to her eyes. They were the conquerors. Germany was defeated and occupied by foreign troops. German pride lay in the dust, and yet in a way it was good to see them—those tall, long-limbed, boyish-looking soldiers who lounged about with their jaws moving. The horror of the war had lifted. No more Peters would be killed. No more bombs would be dropped on German cities. No more crowds of huddled refugees would be slaughtered and buried in the ruins. The years of terror—that kind of terror—had passed.

"That's my father's house!" cried Hilde, clutching the hand of young Hans.

"It's quite a big house," said Hans. "He must be a very rich man."

"He's a Baron," said Trudel. "Don't you know that, silly? One day I'll be a Baroness."

There were two American soldiers at the gate. They barred the way.

Hilde put her head out of the window and spoke in English.

"My father lives here. The Baron von Arnheim."

The American soldier shifted a piece of gum from one side of his mouth to the other.

"Maybe he's a Baron, lady, but he don't live here now. This is the Brigade Headquarters of . . . . . ."

He mentioned some mysterious letters which meant nothing to Hilde who had come home with her children.

The other sentry spoke with a drawling accent.

"I guess there's a Baron up there. With his dame. And that blonde baby who has daggers in her eyes and looks as haughty as the Queen of Sheba. They're living in the stables where all Germans ought to live if they live. See what I mean?"

He looked at Herr Heisenberg and said "O.K." with a jerk of his thumb.

"Better let 'em pass, I guess."

There was a loud cry in a girl's voice. It came from Christel who was walking down the drive in her yellow jumper and blue slacks.

"Hilde! . . . Hilde! . . ."

Hilde sprang out of the car, followed by Hans and Trudel.

"Christel! Oh, my dear!"

She fell into Christel's arms and burst into tears—tears of happiness, tears of relief, tears of remembrance.

She was home at last all the way from Königsberg but not to her father's house. The Baron von Arnheim was living in a stable with a stone floor. History relates that in victorious England other noblemen were living in their stables, but the Germans knew nothing of that.

CHAPTER XVIII

THE years of hunger began.

The War had taken all the able-bodied men from the fields and the harvest had been thin. Germany had always had to import food for her industrial population and now there were no imports. Food had come from the rich soil of East Prussia and now East Prussia was in the hands of the Russian armies who seized what food they could. All over Germany the railway-lines were smashed with thousands of wagons so that provisions could not be moved about from districts which had a surplus. In any case German money was losing its purchasing power.

The farmers hoarded their grain and vegetables, their butter and cheese, refusing to sell it for this paper money, selling it only by barter. A pair of boots might buy a half-pound of butter. A winter overcoat might buy a sack of potatoes. A sewing-machine might buy a good-sized cheese with some eggs and even a bushel of flour. Presently, under orders from the military chiefs in the Armies of Occupation, local governments controlled as far as possible the collection and distribution of food, but the farmers still hid and hoarded all they dared and sold it at Black Market prices, fantastically high. Or they had a secret way of barter, which was not very secret though now and again the police under orders from the military commanders made a show of stopping it.

From the cities men and women streamed out to the villages and farms with rucksacks holding articles for barter which they exchanged for potatoes, bread, cheese, or butter. Furtively they came back with those precious loads. As a rule the German police turned a blind eye to this traffic. Were they not also hungry? Were not their wives and children under-nourished? It took some time to establish a new currency which replaced the worthless marks.

It was the currency of English and American cigarettes. They were not as a rule cigarettes for actual smoking. It was reckoned that a cigarette changed hands eight times before it might be smoked by the ninth person. Other things would have done as well provided they were rare and non-perishable and desirable, such as buttons or needles. The cigarettes were mostly a token of exchange, though it is true that the habit of smoking spread in Germany because it relieved the sense of hunger and steadied nerve-shocked men and women who had been through the air raids. So in due course anyone who could get hold of a carton of American cigarettes or a box of Virginians became possessed of the means of wealth.

For one carton of cigarettes an American typist in Berlin could buy a fur coat from a German woman who would then buy food for her children. A sufficient quantity of cigarettes would buy pearl necklaces, signet rings, silk pyjamas, embroideries, tapestries, antiques. Soon in the time of hunger twenty Virginian cigarettes from England or twenty Chesterfields from the U.S.A. would buy a woman's body and soul, both going cheap in Germany in the years of hunger. Or perhaps they kept their souls and only sold their bodies because pretty girls get hungry like the ugly ones, and God is pitiful.

To Hilde Menzel it was agonizing to see her children underfed and always hungry. When they sat down to a meal their eyes roved round the table to see what there was to eat and often there was very little—the eternal cabbage soup, a few potatoes, two small slices of bread, now and then, but rarely a morsel of meat or cheese.

"I want some more," said Hans after a meal like that. "My stomach is still empty."

"Isn't there anything else?" cried Trudel. "I want to go on eating. I want to go on eating for ever."

The grown-ups starved themselves for the children. Hilde's father slipped his potatoes on to the children's plates surreptitiously. There were quarrels at table.

"Father!" cried Hilde, "you're starving yourself. The children mustn't be greedy. You must keep up your own strength."

"I'm old enough not to matter," he answered. "The children must be fed somehow. Besides you do the same thing. Didn't you give Hans your share of the cheese?"

"I don't need it," said Hilde. "I keep well on very little."

"You're getting terribly thin, Hilde," said Frau von Arnheim. "The children mustn't get more than their right share."

"Mother, you're a hypocrite!" cried Christel. "I saw you give one of your potatoes to Trudel, just now."

Trudel set up a loud wail.

"I'm very hungry! I want some more."

"Shut up!" said Hans, giving her a thump. "You're only a girl. I ought to have twice as much as you."

They had fed better in the covered wagon on the way from Königsberg.

Christel spoke bitterly of the Americans up at the house. She had gone up there again to bring back some more pots and pans and they had not prevented her.

"Those fat boys are wallowing in the flesh-pots while we starve to death," she said. "I never saw so much food—casks of butter, great hams, enormous cheeses, tins of jam, mountains of bread, great packets of shredded wheat, boxes of chocolate. When I went up I heard a loud sizzling noise. It was bacon frying in fat. My mouth watered. My stomach cried out. But I had to look haughty and indifferent while they stared at me and winked at each other."

"If they had any bowels of compassion," said Frau von Arnheim, bitterly, "they would send some food down to the children. They might at least let them have some candies and chocolate."

"I've always heard that the Americans are very good-natured," said her husband. "I can't understand their hostility to us all."

"They treat us as though we were dirt," said Christel.

The Baron von Arnheim knew that there was a general order in the American Army against fraternization but somewhat later he found there was another reason why the Americans, and especially the American officers, were so coldly hostile.

He happened to meet the major who had first come to his house with the two other officers.

He saluted him and then stopped to speak.

"You find my house comfortable?"

The American major flushed slightly as though he were a shy man.

"We aren't here for comfort," he answered, curtly.

"It's a very beautiful countryside," said the Baron von Arnheim. "Have you been up to the mountains yet?"

"I'm rather busy," said the major, icily.

"If you would care to have a guide one day," said the Baron von Arnheim, "I should be glad to take you for a climb."

The American major hesitated and then spoke harshly.

"I don't need you as a guide, sir, and I don't ask for your company."

It was the Baron von Arnheim's face which flushed now. He had wished to be courteous. He had tried to break down this barrier of ice. This officer looked an intelligent type, surely they might have a little conversation without loss of dignity on either side. He spoke with sudden anger.

"Isn't there a quality called chivalry? Don't they teach you that in the United States, sir?"

The American officer's eyes hardened. There was a glint of steel in them.

"They don't teach us torture in the United States."

"What do you mean by that?" asked the Baron von Arnheim.

The American looked him straight in the eyes.

"I've seen your concentration camps—Belsen and Buchenwald. I've never seen anything more horrible."

He strode past the Baron von Arnheim with a hard mouth and that cold steel in his eyes.

Belsen and Buchenwald. The names were almost unknown to Baron von Arnheim. Not quite unknown. Some of his friends had told him that horrible things were happening in the concentration camps, mass murder, mass starvation, torture of German Communists as well as Jews. He had refused to believe such things possible, even under Hitler. The Germans were a civilized people. No German of any decent type would carry out orders involving such hideous cruelty. So he had believed until one day, not long before the arrival of Hilde and her children, a young girl had come back to Kaulbach from one of those concentration camps. She was the daughter of an old servant he had had and he had heard her story told in the presence of her father. She had been arrested for denouncing Hitler as an enemy of the Catholic Church and all good Christians. It was the young schoolmaster, Mundt, who had denounced her to the S.S. She had been sentenced to a year's imprisonment in Belsen. Now she had come back with tuberculosis, telling dreadful things. People were dying of hunger in heaps, she said. Their dead bodies were lying about unburied. Jews and gypsies were put into the gas-ovens. The prisoners were whipped, and savage dogs set upon them.

Was she lying, this girl? Was she neurotic and hysterical? The Baron von Arnheim had tried to believe that for the sake of his own peace of mind, for the honour of Germany. But the look in the eyes of this dying girl—she looked in the last stage of consumption—had made him believe she was telling the truth. That was what her father said.

"Clare is not lying, Herr Baron. She's a truthful girl. These things are happening though most of us never hear of them. They're kept hidden and secret but one day the world will find out."

Now the Americans had found out. Never in his life would the Baron von Arnheim forget the words of that American major.

"I have seen Belsen and Buchenwald."

He had spoken them as a cold and terrible reason for not answering German courtesy with American courtesy. It was a painful incident.

The Baron von Arnheim spoke to Hilde about it.

"Did you know about these fearful things in the concentration camps? Living here in this village I heard nothing."

Hilde told him about the whisperings in Königsberg, about the mass murder of Jews and then about the terrible story told to her one night by a Dr. Goldstein in Quakenbrück.

"Shameful!" said her father in a voice of anguish.

"We had nothing to do with it," answered Hilde, as once she had answered Franz Reber. "The German people are innocent of all that. Many of them were the victims."

"The guilt of it will lie heavily upon our heads," said her father. "We shall all be punished for these crimes. World opinion will be unforgiving and indict the whole German people because of those atrocities."

Hilde spoke many times to Christel about Franz Reber who had been a fellow-student with her sister at the Academy in Munich before the war.

Christel laughed at the remembrance of their comradeship.

"He was a little bit in love with me, I think. He was sentimental now and then, but he was hardly more than a schoolboy. I didn't take him seriously."

"Now he's a man with a tragic mind," said Hilde. "The War

has hurt him horribly and he has a wounded soul. I'm very sorry for him."

"I find it difficult to believe," said Christel. "He was always laughing and playing jokes."

The two sisters were sitting together in their tiny bedroom above the stables. They had a thousand things to talk about and once Christel, generally high-spirited and gay, broke down and wept.

"What's the matter, darling Christel?" asked Hilde, astonished by this passion of tears.

"Life is terrible!" cried Christel. "I'm always hungry, and all the boys I knew are dead, and there's no hope for us."

It was not often she broke down like that. She was the active one with a spirit of adventure and devil-may-care. Twice a week she set out with a rucksack on her back to farmsteads round about, walking ten miles or more and returning, if she had luck, with potatoes and cheese and butter which she had cajoled out of the farmers in return for objects of barter which she had had to steal. She stole them from her father's house at night, slipping in by a back door and creeping like a ghost into the drawing-room and her father's study and a cupboard where he kept his boots and fishing-tackle and other gear. She had to evade the sentries by slinking through the bushes not more than twenty yards away from them. She had eyes like a cat and could see in the darkness and she developed great talent as a burglar. During these adventures she smiled to herself. It was all very amusing, she thought, taking things under the very noses almost of those sleeping Americans.

But one night there was an American who was not sleeping. It was the Major who had been so unfriendly to her father.

She was in the drawing-room putting some silver ornaments into a bag. The room was only lit by a shaft of moonlight coming through the long windows. She was busy with her job when suddenly a harsh voice spoke in English.

"Who's that?"

Someone had come into the room so quietly that she hadn't heard a sound. The door had been ajar and the floor was covered with a thick Turkey carpet.

Christel crouched behind a chair and held her breath.

"Who's there?" asked the harsh voice.

The tiny gleam of a flash-lamp travelled about the room, touching the chairs and sofa. She could see the man now. He was in his pyjamas with bare feet and tousled hair.

He came round to the chair behind which she was crouched and his torch flung its light upon her.

"What are you doing here?" he asked.

She stood up and laughed nervously.

"I hope I haven't frightened you?"

The American officer seemed taken aback by the suggestion that what might have frightened him was this girl with flaxen hair and blue eyes. A smile touched his lips.

"I'm not easily scared," he said. "At least not more than most men who call themselves soldiers. But I'd like to know what you're doing here in the middle of the night."

"Collecting a few of my father's things," she told him.

He was silent for a moment.

"Why do you want them?" he asked. "It's against orders anyhow."

His torch flashed on to her face and into her eyes for a second. Then he lowered it and she saw him only by the moonlight. She noticed his bare feet and the pattern of his pyjamas.

"I want them to get food," she said. "Food for my family and the two children, and food for myself. We're starving while you Amer icans over-eat."

He seemed to think that out, and it was a moment before he answered.

"We won the War, didn't we?" he asked.

"Yes," she cried bitterly. "You don't care if we starve, do you? You would see German children dying of hunger without giving them a packet of chocolate which your fat boys eat after a breakfast of eggs and bacon washed down by grape juice."

The American major grinned at her for a moment and then looked serious. She heard him give a kind of sigh.

"I'm sorry for German women and children," he said. "The Americans are sentimentalists, especially about women and children."

Christel laughed in a shrill voice.

"I haven't noticed any sentiment. You're as hard as nails,

and as cold as ice. You won't speak to us. You look at us as though we were vermin. Your fat boys would like to flirt with the German girls—I've watched them eyeing our girls in Munich but they're punished if they talk to them. We thought you were going to be good-natured. We thought we were going to like you."

The American major seemed amused by this conversation in the moonlight with a young German girl who squared up to him.

"General Eisenhower won't allow fraternization," he said. "Maybe that order will be withdrawn. Then you may get to like us—maybe too much. Meanwhile we have to carry out orders and maintain discipline."

"Discipline!" exclaimed Christel, ironically. "Then why do you let your men loot our houses and rob us of our wrist-watches? Your little brown men, the Hawaians, have been going into houses in Munich and stealing things like monkeys."

"You're a very bold young woman to say things like that," he answered after a moment's pause. "I have the right to arrest you and have you taken to prison. At the moment I'm rather handicapped by being in my pyjamas. I came down to fetch a book. This conversation must cease."

"Are you going to stop me taking these things?" asked Christel. "I could get some potatoes for them. Or do you prefer us to go on starving?"

"It's not worth your trouble," he said carelessly. "My unit is leaving this house. Your family can come back to it unless it's wanted by another crowd."

"Thank God for that!" cried Christel.

The American major let the light of his torch play upon her for a moment. She saw that he was smiling again, a smile that twisted his thin lips and took the cold steel out of his eyes.

"It's lucky for you," he said, "that I'm a respectable married man. You're too pretty to be wandering around at midnight among American soldiers. I wouldn't do it again, if I were you. Well, good night. Can you get out all right?"

"Your sentries are as much use as marionettes," said Christel. "You ought to have them shot."

He gave a quiet laugh.

"I'll see about it tomorrow. Now I must get back to that little bedroom of yours. Good night."

He walked across the room, his bare feet making no sound. At the door he turned and spoke again.

"You speak English marvellously. How's that?"

"My father and mother were in England. I had an English governess."

"I see. Well, good night. Maybe you did scare me a little."

He went out of the room after another laugh. He wasn't quite inhuman, she thought. Perhaps he was more human in pyjamas.

It was glad news about the unit leaving. They were going on to Garmisch. There was a great packing up and the sound of Americans talking, laughing, whistling, singing. Then all was silence. They had gone. Christel's father and mother with Hilde and the children rejoiced to be in the big house again. Christel went up to her bedroom. It was tidier than when she left it, except for the eiderdown on the bed which seemed to bulge. She pulled it off and found a number of packets underneath. They were packets of chocolate and sweet biscuits and American cheese in round boxes. The stony-hearted American major had had a moment of sentimentality. So had his men whom she had insulted by calling them Fat Boys. They had not left much behind, but one thing was precious and beyond price. It was a big tub of fat for cooking and frying.

A few weeks after this homecoming something happened which seemed like a miracle to the family von Arnheim, a miracle of joy. It was Christel who raised her head and listened intently to some sound in the garden. They were seated at table for their frugal meal of soup and potatoes. The children were in bed.

"Did you hear that whistle?" asked Christel.

"What whistle?" asked her mother.

Christel's face had gone white but there was a queer light in her eyes as though she had heard something almost unbelievable, like the pipes of Pan.

She sprang up from the table.

"That's Paul's whistle!" she cried. "Only he and I know it. It was our signal on the mountains."

"It's your fancy, Christel," said her father, but he, too, stood up from the table.

Christel made a rush for the front door. Outside, in the drive, trudging very slowly towards the house was a young man in a tattered uniform. He had a dirty bandage across one side of his head, covering his left eye.

"Paul!" cried Christel. "Are you alive then?"

He laughed as she flung herself into his arms.

"Very much alive, much to my surprise. But dead tired. I seem to have been walking for six months. I shan't be able to take my boots off."

"We thought you were dead!" cried Christel, laughing and weeping at the same time.

"So did I," he answered, grinning under his bandage. "I met an English machine-gun bullet not far from Florence and lay in a shell-hole for three days more or less dead. After that I was taken prisoner by the English, but had the luck to escape. It was then I started walking, mostly by night. The Italians are no fighters but their peasants are kind. They hid me in their barns and gave me food. They did the same thing to escaped English. It was a game of hide and seek on both sides—very comical sometimes."

Christel hugged him tightly.

"Oh, Paul, I can't believe it, having you home again, having you alive! What's the matter with your head?"

"I lost an eye," he told her. "Very lucky not to lose two. I can still see like a hawk. How's everybody?"

Everybody came to embrace him. His mother was weeping. She had given him up for lost, her laughing Paul. His father grabbed his arms and kissed him on both cheeks.

"My turn now," said Hilde, quietly.

"Is that Hilde?" asked Paul, staring at her incredulously.

"I'm not quite the same Hilde," she answered, "but you'll get to know me again, Paul."

"All the way from Königsberg?"

He put his arms round her and she wept on his shoulder.

That evening after a bath he flung away his tattered uniform and put on a suit of his father's clothes. He found his own in his wardrobe but he had grown out of them ridiculously. Four years as a soldier had changed his body, lengthening it and broadening it.

"Any food?" he asked when he came down.

"Not much," answered Christel. "We're all hungry now. I dream of food. I dream of feasts. I dream of the meals we used to have in Munich. Then I wake up hungry."

"One gets used to hunger," he told them. "For more than three months in Italy when I was hiding from the English I had very little to eat. Black bread and peasant wine or black bread and water."

All the same his eye roved round the dinner table where they had been having their meal.

"I'll bake a potato for you," said Christel.

"Make it two, dear sister!"

She made it three in lieu of the fatted calf.

Over those potatoes he told strange stories of his escape and wanderings. He was wounded in an Italian village. It had been an Italian village until wiped out by American bombers. The English had gone beyond it when his own battery retreated to a better position. They had left him for dead in a narrow trench. The English had also left a man for dead, an English boy of about nineteen or twenty.

"We were both in the same ditch. We both looked pretty dead, I expect. There were some real dead with us. Not at all pleasant, you understand."

He looked over to his father with a grin.

"I understand," said the Baron von Arnheim, who had been in the First World War.

"When I began to sit up and take notice I saw this English boy was alive. He was staring at me, I suppose because I moved and groaned a bit. 'Are you a German?' he asked in English, as though not quite sure; perhaps he thought I was Italian."

"Which God forbid!" said the Baron von Arnheim.

His son Paul laughed.

"I came to like the Italians. Not great soldiers, of course—too civilized perhaps—but nice people. I fell in love with several contadine, as beautiful as Madonnas."

"Just like you, Paul," cried Christel. "But what about the English boy?"

"I spoke to him in English, which surprised him a bit. 'Badly wounded?' I asked. 'In the stomach,' he told me. 'Not too good. How are you?'

" 'I seem to have lost an eye,' I told him. 'I think I've an axe in my head. It feels like that.'

"We didn't talk for some time, feeling pretty bad. Then he spoke again.

" 'I could give you a drop of brandy if you feel like it.'

" 'I do feel like it,' I told him. 'Shall I come to you or will you come to me?'

"He said he couldn't come to me. His legs seemed dead.

"I crawled over to him. It took me ten minutes, I should say, to crawl that fifteen yards or so, and my head throbbed like a steam engine. I think I fainted. But I made the distance.

" 'Put your hand in my side pocket,' he said. 'You'll find a flask if it isn't broken.'

"I found the flask and he insisted on my taking the first gulp. It put new life into me. Then I poured some into his mouth which he opened like a baby or a bird being fed by its parent. It seemed to do him good. We talked to each other in a very friendly way."

"He was one of our enemies," said Paul's mother. "Do you think it was quite right to be friendly with him?"

Paul looked at his mother with a smile.

"Do you still feel like that?" he asked. "We might have been dead. We might have been talking on the other side of Time. Anyhow we were comrades now in the same ditch and among the same dead bodies.

"He said, 'I used to know Germany before the War. I did a bit of climbing in the Bavarian Alps.'

"He had stayed in Garmisch and it had left good memories with him. He had stayed in the Vierjahreszeiten in Munich and had a great time there with his mother and sister. Once he had seen Hitler. 'What did you think of him?' I asked."

"And what did he answer?" asked Christel.

"He said, 'He must have been possessed by seven devils'."

"Cheek!" cried Christel. "Why didn't he criticize his own leaders?"

"The boy under-estimated the number of devils," said her father. "Seventy times seven would be more like it."

Paul von Arnheim laughed at this family difference of opinion, and went on with his story.

"We talked all night between spells of silence. I could see he was suffering a lot of pain, but he seemed to stifle it now and then. We talked about English books and he seemed surprised that I had read Dickens and Thackeray and Scott.

" 'You Germans are astonishing people!' he said."

"So we are!" said Christel.

" 'You're better educated than the English,' he said. 'But somehow you seem to get things wrong.' "

"He was impertinent, that English boy," said Christel.

"We do get things wrong," said her father. "That's why we're in this tragic state. That's why we suffer all the humiliation of defeat."

Paul finished his story of the English boy.

"He told me his name. Bernard Lavington. He asked me to take a cigarette-case out of his pocket and keep it as a souvenir. He said if ever I went to England he would like me to call on his mother and give his love to her. 'You'll do that yourself before I go to England,' I said. 'No,' he answered. 'I'm dying.' He died just after dawn. I was sorry."

There was a silence at table. This death of an English boy seemed to stir their pity though they had shed no tears over enemy losses as the English had shed no tears over theirs. But this was one boy with whom Paul had talked in one shell-battered trench on the Italian battlefield.

"Poor boy!" exclaimed Hilde.

Paul took something from his left pocket and laid it on the table. It was a silver cigarette case. He looked at it with a smile.

"A souvenir," he said. "One day perhaps I'll take it to England."

"Tell us about those Italian girls," said Christel.

Several times during the evening she went over to her brother and put her fingers through his hair or took his face in her hands and kissed his cheek or raised his hand and put it against her own cheek .They had been good comrades, these two. They had climbed mountains together risking death. They had laughed at the same jokes. They had read the same books. They had quarrelled, fought, yelled, as younger boy and girl. Now here he was back from the dead with only the loss of one eye.

His mother gazed at him as he told many stories of the campaign in North Africa and Italy. She was wet-eyed, and had a look of adoration for this son who once had been suckled at her breast and who now talked so gaily of his soldiering, though he had lost his left eye and had had such desperate adventures.

To Christel the return of her brother Paul was a source of happiness and laughter and comradeship. He had always been a laughing boy and now the release from war seemed to be a supreme compensation for defeat. The same thing was happening to most other people. The cessation of bombing, the end of fighting, and blood and death was an enormous relief, wiping out for a time all humiliation, wounded pride, and bitter resentment, which afterwards arrived. The younger people like Paul and Christel and their friends in Kaulbach and Munich could make a joke and a laughing adventure even of the restrictions imposed upon them by the occupying troops. There was for instance the curfew forbidding Germans from being on the roads or in the streets after dark. Many times the brother and sister defied this rule, staying late at other people's houses and then creeping out at midnight and dodging the military police on the way home.

It was difficult for the American troops of occupation to understand all this.

"These Germans don't seem to care," they said. "Defeat doesn't mean a darn' thing to them. They don't even seem hostile to us as their enemies and bosses. Where's their pride?"

They were completely taken aback by the sudden outbreak of a Carnival spirit in Munich and the surrounding villages. These Germans seemed to go crazy. It was as though they were celebrating victory instead of bemoaning defeat. They did extraordinary things which the American troops watched with astonishment. Big farm-carts were hoisted up to the roofs of houses. Windows were decorated with green stuff and there was dancing and singing through the streets and in the market-place of Kaulbach. Wounded soldiers who had lost an arm or a leg mingled with these Carnival crowds throwing flowers at the girls. It was the pagan spirit let loose. These German boys and girls who linked arms and marched and sang through the villages had heard the pipes of Pan or they had become bewitched by the enchantment of fairies and gnomes and water maidens of the German forests and streams. There was a wild light in the eyes of German girls like Christel. Ex-prisoners of war like Paul forgot the horrors of the past years and the stench of blood and death. They were alive. The Bavarian air was sweet and soft. Nature had stirred again from its sleep. The myths and legends of the German forests which lurk still in German minds called them back for a few hours of Carnival to the primitive spirit of the old tribes. Something like that happened in the village of Kaulbach and even in Munich.

That evening Paul and Christel visited the houses of two or three friends where Paul was received with warm welcome and embraces. Before the War he had been one of the best young athletes in Kaulbach, renowned for his strength in lifting weights and hurling javelins. He was also an expert skier and mountain climber. Now he met some of his old comrades and the fathers and mothers and sisters of those who were missing.

"I feel like Rip van Winkle," he told Christel. "Some of these girls were only babies when I left for the War. Some of these people look much older, as though they had been buried and dug up again. Have I changed as much as they have?"

"You look a bit older," said Christel, "and your shoulders are broader and your chest deeper. But I fear you haven't grown any wiser."

Paul ignored this doubt about his wisdom.

"Do I look very repulsive with only one eye?" he asked.

He wore a black patch over his left eye.

"These girls don't seem to think so," answered Christel. "They're all ready to fall in love with you."

"I'm ready to fall in love with them," said Paul. "After those years of asceticism. I'm ready to fall in love with any pretty wench who won't mind a one-eyed man."

That evening he fell in love with a pretty girl called Clara.

At least they talked and laughed a good deal on this night of Carnival. This was at their last house of call. The mother of Clara, Frau Kiep, who had embraced Paul on his arrival, had prepared refreshments for her guests, marvellous in this time of semi-starvation. There were fried potatoes, apple fritters, and by some miracle a huge plateful of doughnuts. For drink there was only *ersatz* coffee without milk or sugar.

Christel sat on a sofa with a young man named Otto Kiep whom she had known at the University of Munich before he went to the War. He had lost an arm in Russia but was gay and amusing because of the Carnival spirit.

"Quite like old times!" he said. "How have we got back so easily as though the War had been a picnic?"

"Because we're Bavarians," said Christel. "We forget our woes more easily than other Germans. We're more happy-go-lucky."

"That's true," he agreed. "But there's something fantastic in having this Carnival when Germany lies in ruins and we're occupied by foreign troops."

"Fantastic and amusing," said Christel. "I like the spice of danger when I go black-marketing and stay out late at night dodging the military police."

"Another song!" shouted a voice.

They sang an old students' song in chorus.

Paul was talking again to the prettiest girl in the room who was Clara Kiep. They had been laughing and talking gaily about trivial things and had danced to the music of a gramophone. Suddenly she began to cry quite quietly and he was astonished.

"Why are you crying? Two seconds ago you were laughing."

She dabbed her eyes with a tiny handkerchief. No one noticed her except Paul because they were all talking and laughing loudly.

"I'm crying because of this gaiety. Isn't there something mad about it? How can we laugh when there's so much suffering and when we ought to remember the dead?"

Paul shrugged his shoulders.

"We're alive. Why not be merry for an hour or two?"

"Two of my brothers were killed," said Clara. "Doesn't it seem wicked to laugh and be forgetful?"

"Not in the least. That's the soldiers' way. After a battle we don't sit down and bemoan the dead. If there's a joke to be found we enjoy it. Even in war there's a lot of laughter. Isn't that the right philosophy of life? Come and have another dance."

Christel was dancing again with Otto Kiep whose left sleeve was pinned to his jacket. He was taller than his partner and he smiled down at her.

"The Americans think we're crazy," he said. "I was in Munich today and they were staring with round eyes when the farm-carts were hoisted on to the roofs. If it hadn't been for the order against fraternization some of them would have joined in the fun, but they couldn't understand what it was all about."

"Some of them have been punished for walking out with German girls," said Christel.

Otto Kiep nodded and laughed.

"Human nature can't be repressed by military command. Somehow I can't hate those American boys. I can't even think of them as our enemies. Funny that, isn't it? They look a good-natured crowd of youngsters."

"I hate them," said Christel. "They're very uncivilized. Any-how I hate them because of their bombing. They've destroyed our cities and massacred millions of our poor people."

"We were pretty ruthless," said Otto Kiep. "I helped to bomb London. I saw the fires raging round St. Paul's and it seemed to me a fine sight. I had no pity for the people I was killing when I dropped big bombs on them. Didn't even think of them. It was just my job and I was glad when I got beyond their barrage fire which was as hot as hell."

"The American bombing was indiscriminate," said Christel. "It was just a lust for destruction."

"They were doing their job," said Otto Kiep, with his profes-sional point of view.

Then he added in a lower voice, "Goering let us down." Suddenly he laughed.

"God help me. Why do I talk of such stuff? Let's grab some of those fried potatoes before they're all gobbled up. My stomach craves for nourishment."

It was a night of hilarity and good-humour and release. It was a kind of escape from reality, a German bacchanalia after the long ordeal of war, discipline, rules and regulations, suppression of individuality, Hitlerism with its inhuman disregard of human life and suffering and the liberty of the individual man. Or perhaps it was just youth insisting upon the joy of life for one day and one night.

"Who's going home?" asked a girl's voice at midnight.

There was a burst of laughter.

"We can't go home. We should all be rounded up by the military police. We shall have to sleep here."

Clara Kiep's mother took a practical view of the situation.

"You young people will have to sleep on the floor. I can't provide beds and it's very doubtful if I can provide breakfast. There doesn't seem to be anything left."

Christel spoke to Paul.

"Let's make a dash for it. It will be good fun."

"I don't want to be arrested," said Paul. "Is it worth it? Why not sleep here?"

"The adventure amuses me," said Christel. "Come on, Paul!"

They slipped away and they reached the road which led to their father's house. There was a sickle moon and its faint pale light touched the roofs of cottages and the leaves of some tall poplars. The air was fresh and cool after the overheated atmosphere of the room they had just left.

"It was a great day!" said Christel. "We forgot all our woes."

Paul laughed.

"No wonder the Americans think we've gone mad. Carnival amidst the ruins!"

Suddenly they heard the sound of a motor-car coming towards them and they saw the glare of its headlights. It was an American police-car.

"Quick!" said Paul.

He grabbed his sister's arm and they flung themselves into the roadside ditch three inches deep in wet mud. They lay there like hunted animals crouching low. The military car swept past them. Then they crawled out of the ditch and burst out laughing. By the faint light of the moon Christel saw that her brother's face was smeared with mud and his clothes were plastered with it. Her own frock—an elegant party frock from Paris, cut low at the shoulders with a puffed skirt, was in a dreadful state.

"We look like a pair of scarecrows," cried Christel, still laughing.

"We had a narrow escape," said Paul. "I thought those headlights had picked us out."

"I find this kind of thing very exciting," said Christel. "It makes one forget how hungry one is."

"Not me!" answered Paul. "I feel as though rats were gnawing my entrails."

CHAPTER XIX

ANOTHER American unit requisitioned Baron von Arnheim's big house in Kaulbach and with his family he had to return to the stables. It happened that Christel was alone when they arrived. Hilde and her mother were out in the fields with the children. Paul had gone off to Munich with his father. Christel was in her room reading a German translation of Plato's *Republic*. She heard a car coming up the drive and sprang up from her chair to look out of the window. Three American officers were getting out of the car. A moment later she heard the door-bell ring.

"*Gott in Himmel!*" exclaimed Christel aloud.

She went downstairs and opened the door looking very haughtily at the three young officers.

"Do you want anything?" she asked.

They looked embarrassed at the sight of this girl.

One of them whom she knew afterwards as Captain Robert Lee Welles saluted her in the American way. He was a serious-looking young man with a thin tanned face and keen eyes which gave her one quick searching look.

"I am told you speak English here," he said.

Christel nodded.

"We have orders to take over this house."

The two other officers were fair-faced young men who looked good-natured. One of them gave Christel a friendly kind of grin which made her harden her own expression of extreme haughtiness.

"My father is not at home," she said. "You must wait until he comes back."

Captain Welles thought this out for a moment.

"I'm afraid we can't wait very long. We have to be in tonight. Do you mind if we come in and look around?"

"You will have to wait until my father returns," said Christel firmly. "Good afternoon."

She was about to shut the door in their faces when one of the Americans put his foot forward to prevent it.

"Say, Missy," he said, "who won this war?"

He smiled at her but there was a flash of steel in his eyes.

"The Russians, mostly," answered Christel, who hated the Russians.

The three American officers looked at each other and laughed.

"Well, we won't argue that," said the officer who had put his foot in the door. "We'll take a look round with—or even without —your permission, young lady."

He pushed past her almost roughly and walked into her father's study, followed by the two others.

Captain Welles spoke four words as he passed. They were in German.

"*Entschuldigen Sie, gnädiges Fräulein*..."

It meant 'Excuse me, gracious lady', and she was astonished that any American soldier should know even as much German as that. He spoke with an ironical smile.

Her father returned later with Paul and they heard the painful news that they would have to clear out of the house again. Argument was useless of course. These were the conquerors. They were the conquered. Once again the drive was filled with armoured cars and American G.I.s invaded the kitchen and yard, unloading stores of food, chewing gum, whistling, singing, talking in the American drawl.

Paul stood watching them with a look of amusement and envy. He came back to report his findings.

"Those American boys aren't under-nourished. They've mountains of food. It made my guts ache to look at it."

"What about a midnight burglary?" asked Christel.

Paul shook his head.

"Too strongly guarded, I'm afraid."

Hilde and her mother came back with the two children. Frau von Arnheim wept when she heard the news. The children on the other hand were delighted. They preferred the stables to the big house. It was more of an adventure, climbing up the wooden stairs, playing with some old saddles and harness, watching a little mouse run up and down an overhead beam. If only they had more to eat they would have been perfectly happy.

"I'm hungry again!" announced Hans. "My stomach is empty."

"When are we going to have something to eat, Mummy?" asked Trudel.

It was Hilde's turn for tears. It tormented her to see the children getting so thin and crying out for food. They were both getting weak and tired. They no longer ran about with ceaseless vitality. Half-way through a game Trudel would sit down and say, "I'm tired." Even Hans was beginning to droop and seemed to need a lot of sleep to make up for lack of food though Hilde starved herself for these little ones. Up at the big house the American soldiers were wasting food and sometimes burning it.

They were not starving, these German people, but they were under-nourished. Several times during lectures at the University in Munich Christel fainted. No one took much notice except the girl next to her who propped her up. It was too common an incident now to attract attention or cause consternation. Almost every morning some girl fainted and even a male student now and then. Between lectures conversation turned invariably to the question of food and the Black Market and the way to dodge the police who were ordered to prevent it.

But there were other topics of conversation among the University students. Among them drifting back to Munich and the villages around were ex-prisoners of war who had escaped from the Russians and from the British in Italy, and from the Americans. Those who had been in the hands of the Russians gave horrible accounts of their starvation and ill-treatment though now and then some of them told of the good-nature and kindliness of Russian peasants.

One evening Christel told some of these stories to Hilde and they had an emotional effect upon her.

"If some of our men are escaping from Russia perhaps Peter——"

She hardly dared finish her sentence but looked at Christel with a desperate hope in her eyes.

"You mustn't build up false hopes," said Christel.

"No," said Hilde, in a low voice. "But I don't know for certain that he's dead. Only my dream. . . ."

She put her head down on the table where she was doing some needlework and wept.

"I'm sorry," said Christel, falling on her knees and putting her arms round Hilde. "You've always talked about him as though he were dead but perhaps one day he'll come back."

"It's too late now," said Hilde, after a struggle for self-mastery. "He'll never come back. Only a wild hope leapt into my heart for a moment."

The time came when the Americans became less cold and aloof. The order against fraternization was either withdrawn or ignored. The occupying troops could not live for ever without exchanging friendly words with the German people among whom they were living. It was putting an intolerable strain upon human nature and common sense. German girls walked about openly with G.I.s and their officers took no notice. American food appeared mysteriously in German kitchens. American cigarettes used as tokens of exchange passed secretly to the Black Market in Munich. Half-starved girls gave a little cheap love to American soldiers for a packet of Camels or a bar of chocolate.

The G.I.s themselves were taking a hand in secret trading and buying cameras, field-glasses, fur coats, clocks, and jewellery which they sent home to the United States as spoils of war. In the British zone the same thing was happening on a big scale. A hundred Virginian cigarettes properly laid out would buy things of great value. A thousand was a fortune to any officer or man who knew the trick of the game, not because the Germans smoked the cigarettes themselves, but because they were used instead of money and could buy butter, cheese and eggs, unlike worthless German marks which farmers and shopkeepers would hardly accept.

The United States and Great Britain received other parcels never paid for in any way. It was loot from German houses in which the troops were billeted. The discipline of the First World War, when any form of loot was regarded as a crime, had loosened and departed, from officers to men. Victory was regarded as giving the victors a right to anything they wanted. The old law of *Vae Victis!* was revived and in addition a low sense of honour and morality spread like an infection among the occupying troops and civilian administrators, lowering their prestige in the eyes of the German people who said, "They are no better than our own tricksters and rather worse. They have accused us of many things but we are now the accusers."

After a week or two in the stables again the Arnheim family were allowed to return to some rooms in their own house. This concession was due to the American Colonel in charge of the unit which now arrived. He had a German name, Hoffmann, and German ancestry. Perhaps this strain in his blood made him more sympathetic to a German family living in great discomfort not strictly necessary to his own requirements. If that were so he did not reveal it in his manner or speech. He was a tall, lantern-faced, stern-eyed man who spoke brusquely though without rudeness or incivility, being an educated American of good type. He came down himself and saluted the Baron von Arnheim who was cleaning his boots outside the stable door.

"You speak English I understand," were his first words.

"Not too badly perhaps," answered Herr von Arnheim, curtly.

"I dislike the idea of you living in these stables," said Colonel Hoffmann, "especially as I shall not need the whole of your house for my officers and clerks."

"Does that mean that we have permission to return?" asked Arnheim, hiding the glint of gladness in his eyes.

"Within certain limitations which I will discuss with you. I should be glad to place the top floor at your disposal. You may also have the use of your study."

The Baron von Arnheim spoke with less coldness.

"That would be a great favour, sir."

Colonel Hoffmann made a slight gesture of denial.

"I don't wish to confer a favour, Baron. But as an American I do not wish to take unnecessary advantage of my authority. I should feel uncomfortable if your family were crowded into these stables while the three officers under my command have more rooms than they need for their own comfort and duties. We're a small unit and yours is a big house. That is all I have to say at the moment."

"I am greatly obliged to you, Colonel," said Arnheim.

"Good morning," said Colonel Hoffmann, saluting, and striding away.

It was with joy that the family trooped back to the big house. Christel had her own room again. Paul was in a little room next door. Their father and mother had a room which once had been the children's play-room. Hilde had a tiny room next to one of the same size where Hans and Trudel slept in two small beds. To Herr von Arnheim the return to his study was like paradise. He could get into it by french windows leading on to the lawn so that he need not meet the American officers or their soldier servants, and it was astonishing how separated they were from their unwelcome guests.

Now and again Christel met Captain Welles on the stairs. Always he gave her that ironical smile which she resented because it seemed to her contemptuous, and always he greeted her with those words in German as he passed her:

"*Entschuldigen Sie, gnädiges Fräulein.*"

"Are those the only German words you know?" she asked him one day.

He laughed at this question which seemed to amuse him.

"Not many more. I know *Danke schön* and *Bitte schön*. As a matter of fact I'm mugging up a bit of German when I get time. I would rather like to read Goethe's *Faust* in the original."

Christel laughed incredulously.

"You'll never do that!" she told him. "You're too ambitious."

"I want a good teacher," he answered. "Any volunteers in this neighbourhood?"

His keen eyes looked into hers with a smile. It was of course a suggestion that she should volunteer. There was nothing doing, she thought, as far as she was concerned.

"There are lots of girls who would be glad to teach you for a few cigarettes or a packet of chocolate. They're all half starved."

For a moment he spoke seriously.

"I know. I'm sorry about that."

Christel laughed again, rather bitterly.

"It's easy to be sorry so long as you're well fed yourself. Why don't you hand over some food to the women and children, instead of wasting it and burning it?"

"We're not allowed to do that," he told her. "Personally I wish we were. But I think some of our G.I.s hand over a bit now and then, don't they? Against orders, of course."

"When they want to buy a girl's body and soul," said Christel. "Cheap love for the price of a packet of Camels. How charming of them! How generous!"

Captain Welles gave her one of his keen looks and his thin lips lengthened to a smile.

"Pretty bitter, aren't you? You're not friendly towards the Americans."

"I happen to be a German," said Christel. "I happen to have some pride."

"Quite a lot, I should say. Well, I must get on with the day's work. *Auf Wiedersehen, gnädiges Fräulein.*"

It was some weeks later when Christel had another conversation with Captain Welles. He met her in the hall and stood in front of her smiling.

"I'm still keen to learn German," he said. "But I want someone to teach me the pronunciation."

"I'm afraid I can't recommend anyone," said Christel, coldly.

"What about you?" he asked bluntly. "Couldn't you help me out a bit? An hour every evening for instance after *Abendessen*?"

"I'm afraid not," answered Christel, even more coldly.

"Think it over," he said. "I'm quite serious. I'd pay for the privilege of course. How about a carton of cigarettes now and then? They seem to be the new tokens of exchange."

Christel's face flushed.

Was this American officer trying to buy her, she wondered. Did he think she was a slut who could be tempted by his filthy cigarettes?

"You're being impertinent," she told him. "Kindly let me pass."

She was about to walk past him but he answered rather hotly.

"No impertinence meant," he said. "There's no need for you to take it that way. It's a fair offer meant seriously. I want to learn German. Why shouldn't you give me some lessons in return for a fee? What's wrong with that?"

"It's a pretence," said Christel. "It's just an excuse for getting hold of me. You forget that I'm a lady, Captain Welles."

He looked distressed and angry.

"Say now, that's getting it all wrong. I don't like that way of putting it. I don't doubt you're a lady—the daughter of the Baron von Arnheim and all that snob stuff, but that's no reason why you should think I'm a cad."

"You're an American," said Christel.

"By Jeminy!" exclaimed Captain Welles. "If I were to lose my temper. . . ."

He controlled his temper very successfully and even laughed in a harsh way.

"You're a little spit-fire," he said. "I wanted to be kind to you but you don't give me much encouragement. You Germans. . . ."

He controlled himself again and strode past her and went upstairs to his own room.

Christel spoke to Hilde about this incident.

"I'm afraid I was rather rude to him," she said.

Hilde agreed that her sister had not behaved very politely.

"Christel," she said presently, "it would help us all very much if you would give him those lessons in German. Did he say a carton of cigarettes now and then?"

Christel nodded.

"I'm not to be bought for a carton of Camels."

"But, Christel," said Hilde, "think what you could do with a carton of cigarettes! It's like a fortune. You could buy food for Hans and Trudel, and all of us. I'm terrified about the children. They have never enough to eat. It breaks my heart."

"Do you want me to sell myself?" asked Christel, flushing angrily.

"He may be quite serious," said Hilde. "That kind of thing may not be in his mind at all. He looks charming and thoughtful. Christel, my dear, for the children's sake . . ."

"I won't be the plaything of any American," said Christel. She spoke firmly, but as the weeks passed she became less convinced that Captain Welles had evil designs upon her, and in any case less obstinate in refusing to teach him German. Like Hilde she could not bear to hear the children whimpering for food, and to see their eyes wandering about the table for something to eat. She spoke to Paul about it.

"Paul, what do you think? Shall I risk it?"

Paul took a light-hearted view of the situation.

"Not much of a risk," he said. "You're a hefty wench. If the fellow makes improper advances give him a punch on the jaw. Besides I've talked to him now and then. I like him. He has good manners and a straight look in his eyes."

"A contemptuous look," said Christel. "He despises us. And he looks at me as if I had no clothes on."

Paul laughed loudly.

"Well, he would only see a scraggy female without any flesh on her bones. And it's all imagination on your part. All you girls think the Americans want to make you their mistresses."

"So they do," said Christel. "But perhaps I'll risk it. A carton of cigarettes. . . ."

"Exactly," said Paul. "Worth their weight in gold. We could buy a lot of food. I could have a good meal for once instead of tightening my belt until I can feel my backbone. My legs don't seem to belong to my body."

Certainly he looked very thin, she thought, smitten by the sight of his leanness.

It was an extreme humiliation to Christel to reopen the matter with Captain Welles. For some days she did not meet him in the hall or on the stairs though she lay in wait for him. Then she came face to face with him in the garden. He just raised a hand to his cap and would have passed her but she stopped and smiled. Her face flushed despite her effort to keep cool.

"Are we on speaking terms?" she asked.

He hesitated for a moment and then smiled at her in his ironical way.

"As you like," he answered. "I should be glad to have an apology."

"Oh, I never apologize," she said hastily. "Besides I have nothing to apologize for."

"No? Not insulting suggestions? No insinuations that Americans are cads?"

"You may have misunderstood me," said Christel. "I speak English but do not express myself good at times."

This was as far as she would go in the way of an *amende honorable* to his wounded feelings.

"You speak English miraculously well," he told her. "I think you can say precisely what you intend to say, including a subtly conveyed insult."

Christel shrugged her shoulders.

"If you like to think so. As a matter of fact I have changed my mind about those German lessons. I should be glad to give you some lessons if you still care to have them."

He did not show any joyous enthusiasm. He hesitated for a moment and she saw his penetrating eyes fixed upon her.

"Certainly I still want to learn a bit of German. But I'm not sure that you would be a good teacher, if you'll forgive my saying so."

Christel's face paled slightly. She had not expected this rebuff. It was like a slap in the face.

"That's quite all right," she said. "I hope you will find someone else. Good morning!"

Captain Welles stood in her way.

"Don't let's be hasty about it," he said. "Let's give it a trial. On second thoughts I think you'll be quite a good teacher."

"I value your good opinion—on second thoughts," said Christel with mock humility.

"When shall we start?" asked Captain Welles. "Tonight if you like. Would eight o'clock be convenient?"

Christel paused. Her next words were rather difficult to say. "I suppose it's a business arrangement? You said something about a carton of cigarettes. Once a month do you mean?"

"That's O.K. with me," he answered. "Five hundred cigarettes a month."

Christel could not resist giving a little gasp. He was offering her incredible wealth. With five hundred cigarettes a month she could buy food for Hans and Trudel and Hilde and Paul and her father and mother. She forgot herself for a moment in this list of hungry ones. She swallowed as though she had a lump in her throat.

"That is quite satisfactory," she told him.

Then for a moment the horrid suspicion possessed her mind. Was he trying to buy her with this prodigal offer? Was he trying to seduce her by this terrific bribe? Did he think she was one of the sluts who since the withdrawal of the fraternization order were selling themselves to American G.I.s.?

"You are not asking me to give you more than German lessons?" she asked, raising her eyes to his.

He answered carelessly but she saw his smile and knew that he read her thoughts.

"Nothing more. Not Ancient Greek or Chinese or Persian. German will take me all my time. Tonight then at eight?"

"In my father's study," said Christel. "He will be in my mother's room."

"Fine!" said Captain Welles.

Christel was very nervous when she went into her father's study at two minutes past the appointed hour. Captain Welles was waiting for her there, examining the books on the shelves.

"You're two minutes late," he said.

"Yes. Does that matter?"

"Not much. But I believe in punctuality. Shall we begin?"

He sat at her father's desk and made a sign for her to sit opposite.

"How much German do you know?" she asked, opening a German grammar. His mouth twitched into a smile.

"I know the verb to have, the verb to be, *der die* and *das*, how to take a railway ticket, how to order a meal, how to get one's hair cut, and to ask the price of potatoes, bread, butter, milk, umbrellas and pen-knives."

"You know quite a lot," said Christel. "Where shall I begin?"

She began according to his wish by reading a German story for children. He made a note of the words that were new to him. *Witch*, *ogre*, *step-mother*, *pumpkin* and *toadstool*.

"Very useful words," he observed drily, "especially if I do a trip to fairyland."

"Perhaps you would care to read the story to me," said Christel. "For pronunciation's sake."

"Great idea!" he answered, "if you can bear it."

She found it difficult to bear. He pronounced German with a strong American accent.

"That's terrible," she told him. "It's enough to make a cat laugh."

"A German cat?" he asked. "Have they a sense of humour, your German cats?"

"Your intonation is horrible," she said. "Have you an ear for music?"

"I can tell the difference between Schubert and Bach," he answered.

"Well, then, listen to the vowel sounds and the tone of the voice."

She read out the German fairy tale again, and he listened intently.

"I come from Kansas City," he said. "If I speak German

I shall speak it with a Kansas City accent. What's wrong with that?"

"It's an insult to the German language," she told him. "German is the most beautiful language in the world. It's a shame to murder it."

He gave what the dramatists call a 'hollow laugh'.

"We won't argue that point about the most beautiful language," he said. "You might think I was being uncivil. But I propose that you now read out a bit of Goethe's *Faust*."

"No, no!" she cried. "You wouldn't understand a word of it. It's extremely difficult."

"Of course I shan't understand a word of it," he admitted. "But I want to hear what it sounds like. I've read it in an English translation. I was much impressed."

She found a copy of *Faust* on her father's shelves and read out several long speeches giving them great dramatic value and losing herself in them until presently he stopped her.

"It sounds better in English," he said calmly and firmly.

"No!" she cried. "In German it's magnificent. It rolls like thunder. It flashes like lightning."

"I don't like thunderstorms," he said, and she saw him give a little smile.

She sprang up in anger.

"You're mocking at me!" she said. "If you make a mockery of German I shan't give you any more lessons."

"Now look here," he said. "I want to learn German. I'm taking this quite seriously. I'm willing to meet you half-way and admit that German is a mighty powerful language and probably spoken by my ancestors away back in history—I come from Anglo-Saxon stock. Maybe it's the call of the blood that makes me want to learn German. Now let's get on with it. What about a little conversational exercise in railway-stations or hotels?"

She sat down again. For the rest of the hour he behaved very well, not mocking at her though now and then she saw the glint of humour in his eyes.

He glanced at the clock in her father's study.

"Thanks a lot," he said, rising. "Tomorrow evening? Same time, same place?"

It was agreed.

After further lessons she admitted to herself that her suspicions of him had been unjustified. Always he behaved correctly. Never once did he attempt any foolishness. He really wanted to learn German and made considerable progress in quite a short time. He seemed to have an astonishing memory, never, or seldom, forgetting the notes he made or her correction of his mistakes. There was no doubt that he was studying, apart from these lessons, in his own room upstairs. She felt at ease with him now though still on her guard and still careful of her own pride. He was an American officer. He belonged to the Army of Occupation. He was one of those who had their heels on the neck of Germany.

It was a long time to wait for his first payment of cigarettes. She had been unsuccessful lately in getting food for barter, and Paul's appetite carved a hole in the day's rations. Hilde was getting desperately anxious about the children though all the grown-ups still conspired to pass some of their food to them. She herself was always hungry. Sometimes she awakened in the night with gnawing pains in her stomach.

Four weeks German lessons. One more week to go.

She felt tired in her limbs when she gave the first lesson of the fourth week. That evening Captain Welles was looking at her father's bookshelves again when she came into the room.

"What a lot of books I haven't read!" he exclaimed with a kind of humorous groan. "What a lot of wisdom I've missed!"

He was astonished at the number of English books on these shelves. Dickens, Thackeray, Scott, John Galsworthy. Even Sinclair Lewis.

"Have you read them?" he asked.

"Of course."

He turned with raised eyebrows.

"How have you found time? With all the German books to read as well. Kant, Hegel, German history, German philosophy."

"One reads," said Christel. "My brother Paul is a great reader too."

"You Germans are astonishing," said Captain Welles. "How is it that you read so much and know so little? I mean know so little about other people's psychology and the way to rule, and the way of liberty and democracy?"

Christel flared up instantly.

"It's not for Americans to teach us that," she said. "You are only beginning to be civilized. You're an uncultured people. How dare you come and insult us Germans who have been great scholars for centuries, producing the greatest genius in the world."

He turned round on her with his mocking smile.

"I suppose I asked for that. One day, maybe, you and I will have to argue things out. One day, maybe, I'll tell you what I think of the truth of things and you'll tell me. I doubt whether we shall agree. But tonight you're here to give me a German lesson and we'll keep to that. Are you ready, *gnädiges Fräulein*?"

The lesson had been going smoothly for three-quarters of an hour when Christel had to go to the bookshelves to find a German dictionary. She didn't get as far as the bookshelves. Her legs seemed to be walking on air. The room seemed to swim about her. She felt faint and ill and suddenly she swayed and fell.

When she came to herself again and opened her eyes she saw Captain Welles kneeling by her side. He was dabbing her forehead with a wet handkerchief.

"Better?" he asked.

"I'm sorry," she answered. "It was silly."

She tried to sit up and he lifted her up in strong arms.

"Better rest a bit," he said.

He half carried her to a leather couch and dumped her into it, standing in front of her and looking at her anxiously.

"I'm all right now," she told him.

"Glad to hear it. Why did you go off like that?"

She began to cry a little.

"I suppose I'm weak," she said. "Most German girls flop like this sometimes. We don't get enough to eat. We're half starved. Don't you know that?"

"Good God!" he said. "Good God!"

It seemed to come to him as a revelation that German girls did not get enough to eat.

"I didn't know it was as bad as that," he said in a low voice as though speaking to himself.

He went towards the door and then came back a step or two.

"Say, don't go fainting again. I'll get you something."

He went out of the room while Christel wiped her wet forehead with a handkerchief and licked her lips with a dry tongue.

She hated having made a scene like this. She hated being so weak before this American.

He came back in a short time carrying a tray on which there was a bowl of soup and some cracker biscuits.

"Get this down," he said. "It will make you feel a lot better."

"No thanks," said Christel. "I would rather not."

"Get it down!" he said in a commanding way. "Don't be silly."

"I don't want it," said Christel firmly. "Thank you very much all the same."

"Drink it!" said Captain Welles. "You want it like hell. Open your mouth."

He held a spoonful of soup to her lips and she opened them feeling too weak to resist. The hot soup went down and she felt the glow of its warmth and her strength coming back through her veins.

"That's better," said Captain Welles. "Are you strong enough to hold the spoon or shall I feed you like a baby?"

"I'll hold the spoon," she said.

She felt that the situation was idiotic and humiliating. She also felt that this soup was marvellous and almost intoxicating. Those biscuits looked very good too. She began to nibble them. Captain Welles watched her. Once she raised her eyes and saw his grave serious look. He was like a doctor watching a patient coming back to life.

"I had no idea," he said presently. "I ought to have noticed that you were undernourished."

"No worse than the others," said Christel. "Many of my friends at the University. . . ."

"It makes me feel bad," said Captain Welles. "I'm not soft-hearted about the Germans, but it makes me feel bad. We get more food than is good for us. It's not amusing to eat in a country where the people are undernourished. It makes one feel darned uncomfortable."

It made him feel so uncomfortable that he left her again for a few minutes and came back with a carton of Camels under his arm and six packets of chocolate.

"I ought to have given you these cigarettes in advance," he

said. "It was very thoughtless of me. One doesn't realize that you people are not living on the fat of the land."

Christel's eyes fastened on the cigarettes and chocolates. She would have to hide some of the packets from Paul who was a voracious eater. She would give him two. The others she would give to Hilde for the children. With the cigarettes she could do some wonderful marketing.

"*Danke schön*," she said.

He answered with a laugh.

"*Bitte schön*."

Then he looked at her searchingly.

"How do you feel?"

"Quite restored. It was nothing. I'm ashamed of myself."

She shook hands with him before she left her father's study. It was the first time she had shaken hands with him or with any American. He had behaved very nicely, she thought. Her dark suspicions had been unjustified. He was, she was bound to admit, quite civilized.

Denazification courts were set up in Munich. The Americans were arresting people denounced by their neighbours as notorious Nazis and petty tyrants. They were also arresting Germans accused of war crimes and those whose records convicted them of being members of the Party or S.S. men. Everybody was to be examined or 'screened' as it was called. Most of the German leaders at the very top—Goering, Ribbentrop, Schacht, Schirach, Hess, with German Generals and Admirals—were already in prison awaiting trial for 'crimes against humanity'.

In the opinion of many Germans, even those who had been hostile secretly to Hitler's regime, these trials could not uphold the code of justice because the verdict and condemnation would be decided beforehand by judges who were also victors trying those already condemned in their minds. Among those judges would be Russians. Were they innocent of crimes against humanity? Did not torture prevail in Russian prisons and concentration camps? Was not the U.S.S.R. guilty of frightful crimes and atrocities in Estonia, Latvia, Lithuania and Poland? Were they fit judges to decide the guilt or innocence of German leaders? . . .

So the Baron von Arnheim, who had been hostile to Hitler's way of rule, though he had accepted service under its authority, talked and argued with his son Paul and other members of his family.

This hearing of denunciations opened the door to many abuses and evil minds. How easy to denounce a neighbour against whom the denouncer had a private grudge! What a temptation there was to craven and guilty men to curry favour with the military commandants in their own district and to cover up their own misdeeds by acting as informers against men whom they envied or hated. Here indeed was a wonderful opportunity for private revenge or the malice of the weak and evil-minded.

It was a mistake of the Occupying Powers to attempt any distinction between one kind of Nazi and another, the bad and the not so bad. How were they to draw this fine distinction when every German man and woman, boy and girl, apart from a heroic few like Ulrich von Hassell and his friends, had accepted the way of life and service prescribed by the Führer and supported with enthusiasm by German youth, duped and doped by an irresistible propaganda. They were all Nazis in the mass apart from secret critics and unbelievers of older years. To get a job or to get a food-card it was necessary to shout 'Heil Hitler!' with the rest. The concentration camp or the headsman's axe awaited those who dared to resist the rule of Caesar, or rather this supreme Chief of the German tribes by the name of Hitler.

"In any case," said Christel's brother, Paul, discussing these things with her one day after a mountain climb, when they sat on the summit of the Zugspitz, "we had a good time before the War. We enjoyed all that marching about and banner carrying. It was youth's day out in Germany. The Führer was our God. Now we all pretend that we were never Nazis and that we hated him. A bit cowardly, don't you think?"

"There are a lot of cowards about," said Christel. "It makes me sick to see young men in Kaulbach and Munich fawning upon American soldiers, crawling to them for the sake of a cigarette, running errands for them, bowing obsequiously if an American officer looks them in the eyes. Disgusting."

Paul laughed carelessly.

"I've no sense of hostility to the Americans. I don't crawl to them, but I don't scowl at them. They'd like to be friendly with us."

"They just want our girls," said Christel.

She made one exception to this sweeping statement.

"Captain Welles has behaved very nicely."

Paul ignored these remarks. He was sitting with his hands clasped round his knees looking across the mountains with his one eye.

Presently he asked a question which startled Christel.

"Do you think Father will be all right?"

"Father? Why not?"

"They're sure to examine him."

"Well he has nothing to hide. He's always been hostile to the Nazis. I used to quarrel with him over that until we began to lose the War, as he always said we would."

"All the same he was in charge of some of the Labour Camps."

"Oh, he will be all right," said Christel. "All his friends will vouch for him."

"Perhaps he has one or two enemies," said Paul.

He said no more on that subject but sat on the mountain-top breathing in the clear air, drinking in the beauty of the scene around him. Here was peace. Here at this altitude the troubles and agonies of mankind seemed ephemeral and far away. These old rocks had stood through timeless ages while below them men slaughtered one another for religion and power. Paul von Arnheim was not a poet or philosopher, but like his sister, like every Bavarian peasant, he felt a sense of joy and liberation when he reached a high peak and surveyed the world with an eagle's eye.

When the brother and sister returned home that evening they heard from Hilde and their mother that their father had been summoned to Munich for an examination by the Military Commandant and had not yet come back, though he had been away for some hours.

Frau von Arnheim was getting anxious but Christel tried to reassure her.

"They can't have anything against him, Mother."

"These things take a prodigious time," said Paul. "A long, long way to Tipperary. He'll be home before long—that is to say before midnight."

He said this to comfort his mother, but secretly he was disturbed. His father had certainly been in charge of Bavarian Labour Camps, and outwardly, at least, had conformed to the required code.

But it was Christel who heard worse news than that. When she went into her father's study for the German lesson she saw Captain Welles give her a look as though for some reason he was sorry for her.

"Do you know anything about my father?" she asked.

She was suddenly frightened by that look in his eyes.

"Somebody has denounced him," answered Captain Welles. "I've just had a message from the Colonel. He has been detained. You had better tell your family. We won't have a lesson tonight."

"Detained?" cried Christel. "Do you mean they have arrested him?"

"Detained for further examination," he answered. "But I'm not supposed to answer questions."

"Who has denounced him?" asked Christel excitedly. "It's shameful. He has been kind to everyone."

"I hope he will be cleared by his examination," said Captain Welles.

But Herr von Arnheim was not cleared by his examination. It appeared that he had been denounced by the schoolmaster—Mundt—on account of the girl sentenced to a term of imprisonment in the concentration camp from which she had returned with terrible tales and broken health. This schoolmaster, who was a cripple, had been befriended from time to time by Herr von Arnheim who had given him some of his clothes and sent him books until he suspected this young man of being a Communist. Now he had turned round venomously to denounce his benefactor, perhaps in order to cover up his own political views or from some black prejudice in his own mind against a German of high rank who once had been rich. He had presented a report setting out a series of lies designed to portray the Baron von Arnheim as a brutal Nazi, harsh in his treatment of the villagers of Kaulbach, and the callous inquisitor of the young girl who had suffered torture for a few words of criticism against Hitler and his S.S. With other Germans accused of similar actions by secret informers the Herr von Arnheim was sent to a prison near Frankfurt, leaving his family sorrowful and indignant.

"If he is innocent he will be cleared pretty soon," said Captain Welles by way of consolation to Christel who was overwhelmed with grief. "We Americans believe in justice."

"Justice!" cried Christel. "Is it justice to believe the denunciations of crawling informers? Is it justice to believe lies and to disbelieve a man of honour like my father?"

"These things have to be sorted out," answered Captain Welles. "Our military commandants have to take notice of definite charges."

He was genuinely distressed when Christel broke down and wept one evening because of a letter received from her father saying that he was being terribly underfed and was rapidly losing weight.

"You denounce our concentration camps," she cried. "Now you make your own, and starve your prisoners."

"We don't torture them," answered Captain Welles, quietly.

It was then that she began to weep.

He was much distressed by that. "I'm terribly sorry," he said. "If I can be of any help I shall be mighty glad because I have a respect for your father and because I like your courage and high spirit."

From the top left pocket of his tunic he pulled out a large clean handkerchief to stop her flow of tears.

She flung it on the floor and sprang up and rushed out of the room.

Captain Robert Lee Welles had to go without his German lesson that evening and he regretted it because he was making steady progress in that language.

CHAPTER XX

It was while her father was in prison that Hilde Menzel received a letter from Franz Reber after a silence of many months.

Forgive me for not writing [he began]. *I have been living an underground life in this mad-house of Berlin. My mind has also been underground in tunnels of darkness from which I am just crawling out. My remembrance of you on that journey from Königsberg and during that time at Quakenbrück when we talked without any masks on our faces or any concealments, has come back to me lately as a kind of revelation which lay only in my subconsciousness, but now has leapt into the forefront of my thoughts. It is again a question of Destiny—the logical sequence of events. I see now that step by step through many events which seemed accidental, I was led to meet you and to form a spiritual friendship with you which for a time I have utterly neglected and thrown away. Now I need you with a sudden intensity of longing. I need your tenderness and courage and wisdom. I dare to ask for it though I don't deserve it. I must get away from Berlin and come to Munich. I believe there is more sanity in Bavaria and that in the pure air of the mountains I shall find a cleansing of the mind from the filth and degradation of a city in which the blackest of Black Markets is very flourishing and in which luxury and corruption are beginning to rear their heads above the hunger and suffering of the decent folk whose courage and patience are miraculous. Anyhow I shall come to Munich and hope to have your forgiving friendship.*

Hilde read this letter with emotion. She had been hurt by the long silence of Franz Reber. She had not forgotten their comradeship in time of terrible danger when she was fleeing from the Russians. A thousand times she had thought of their evening talks when he had revealed his troubled soul to her and she had given him, it seemed, a little comfort. Now her heart beat rather faster with a little fear in her mind because of this letter. To be needed so much by any young man, and one like Franz Reber.

was disturbing and perhaps alarming. He spoke of Destiny as though their fate were intertwined. But was she not still the wife of Peter of whose death she was uncertain? She would not deny Franz a spiritual friendship but it must never be different from that. It could never be love in its fullest sense, though in her heart she knew that she loved him as a comrade, as a mind in tune with hers. She kept her letter hidden from Christel and the others. . . .

My mind has been underground in tunnels of darkness, he wrote.

Franz Reber lived underground like many others in Berlin. He remained in his father's cellar with Baümer and the two girls after the occupation of the city by Russians, British and American troops. It was a relief when Winkelnkempler departed for another hole in the ground where he had friends more suited to his dark and sullen spirit dedicated to hatred and revenge. Franz had had a fierce quarrel with him one night, calling him a madman and a homicidal maniac. Winkelnkempler had had murder in his eyes for a few seconds and drew a knife with which he would have stabbed Franz but for Baümer gripping his wrist and flinging him against the wall.

After that he had slouched up the cellar steps and had not come back again. His last words had been a sneer and a threat.

"I prefer to keep company with men of spirit. One day when another Hitler calls to the German soul, the cowards and collaborators will have their heads lopped off by the headsman's axe. Take care of your neck, Franz Reber!"

"Thank God he's gone!" laughed Elsa. "That man makes my blood run cold. He has no sense of humour."

No sense of humour had availed to beat back Terror—a quaking animal blood-freezing terror—in the first days of occupation by the Russian troops. People hiding in cellars, or crowded into Bunkers, as the Germans call their air-raid shelters, heard the roar of gunfire in Unter den Linden, the Wilhelmstrasse, the Friedrichstrasse, and all parts of the Capital.

Close to them wherever they crouched was the ceaseless tattoo of massed machine-guns. Berlin was on fire. The sky above it throbbed with scarlet light, pulsating like blood and touching great pillars of black smoke. The Russians were blowing up buildings left undestroyed by British and American air raids. Like the Goths and Vandals storming ancient Rome they were smashing and destroying palaces, churches, statues, and public buildings with industrious ferocity. So Carthage had fallen and disappeared from the earth.

The capital of the German Empire was being blasted down stone by stone, column by column, street by street. Now and then there was silence almost more frightening than the tumult of gunfire and out of these silences came blood-curdling shrieks of women or the yells of hoarse-throated men. Then presently after a week or so deep silence prevailed over this destruction, except for the tramp of Russian soldiers, or the grinding wheels of monster tanks or single shots fired in the streets.

On such a night of silence Franz left his cellar and went out into the ruins of Berlin. It was a moonlight night casting black shadows from gaunt ribs of masonry sticking up into the sky with great gulfs of darkness between mountainous piles of masonry while the moon shone through the holes of windows in skeleton houses touching with a silvery luminance these tatters and rags of massive architecture which once had been the churches, monuments and mansions of Berlin.

Franz Reber tried to walk down the Uhlandstrasse but it was blocked with fallen masonry. Climbing like a lean wolf over these mountainous heaps of rubble and stone and twisted iron he came at last into the Kurfürstendam—that long highway which once was the Broadway of Berlin whirling with illuminated signs over cinemas, theatres, dancing-halls and restaurants. Now only the light of the moon revealed its ruination. In the middle of it two German tanks had been buried up to the level of their gun turrets. It was only possible to walk a little way because of its high piled litter of fallen houses.

Franz Reber spoke aloud in this solitude of ruin. He seemed to be the only soul alive in this city of Berlin. It was as though he were the last man on earth. His own loneliness frightened him. This awful picture of ruin under the bright moon where once had been a civilization which he remembered as in a former life was very dreadful to his soul. He spoke aloud.

"This is a tomb," he said. "Berlin is a tomb. Here lies buried all that we were."

Suddenly he cried out two words followed by a harsh and terrible laugh.

"Heil Hitler!"

He flung out his arm in the Nazi salute, and then put his arm over his face and wept in a convulsive body-shaking way like a man torn with agony.

Once he had been a soldier of Hitler's armies. Sergeant Reber. Now he was a lean lone wolf prowling about the ruin of German civilization. Destiny had led to this.

He went back to his cellar. . . .

The food situation was bad and remained bad. There came the time of rationing when the Municipality under the orders of the military commandants of the Occupying Powers tried to control the supplies of food and gave coupons for so many 'calories', just enough for life, if they were obtainable, but not enough to sustain the strength of German workers nor of the unemployed of whom there were millions. After the flight from the Russians which had crowded Berlin with refugees there was now another tide almost unceasing when the population of East Prussia were forced to abandon their land handed over to Poland by the Allied Powers. These wretched people arrived in cattle-trucks and wagons so overcrowded that many died on the way. For hundreds of years their forefathers had been prosperous farmers or well-to-do merchants in cities and townships. Now they were forced away from their farmsteads with only what they could carry in a few bundles, and they poured into Berlin, already over-crowded, already crammed with unemployed, already half starved, without reserves of food for the empty stomachs of the new arrivals.

Baümer had something to say about it. That straw-bearded young man for whom Franz now had a comradely affection was walking with him in the Leipzigerplatz when a crowd of these East Prussians were moving away from the railway-station. The women were haggard with a bewildered look in their eyes. Children dragged at their skirts, whimpering. Elderly farmers strode by with packs on their shoulders and dull sullen eyes.

"One day," said Baümer, "what is happening to these people will be the cause of another war. Those who have carved up Germany have not only committed a crime but a folly. A new generation of Germans will fight to get back East Prussia and all the fat will be in the fire again. Thanks be to God I shall be a dead man before that happens."

"How do you know?" asked Franz. "You're still a young man, Baümer."

"I'm nearly dead now," said Baümer. "I haven't the strength of a louse. How can a man live on potato soup?"

Franz Reber gave a queer kind of laugh which was half a groan.

"Hunger helps one to think! I'm becoming a deep thinker! My mind ignores my stomach-pains and goes on thinking."

"That's unfortunate," answered Baümer. "What the hell are you thinking about? When I start thinking I know I'm going mad."

"Sometimes," answered Franz, "I think about the reason for my being alive."

"There's no reason," answered Baümer.

Franz shook his head.

"There must be some reason. There's a reason for everything. Most of my comrades were killed. Why should I remain alive?"

"Just bad luck," said Baümer. "The same as mine."

"No," said Franz. "Everything is dictated by Destiny. I was meant to stay alive. Why? That's what worries me. I can't find the answer."

"You're going mad, like me," said Baümer. "Sometimes when I'm very hungry I see queer things—reptiles and prehistoric monsters. I yelled out last night because I saw them coming down the cellar steps."

"I heard you," said Franz. "You frightened Elsa."

"I don't suppose those things were really there," said Baümer half doubtfully.

Franz put his hand on the shoulder of his straw-bearded friend and laughed at him.

"If they had been there we might have killed them and eaten Megatherium steaks or Pterodactyl cutlets."

Baümer echoed his laugh.

"*Gott in Himmel!* That's an idea. Of course we're both mad, my friend, but we can still laugh. That shows we're mad. No-one but a madman could laugh in Berlin."

"Elsa laughs," said Franz, "and she's not mad."

"She gets food," said Baümer. "Many times she doesn't come

back to the cellar at night. She comes back in the morning well fed and doesn't look us in the eyes. She still has a little shame."

"It's none of our business," said Franz.

"She brought back two tins of beef a morning or two ago," said Baümer. "Army rations. She said an English sergeant had given them to her."

Franz nodded.

"I know. She shared them with us. That was kind. Perhaps God will forgive her because she was kind."

Baümer raised his eyebrows.

"God? I used to believe in God. I was a Catholic. I think I told you. Now I believe only in the Devil."

"If you believe in a Devil you must believe in a God," said Franz. "Everything has its opposite. The pull between opposites creates an equilibrium. That's what holds things together. I've been thinking about that. If there's Evil there must be good. Isn't that logical?"

"It's logical but ridiculous," said Baümer, "where's the opposite to the Evil in Germany? It's all evil. This misery, this hunger, those starving children, the fainting women, this unemployment, this chaos of what was once a civilized land—where's the balance?"

He stood still by a pile of rubble and stared into Reber's eyes sombrely.

"All this evil may produce some good," said Franz. "Germany isn't alone in the world. The victors will suffer as well as the vanquished. Perhaps out of this general suffering may come some new kind of revelation, some comradeship among nations, an era of peace, and renaissance of the arts and things of beauty."

The sombre look left Baümer's eyes and he grabbed his friend's right arm and laughed.

"You have more beautiful dreams than mine! But they're equally unreal."

Franz had taken Winkelnkempler's iron bedstead in the cellar after offering it to Baümer. Sometimes he lay on it until late in the morning, or even late in the afternoon, because lack of food made him lethargic and because he wanted to think and sometimes read. From the rubble which once was his father's house he had picked up an old copy of Aristotle's *Ethics and Metaphysics* in a German translation and found it illuminating. That old Greek seemed to have found out a lot of truth about life and had analysed almost every human relationship and the pursuit of happiness. He had eliminated pleasure—all physical pleasure—from the way to ultimate happiness. Philosophy itself, the quest of truth itself, seemed to be the highest attainable happiness for an educated man. On the other hand he seemed to be in agreement with the Nazi view of life in some respects. He believed in pride rather than humility and condemned pity as a weakness in the magnanimous man, though he extolled magnanimity—greatness of soul—as the attainment of the highest virtue.

'He's wrong about pity,' thought Franz. 'It's lack of pity which creates cruelty and torture—the two deadly sins of the modern world and of Hitler's rule. I believe in the pity preached by Christ. If Christ came to Berlin . . .'

His thoughts followed out that idea. If Christ came to Berlin he would be pitiful of the hungry refugees. He would be pitiful of the young women like Elsa who sold themselves for a meal or a tin of bully beef, especially if they shared it with their comrades.

Lying on the iron bedstead he watched those two girls, Elsa and Erike. They remained in the cellar most of the day. Behind the curtain they whispered and laughed and cooked little bits of food on an oil-stove, or slept if there were no food. Then in the afternoons they emerged with polished finger-nails, neatly brushed hair, and a touch of colour on their cheeks and lips. It was astonishing how well they turned out from this damp dark cellar. Often they went out together but sometimes separately. One evening Elsa let her friend go out first and sat on Reber's side of the curtain polishing a pair of shoes which were down at heel.

"Let me do that for you," said Franz, who was sitting on the side of his iron bedstead.

"I'm strong enough to do my own dirty work," said Elsa. "Thanks for the offer all the same. I see you were brought up as a gentleman. A bit old-fashioned, isn't it?"

"The male is supposed to be the stronger animal," answered Franz carelessly.

"Some men behave like apes," said Elsa. "That's why I'm beginning to like the English. They've no morality but nice manners."

"Do you meet many?" asked Franz.

She looked at him and then lowered her eyelashes.

"Now and again."

"What do you think of them?"

Elsa laughed and shrugged her shoulders.

"They're all gambling on the Black Market. They send home for cigarettes—thousands of them—and buy up everything or change them into German marks and then back into English money. It's what they call 'a racket'. They're all doing it."

"I thought the English had a sense of honour," said Franz. "Although the English were our enemies I had a secret admiration for them. I used to read the books of Dickens and that made me love them before I was taught to hate them."

"They've gone bad," said Elsa. "Boys of eighteen are learning all the vices. I'm sorry for them. I'm sorry for myself because I teach them a bit. See what I mean?"

Franz Reber glanced at her. He liked this girl. She had a laughing spirit. She was kind. She was generous when she had a little food.

"I wouldn't if I were you," he said. "It isn't good for your soul."

Elsa stared at him and then gave a shrill laugh.

"Are you preaching at me?" she asked.

"No," said Franz. "I'm not a preacher. But we've become comrades in this cellar."

Elsa's voice became a little harsh.

"How do you think I'm going to live? How do you think any of us German girls are going to live unless we play about with English or American soldiers and get a meal now and then? Funny, aren't you?"

She spat on her pair of shoes and then rubbed them with a dirty cloth.

"I'll get a job somehow," said Franz. "I'll share what I earn. Then you needn't humiliate yourself."

Elsa's face flushed and she spoke angrily.

"Shut up! If you don't like the morals in this cellar go and find another hole in the ground."

"Forgive me," said Franz. "I've no right to interfere. I have to find my own soul first. I have to clean myself before I can talk morality—and not even then."

Elsa put on her shoes and was silent until she was ready to go out after a minute or two behind the curtain. She went towards the steps with a hard expression on her face. Then suddenly she came and fell on her knees and put her head against Franz who was sitting on the bedstead.

"What's the matter?" he asked.

"I'm sorry!" she cried.

"Sorry for what?"

"For being such a dirty little cat."

"Don't be a dirty little cat," said Franz.

"How can I help it?" she cried. "I didn't make the War. I didn't ask for all this? Why should I have to pay?"

"I don't know," answered Franz. "I suppose Fate has something to do with it. The vengeance of the Gods. There was a fellow called Aristotle. . . ."

He smiled to himself. It was no use talking to Elsa about Aristotle.

Presently she started up and mopped her eyes, half laughing and half crying.

"*Mein Gott!* I've made my face all messy. It's because my stomach's empty."

She went behind the curtain again and he could hear her humming *Lili Marlene*.

Then she came out putting on a smile as part of her make-up.

"Shan't be home till late. Sergeant Brown is taking me to an underground cinema. Very expensive!"

"What's he like?" asked Franz.

"One of the baby boys. He blushes when I kiss him."

"Poor little devil!" said Franz. "Ask him if he's read *David Copperfield*."

"I'm in a hurry," said Elsa. "If he doesn't wait I shall have to go hungry."

She ran up the steps into the outer world which was Berlin in ruins.

Franz walked through those ruins day after day, and became familiar with the sight of the occupation troops and their civilian missions. Among them were English girls in khaki and presently English women in civilian clothes who were the wives of British officers, or typists and secretaries in the Allied Control. The

English Tommies were very young, mostly fresh-faced boys who looked like school cadets more than fighting soldiers. Their officers also looked young and inexperienced in comparison with Germans like himself who had been through the War and bore the marks of it on their faces and on their bodies. The British officers generally walked about in couples, looking about them with smiling interest, prodding the rubble with their sticks, stopping to look at gaunt ruins. Once he lingered by two of them who were staring down the Wilhelmstrasse and his knowledge of English was good enough to understand what they were saying.

"That was Hitler's Chancellery. That's where he committed suicide with his woman, Eva Braun."

The other officer nodded and spoke in a clear English voice.

"Will there be another Hitler? These Germans will try to make a come-back one day. You can't keep sixty million people down for ever."

His friend turned round on him and answered sharply.

"Why not? I hope to God we don't weaken. They don't admit their war guilt even now. They've no sense of shame for putting Jews into gas-ovens and all the other atrocities."

"I can't help feeling sorry for the women and children," said the other officer. "They're all pallid and undernourished."

"There you are! Going weak already! It's the English vice. We're always sorry for the enemy when we've beaten him. We forget and forgive a damn' sight too quickly. Soon we shall be feeding the Germans while our own folk are undernourished. I know! We're crawling sentimentalists."

The other officer laughed.

"All the same I'm sorry for the German women and children. I'd rather be a crawling sentimentalist than a hard-faced brute without bowels of compassion. Besides we've got to think of the future. One day we may need the Germans to keep back the Russians."

His friend answered impatiently.

"Oh hell! That's German propaganda. They're already playing that card."

They moved on. Franz had not understood every word but had followed the drift of them. Very clearly he had understood those words about the future of Germany. "You can't keep a people of sixty million down for ever."

This young English officer was looking ahead—far ahead. How could Germany build up these ruins which once were Berlin and all the other ruined cities? How could they build up the spirit of a people slowly starving, as now they were?

"They've no sense of shame for putting Jews into gas-ovens." Didn't one of them say that? He, Franz Reber, had a sense of shame, but few others to whom he spoke, not Winkelnkempler, not even Elsa with whom he had talked about it. She had merely shrugged her shoulders and said, "We suffered much from the Jews," as though that excused mass-murder and torture. Somehow the German mind, or many German minds, were proof against compassion and against self-accusation of war guilt. Defeat, and the frightful price they were paying for defeat, seemed to them to outweigh any evil on their side. "Hitler made mistakes," some of his friends said; or others more violent said, "Hitler was a madman. He over-ruled his Generals." None of them said, "We were guilty"—none of them, except Franz Reber himself who had this sense of guilt heavily upon him—this sense of having served the powers of Evil.

'Why do I think like this?' he asked himself in his introspective way, as he strode through the ruins of Berlin. 'Is it because I lack a sense of patriotism? Is it because I'm a weakling and a coward? Or is it because I follow a flicker of light in this dark tunnel of human ignorance and blindness? Perhaps it's only because I never get enough to eat and my belly is empty like my brain. But others are like that—they don't think like that. Only Hilde Menzel thinks like that.'

So a bewildered man walked alone through the ruins of Berlin.

In those ruins one morning he met Magda Hessell.

"How are you getting on?" he asked.

She looked ill, he thought. Her face was pale and had a pinched look, but for the first time he was struck by a kind of tragic beauty in her face. With a little colour, he thought, she would be beautiful. As a young girl before the war she must have been rather distinguished—even in a shabby frock, badly stained, she had a touch of elegance.

She answered his question with a laugh in which there was not much mirth.

"I'm getting on—towards the unpleasant end of all things."

"As bad as that?" he asked. "Let's sit down on this block of stone."

They were in the Tiergarten, looking like a battlefield, not long ago a battlefield. A few hundred yards away was the tall column of the Siegessaüle on which was poised the Angel of Victory for the war of 1870. The Angel of Victory with its outspread wings of gold glinted in the sunlight high against a blue sky looking down upon a city destroyed by war. Franz stared at it a moment. As a child he had often stared up at it with awe. He noticed now that the tip of its left wing had been knocked off by gun-fire. Away through a thin blue haze was the wreck of the Kaiser Wilhelm Denkmalkirche and near to them were the statues of German heroes in the Siegesallee, some of them battered and broken and toppled from their pedestals. So had the German gods fallen into the dust. A few people passed dragging along bits of wood. Then came some refugees with shawls round their heads though the weather was warm. Then passed two smartly dressed girls chatting and laughing as though all were well with the world.

"It's nice to see you again," said Magda.

"And you," he answered. "Where are you living now?"

"In the same old Bunker. Just over there."

She pointed to the edge of the Tiergarten.

Franz nodded. It was the Berlin way of life. Thousands of people had no other home but these grim Bunkers.

"Nice people with you?" he asked.

Magda laughed bitterly.

"Oh, charming! Some of them verminous. Some of them in the last stages of tuberculosis. At night the atmosphere isn't too sweet. Coughing, spitting, snoring. Children crying. Old people quarrelling. Yes, it's very pleasant down there!"

"It's very hard on you," said Franz. "You haven't been used to that kind of thing. As Otto Hessell's wife . . ."

Magda shrugged her thin shoulders.

"It's no use thinking of the past. People saved from shipwreck on a raft in rough seas don't think of soft beds. They think only of how long they'll keep alive."

Franz put his hand on one of hers.

"I hate to think of you in such misery."

"It's the hunger that gets me down," said Magda. "Always

the nagging thought of food. Just enough to keep alive and nothing more."

Franz nodded. There was nothing he didn't know about that.

"I used to be rather fond of cooking," said Magda. "I used to make fruit cakes and cream buns. Otto used to like them. Sometimes I dream of them. Beautiful dreams!"

"Yes," said Franz with a laugh. "I sometimes dream of meals I used to have in Munich—plates crammed with food and piled high."

Magda became reminiscent and spoke dreamily as though seeing a vision.

"There used to be a restaurant in Königsberg where the food was marvellous. They had a French *chef*, a prisoner of war. He was a genius. I used to watch him cooking *crêpes Susettes*, on a little brazier in front of the guests. It was a work of art."

Franz also became reminiscent.

"I once had a memorable meal in Garmisch. At 'The Three Grenadiers'. I remember it now. *Gott in Himmel!*"

He gave details of this dinner which he had shared with a girl named Christel and her brother Paul.

Suddenly they both laughed and looked ashamed.

"We're like two children," said Magda.

"Like Arctic explorers on the last lap," said Franz.

It was pleasant sitting here with Magda, he thought. They were like old friends after that journey from Königsberg. It was good of her to be pleased to see him again. Down there in the cellar with Baümer and Elsa and the other girl it was very squalid and primitive. He had missed the company of a woman like Magda, one of his own class. Elsa and Erike were uneducated little creatures, though he had become fond of them.

"Some people are getting parcels from America," said Magda. "I know a girl who gets wonderful parcels from an aunt in New York. Now and again she gives me a few things—a bit of soap the other day and some American cheese. I nearly wept at the splendour of the gift."

"I wish I had an American aunt," said Franz.

"I wish I had two American aunts!" said Magda.

Presently she mentioned another way of getting food.

"The American and English pick up German girls. They have a fine time. Good meals, cigarettes, candies."

"I know," said Franz, thinking of Elsa. "They sell themselves for the price of a meal. It's terrible. But I can't find it in my heart to blame them. It's an easy way of escape from starvation."

Magda glanced at him with raised eyebrows.

"You don't blame them? I thought you were a moralist, a high-souled young man."

"How can one blame them?" he asked. "I feel only pity. But I don't pretend to be high-souled."

"Jesus Christ was pitiful of the Magdalen," said Magda. "Perhaps you're a better Christian than those who blame them."

A blind man wearing his old tunic without badges passed them where they were sitting on the block of stone. His mother, a gaunt, haggard looking woman, was leading him by the hand.

When they had passed Franz groaned quietly.

"The sight of our blinded soldiers freezes my blood," he said. "Blindness is the worst of all. Never to see the sky, never to see the trees and the grass, never to see a woman's face. . . ."

He looked at Magda's face as though thankful for his sight. She had a good face, he thought, good in the sense of being very paintable. He would like to do a head of her one day. He would like to get the sense of tragedy behind her smile. Only Leonardo could do that. Now he came to think of it Magda was a Leonardo type.

They talked for an hour or more with many silences. Then she had to go. She was joining two girls who were lining up for their rations.

"By kind permission of our conquerors," she said. "Enough calories—isn't that the word?—to keep a canary alive while they wallow in the flesh-pots."

"They seem to be on meagre fare in England," said Franz. "So the papers say."

Magda laughed contemptuously.

"Let them try our meagre fare! As for the Americans they've all the food in the world. That girl with an American aunt tells me fantastic stories of luxury in New York."

She rose from the block of stone and smiled at Franz.

"A pleasant interlude. Let's meet here again. Let's remember some more good feasts we had in the days of plenty."

He held her hand for a moment, a thin delicate hand and very cold.

"I'll wait for you tomorrow at the same time," he said. "On this block of stone. I've enjoyed our talk."

"I won't promise," she told him. "I may pay a visit on the girl with an American aunt."

But she came next evening and he sprang up to greet her surprised by his own eagerness. He found her unusually attractive now, though he had paid no attention to her when she was in his car on the road from Königsberg. There was some grace about her, he thought. The poise of her head gave him a sense of pleasure from an artist's point of view. There was a kind of desperate courage in her spirit which made her almost gay now and then. She could talk about books and pictures. Anyhow she was a pretty woman in this desert of his loneliness and perhaps some weakness in him needed the company and comfort of a woman. He had found that in Quakenbrück with Hilde Menzel who was often in his thoughts.

They walked in the Tiergarten on these Summer evenings, though not very far because Magda pleaded weariness. Sometimes they went hand-in-hand like brother and sister, like lovers, as those who passed them may have thought. Several times they sat on the grass together and once he watched her for an hour or more while she slept with her face turned sideways. She looked very thin under her frock. There was no flesh on her bones. The lines of her body were revealed by her flimsy frock which she wore in these Summer days now getting hot.

'Perhaps I'm falling in love with her,' thought Franz. He altered the tense of his sentence. 'Perhaps I have fallen in love with her.'

The idea came to him as a sudden surprise, almost as a shock. He had a sudden desire to kiss her and hold her in his arms. He moved from where he had been sitting with his rough hands clasped round his knees. He knelt down and bent his head and kissed her lips. She stirred and opened her eyes and spoke one word.

"Otto!"

It was her husband's name.

Franz rose from his knees and stood looking down at Magda who slept again. Otto had been his friend. Several times he had talked of Magda with devotion. "If I don't get back from Russia," he had said once, "go and see Magda if you can find her. Tell her that she was always in my heart." Now by a strange chain of happenings he was looking down on Otto's wife, lying there in the sunburnt grass of the Tiergarten. Would it be disloyalty to his dead comrade if he were to make love to her? Love in the ruins! Love on a hungry stomach! Love as the only happiness and warmth of life in a cold, comfortless world.

'Otto would only wish for Magda's happiness,' he thought. 'If he looks down on us—if his spirit walks—he won't be angry with me. The dead understand more than the living, if there's life after death.'

Presently Magda opened her eyes again and then rose from the grass at first on her knees.

"I've been sleeping!" she said as though he didn't know. "I've been dreaming. My mind escaped from that dreadful Bunker."

"Certainly you've been sleeping," agreed Franz, laughing at her. "For more than an hour."

"And you?" she asked.

"I stood guard on the sleeping beauty," he answered.

"Not a very beautiful sleeping beauty," she said. "A miserable hag as ugly as sin."

"I liked the look of you," he told her. "I liked watching you asleep."

A faint colour crept into her pale face and she laughed.

"I don't think that was quite decent of you. Gentlemen shouldn't watch ladies in their sleep—I mean unmarried gentlemen and virtuous ladies."

Suddenly she put both her hands to her waist.

"*Gott in Himmel!*" she cried. "I starve. There's a knife in my stomach. Hunger gnaws at me."

"Come back to my cellar," he said. "I'll give you some soup."

She shook her head.

"You'll need it yourself. I've promised to go to a basement room where they may have a bit of food. Three girls I know live down there. One of them is comradely with a Russian officer who is quite good-natured."

"Degrading!" said Franz. "Horrible!"

"He gives her tit-bits," said Magda. "She shares them with her friends. Isn't that rather sweet and kind?"

"Our German women are lowering themselves," said Franz. "To the very depths. God help them."

Magda glanced sidesays at him.

"Doesn't charity cover a multitude of sins?" she asked. "I thought it wasn't in your heart to blame them."

Franz walked with her in silence for a while as far as the edge of the Tiergarten and then down the ruins of the Leipzigerstrasse.

"Magda," he said. "I wish you wouldn't go with loose women."

"I don't!" she answered quickly. "What makes you say that, Franz?"

"That woman who is comradely with a Russian officer."

"He's quite a nice Russian officer," she told him. "And she's one of my best friends. It's Theresia Koch, the opera singer You must come and meet them one day. And here we are. Come in now, won't you? Meet the Russian."

"No," he answered. "I'll go back to my own cellar."

He held her hand for a moment and then made a confession.

"I kissed you when you were asleep."

She looked at him with surprise and reproach.

"That was taking an unfair advantage. Did it give you any pleasure?"

"To the very depths of my being," he answered.

"I don't believe it," Magda jeered at him. "An ugly hag like me?"

"You're beautiful," he told her.

"No, no!" she cried. "I still have a mirror. I see my sunken eyes and the little lines about them."

"I like the little lines," he said. "They give character. They tell of experience and life. Doll's faces have no lines."

She made a little curtsey and said, "Thank you, kind sir!"

Then she turned away from him and went down some steps.

The next time he met her in the Tiergarten she was waiting for him on the same block of stone.

It was a warm Summer evening. The ruins of Berlin were

bathed in a golden haze. Even the dead trees in the Tiergarten, lopped by Russian gun-fire, had a kind of beauty, etched against a blue sky and touched with gold. It was a week since he had last met her though he had walked this way each evening hoping to see her.

"Where have you been?" he asked. "I thought you had deserted me."

"Why should I?" she asked in return.

"I thought you were angry with me for kissing you when you were asleep."

"Oh, I had forgotten that. I wasn't angry. I was only surprised."

"Why surprised?"

"You don't look like a man in need of kisses."

She looked at him as though seeing him for the first time.

"How do I look?"

"You look a very serious young man and rather austere. You look like a monk in a picture by Pacher."

"*Gott in Himmel!*" he exclaimed with a laugh.

"You look like Saint Sebastian," said Magda. "After his martyrdom."

"I don't feel like it," said Franz. "I feel very unsaintly and very full of human desire. I'm a lonely animal. I'm spiritually alone. That's why I come here; to talk to you and to walk with you hand in hand. I've kissed you asleep. May I kiss you awake?"

Her eyelids fluttered for a moment.

"It's not worth it," she said. "But if you like I don't mind. I'm hungry for food, not for kisses."

"Did you get anything to eat with Theresia Koch and her Russian officer?"

"That was a week ago," she said. "Now I'm starving again. Aren't you starving too, Franz?"

"I feel a bit weak," he admitted. "Potato soup isn't very sustaining. Nor two thin slices of bread."

"Let's forget it," she said. "Let our souls rise above our bodies. Let's talk about old times when Germany was a happy land."

She spoke with a kind of mockery and bravado.

"Tell me about your girlhood," he said. "I want to know more about you. Tell me about Otto."

"That would make me weep," she answered. "And I don't feel like talking anyhow. How silent it is here! In this light Berlin looks like a dream city."

He took her hand and they walked by the relics of the Siegesallee where broken bits of statuary lay on the ground, once the avenues of German heroes sculptured in marble. A few people passed, shabby looking and pallid with the pallor of all Berliners at this time.

"This solitude gives me a queer feeling," said Franz.

"In what way?"

"It's as though you and I were the last survivors of an ancient civilization once called Germany. My comrade Baümer thinks all Europe will be like this one day."

Magda shrugged her shoulders.

"I don't care! I'm past worrying about that."

Presently she interrupted something he was saying.

"I think I must be going back, Franz."

"Why? We haven't been here long."

She put her hands to her forehead.

"I've a headache. I don't feel too well."

"Oh, I'm sorry. Let's walk back slowly."

She rose to walk back but only went a few steps. Then she swayed and cried out.

"Hold me, Franz! I feel faint."

He put his arms round her but only just in time. She had fainted and he felt the weight of her body in his arms, though not a very great weight.

He was alarmed. She lay with her head on his shoulder and he saw the whiteness of her face and lips.

"Magda!" he cried. "Magda!"

He laid her down on a weedy path and with a dirty handkerchief from his pocket dabbed her forehead which was wet with tiny beads of sweat. Soon she became conscious and her faintness passed.

"How silly of me!" she exclaimed. "Help me up, Franz."

"Can you walk?" he asked anxiously. "What made you go like that?"

"It's the German disease," she said, trying to smile with her white lips. "*Unterernährung*."

Undernourishment. Many German girls in Berlin were fainting like that, she told him. Franz put his arm about her—his unwounded arm—and walked slowly with her out of the Tiergarten.

"Come to my cellar," he said. "You need food. I'll find something."

She laughed at his diagnosis.

"Of course I need food! But I can't get as far as your beautiful cellar. I can't get farther than my dirty Bunker."

Her Bunker was quite close now.

"Will you get anything to eat down there?" asked Franz.

She told him that she had some slices of bread and a piece of cheese. She had saved them for her supper. And other people in the shelter would share some of their rations. They were always generous like that.

"Are you all right?" he asked when they reached the steps going down to the shelter.

"I feel much better," she told him.

She smiled and seemed to remember something.

"I didn't give you that kiss."

"No. I shall miss it."

"Another time. But kisses are a poor fare these days, and very cheap in Berlin."

She went down the steps. Franz noticed that a little colour had crept back to her face. For a few moments in the Tiergarten she had lain like a dead woman in his arms.

CHAPTER XXI

He met Ursel in the Grünewald. She called out to him.

"Franz! . . . Franz Reber!"

She ran towards him and flung her arms around him and kissed his cheek.

"How good to see you again," she exclaimed. "What have you been doing all this time?"

"And you?" he asked. "You look marvellous."

She was in a smartly cut frock and her complexion was not the grey pallor of the Berlin face.

"I'm working for an English officer," she told him. "Our house is now occupied. We have only three rooms left to us."

"You get food?" he asked. It was the inevitable question.

Ursel laughed.

"A little barter now and then. But it began only a few weeks ago. Before then we starved."

"And now?"

She looked mysterious as though hiding a secret but then blurted it out.

"One of the officers has come to a little arrangement. He's interested in the Black Market."

She laughed again.

"They're all in it! Officers and men."

"What kind of arrangement?" asked Franz.

Ursel lowered her voice and glanced over her shoulder as though she might be overheard.

"It began with cigarettes. I paid for them with a fur coat and a pair of field glasses belonging to my uncle. Hermann said I could have them for the sake of food. Now every week he gives us English rations in return for bits of jewellery belonging to my aunt and silver ornaments out of the cabinet. They would have been stolen anyhow. One of the sergeants took away the drawing-room clock under my very nose. When I grabbed his arm and said, 'What are you doing?' he said, 'We won the war, didn't we? Everything belongs to us, doesn't it?' "

"It's incredible!" exclaimed Franz. "The English? Where is their discipline?"

"Some of them are making fortunes on the Black Market," said Ursel. "And it's so easy for them when we're all starving and will give anything for a little food. But some of them are very nice. There's an English lieutenant in the house who gives me chocolate sometimes."

She seemed amused at the thought of this English lieutenant and blushed a little.

"With or without payment?" asked Franz.

Ursel gave a little laugh.

"Just a kiss now and then. It's not much to ask, is it?"

"Sometimes it means a lot," answered Franz. He thought of Magda and his desire to kiss her. It meant a lot to him.

"He's very nice-looking," said Ursel. "He has a tiny moustache and rose-red lips and brown eyes like a deer's eyes."

"He sounds detestable," said Franz. "Effeminate."

Ursel shook her head.

"No, he's extremely charming, I assure you."

"How's Hildegard?" asked Franz.

Hildegard, it seemed, was ill in bed. It was a bit serious. Aunt Tessa was getting anxious about her. She mentioned a frightening word. Tuberculosis. So many girls were going down with that. Many of Ursel's own friends. It was terrible.

"Come and see her," said Ursel. "Come and see Aunt Tessa. She often talks about you."

Franz went with her to the house in the Grünewald.

Some English officers were in the hall hanging up their belts before going into the dining-room where they had their mess. One of them smiled at Ursel. He had a tiny moustache above rose-red lips. It was obviously her lieutenant who handed out chocolate in return for a kiss.

"We live at the top of the house," said Ursel.

She led the way up and took him into a small room where Hildegard lay in bed. Frau von Grottenbach, whom he had known as Aunt Tessa, was there sitting by the bedside.

"An old friend to see you!" said Ursel.

Aunt Tessa flung her arms about him and kissed him on both cheeks as Ursel had done and Franz was touched by this greeting.

"Hildegard is not very well," said Frau von Grottenbach. "You feel tired, don't you, my darling?"

"Lazy!" said Hildegard with a smile.

She looked extraordinarily well. Her face was without the Berlin pallor and was flushed with the delicate colour of a rose petal. Her eyes were very bright. But she didn't seem to have much strength and could hardly lift her hand to greet Franz. She had a nasty cough, low and hollow.

Franz sat on the end of her bed and chatted with her. Ursel slipped out of the room. She had to do some work for the English colonel. Franz asked after Hilde and the two children who were now in Kaulbach near Munich. He heard the news about her father's arrest by the Americans and his imprisonment in a concentration camp

"He doesn't get enough to eat," said Aunt Tessa "They're starving him to death, after all their talk about Belsen and Buchenwald!"

Presently Hildegard turned her head to the pillow and seemed to fall asleep. Aunt Tessa put a finger to her lips and then beckoned Franz to come out of the room.

They tip-toed into the passage.

"How is she?" asked Franz in a low voice.

Aunt Tessa looked at him with tragic eyes.

"She's dying. The doctor says three months more perhaps. We haven't told Ursel."

"Oh God!" cried Franz.

"We starved," said Frau von Grottenbach. "Now we're getting some food. Ursel arranges that."

She took his hand and led him down the passage.

"You must come and see Elizabeth and Hermann."

They went into another room which was a bed-sitting-room.

"Here is our comrade who was with us on the roads from Königsberg," said Aunt Tessa. "We knew him then as Sergeant Reber."

Hermann rose and shook hands with him.

"We have heard about you so many times," said his mother.

Franz remembered the tragedy of the Baron von Meissner like his own father executed for the plot against Hitler, and he raised her hand to his lips with a sense of deep emotion.

"Germany sinks deeper into the abyss," said Hermann presently. "We're reduced to a struggle for animal existence."

"It's worse in the Russian zone," said his mother. "Terrible things are happening there."

"We are being crucified," said Franz. "One day we shall rise again perhaps. Doesn't one learn by sacrifice and pain? Mustn't one get down to the depths—this dark pit of ours—before one can reach up to a new philosophy of life? Otherwise all this has no meaning—all this agony. I'm trying to find some meaning."

His words seemed to startle Hermann.

"You talk like my father," he said. "I wish I could hold on to any such faith. Looking at this frightful world, this world of blood and torture and mass-starvation and devilish evil—I can't see any hope."

"I'm only wondering," said Franz. "I'm only groping my way like a drunken man. Sometimes I seem to look ahead a bit beyond this misery. It can't last for ever, can it? Things must get better, don't you think?"

"I see no reason to believe it," said Hermann with utter pessimism. "They may get worse. Civilization may perish like Germany. Hasn't it gone already over a large area of Europe?"

His mother spoke to Franz.

"What you have said is like striking a light in a dark cellar. Thank God you have said it."

Franz was abashed by those words.

"Forgive me!" he said. "It was only a cry of bewilderment. I know nothing. I've no lighted torch. Not even half an inch of candle."

"You're trying to find a light," said Hermann's mother, "and one day the candle will be lit—perhaps a flaming torch. If other young men like you grope towards the light my husband and his friends will not have died in vain. Talk to my Hermann who gives way to despair."

"I've nothing to say," said Franz. "I only blurted out things that haunt my mind."

Presently he took his leave. Hermann walked with him for some way.

"I must see more of you," he said. "You seem to be thinking things out."

Franz laughed and shrugged his shoulders.

"I'm no thinker. But it would be good if you would come round to my cellar now and then."

They separated. Hermann apologized for not coming farther. He felt weak about the legs. He felt like an old, old man, he said.

Darkness was creeping into the ruined streets of Berlin when Franz was walking down Unter den Linden on the Russian side of the Brandenburger Tor. A few lights gleamed from basements and cellars. A police-car had just passed with a screeching horn. A few shadowy forms hurried by and disappeared. Two figures stood in the archway. One was a Russian soldier. He was having some altercation with another man and suddenly seized him by the arm shouting out something in Russian. Franz heard some words in English.

"Let go, can't you! What the devil do you want?"

Coming closer Franz could see a young man in civilian clothes struggling with the Russian who struck a heavy blow at him in a staggering drunken way. The young man dodged it and hit the Russian full on the chin sending him lurching back, but he regained his feet and made a rush like a bull at his opponent. It was then that Franz came to the rescue. He put his foot out and the Russian went over sprawling heavily to the ground.

"Thanks very much," said the young man. "*Danke schön!* That fellow wanted my wrist-watch."

Franz spoke to him in bad English.

"It is good to run. We find ourselves in the Russian zone. Come quick."

They both started running. Behind them a rifle-shot rang out.

On the other side of the Brandenburger Tor Franz dragged the young Englishman behind a heap of rubble where they both fell.

"Excuse me!" said Franz. "It is good—it is better—to avoid trouble. The Russians are not always reasonable."

"They certainly aren't!" said the young Englishman with a laugh. "That fellow was a drunken brute. I'm much obliged to you for coming up at the nick of time."

"The nick of time," said Franz, "is a very good time. Excuse my English. I only learned it by reading. Have you read *David Copperfield* by your great author Charles Dickens?"

He could hear the light laugh of this Englishman though his face was hardly visible in the darkness behind the heap of rubble.

"Yes, I've read *David Copperfield*. But isn't this an odd place to discuss literature? Come and have a drink with me——"

"Where if you please?" asked Franz.

He found it exciting to be talking to this Englishman. He was the first to whom he had ever spoken. He felt no enmity towards him. He had no desire to kill him.

"There's an underground place round the corner. Rather a hot spot, but we can have a drink. What's your name, by the way? Mine is Julian Romilly."

"Mine is Franz Reber. I was a sergeant."

The Englishman laughed.

"I was a captain. Now I'm a civilian in the Allied Control. If you like we'll speak German but your English is remarkably good."

"You speak German?"

"*Nicht besonders gut, aber* . . ."

He spoke better German than Franz Reber's English.

Romilly had an electric torch and by its little circle of light they groped their way to a heap of ruin which had once been a Government office block.

"Here we are," said the Englishman presently.

He led the way down some steps and into a big basement room furnished with small tables and chairs. It was lit by electric lamps with pink shades.

There were several waiters in white jackets. One of them, the head waiter, came up and bowed to Romilly and presented him with a menu.

"We have excellent roast chicken tonight."

Julian Romilly glanced at Franz Reber with a look of inquiry. "Do we want to eat?"

He seemed to read Franz's face, thin and drawn. His glance took in the shabby figure of his new acquaintance in his old service uniform without badges.

He answered the head waiter.

"The roast chicken sounds good. But first of all two cocktails, please."

"Two Martinis?"

"Martini?" asked Romilly, looking at Franz Reber.

Franz felt ill-at-ease. He was conscious of his shabbiness in this place where two English officers sat with two German girls in evening frocks. Three other well-dressed people—English civilians—entered the basement room talking and laughing.

"I prefer not to eat," said Franz. "If you will excuse me."

"Oh, we had better eat something," answered Romilly. "They expect it. It's not too early."

He glanced at his wrist-watch and then laughed.

"I nearly lost that! Thanks to you I can still tell the time."

He knew the two people who had just come down and raised a hand to greet them.

"Hullo, Julian," said the English girl, waggling two fingers at him. She was tall and thin and unbeautiful with a voice too highly pitched in artificial gaiety.

"I'm dying for a cocktail," she told her friend, a serious looking young man with horn-rimmed glasses.

"I decline to let you die, dear lady," he answered. "Herr Ober!"

He snapped his fingers at the head waiter.

The two German girls with the English officers were drinking champagne. The long neck of the champagne bottle rose from a silver bucket. The English officers were talking to the girls in broken German. One of them was smoking a cigarette and for a moment she looked towards Franz and their eyes met. She smiled at him but he didn't return the smile.

'German girls earning their meal from their ex-enemies,' he thought. 'Who can blame them? And yet somehow I find it humiliating and a little shameful. I don't like this place. It's too much of a contrast with the starving refugees and all the misery in Berlin.'

The young Englishman was asking him a question.

"Where do you live in this devastated city?"

"In a cellar under my father's house in the Fasanenstrasse which is now in ruin, of course."

Julian Romilly looked at him across the little table. Franz knew that he was being scrutinized by this young Englishman who had a delicately cut face, almost feminine in its features and yet with some intellectual strength. He had shown courage when the Russian soldier had attacked him.

"Rather uncomfortable, no doubt," he said. "And the food situation is difficult for the Berliners."

"We starve," said Franz.

The young Englishman nodded.

"Not enough calories, I'm afraid."

"This place," said Franz, "must be supplied by the Black Market."

His new acquaintance smiled at this very obvious statement of truth.

"Of course! The Black Market flourishes. Have a cigarette?"

He opened a silver cigarette-case and pushed it over to Franz.

Franz hesitated and then refused politely.

"Cigarettes are the new currency," he said. "Your soldiers get rich on them, I'm told."

"Perfectly true," said Romilly. "It's a racket of the first water."

He used the word 'racket' which Franz had heard for the first time from Elsa.

"It's not very good for the prestige of England," said Franz. "Forgive me for saying that."

The young Englishman gave him a quick glance and laughed.

"Lots of Germans are up to their necks in it."

He did not pursue that subject but asked Franz what he had been before the War, and seemed interested to hear that he had been an art student in Munich. He became enthusiastic about the pictures he had seen in the Alte Pinakothek and astonished Franz by his knowledge of German painters. He mentioned Grünewald and Pacher.

"Marvellous!"

Franz observed him closely while he talked. He had beautiful hands unspoilt by any rough experience. He wore a suit of English cloth. There were gold links in his shirt-cuffs. He had, Franz thought, a kind of elegance in his civilian clothes. He spoke sometimes with a smiling cynicism, except when he talked about Art, and he spoke German remarkably well.

Franz faced his wing of chicken. He had eaten nothing all day but for some reason his stomach, or perhaps his mind, revolted against this food. On the way here, before the incident in Unter den Linden, he had passed a party of refugees dragging their feet wearily, overburdened by their baggage, sallow-faced, lean and hungry-looking. How could he sit in this over-heated room, too brilliantly lit, and find any appetite for this rich food? He noticed that his finger-nails were dirty and that his old tunic was stained. He sat with the plate in front of him pretending to eat but uncomfortable. This was an objectionable place, he thought. Those waiters bowing and scraping to the English officers and women had been German soldiers. Now they were fawning on their conquerors. But wasn't he doing the same? Wasn't he accepting food from an Englishman who was patronizing him, or, at least, giving him a meal because he had done him a small favour? But he had to admit that he was sitting next to a very pleasant young man who came up to his ideal of an English gentleman.

Other Englishmen and women had come into this restaurant. They all seemed to know each other. There were exchanges of "Hullo, old boy," "Hullo, my dear." The women tittered and laughed in high-pitched voices. "Good evening, Mary! . . . Good evening, Betty!" Two French officers arrived and sat at one of the little tables, then an American officer came in and ordered his meal and looked round the room until he met the smile of a German girl who was alone at another table. Presently he moved his place and sat opposite the girl, and ordered a bottle of wine for her.

The young Englishman seemed to be amused by the scene around him. Several times he raised his delicate hand to friends who greeted him.

"I'm afraid you don't like your chicken," he said after some time.

Franz felt his face flush.

"I have no appetite," he said. "Excuse me."

He had no appetite because he hated this hot room with its rose-coloured shades. It was a market-place in which German girls were selling themselves to the English and Americans. It was a place of degradation.

"Shall I order you something else?" asked the young Englishman.

"Pardon me," said Franz. "I'm putting you to shame because I'm badly dressed. Your friends don't like the look of me. I see their contempt. I see them whispering among themselves and smiling at you with raised eyebrows. Why did you ask me here?"

Julian Romilly glanced at him as though faintly surprised by this sudden emotion from his guest. He was surprised and a little amused perhaps.

"I owe you a debt," he answered. "It's quite likely you saved my somewhat worthless life. Don't worry about the people whom you call my friends. With few exceptions they have no intelligence."

"*Entschuldigen Sie*," said Franz. "You're very kind but I'm out of place here. My place is in a cellar with an iron bedstead and an oil-lamp. I feel more honest there as an ex-German soldier. I hope you understand and don't think me impolite."

Romilly flicked the ash off his cigarette and answered good-humouredly.

"Not at all!"

He referred for a moment to Reber's remark about being ill-dressed and tried to put him at ease.

"That uniform is all right here. What's the matter with it? I wasn't exactly elegant when I was a Desert Rat in Africa."

"You were in the North African campaign," asked Franz. "Against our General Rommel?"

He was astonished that this young Englishman with his delicate figure and features should have served as a soldier in the desert.

Romilly nodded.

"Until I was a prisoner of war in Oflag 6. That's where I learned German. It saved me from being bored to death behind barbed wire."

"You learned it very well," said Franz.

Romilly shook his head and smiled.

"Not too well! But it comes in useful now."

He saw that his guest was still distressed and hardly touching the food on his plate.

"Isn't it a pity to waste that food?" he asked. "It's an excellent chicken."

Franz was ravenously hungry. It was only pride in him which made him revolt against this food which would cost a lot of money in German marks. His pride broke down. The temptation was too great. He began to eat.

"What's the address of your cellar?" asked Romilly, who had

observed this surrender. "Perhaps you would let me come and sit on your iron bedstead one day."

Franz gave him his address on the Fasanenstrasse.

"For what purpose would you come?" he asked.

The young Englishman seemed amused by this blunt question.

"Oh, just a friendly visit. No sinister motive! As a matter of fact I'm interested in what Germans are thinking about just now —what's going on in their minds. I have the journalistic instinct."

"They're not thinking," said Franz. "Nothing is going on in their minds. They're only trying to get shelter, to get food, to keep warm, to find their lost relatives, to search for bits of furniture in the ruins, to adapt themselves to defeat. Presently they'll begin to think."

"And then?" asked Romilly. Perhaps he was not really interested. His glance travelled around the room and he smiled at a new arrival.

Franz paused before answering. There was not much left of the chicken on his plate. He decided to leave a bit lest he should appear too greedy. This young Englishman, he noticed, was not eating much.

"Then they'll think in many different ways, mostly foolish. Some will regret the Nazi regime, forgetting everything that was bad in it. Some will begin to plot for revenge forgetting where this war has led them. Some will search for a new hope and a new faith. I'm one of those."

"That's interesting," said Romilly, politely. "What kind of hope and what kind of faith?" There was a note of satire in his voice as though sceptical of faith and hope.

"We have to regain our soul," said Franz.

Romilly gave a light-hearted laugh.

"Oh well, we've all fallen pretty low I'm afraid."

"You are a philosopher?" asked Franz.

Romilly raised his hands and laughed.

"Good heavens, no! Nothing like that!"

'He's not serious,' thought Franz. 'He's mocking at me. I'm a fool to talk of serious things in a place like this. I wish I hadn't come.'

He saw that the young Englishman had lost interest in the conversation. He was looking towards the curtained door of the basement room and watching somebody coming in.

"That's a pretty lady," he said in a low voice. "Very charming, don't you think?"

Franz followed his glance. Through the curtain came a young woman in a black frock cut low at the neck. She was wearing little blue ear-rings. She stood there hesitating as though half afraid to come in. Her face was dead white except where she had touched it with rouge on her cheeks and lips. Her eyes seemed unnaturally bright and glittering but she looked round nervously like an animal walking warily out of darkness into light. Franz Reber knew her. It was Magda Hessell.

She left the curtain and walked farther into the room, looking for an empty table.

Franz spoke to the young Englishman.

"Excuse me! I must speak to that lady."

He left his chair and went quickly over to her.

"Magda!" he said in a whisper. "What are you doing here? *Um Gottes Willen!*"

She was startled to see him and her white face flushed.

"You here, Franz?"

"Why do you come here?" he asked. "This is a vile place."

She looked him in the eyes in a challenging way. The false smile left her face.

"I'm hungry. I want some food."

"Do you sell yourself in this market-place?" asked Franz, in a voice of horror. He had not blamed Elsa for giving a little cheap love in return for food. He had said that he was not a preacher of morality. He felt only pity for these girls. But Magda Hessell whom he had held in his arms, whom he had kissed when she lay asleep. He was staggered and horrified by her presence here.

"People are looking at us," she said.

The head waiter came up and spoke to them.

"This lady is joining your table?"

"No," said Franz. "I'm leaving with her."

"You're not finishing your dinner?" asked the head waiter. "Your English friend——"

The young Englishman stood at their side. Perhaps he had

guessed what was happening, or perhaps he was a connoisseur of women's beauty and liked the look of Magda Hessell.

"I should be delighted if this lady would join us," he said. "Perhaps you will introduce me."

"We must go," said Franz. "If you will excuse us——"

Romilly answered good humouredly.

"Oh, that would be a pity. It would spoil my evening."

He turned to Magda with a smile.

"Do please join us. My name is Romilly. Your friend helped me out of a tight corner tonight."

"Thank you," said Magda. "I shall be very glad to dine with you. I am Magda Hessell."

"Fräulein Hessell?"

"Frau Otto Hessell."

"I'm delighted to meet you," said Romilly. "Let's go back to my table."

He spoke a word to the head waiter.

"The menu, Herr Ober."

Franz followed the young Englishman and Magda to the table. He felt sick. His heart felt as though it had been stabbed.

"You know this place?" asked Romilly when they were seated.

Magda answered him after a moment's hesitation.

"I've been here once before."

"They provide excellent food," said Romilly.

Magda smiled at him. She was acting a part, thought Franz. Her smile was artificial.

"One has to pay for it, of course. In this life one has to pay for everything, doesn't one?"

Romilly nodded and laughed.

"That's one of the snags. But we'll forget that. You will take a glass of wine, *gnädige Frau*? *Nuits St. George*. Very good Burgundy."

"Thank you," said Magda.

Franz remained silent. So she had been here before. That also was terrible. He felt his hands trembling. His nerves were on edge. He had loved her. He had held this woman in his arms.

The young Englishman had very charming manners. He was talking to Magda in an easy natural way as if he had known her for some time. At first Magda only answered with a few words but presently, perhaps because of the wine, she responded more easily and smiled less nervously.

"It's astonishing how the German girls turn out so smartly," said Romilly. "It's difficult to imagine that they come up from over-crowded basements in a city of ruins. I must say I admire them."

"It needs courage," said Magda. "It's the struggle for life."

Romilly agreed but took a less tragic view.

"Some of them seem quite happy. I heard a group of young people laughing in the Tiergarten yesterday as though they hadn't a care in the world."

"They're the very young ones," said Magda. "The very young adapt themselves to everything and make a joke of it. Because they're alive they laugh. Those of us who are not so young find life less amusing."

Romilly was studying her face and her thin white shoulders.

"A sense of humour helps a good deal," he said. "Perhaps the English have more sense of humour than the Germans, though I ought not to say that."

Magda answered with a note of bitterness in her voice though her lips smiled.

"The English have enough to eat. It makes a difference, don't you think? A sense of humour is difficult to keep if one is starving. You think we Germans ought to laugh and be gay?"

Romilly smiled at her for this unanswerable retort.

"That would be expecting too much."

"We're also the Defeated," said Magda. "Germany is occupied by foreign troops. That doesn't make us very happy. In the Russian zone—why did you allow them to get into Berlin?—horrible things are happening."

Romilly did not dispute these horrible things. Perhaps he had heard of them all.

"Some of the Russians are not highly civilized," he agreed. "One of them wanted to have my wrist-watch this evening. Your friend here helped to rescue it."

Magda looked at Franz but he avoided her eyes and she knew that he was angry with her. She had known that by the look of horror in his eyes when he had seen her come into this restaurant. But she did not know what was in his mind at that moment.

'She has come to this place like a street-walker,' he was thinking. 'The wife of Otto Hessell is degrading herself to the level of a slut. A week ago I held her in my arms. A week ago I desired her kisses.'

"One day," he heard her say, "there will be trouble between Russia and the Anglo-Saxons. That's inevitable. Then there will be another war. Perhaps England will be occupied by the Russians. Then they will know the meaning of it."

Romilly smiled at this frightful prophecy.

"If that happens it will be the last war. It will wipe out this so-called civilization."

"That also is inevitable," said Magda. "The atom bomb will see to that."

She seemed to be talking seriously. She seemed to have forgotten the reason for coming to this restaurant. She was not seductive in her manner to this young Englishman. She did not beguile him by languishing looks or the tricks of the trade. She was behaving like a lady, thought Franz, who was listening with a sense of anguish.

Romilly laughed in his quiet easy way. He too was behaving like an English gentleman.

"Unpleasant thought! Let's talk about something pleasant."

Magda raised her eyebrows. She was playing a part, thought Franz. She was like an actress in a stage play. She was doing it marvellously well. What was happening behind the mask of her face? What was happening in her soul? She had looked frightened when she first came in.

"Can you suggest anything pleasant?" she asked. "Does it exist?"

Romilly looked round the room as though searching for something pleasant. The German girls were getting a little intoxicated and laughing in shrill voices. The American officer had ordered another bottle of champagne. Other German girls had come in. The English people were talking at the tables. The two French officers were having a political argument.

"It's not too bad here," he suggested. "This wine is quite good. That pêche Melba is excellent, don't you think? This is a pleasant meeting across a little table. I find it a charming interlude. A cigarette?"

Magda took a cigarette and Romilly lighted it for her.

"Those blue ear-rings are very seductive," said Romilly. "Chinese?"

Magda touched one of her ear-rings.

"Italian. My father gave them to me on my twenty-first birthday. He was German Consul in Naples. I was with him there for five years."

"I was in Florence with my mother for a time," said Romilly.

They talked about Italy as though it were Paradise, and Franz, still sullen and silent, noticed that Magda became more natural and that her eyes brightened and that she was not so dead white under her rouge. She had eaten a good meal. She had drunk two glasses of wine. Her memories of Italy—Florence, Venice, Rome, Sienna—seemed to have blotted out her misery and brought back a brief vision of the joy and beauty of life.

Once or twice Romilly tried to bring Franz into the conversation but without success. Did he guess what emotion was raging in the mind of this ex-soldier sitting next to him? If he guessed he did not show it by the flicker of an eyelid.

It was ten o'clock when Magda gave a kind of laughing sigh.

"I must go back to my Bunker or I shall be locked out. I feel like Cinderella after dancing with the fairy prince. The clock struck twelve. She must go back to the cinders and the rats."

Romilly looked surprised and disappointed.

"Oh, it's early yet! Two hours before the clock strikes twelve. Do stay a little longer—much longer."

"I must go. Franz will take me back. Thank you for my dinner."

She held out her hand and Romilly took it and raised it to his lips as though she were a princess.

While he held her hand she gave a little uneasy laugh.

"Didn't we say something about having to pay for everything in life? I'm afraid I'm cheating. Forgive me."

"I hope we meet again," he answered. "But I'm not a Shylock. *Gute Nacht, gnädige Frau. Auf Wiedersehen.*"

"*Auf Wiedersehen.* Will you come with me, Franz?"

Franz shook hands coldly with his host and said *Danke schön.* Then he left the restaurant with Magda. He was aware that the other people were watching them. Magda Hessell with her blue ear-rings seemed to have made a sensation among them. He had seen that while she sat at table with the young Englishman—because she was sitting at his table. When they had passed beyond the curtain one of his friends spoke in a high clear voice plainly audible.

"Who's your pretty lady, Julian? A new one, isn't she?"

They went up the steps into the darkness and Franz felt Magda's hand take his arm. They walked on silently for a few moments and then he stopped and he felt her hand drop away from his arm.

"Magda," he said in a low voice. "Why did you go to that place? Why did you go there once before?"

"It's quite a pleasant place," she answered. "What's wrong with it?"

She was trying to brazen it out, he thought.

"Why did you go there?" he asked again. "Alone!"

"It's not too bad," she said. "There were nice people there. Your English friend is very charming, don't you think?"

"Magda," said Franz, drawing a deep breath and struggling to speak quietly, "you know that place isn't respectable. Women don't go there alone except for one purpose. Those other German girls were selling themselves for the price of a meal."

"Of course," said Magda. "Do you think I don't know?"

"Have you become one of those?" asked Franz, harshly. His voice softened and he gave a broken cry. "Oh, Magda!"

"I'm no better than they are," said Magda.

He could see the whiteness of her face through the darkness and the glitter of her eyes.

"Why should I be? I live in an air-raid shelter as many of them do. I'm dragged down to the same level. I have the same kind of body. I starve, as they do."

"You were Otto Hessell's wife," said Franz. "When I saw you come into that place alone something broke inside me."

"I was Otto Hessell's wife," she answered, "but that was in a different world. Otto is dead. That world is dead."

They were still standing there in the darkness. A group of people hurried by. Franz could see the dim beauty of her face and hear a kind of sob in her voice.

"Magda," he said more gently, "I've no right to reproach you."

"No," she said harshly. "You've no right. I'm free to do what I like. Have you no pity?"

"I shed tears of blood for you," he told her.

She had a change of mood unless she was acting again.

"You make too much fuss about this, Franz. Why do you make a tragedy of it? Those English women—how ugly they were—are quite respectable and tonight we met a very nice English gentleman who liked my blue ear-rings and talked about Italy. What harm has been done?"

He was silent. He knew this defence was false. She had gone there alone to be picked up like a common slut of the streets. But now he too had a change of mood. His anger ebbed away. She had asked 'have you no pity?' His heart was drowned in pity which was partly self pity because he loved her.

He told her that.

"Magda, my dear, I love you. Don't go with that Englishman. Starve with me if we have to starve. Come to my cellar and I'll take care of you."

She caught hold of his arm and tucked her hand through it and laughed a little in a strained voice.

"Franz, it's not my fault if you love me. I haven't been the temptress, have I? We were just comrades, weren't we? Don't spoil our comradeship by getting emotional. If you want my kisses you can have them, but love in a cellar doesn't help very much if we starve there. I should only drag you down. Let me be free, Franz. Let me make my own friends and make my own way of escape."

"What way of escape?" he asked. "By selling yourself to some immoral Englishman?"

"Mr. Romilly was charming," she said. "He kissed my hand in the old German style as though I were a princess."

"Curse the fellow," said Franz. "I wish I had never met him. I wish I hadn't saved him from that Russian."

His own sense of fairness rebuked these words as soon as he had spoken them.

"I've nothing against him really. I admit he behaved very well."

"Take me home, Franz," said Magda. "It's late and I shall be locked out." She gave a long-drawn sigh and cried out, "Oh, I'm tired! I've no strength in my bones."

They walked on to her air-raid shelter by the Tiergarten and she clung to his arm as though she needed support. At its entrance she held up her face.

"Kiss me, Franz, if you like. I won't go to that place again—alone. I'll be very discreet!"

She gave a laugh in which there was a little mockery.

He kissed her and held her until she pulled herself away and went down the steps into the darkness of the air-raid shelter.

They were beginning to shift the rubble away in the streets, or at least to tidy it up, numbering blocks of any size. Franz volunteered for this work but after a few weeks had to abandon it because it was beyond his strength. Potato soup was not a good ration for hard manual toil, especially for a man with a smashed arm. He had discovered also by meeting a friend employed in the Deutsche Bank that there was money waiting for him there bequeathed by his father. There would be certain legal formalities necessary before he could draw it and a heavy percentage of it would be seized by the Occupying Powers. But the Bank might advance small sums on the security. This news excited him.

'I shall be able to get food for Magda,' he thought. 'It will save her from humiliation. It will give her new strength, and take away her pallor.'

He did not see her for some time and was anxious about her. She might be ill. When he had taken her home that evening her footsteps had dragged. She had leaned against him as though exhausted. He tried to find her in the Tiergarten but she did not come to sit on the block of stone near the broken statues of the Siegesallee.

He caught a glimpse of her one afternoon in the Leipzigerplatz, and his heart turned to stone. She was walking with the young Englishman, Romilly. They were going into some underground café which had a painted sign in the street outside. Romilly said something to her and she laughed and shook her head. Then they both went in and Franz stood for a moment with a heavy frown on his face, motionless until he was jostled by passers-by —more of the refugees who came into Berlin day after day, week after week, month after month, laden with bundles and luggage in exile from their homesteads in East Prussia which had been given to the Poles or from the other side of the Oder in the Russian Zone.

So Magda was meeting that young Englishman. 'Why not?' he asked himself, trying to stifle the pang of jealousy, trying to be reasonable and fair-minded. If that fellow behaved like an English gentleman there was no harm in it. Women were no longer kept in harems. He mustn't behave like a Moroccan Sheikh. He mustn't think dark thoughts because Magda went into a café with an English friend at four o'clock in the afternoon. It was perfectly natural and innocent. In any case he had no right to interfere. Magda claimed her liberty. He had no claim upon her beyond his love, beyond his desire to help her and be her comrade. So he argued with himself, but could not kill the little devil Doubt which gibbered inside his mind.

She was looking ill, he thought. When she turned her face to that young Englishman and smiled and shook her head, he had seen the thin line of her neck, the thinness of her body, the pallor of her skin, like old ivory. It was only the people who were getting food parcels from relatives and friends in America who lost this pallor. One could always tell.

'If I can get that money from the Bank,' thought Franz, 'I'll feed her up. I'll take her to Black Market restaurants. She won't need to accept the Englishman's invitations. Perhaps, after all, he is just a good-natured fellow. Why not be friends with him?"

But the little devil, Doubt, gibbered again.

One evening he was in the cellar with his comrade Baümer, who was sitting on a low stool near the stove with his hands between his knees. Franz was making a charcoal sketch of him by the light of the oil-lamp which revealed the man's sharp cheek-bones and touched his straw-coloured beard, and made a deep shadow on one side of his face. Neither of them had spoken for half an hour when they heard somebody coming down the stone steps.

"It's not Elsa," said Baümer. "She wouldn't be back so early."

"May I come in?" asked a man's voice, speaking in German with an English accent.

Franz put his drawing on one side and stood up, recognizing Romilly's voice.

"*Herein!*"

Romilly pushed his way past the curtain and entered the dim room.

"Do you mind my coming?" he asked.

"It's good of you to come," said Franz, who had once cursed him to Magda and then withdrawn the curse. "We don't live in luxury, as you see."

"That's all right," said Romilly. He glanced round the cellar with smiling eyes, and then glanced at Baümer who had remained seated.

"Konrad Baümer," said Franz. "My comrade here."

Baümer rose slowly but did not hold out his hand.

Romilly nodded to him and looked round for somewhere to sit.

"Any room on the iron bedstead?" he asked.

"The best place perhaps," answered Franz.

Romilly sat down holding a black felt hat and a crooked stick.

Baümer watched him as if he might have been studying a rare species of the animal world.

Romilly glanced at the charcoal drawing which Franz had dropped to the stone floor.

"May I see?"

"It's nothing," said Franz. "A rough sketch."

Romilly picked it up and studied it attentively with one quick look at Baümer.

"Remarkably good!" he said. "Very strong indeed, the Rembrandt effect."

Inwardly Franz was pleased with this praise but he shrugged his shoulders and repeated words he had spoken before.

"It's nothing."

"I'm fond of drawings and sketches," said Romilly. "Sometimes they're so much better than finished work. I once saw a lot of drawings by Leonardo da Vinci. They're in Windsor Castle, in England."

Franz Reber nodded.

"I've heard of them. I've seen reproductions."

"There are some fine Rembrandt drawings in the British Museum," said Romilly.

He talked for some time about pictures and drawings and seemed to know a lot about Art.

"I confess I'm not much of a modernist," he said. "I abhor Picasso and Matisse."

"They have their value," said Franz.

Romilly challenged him with a laugh.

"What value, except decadence?"

"Decadence may have a value," said Franz. "All art reveals the spirit of the time. Picasso represents chaos and lawlessness and revolt."

"It's all very disgusting," said Romilly. "It's also a pose to shock the bourgeois mind."

"No, no!" said Franz, hurriedly.

They had an argument on the subject, modern versus academic art. Franz spoke with more heat than was quite polite but the young Englishman remained good-humoured and spoke always with a touch of humour and satire which Franz found annoying. Art, he thought, could not be treated flippantly.

It was Baümer who intervened and spoke for the first time.

"It amuses me to hear this argument in a cellar under the ruins."

He gave a harsh laugh and looked from Franz to Romilly.

"What amuses you?" asked Romilly politely.

"It's an argument about unreality. You talk about pictures when most of them have been destroyed or will be destroyed. Here in Berlin pictures used to hang on the walls. Now there are no walls! When the Atom bomb blasts everything off the earth, including the painters as well as the pictures, there'll be no more argument."

Romilly laughed again. He refused to envisage complete annihilation.

"There are still many pictures left," he said, "and a new age will produce artists of genius. We must prevent the Atom War."

Those last words seemed to strike the two Germans into silence. They bent their heads and seemed to be thinking very deeply. It was Franz who answered first.

"I agree. But how?"

"I have an idea," said Romilly lightly, "—it may be quite wrong of course—that the last war has been fought because no nation will dare to risk atomic warfare."

Baümer disagreed.

"The Russians will risk it when they discover the secret and make a mass production of atomic bombs larger and better than the American types."

Romilly laughed involuntarily.

"Do you think mutual extinction would attract them?"

"It's possible," said Baümer after a pause, "that you are right in saying the Atom bomb may never be used. That's not because the Russian leaders would hesitate to use it, but because they'll conquer the world without it. Communism is even more deadly than the Atom bomb and equally destructive of Art."

Romilly raised his eyebrows with his superior satirical look.

"You think Communism will conquer the world?"

"Of course."

Romilly shook his head.

"Western civilization is already putting up barriers."

"Barriers?" asked Baümer contemptuously. "Even now they would be swept down like straws if the Russians put on their boots and marched westwards. Who could resist them? Not the French. Not the English. Not the defeated Germans, disarmed by their conquerors."

The young Englishman made a gesture as though sweeping away that argument.

"I'm still hoping that Russia will co-operate in establishing world peace."

Baümer stared at him and laughed harshly again.

"A delusion! They'll never abandon their religion. They're like the Mohammedans. And it has a lure for the modern mind. We shall have to be converts to Communism or be shot in the back of the head after being tortured a bit if we resist."

Franz intervened between Baümer and Romilly.

"Some of us Germans know too much of what is going on in Russia."

"Many of us Germans don't know," said Baümer stubbornly, "or if they know they like it. Many Germans will see that an acceptance of Communism and a linking up with Russia will give them power again and revenge."

"I see no sign of it," said Romilly, in his mild tolerant way.

"It's for you to decide," said Baümer.

"Me?" asked Romilly with a look of amused surprise.

"You English and the Americans. If you keep us down in these cellars too long, if you keep us hungry, if you give us no peace and no hope, our people will stretch out their hands to the Russians and say, 'We're with you, Herr Stalin. Give us the hammer and sickle.'"

Franz looked at his comrade with astonishment. He had never spoken like that before. He had never heard him argue like that.

"Baümer," he said, "you're talking like a lunatic."

"I am a lunatic," said Baümer. "I've told you so many times. I have bad dreams."

Romilly laughed quietly.

"That's a very bad dream! For a moment it gave me a touch of gooseflesh."

Franz was listening towards the curtain.

"Someone else is coming," he said. "We have a reception tonight."

It was a woman's voice this time which said, "May I come in?"

It was Magda Hessell who drew the curtain on one side and stood there smiling. Her eyes glistened in a dead white face touched by a little rouge.

"*Lieber Gott!*" exclaimed Franz, in a low voice.

"I thought I would pay you a visit—without invitation."

She was in the same black frock cut low and square at the neck. Perhaps it was her only evening frock. This time she was not wearing her blue ear-rings. Her gaze fluttered over to the young Englishman.

"You here?" she asked.

"Very luckily," he answered. "How delightful to meet you again!"

He went forward and kissed her hand as he had done in the restaurant.

Franz looked at them both suspiciously. He was convinced that they had made a rendezvous here. Somehow they had known that they would meet here. The sharp knife of jealousy stabbed his heart.

"May I sit down?" asked Magda. "Am I breaking up a bachelor party?"

"There's the iron bedstead," said Franz.

She glanced at Baümer expecting to be introduced.

He introduced himself.

"Konrad Baümer. A lunatic and dreamer of bad dreams."

"They couldn't be worse than the bad reality," said Magda.

She sat on the iron bedstead next to Romilly with whom she exchanged a glance, a secret glance, as Franz saw, or thought he saw.

"We were talking about Art," said Romilly. "We had an exciting argument."

"Oh, a pity I wasn't here," cried Magda. "I should have been on your side."

"Which side is that?" asked Romilly.

"The side of Academic Art."

"How do you know?"

"You're an Englishman. All Englishmen dislike change and modernity and revolutionary experiment. So I've read in German books."

Romilly denied this diagnosis of the English character.

"Quite untrue. We adapt ourselves to new ideas very readily."

"I can hardly believe that," said Magda. "You believe in the old traditions. You've kept your King and your aristocracy."

"It's a new aristocracy with Labour peers," he told her.

They had a little fencing with words. Then Magda turned to Franz, not wishing perhaps to leave him out of the conversation too long.

"This is a very superior cellar! It's luxury compared with my dirty Bunker."

"We're lucky here," said Franz, gloomily.

He was angry with her for coming when Romilly was there—coming because Romilly was there. He was almost certain of that. Jealousy gnawed at him until he rebuked himself. There seemed to be nothing vicious about this young Englishman. In any case Magda must follow her own Destiny. He couldn't behave like a cave-man.

"We must get you out of that Bunker," said Romilly. "It's too dreadful to think of your being there."

"There are hundreds of thousands like me," said Magda. "It's the Berlin way of life."

"You are different," said Romilly.

"Not in the least, I assure you. But of course if you can find me a spacious apartment——"

She laughed at this preposterous dream.

Presently Franz interrupted them.

"I could make you a little soup. It's all I can do in the way of hospitality."

"How good of you!" exclaimed Romilly. "But I haven't come to eat your food. Won't you come and dine with me? I know a little place, quite respectable."

It was Magda who accepted his invitation. She pleaded with Franz to go with her but he refused sulkily, though inside himself he was tempted. When he saw them going up the steps together he felt strangled by jealousy. If Baümer hadn't been there he would have wept.

"That Englishman has taken a fancy to your lady friend," said Baümer. "Are you going to break your heart about it?"

He grinned over his bowl of soup.

"I've other things to think about," said Franz, lying to his friend and partly to himself.

"Why think?" said Baümer jeeringly. "I've asked you that question before."

Franz was silent and after a while Baümer spoke again.

"This soup is very warming to the belly. Why don't you get on with it?"

Franz had no appetite. His mind had followed Romilly and Magda. They would be sitting in a restaurant together. They would be talking and laughing. Perhaps he would take her home with him that night. That would be her way of escape.

After her first visit to his cellar Magda came again one evening. Baümer and the two girls were out and Franz was half asleep when he heard her voice.

"Are you there, Franz?"

He sprang up and went towards her.

"Come in and stay," he said. "Don't go away again."

She looked round the damp dark cellar.

"Very tempting. But what about food?"

"I'm getting some money," said Franz. "It's in the Bank. I might get it soon. And I'll get a job somehow."

"What kind of job?" asked Magda.

"In the market perhaps. As a porter. Fifteen marks a day."

"Just enough to keep you alive. Not enough for two. I can get you better work than that, Franz."

"You?" he asked, showing his astonishment.

She smiled at him again. There was a little excitement in her eyes.

"Mr. Romilly admired your drawing, Franz. He wants you to do a sketch of me. He would pay you for it. Then he could get you some commissions."

Franz stared at her suspiciously.

"When did he tell you that?"

She hesitated for a moment and then answered:

"I went to his rooms last night. He was very charming."

Franz caught hold of her arm in a tight grip.

"Magda! What's that man playing about with you for? Why did you go to his rooms? These Englishmen don't give anything for nothing."

He saw her face flush and she answered him angrily.

"I can do what I like. You've no right to say such things."

He let go of her arm and stared at her silently for a moment. She was looking ill and worn and his anger was disarmed by a sense of pity.

"No. I've no right, except that of friendship. Doesn't that mean anything to you?"

"I shouldn't be here unless it meant something to me," she answered.

She sat on his iron bedstead and looked round the cellar again.

"Franz," she said. "I want you to be reasonable."

"In what way?"

"I don't want you to lose your head about me."

"My heart," he said. "It's lost."

"No!" she answered. "We can't live on dreams. And anyhow you're no longer a jealous boy. Haven't you been through frightful things? Aren't we both dragged down to the very depths?"

"In the depths," said Franz, "love between you and me would give a little warmth to life, some radiance in this darkness."

She gave a laugh of mockery and impatience.

"How old-fashioned! It's the sentimentality of the days before the war. You're a sentimentalist, Franz. I thought you were a philosopher, and a bit of a saint."

"My philosophy breaks down when I'm with you," he told her. "I'm jealous of that damned Englishman, and I'm no saint."

"You might at least be grown-up—a man and not a sulky boy."

He felt a little guilty. Her words and challenge had touched him. Perhaps he was behaving like a boy of eighteen instead of as a man who had waded through blood and horror.

"That young Englishman," she said, "behaves like a gentleman. He is a gentleman. He hasn't asked for anything—yet."

"Why did you go to his rooms?" asked Franz.

She shrugged her thin shoulders and gave a long drawn sigh as though very tired. She looked very tired.

"Do you live in the eighteenth century?"

"He's English and you're German," said Franz. "The English treat German girls as cheap goods."

"Oh well, if you want to know I wasn't alone in his rooms, though I wouldn't have been worried about that," said Magda. "He introduced me to his friends. We had a little party. There were two others there—an English officer and his wife. You see how wrong you are—how very foolish, Franz! Herr Romilly wants to make a friend of you. He thinks you have a great talent. He wants you to do that sketch of me."

"If I do a sketch of you," said Franz, "I shall keep it for myself."

"You're throwing away a chance," she told him. "You might earn your living as an artist. Herr Romilly wants you to do sketches of some of his friends."

Franz was silent for a little while. It would be wonderful if he could earn a living as an artist. It would be better than clearing rubble from the streets, or being hired as a porter in the markets.

"If I could believe that fellow was an honourable man," he said, "I might think about it."

Magda smiled in her ironical way.

"Honourable? How do I know? He has very good manners. He belongs to a good family in England."

"How do you know that?"

"His friends told me so when he left the room last night to make some coffee."

"That doesn't make any difference," said Franz. "Good families don't possess a monopoly of morals."

Magda's eyes were roving and she asked a question with half a laugh.

"Any food, Franz?"

He looked round and shook his head dolefully. "Only some stale bread and some cabbage soup."

An idea came to him suddenly.

"I might do a bit of looting. Those girls who sleep behind the curtain bring back English rations. Elsa wouldn't mind——"

He strode behind the curtain carrying the oil-lamp and leaving Magda in darkness.

On the shelf above Elsa's bed were two or three tins. One of them was labelled *Spam*. He knew the meaning of that strange word. Elsa had opened a tin of the same kind one evening. It was when Baümer hadn't had anything to eat all day.

He brought it back and said, "This is marvellous."

Magda's eyes gleamed but she hesitated.

"Is it quite fair, Franz? Isn't it like thieving?"

"It is thieving," he admitted carelessly. "But Elsa is a friend of mine. I can put it all right with her."

He opened the tin, spread a newspaper on a small table, pulled up two chairs and laid the table while Magda warmed up the cabbage soup on the oil-stove.

"What about putting this meat in the soup?" she asked. "Wouldn't it be rather delectable?"

"A Lucullan feast!" exclaimed Franz.

They sat down opposite each other. The dim light of the oil-lamp touched Magda's hair and revealed the sharpness of her cheekbones and the thin lines of her neck.

"This is good!" she cried.

"As good as dining with that Englishman?"

"Almost!" she answered teasingly. "But no wine on the table, Franz!"

"The wine of love," he answered.

"Thin stuff!" she exclaimed in her mocking way.

She stayed talking after the meal until she drooped like a withered flower.

"Stay here tonight," said Franz. "Don't go back to that old Bunker. You can sleep on the iron bedstead."

"And you?"

"On the floor at your side," he told her. "Baümer dosses down over there. The two girls will be back late. They're dancing in some underground place with English soldiers."

Once or twice Magda said, "I ought to go."

"Don't go!"

Several times she shut her eyes as he talked to her.

"I'm sleepy," she admitted. "I'm as tired as death."

Then at last she surrendered to his plea.

"Forgive me if I lie down, Franz."

He put his arm about her and helped her to lie down on the iron bedstead, covering her with his own blanket. That night he would have to sleep without a blanket.

She slept almost at once and he sat on one of the kitchen chairs watching her. Her dark hair looked black against the tattered cushion covered with dirty red silk. He studied the lines of her face lying sideways. He thought again that she was of the Leonardo type. He would like to do a head of her in oils but that would cost money and in any case oil colours were unprocurable in Berlin.

Somebody came down the stone steps. It was Elsa. She pulled the curtain on one side and came into the cellar rather breathlessly.

"A military policeman came after me," she said. "I had to run."

Suddenly she saw Magda lying on the iron bedstead.

"Who's that?" she asked in astonishment.

"A friend of mine," said Franz. "Keep quiet. She's asleep."

"Mother of God!" exclaimed Elsa, who had been a good Catholic but was not so good now.

She seemed annoyed and even angry.

"Can't we keep this place to ourselves? Are you going to bring your women here?"

"I don't like that way of putting it," said Franz. "She is a lady—Frau Magda Hessell. I want you to be kind to her."

"Oh you do, do you? I thought you were a saint, but I suppose you're just like other men."

"Be quiet," said Franz, in a low voice. "Don't wake her up."

"It's damn' silly bringing her here," said Elsa, sulkily.

She flung herself through the curtain which screened off her part of the cellar and lit her oil-lamp. Franz could see its glow through the thin bit of chintz. A few minutes later she came out again with a furious look.

"Somebody has stolen a tin of Spam. Who did that, I'd like to know."

"I did," said Franz. "You're always so generous I knew you wouldn't mind. You get so much now from those English friends of yours."

"Did you feed your woman on it?" asked Elsa, glaring at him fiercely.

He had never known her like that. She had always been so gay and good natured. What had happened to her? What had turned her suddenly into a little tigress?

"Don't call her my woman," he said. "I came with her from Königsberg. She's a refugee. She starves here in Berlin."

Elsa gave a shrill laugh.

"Let her do as I do! Wasn't I starving? Let her go on the streets."

Franz was stricken into silence. Magda had gone into that restaurant to sell herself. She was no better than this girl who made no secret of her relations with young English soldiers, those boys of eighteen who blushed when she kissed them.

"I pity all women in this tragic city," he said. "We're all in the dark pit together. We can't blame each other or hate each other. We can't escape from the evil Destiny which has overtaken Germany. We're all trapped. We're all like rats in the underworld. Only the spirit will make us different from the rats. I'm sorry about the tin of food, I oughtn't to have taken it."

"Oh, shut up!" she said angrily. "You talk like a Carmelite monk with that woman lying on your bed. You're a hypocrite and a liar. You're no better than the rest of us. Save your own soul first, can't you?"

She dashed her flimsy curtain on one side and then pulled it behind her with an angry tug, shutting herself off from his vision.

Magda had not stirred during this talk. She was sleeping heavily as though she had been drugged.

Elsa had called him a hypocrite and a liar and in his queer introspective way he wondered how much truth there was in that portrait of him. Had she torn down a veil, hiding his hypocrisy? Did this girl in her rage see through him as he failed to see himself?

'She may be right,' he thought, as he sat there on the kitchen chair a yard away from the iron bedstead where Magda was asleep.

'My love for Magda fills me with jealousy and desire. I talk about the spirit but I'm becoming an animal. I robbed that girl's food. Presently I might kill a man or rob him on a dark night if I get a bit more hungry or want to feed Magda. I live in the underworld and I'm being dragged down to the morality of a cellar rat. "Save your own soul first," she said. Have I any soul to save? Isn't it an illusion, this belief in a soul? Aristotle believed in something like a soul and something like God, but he didn't live in the ruins of Berlin with an empty belly and a hungry heart.'

Erike came down the steps and entered the cellar.

"It's dark tonight," she said. "I went to a cinema with a boy friend."

She didn't even notice Magda but said 'Good night' and went beyond the curtain. He could hear Elsa whispering to her. Presently Erike drew the curtain on one side and looked towards the iron bedstead and gave a little mocking laugh. Then the curtain hid her again.

Baümer came in and sat down heavily to take off his boots.

"Don't make a row," said Franz. "Magda is here. She's asleep."

Baümer looked at the iron bedstead, peering through the semi-darkness. Then he gave a quiet laugh.

"The Sleeping Beauty! Berlin is like a fairy tale. One never knows what's going to happen next in this romantic city!"

He was very decent about it—he was always decent—and lay down on his mattress without making a noise. Franz slept next to the iron bedstead on the stone floor of his father's cellar.

He had a scene with Elsa when Magda had left next morning. She was still sullen and angry and answered him rudely when he apologized again for taking her tin of meat.

"I didn't think you'd begrudge it," he said. "You've always

been so comradely. You quarrelled with me once when I refused to share your gifts because they came from English soldiers who had no right to give them."

She became very red in the face and went towards the door, then suddenly turned on him.

"Do you think I begrudge it to you? You can take everything you like."

"Well then——"

He couldn't understand her fury because he had taken one tin.

"You didn't take it for yourself. You took it for that woman. I don't hand it out to stray cats."

He was silent for a moment and then some glimmering of the real truth came to him, and he laughed uneasily.

"You're not jealous of her, are you? You don't think——"

Her voice rose to a shrill tone.

"Why do you bring her here to spoil everything? Haven't we been happy in this cellar by ourselves? Haven't we all been good comrades after that beast Winkelnkempler went away?"

"Yes," said Franz. "You've kept a brave spirit, Elsa. You've been a gay little comrade in dark days."

"And now you bring in that white-faced woman. She's a lady of course, and I'm only a little slut. If you bring her here again I'll scratch her face. She won't look like a lady after I've done with her."

Franz went across to her and took her arm and pulled her towards him.

"You little fool!" he said laughing at her. "There are no differences of class in this cellar. We're all in the dirt together. We're like people shipwrecked on a desert island. Germany is shipwrecked. We're just struggling to keep alive. That's not a time for jealousies and quarrels."

Elsa began to cry. A hot tear fell on his hand as he held her against his body.

"I don't want anybody to come and spoil things," she cried. "I loved you because you seemed better than other men. I felt like Mary Magdalene when Jesus spoke to her. Now you've let me down by bringing a strange woman and letting her sleep on your own bed. It was I who loved you first."

"Elsa!" exclaimed Franz. "You're talking nonsense. For

God's sake be sensible. Haven't we been good comrades here? You've said so yourself. Nothing is changed because Magda Hessell has spent a night with us."

"Tell me you don't love her," cried Elsa.

Franz hesitated. He didn't want to lie to this girl who had called him a liar and a hypocrite. He didn't want to lie to himself.

"You're ridiculous," he said with a harsh laugh. "You haven't spoken a single word to her. What makes you think I'm in love with her?"

"I saw it in your eyes," she told him. "When you talked to her this morning there was a softness in your eyes. You've never looked at me like that. She's a lady, of course, with a fine way of speech! I'm only a dirty little cat. Do you think I don't know?"

"You've got some bee buzzing in your head," he told her.

"You despise me!" she cried. "You treat me like dirt, and I used to be a good girl once."

She began to weep bitterly and he felt her body shake against him.

"I don't despise you," he said. "If there's a God who looks down upon us He will pity us all—the starving, the desperate women, the refugees and those who are hopeless like ourselves. If there's anyone whom I despise it's myself and I can even find it in my heart to pity myself!"

He spoke these last words with a harsh laugh again.

Then he gave the girl a little push.

"Go and dry your eyes, my child. Aren't we both behaving very foolishly? Aren't we talking the greatest nonsense?"

She gave a tearful kind of laugh, and made a rush for the curtain which hid her sleeping place, leaving Franz perturbed and distressed by this new complication in his life, the mad jealousy of this little creature in his cellar. Wasn't his own mind possessed by the same demon?

CHAPTER XXII

THE young Englishman, Romilly, came round again one evening and then on other evenings. He was always polite, intelligent and unpretentious, almost breaking down the secret hostility which Franz had felt for him, almost disarming his suspicions.

Other people came while he was there. One was a war comrade of Franz, named Gustav Arnold, who had been living in the Russian sector of Berlin but had decided that conditions were better on the British side. The boundaries between these two sectors were hardening. Another was a young doctor from Danzig, Wilhelm Metzing, who was now attached to a clinic in Berlin. That evening Magda also appeared again so that the cellar was unusually crowded, especially when Baümer joined them.

Romilly had brought some chocolate and a tin of coffee which excited his German friends almost as much as if he had brought a gold nugget or the Koh-i-Noor diamond.

"But that is worth a fortune!" exclaimed Dr. Metzing, a youngish bald-headed man with a pair of steel-rimmed glasses.

"One could barter that pound of coffee for pearls and precious stones!"

Gustav Arnold took off the lid and smelt the brown powder.

"*Ach, Wunderschön!*"

Romilly smiled at this excitement.

"Let's make some and drink it."

"There's no coffee-pot," said Franz.

"A tin can?" suggested Dr. Metzing. "Here is coffee. There's a stove. Where is water?"

"We have only four cups," said Franz, "and two of them are cracked."

"We will share cups," said Dr. Metzing. "In time of defeat one has to improvise and make the best of a bad business. Germans are learning to dispense with luxury."

There was no trace of hostility in their manner towards Romilly, one of the conquerors and representative of the Occupying Powers.

Dr. Metzing spoke to him in excellent English.

"In England there are few privations, I expect."

"Quite a few," said Romilly. "Everything is rationed. Nothing much to buy in the shops. We call it 'austerity'."

Dr. Metzing's eyes twinkled behind his steel-rimmed glasses. "Just a little less luxury. Just a little less food. I was reading that the health of your children is marvellous." He gave a quick sigh and the twinkle left his eyes. "Here the children's faces are pallid. Many of them have tuberculosis like so many of our young girls." He looked over at Magda and lowered his voice: "That beautiful lady has the Berlin pallor. She's undernourished like most of us. But don't let us think of miserable things tonight. I look forward to that cup of coffee. In a little while the kettle will boil. Then we shall have a treat."

It was he who made the coffee in an old tin pot. Romilly handed the first cup to Magda.

"We must share the cup," she told him. "Do you mind?"

"It will make it sweeter," he said, gallantly.

Franz overheard this and was conscious of an absurd pang of jealousy again. Magda noticed his look and smiled at him and raised her cup after touching it with her lips.

Gustav Arnold took a cigarette offered to him by Romilly from his silver case.

"With one cigarette," he said, "one can begin a Black Market operation. With a hundred one can be lord of one's fate or at least fill one's stomach. It's the new token of real wealth."

Romilly was generous with his cigarettes, offering them round until his case was empty. Then he put his hand in his jacket pocket and produced a packet of twenty which he held out to Magda.

"I've plenty more," he said.

Magda's face flushed.

"No, no!" she cried. "Please. That's too much!"

"Oh, it's nothing," said Romilly, carelessly, "I have a thousand in my rooms."

A thousand! For a moment all the people in the cellar stared at him as though he had told them that he owned all the gold mines in South Africa.

"With a thousand cigarettes," said Dr. Metzing, "one could get the wedding-rings off all the married women I know, or the fur coats off their backs."

Gustav Arnold gave a loud laugh.

"In the Russian zone many women have given up their wedding-rings without payment. The Russian soldiers collect them in handfuls. Rings and wrist-watches."

"But for our host tonight," said Romilly, "I should have lost mine."

He looked over at Franz and smiled at the recollection of their first encounter.

He turned to Arnold again.

"What do you make of the Russians?"

Arnold shrugged his shoulders and then looked round the cellar as though wondering whether there might be an eaves-dropper.

"We're all friends here," said Dr. Metzing, cheerfully. "No spies in this cellar! Here we can talk freely."

"It's not wise to talk freely anywhere," said Arnold.

But he talked freely later in the evening as though reassured by this company.

"One doesn't notice much difference outwardly in the Russian zone. Things happen quietly and secretly. Men disappear mysteriously—mostly young men. Nobody ever hears of them again. There are midnight arrests. More of one's friends disappear. That's the last one hears of them. Young women and girls are taken away. God knows what happens to them. It's better to be in the British zone."

"Are they making converts to Communism?" asked Romilly, who seemed to take a mild interest in this conversation.

Arnold answered ironically.

"It's easy to convert people who will die of starvation or be dragged off to the mines if they're not converted. Of course there are some who are lured by the new religion which seems to be like an infectious disease."

Dr. Metzing had something to say.

"The Russians are bad missionaries for their own religion, at least in Berlin. Escaped prisoners of war are coming back with tales of brutality and starvation and forced labour."

Baümer spoke almost for the first time that evening. He had been a listener sitting on a low stool by the stove.

"I was a prisoner in Russia. It wasn't amusing. But we didn't treat Russian prisoners as though we loved them."

"That's true!" said Dr. Metzing, who seemed in a mood to agree with everybody. Was he not drinking a good cup of coffee? Was he not enjoying Romilly's chocolates and cigarettes? "The fact is, my dear friends, total war is total cruelty and the scum of humanity rises to the surface. The human beast is let out of its lair. But in every country, even in Russia, the ordinary folk—the peasants, the craftsmen, the toilers—are decent friendly human beings who don't want to kill anybody and don't want to be killed. The guilty men who make all the trouble in the world are those who want power and those who are fanatics of some political creed."

"The homicidal maniacs," said Baümer.

Romilly came over to Franz leaving the iron bedstead where he had been sitting beside Magda.

"I was greatly impressed by your drawings," he said.

"It's good of you to say so," answered Franz, rather coldly.

"If you would do a portrait sketch of Frau Hessell, I should be very glad to buy it—if the price is not too high!"

He smiled at his last words, as though to soften a business offer.

"I might make a shot at it," said Franz, grudgingly.

Why should this Englishman want a portrait of Magda? he wondered. Wasn't it rather impertinent? Wasn't it a kind of claim to her?

"It's a good subject," said Romilly. "Sitting there on that bedstead with a shadow world around her and the light of the oil-lamp touching the right side of her face, I find her very striking. Don't you agree?"

"Naturally I agree," answered Franz.

He was inclined to resent this admiration of Magda. Yet he had to admit to himself that there was nothing offensive in his words or in the tone of them. They had been spoken in a frank and friendly way. A sudden wave of contrition smote him for his lack of courtesy to this English visitor who had come into his cellar with so much indifference to its squalor and such friendly overtures.

"I'll do my best," he said. "I'm out of practice, you know, and I was never more than a student."

While the talk was going on he did a charcoal portrait of Magda, whose face touched only by the colour of her lipstick was framed in darkness. She was looking tired again and ill. He was startled for a moment by her extreme pallor. The others took no notice of him. Dr. Metzing was enunciating some theory about the future of civilization.

"It will be a struggle between the white and coloured races. It will be a life and death struggle. The surrender of India by the British is a great retreat, inevitable, perhaps, but terribly significant. In South Africa the white people are a small minority among millions of black folk, restless and in secret revolt. The cry of Asia for the Asiatics is setting the East on fire. The Chinese are learning to use machine-guns and aeroplanes. There are four hundred million Chinese. The population of the coloured races increases by something like twenty million every year. The world's food supply can't keep pace with this increase in fertility. The White races clinging to their own food supplies, will be threatened by hungry hordes. It is in fact an ominous outlook. The conclusion of my argument? The White races, especially in Europe—a frontier of the Asiatic continent—must hold together for self defence or perish separately."

"All very gloomy!" said Romilly, with a smile, as though dismissing this dark pessimism. "What about Russia? Half Asiatic but with spearheads deep into Europe?"

Dr. Metzing laughed.

"That's the great enigma. The answer to it will decide the Destiny of Europe and of the world. If Lenin's dictum is true that there must be an inevitable clash between Communism and Capitalism—Stalin has echoed it—then Europe will be a battleground again and there will be few survivors among its ruins."

Out of the darkness where he sat by the stove Baümer laughed.

"Aren't we sitting in ruins now?" he asked. "Isn't the whole of Germany a ruin? Here we are in this cellar talking as though nothing had happened to civilization. Isn't Germany itself a blue print of what Europe will be like when the Atom bomb is dropped from a sky full of planes?"

Romilly intervened again.

"I deplore this conversation," he said with his light laugh. "I don't think those horrors are going to happen. In any case don't let's talk about them!"

Dr. Metzing smiled at him.

"The policy of the ostrich?" he asked. "Is that the English philosophy of life?"

"We don't meet troubles half-way," answered Romilly. "One day Germany will rise again and be strong again. Then I hope that your people will be on the side of freedom and civilization."

"On your side you mean," said Dr. Metzing.

There was a note of irony in his voice, of which Romilly was aware.

"One day," said Dr. Metzing, "the English will want us to love them although they destroyed our cities, cut down our forests, dismantled our factories and put our best men into concentration camps. They will expect us to fight for them against Russia. The English will want us to forget."

"We have something to forget too," answered Romilly. "The Germans——" He checked himself and laughed and went over to look at Franz's drawing.

"That's good," he said. "Congratulations!"

"A rough sketch," said Franz.

"May I see?" asked Magda.

She looked at this study of her head and raised her eyebrows.

"Do I look like that?" she asked. "Do I look so ill and hungry?"

"Portrait of a beautiful lady," said Romilly in his charming way. He turned to Franz again.

"Is it for sale?"

Franz hesitated and then handed it to the young Englishman.

"It's worthless as a work of art. I'll do another for myself."

Romilly looked at him doubtfully and then accepted the drawing.

"You're too generous. But thanks very much."

They stayed late that evening until Magda rose from the iron bedstead.

"I must go home to my beautiful Bunker," she said. "Who will come with me? It's dark and dangerous for a lonely female."

"I shall be delighted," said Romilly.

"We will all go," said Dr. Metzing. "Berlin by night is like a jungle. Coming, Arnold? We have stayed too long, perhaps."

"Stay all night," said Franz, "if you don't mind sleeping on a stone floor."

Romilly laughed at this invitation.

"I've slept in worse places than this, but it's not far to my rooms."

Franz was watching Magda. Her face had suddenly become dead white. As she walked across the cellar towards the part curtained off she swayed and put her hands out. In three strides he had caught her before she would have fallen.

"Magda!" he cried.

She lay limp in his arms as that time in the Tiergarten.

"Good God!" said Romilly. "What has happened?"

Dr. Metzing rushed up.

"I'm not surprised," he said. "Put her on the bed."

He put his hand into her bodice and felt her heart. Then he held her hand and felt her pulse.

"She's very weak," he said. "It's the same thing of course. All these women are going down with it. I knew at once by the look of her."

Franz stared at the doctor.

"She is very ill?"

Dr. Metzing nodded.

"She had better stay here tonight. I will give her an injection. Her heart is very weak."

"We had better go," said Romilly.

He looked distressed and spoke in a low voice to Franz. "I'm extremely sorry. If there's anything I can do——"

Magda did not leave the cellar next day, nor for other days and nights. The hospitals and clinics which had survived the air raids were overcrowded and there was no room for her.

"She's better here," said Dr. Metzing, who came to see her. "It's not ideal of course. . . ."

He looked round the cellar and gave a gruff laugh.

"Better than a refugee camp!"

She was no longer on the iron bedstead. Elsa and Erike had given their place behind the curtain. Now that Magda was ill Elsa's hatred and jealousy had left her and Franz was astonished by her devotion as a nurse. The natural goodness of heart in this girl who had called herself a dirty little slut was touching. She found some craving for goodness which might blot out the smudges in her soul. So she told Franz one day with a laugh when he thanked her.

"I like to be good sometimes! Perhaps I'll go to heaven one day. You never know your luck."

"You'll wear a golden crown," said Franz. "Wings are sprouting from you."

He smiled at her and then spoke anxiously.

"How's Magda today?"

Elsa gave a little shrug.

"She can't last long. Don't deceive yourself. She's dying."

"For heaven's sake don't say that," he answered in a low voice.

"You know she's dying," said Elsa. "And she knows."

"She'll get better," said Franz. "She's getting better."

He knew she was not getting better. Every day she became weaker. Baümer had cleared out of the cellar. He was sleeping in one of the Bunkers but he came in every day bringing some food with him which he had bought out of his poor wage for clearing rubble.

There was another visitor who brought food several times. It was the Englishman, Romilly. He brought chocolates and biscuits and fruit.

Always he asked after Magda, very politely.

"How is Frau Hessell?"

"A little weaker perhaps."

"I'm terribly sorry. Give her my kind regards."

Once Franz asked him whether he would care to see her. He asked for Magda's sake.

Romilly looked embarrassed.

"Oh, no, I don't want to be a nuisance."

Franz went to the other side of the curtain.

"Magda," he said softly. "Herr Romilly is here. Would you care to see him?"

She raised her head slightly and smiled.

"Yes, of course! I want to tell him something."

Franz put a chair by the bedside so that Romilly could sit there and then took him in.

Romilly was shy and embarrassed but raised Magda's hand to his lips.

"You're looking wonderful," he said. "You have an exquisite colour."

"I'm dying," she told him. "I shall never be your mistress, Herr Romilly."

For a moment Romilly was silent. Perhaps he was thinking out a lie or a protest but he bent his head and said, "I'm sorry."

Franz went to the other side of the curtain. He felt stricken by those words, but without anger. He felt only a great anguish.

Romilly stayed only a few minutes and came out with a grave face. "Thank you," he said to Franz. "It was kind of you."

Franz walked up the steps with him.

"How do you think she looks?" he asked.

"Very beautiful but very weak."

"Yes," said Franz. "May I ask you something?"

"Do," said Romilly.

"Did you want her to be your mistress?"

Romilly looked at him and hesitated.

"Must you ask that question?"

"I would like to know."

Romilly hesitated again and then answered.

"It was an idea at the back of my mind. Nothing more than that. She attracted me, and I was sorry for her. When she came into that restaurant one night I was shocked. I might have saved her from this. If she had lived with me . . ."

"I love her," said Franz. "I should have killed you. Then I should have regretted killing you."

"Why?" asked Romilly, as though interested in an abstract problem.

"I've become a pacifist. I'm against killing. It does no good. It's the ape in us that makes us kill."

"I agree," answered Romilly. "We ought to become civilized."

The two men were silent for a moment at the top of the steps which led into the street of skeleton houses.

"I should like to remain friends with you," said Franz.

"Why not?" answered Romilly.

"I've no hatred now," said Franz. "That has passed."

"Thanks. I'm glad."

"*Auf Wiedersehen.*"

The young Englishman walked away into the ruined street. Franz went back into the cellar and pulling the bit of curtain on one side stood by Magda's bedside again. She was lying back with a smile on her lips.

"He's nice, isn't he—our Englishman?"

"He's a good type," said Franz.

She put her hand outside the bed-clothes and he held it.

"Franz," she said, "you're very kind to me."

"I love you."

She held his hand more tightly.

"I like you to love me. I should have been Herr Romilly's mistress but I should have gone on loving you. Now nothing is any good like that. I'm dying, I know."

Franz went down on his knees and put an arm—his unwounded arm—about her.

"Get better," he said desperately. "Get better quickly, Magda. I love you. We'll be happy with our love. I'll work for you and earn money. I'll make you well. I can't do without you, Magda."

"My poor Franz!" she said. "You'll have to do without me. I'm going away. Perhaps I'll see Otto again. He loved me too. It's funny how men have loved me!"

She closed her eyes still smiling with her lips. She seemed to be asleep. Presently Franz took his arm from her and crept away.

Baümer came in bringing some apples wrapped in an old newspaper.

"Would she like one?" he asked. "They're cooking apples. I could stew them on the stove."

"She's asleep," said Franz in a low voice. "How can you afford to buy apples? Don't they cost a fortune?"

"I can afford it," said Baümer. "I'm earning fifteen marks a day."

Franz looked at him. Baümer who was as thin as a rake. His shabby old uniform with its badges torn off was covered with white dust from the cement and rubble of the streets. It had worked into his straw-coloured hair and beard. His long, lean hands were dirty.

"You're starving yourself," said Franz. "You bring food for us and don't eat a morsel of it."

Baümer shrugged his shoulders.

"I'm all right," he said. "I get enough bread."

Franz put his hand on Baümer's shoulders as he unwrapped the apples, mostly bruised and going rotten.

"You're a good comrade," he said in a broken voice. "You're one of the saints of God. I've seen you give food to the refugees when your own belly was empty."

Baümer's face flushed. The colour crept up from his neck.

"You're talking like a lunatic," he said.

He stayed for twenty minutes, peeling the apples and putting them into the saucepan with some water on the top of the stove. Then he went off to his work again.

That evening Franz heard Magda call him and he rose from his chair where he had been reading *Faust*, a tattered book he had picked up from the rubble outside.

"Franz."

"Yes, Magda."

"Come to me."

He bent over her bedside and put his arm below her shoulders, raising her up a little.

"Are you hungry?" he asked. "Baümer has brought some apples. They're cooking on the stove. I expect they're done by now."

"No, I'm not hungry, I just want to talk to you."

"Talk to me then, dear heart."

She did not talk for some time but lay there holding his hand. Presently she spoke a few words.

"When I'm gone you must get out of this cellar, Franz; it's silly staying here."

"You mustn't go," he said with an emotion which he tried to hide. "Don't leave me, my beloved."

"You could be a great artist if you liked," she said. "People would buy your pictures."

"That's unimportant," he said. "Only you are important. My love for you is enough—enough for me."

He felt her hand tighten on his.

"Kiss me," she whispered.

Her voice was getting fainter.

He was down on his knees now. His arm lay across her breast. His lips were against her forehead.

"I'm tired," she said.

She closed her eyes. She seemed to be sleeping. He dared not move lest he should wake her. Perhaps it was twenty minutes that he stayed like that. Then suddenly he moved and stood up and gave a cry.

"Magda!"

Her forehead had become cold against his lips. Her hair had become cold. He stooped and put his hand below the bed-clothes and felt her body. Her body was cold.

He cried out again.

"Magda! My love!"

She did not answer him.

A sudden rush of tears came to his eyes. His body was shaken by harsh sobs. He clasped his hands together and raised them above his head and leaned against the wall, weeping. He was alone in the cellar.

CHAPTER XXIII

HILDE MENZEL was cutting out a piece of cloth from one of her father's old suits to make a jacket for young Hans when Christel came into the room excitedly.

"There's a friend of yours downstairs. He wants to see you. It's Franz Reber."

Hilde dropped the piece of cloth and her face flushed slightly. It was two months now since she had received that letter which had disturbed her mind because of its emotional craving for spiritual help. Now he had come and might ask from her more than she could give because he put her on a pedestal as a kind of saint with a spirituality which she did possess, in her own self judgement. But she could not conceal her joy at his coming. She had been hurt by his long silence. He had been very much in her mind all that time. Their comradeship at Quakenbrück, their long talks on Winter evenings when the others had gone to bed, their self revelation one to another in those days of flight and terror had remained in her heart.

"He remembers me," said Christel, "but he means nothing to me. I can't connect him with the boy who used to dance with me in Munich and wanted to kiss me when we went climbing. He looks as if he had just escaped from a concentration camp—lean and haggard with sad eyes and a broken arm."

"That has happened to many poor boys," said Hilde. "Where is he?"

"In Father's study."

Hilde went down and opened the study door.

"Franz!" she said. "How good to see you. After all this time!"

He took both her hands and raised them to his lips.

"You haven't changed," he told her. "You're still beautiful as I've always remembered you."

"I thought you had forgotten me," she said. "Not a word from you, Franz, for a long time."

He released her hands and struck his chest.

"I know. I feel guilty and ashamed. But I've been living in the underworld of Berlin. There are many things to tell you. I fell in love and my love died."

"I'm sorry," said Hilde.

She did not feel hurt because he had fallen in love with another woman. She had no jealousy of him that way. Their comradeship had not been of that kind.

"That page has been turned over," he said. "It belongs to the past—one of the dreams, one of those memories which are like open wounds until presently they heal, leaving just the scars and some wandering ghosts whom one meets at night."

"What are you going to do now?" asked Hilde.

Franz spoke less gloomily, dragging himself out of his tragic mood.

"I want to talk to you now and then. I want to climb the mountains again after living in a cellar too long. I want to do some drawing and painting. I have a sudden and terrific urge to find my way out of the dark tunnel by way of creative art. Do you think that's of any importance, or is it just egoism and lunacy?"

"It's very important," said Hilde. "In this time of world chaos and ruin the artist and the poet must come into their own again. They will light the lamps in our darkness. I truly believe that. It can't be done by politicians."

She laughed a little at her own words.

"You make me speak as though I were a wise woman, instead of one who knows nothing!"

Franz shook his head and answered emotionally.

"You have a spiritual wisdom. That's why I've come to you. At Quakenbrück you helped me more than I can ever forget. The War had left me with raw wounds. I was utterly bewildered and embittered. Somehow you were a healer. Do you remember our long talks? Do you remember my raving nonsense?"

"I remember very pleasant conversations," said Hilde. "I remember we leaned on your strength and comradeship."

"Tell me about yourself," said Franz. "I've been talking like an egoist as though my affairs mattered most. What's happening in your own life? How are you getting on with the Americans? How are Hans and Trudel? What's the pretty Christel doing in this difficult world?"

In this first conversation with Hilde Menzel, in this renewal of a friendship which he had neglected but never abandoned, he heard the answers to his questions. Hilde was devoted to her children's welfare, sewing, knitting, cooking, in a constant drudgery which she found was the way to consolation and happiness. The children were well and full of spirit after lean and hungry days when she had been terrified because of semi-starvation.

The food situation was better in Bavaria, helped to some extent by the Americans who had brought pressure on the farmers to prevent hoarding and the worst abuses of the Black Market. The withdrawal of the ban on fraternization had made more friendly relations possible, anyhow as far as they were concerned. Christel was studying hard in Munich but in the evenings gave German lessons to one of the American officers who was now friendly and helpful. Christel still hated the Americans, or at least was very critical and supercilious, but she made an exception in the case of the American officer who was her pupil and who paid her more than generously so that they could get food and many little comforts. They had terrific arguments—those two.

The one dark shadow which lay upon them all was the imprisonment of Herr von Arnheim who was still held in prison on a false charge. But Christel's American officer—the one to whom she taught German—was working for his release. Hilde's father had already lost six stone in weight and complained of ill-treatment. They were all praying for an end to his captivity.

"That's our family history up to date," said Hilde. "Now you know about us. Tell me about Berlin."

But it was not then that he told her much about Berlin or his love for Magda. Christel came into the study in her slacks and yellow jumper and Franz found himself laughing with her, remembering their flirtation as boy and girl. She hadn't changed much since then. The war years and what had happened afterwards had not carved any lines on her face. Nor, it seemed, had they left any dark shadow on her spirit which was gay and light-hearted except for a bitterness about her father's imprisonment.

Franz took his leave of these two sisters.

"May I come again?" he asked. "May I weary you with my woeful visage—a Rip van Winkle with a broken arm and a broken heart?"

"Broken hearts get mended very soon," said Christel, laughing at him. "As a student of philosophy and history I've become aware of that. Men's hearts, especially, mend with great rapidity."

"We must talk about philosophy," said Franz. "I've been studying Aristotle."

He left them with a new sense of cheerfulness and hope which startled him. He even rebuked himself because of this release from despair and grief. Was it possible that he could ever recover from the loss of Magda? Christel had made him laugh and now it seemed like treachery to his dead love. It had been good to see Hilde again but he had no sense of guilt because his heart had been moved by joy. For Hilde he had, he thought, a spiritual love beyond the endearment and ecstasy and warmth of man's love for woman.

CHAPTER XXIV

CHRISTEL came back from Frankfurt late one afternoon. She had had to spend the night there. Once a fortnight she made this journey to take food to her father who had been under arrest for several months. It was always a painful journey, almost unendurable in the heat of Summer. The train was like a furnace in which human beings were being roasted. It was an actual fight to get into a carriage. Masses of people lined the platform and made a rush for the train when it came in. Women laden with babies and baskets shoved and pushed each other, desperate to get a place. Men lost their tempers and used their elbows to wedge inside, or flung their full weight against those who were standing in the carriages to force themselves into another square foot or so of cubic space.

Christel, with a heavy basket full of potatoes, was agile and crafty, adopting her own technique which was to board the carriage next to the engine and climb through the window before the door was unlocked. But once inside the carriage her feet were trampled upon in the wild scrimmage, and not seldom she was sat upon by heavy men or fat women struggling for seats. Those who failed to get seats stood squeezed together for the duration of a long journey. Women fainted, men perspired, children wailed, and only the most patient or the most good-natured could prevent a loss of temper or endure this suffocation. Journey's end was even more painful to Christel on this pilgrimage to her father's prison She was not allowed to see him. The American police, who always looked to her grotesque and hideous in their white helmets and white belted uniforms, refused her pleading for a short interview with her father.

"Nothing doing, girlie. Against the rules."

They even weighed out her load of potatoes and handed back half a basketful.

"No good bringing such a lot," said one of them. "Political prisoners are rationed, you know."

"You mean they're starved," she said angrily.

"Better keep a civil tongue, lady. Better remember Belsen and Buchenwald."

On her last visit she burst into tears when handed back this excess of potatoes. She had brought them a long way. They had weighed heavily on her lap in the overcrowded carriage, hot and stinking in the heat of Summer. Inside the prison her father was underfed and always hungry. Now half her load was rejected.

"Tears this time, eh?" said one of the policemen at the gate. "Last time it was insulting language. Give a chance to the others, won't you?"

The others were girls like herself, of good class, the wives, daughters, or sisters of men held back for 'screening', or arrested on the denunciation of Communists and informers. Christel knew some of them. They spoke in low voices to each other while waiting to hand in their parcels. They too were angry, tearful, and exasperated.

"My husband," said one of them, "was always anti-Nazi. Now they treat him as a criminal."

A girl next to her laughed scornfully and spoke in a loud voice as though addressing this queue of waiting women.

"We all pretend to be anti-Nazi! Weren't we all Nazis unless we were dirty Communists and traitors? Why should my brother be imprisoned because he served in the Foreign Office? Do they think all Foreign Office men are murderers? My brother is a patriotic German. Since when has it been a crime to serve one's country?"

"It's the day of the dirty dogs," said another girl who was smartly dressed except for down-at-heel shoes. "The men who get to the top in Germany now are the fawners who bow low to their conquerors and the filthy scum in the Black Market and the secret agents of Russia who call themselves democrats and dupe the simple-minded Americans."

A more elderly woman spoke to this one.

"We have to pay the price of defeat," she said with a kind of tragic resignation. "*Vae Victis!* It always has been like that. We were no better in our time of victory."

"You're one of the crawlers," cried the younger woman. "Why do you crawl?"

"I happen to be the wife of——"

She mentioned a name which made the young girl stare at her. It was the name of a German Field Marshal who had been cheered by the German people as one of the heroes of Hitler's early victories, and then had been dismissed.

"I'm sorry!" said the young girl who had spoken so fiercely. "Forgive me, *gnädige Frau.*"

She burst into tears as Christel had done outside the prison gate.

When Christel arrived home again after this last journey to Frankfurt she remembered that it was her evening for the German lesson to Captain Welles and after supper with Hilde and her mother she went into her father's study, still angry and distressed.

He was there waiting for her as usual on the tick of time.

"Glad to see you back," he said. "A bad journey?"

"I'm furious," she told him.

They spoke German now. These lessons were hardly necessary except as good practice. Captain Welles had been a diligent student in his own time and could speak fairly correct German with considerable ease.

He smiled at this introduction to a German lesson.

"It sets your eyes on fire when you're furious. It's an aid to beauty."

"You Americans are disgusting," said Christel. "I hate you all with a deadly hatred."

Captain Welles laughed good-humouredly.

"Then you're hating your best friends."

"Friends!" she exclained scornfully. "You tread on our necks with your clumsy boots. You talk of democracy and behave like tyrants. Your women who come to join their hen-pecked husbands turn us out of our houses and treat us as though we were dirt. You put our men in prison on false charges and treat them like convicts—my father who hated Hitler and has never done a cruel or ignoble thing. Your American police are brutal. You starve your prisoners. You have the impertinence to lecture us on culture and make out plans for the re-education of the German people who despise your dollar civilization and your low grade standard of education. Is it any wonder that we hate you?"

Captain Welles looked at her humorously.

"A very good exercise in German vituperation," he said. "A very candid revelation of the German attitude of mind."

She caught his smiling glance and against her will gave a little laugh.

"Isn't all that true?" she asked.

Captain Welles handed her a cigarette from his case.

"Calm down," he said. "Now that you've got all that off your chest after a hot and tiresome journey we may as well talk reasonably."

"Do you deny the truth of what I've said?" she asked in a challenging way.

"I'm prepared to agree with some of it," he said. "I agree that some of our American women over here are lacking in good manners, but I'd like you to admit that others go out of their way to be kind and generous."

"I haven't met them," said Christel.

"I'm willing to admit," said Captain Welles, "that we're making plenty of mistakes and act now and then on false information, but I'd like you to admit that we try to establish rough justice and fair play. It's not easy for ourselves or the British to sort out the bad Germans from the good Germans. I'm one of those who believe that here and there there are good Germans."

She saw the glint of humour in his eyes again.

"Thanks for the admission," she said. "Very kind of you, I'm sure."

"I'm also one of those who believe that there are good Americans, profoundly anxious to help you people to get on your feet again, deeply pitiful of unnecessary suffering, trying to work for peace and good will."

"They're not succeeding," said Christel, stubbornly.

"Not yet," said Captain Welles. "It takes time to sort all this out. But at the back of everything—all the mistakes, all the failures—that's our hope and that's our policy. Don't you believe that?"

"You want us on your side because you hate Russian Communism," said Christel. "One day you'll want us to fight for you and make Germany a new battlefield, holding the Russians until you get your Atom bombs going."

He looked at her sharply and gave an uneasy laugh.

"Is that the kind of thing your fellow students are talking in Munich?"

Christel nodded.

"Yes, they're talking like that."

"I'll tell you something," said Captain Welles. "Those fellow students of yours are talking about the wrong things in the wrong way."

Christel raised her eyebrows.

"Really?"

"Yes, I'll say they are. And so are many Germans with whom I talk now and then thanks to your conversation lessons. They're talking about their grievances and their sufferings as though the Americans and British were responsible for all that. They forget that they followed a man named Hitler who led them down the road to ruin. They forget that their leader inflicted atrocious sufferings upon other peoples whose only crime was defence of their own soil and liberties. What they should talk about is the wickedness of all that and the need to pay the price of defeat, and their future chance of regaining the confidence of the world by working for peace and democracy and international team-work among free peoples. That chance will come to them. I hope to God they'll take it."

"A moral lecture!" said Christel. "Captain Welles of the American Army tries to re-educate the German mind. How very touching!"

Captain Welles of the American Army stubbed out the end of a cigarette into one of her father's ash-trays and fixed his smiling glance upon her.

"Christel," he said, "let's drop all this sham fighting. Sometimes you behave like a schoolgirl in a temper and sometimes I treat you as such. It's a kind of game which amuses me. But you're a grown-up young woman. You're a student of history and philosophy. You've not only a well-trained intelligence but you have a fine spirit, full of courage, and now and again I've been startled by something you try to hide from me."

Christel's face flushed slightly.

"What's that?" she asked. "What do I try to hide?"

"The agony in your soul," he said. "Your yearning for the beauty of life. Something very lovely in your mind. When we went mountain climbing one day I caught a glimpse of that. You were what we call 'fey'. There was something ethereal in your ecstasy with nature. The hardness and the bitterness dropped away from you. You were lovely and I saw the real Christel, free from the hatreds and hardships of a nation in defeat. You were above all that for a while. It's because you love Germany so much, the Germany of the mountains and the forests and the streams that you hate the Americans who come as conquerors and are rather clumsy at the game because it doesn't belong to their make-up or their tradition."

Christel's face flushed very deeply this time and a sudden rush of tears came to her eyes.

"Why do you say these things?" she asked. "Why do you call me Christel? Why do you think I have a lovely soul when I insult you and quarrel with you and show no gratitude at all for all your kindness?"

Captain Welles was silent for a moment and then spoke quietly. "Somehow I thought it's about time to take the masks off our faces. For quite a long time now you've been giving me these lessons. I've looked forward to them more than I can say. But we've always kept our distance. We've been absurdly formal. You've treated me always with the hostility due to one of the Occupying Powers, mightily afraid lest you should demean yourself to one of the conquerors. Isn't it like that?"

"Of course it's like that," said Christel. "It must be like that. I'm not one of those who fawn upon the victors. My father is the Baron von Arnheim and the Americans have put him in prison."

Captain Welles hesitated and gave a quiet laugh.

"What would you say if an American got him out of prison?"

Christel stared at him with excitement in her eyes and a desperate hope.

"What American? Is there any chance? Are you kidding me, as you call it?"

"Now, look here," answered Captain Welles in his quiet way. "You deny the American sense of justice but I've been getting busy on your father's case, with full consent of the Colonel who has given me time off to do it."

"What have you done?" cried Christel. "Is there any hope? Oh, I would go down on my knees to you if you could get my father out again."

"I won't ask you to go down on your knees, my dear," said

Captain Welles. "But your father will be back in a few days now."

"Is that true?" asked Christel. "You're not trying to comfort me by false hopes?"

"What do you take me for?" asked Captain Welles. "I've been pretty darned busy on this case and haven't said a word so that you wouldn't have false hopes. I've hunted out the witnesses who gave evidence against your father. I've tied them up in knots and proved the falsity of their accusations. That scoundrel, Mundt, the Communist, was the nigger in the woodpile. He was arrested yesterday and confronted with your father. The order of release is on its way. Herr von Arnheim will soon be home and it's going to be a pleasure to the Colonel and myself."

"How can I thank you?" asked Christel in a low voice. "How can I ever thank you enough?"

She came over to him holding out her hands and her eyes were wet and shining. He took both her hands and raised them to his lips.

"No need of thanks," he said. "I did it as a duty. Some of us Americans are on the side of Justice. Won't you believe that?"

"One American," she answered.

She laughed but he could feel the tears wet on his hands.

"I thank God for one dear American who believes in Justice."

"Well, I'm satisfied with that," he said. "It's what I call generous of you. One American among a hundred and thirty million believes in Justice and the lady calls him a dear American. Is that dear American dear enough to have one kiss as a reward for a small service?"

Christel flung her arms about him and kissed his cheek. Then as though frightened by this abandonment of formality, this surrender of pride, she fled from the room.

Captain Robert Lee Welles stood in the Baron von Arnheim's study with a smile on his thin lips. Then he went to the bookshelves whistling a little tune and took down a book and tried to read it. But it was difficult to read because he was holding it upside down. There was no German lesson that evening, but on the top floor of the Baron von Arnheim's house, his family wept for joy.

CHAPTER XXV

GRADUALLY as the months passed Franz Reber lost his haggard and haunted look and the grey pallor of his skin and the despair which had been his bedfellow in a Berlin cellar. In Bavaria conditions were better and it was possible to walk away from rubble and twisted iron to villages untouched by war, and better still to the mountains where in the solitude of high peaks looking down to green valleys, looking away to the splendour of the hills and the glory of the sky human suffering and folly the blood and filth of war, became remote and insignificant in relation to eternity which here took possession of the lonely mind.

He did some mountain climbing alone, but sometimes with Paul von Arnheim and his friends who were all ex-soldiers like himself. As Bavarians they had a passion for the mountains. They were daring climbers and daring skiers. They would rather go without food than stop climbing, yet in a way they were mostly unconscious of the cause of ecstasy which urged them to scale the high peaks, taking great risks from avalanches and crevasses and falling rocks. Never once did a man say 'this is beautiful', or 'this is a marvellous panorama' or call attention to some magical light touching a distant range. They took it as men draw breath. This to them was life at its best. It was life itself. They were mountaineers from boyhood.

Franz Reber from Berlin was more conscious of the beauty around him, more awed by its glory. Climbing with these other men, sharing sleeping huts with them, listening to their talk and songs, he felt old in their company though in years he was not older. Paul was gay with irrepressible spirit, yet they had all been through the War, seen the death of many comrades, crouching under bombardment, fighting through flaming cities.

How was it they had remained young in their minds, he wondered, thinking only of the immediate present, not worrying about the future of Germany—their way along the road of Destiny? Perhaps he misjudged them. Perhaps each man among them had some chamber of horror in his soul or some frightful experience which he kept secret.

Once with four of them on the slopes of the Zugspitz above Garmisch he asked a question which made them all stare at him incredulously.

"What kind of Germany are you fellows going to shape out?"

Paul was the first to laugh.

"We didn't know you were a humorist, Franz! Damned funny, Comrade Reber!"

One of the others echoed his laughter.

"It's not so much a question of shaping a new Germany as of getting a new pair of boots or deciding whether the holes in one's socks can be mended without making new socks."

"In any case what is Germany?" asked one of his comrades. "A prison camp, occupied by foreign Powers. The ruin of an ancient civilization."

"All this is temporary," said Franz. "The German people still have a great destiny. It's up to men like ourselves to be the path-finders beyond the ruins to a new highway of human progress."

Paul clapped him on the back and laughed jeeringly.

"You talk like Adolf the Great! Have you been seeing visions, comrade? Don't tell me you're one of the carpet-biters."

"It's not difficult to see visions from this slope," answered Franz. "Look how peaceful it is down there. If the Western nations get together and make a friendly peace themselves——"

It was unfortunate for his vision of peace that his words were interrupted by three or four shots in the valley.

There was a chorus of laughter from his comrades.

"Peace, beautiful peace!" exclaimed Paul. "It's those damned swine again, attacking an undefended farmstead. Czechs, Poles and other ruffians."

One of his comrades spoke angrily.

"No German is allowed to have a firearm. How do those Americans think our peasants can defend themselves or their womenfolk? Every day there are stories of rape and looting by these so-called Displaced Persons who ought to be called bandits."

"We brought them here," said Franz. "We have to pay for our mistakes and a bit more for our crimes."

"Crimes?" asked one of the young mountaineers angrily. "What crimes? Are you prosecuting counsel at Nürnberg—that parody of justice?"

"We shall never get anywhere," said Franz, "unless we regret the atrocities committed by Hitler and his ruffians. We shall have to work our way back to the respect and admiration of neighbour nations."

"*Um Gottes Willen!*" cried one of his comrades. "Our neighbour nations are not doing much to earn our respect and admiration. They dismantle our factories. They underfeed their prisoners. They put our dirtiest dogs into places of authority. They're up to their necks in the Black Market. Do they expect us to love them? Are you one of the crawlers and collaborators, Franz Reber? If so I'll chuck you over that mountain-side."

Paul roared with laughter and put his arm round Reber's shoulder.

"No attack on a one-armed man," he shouted, "and no political argument at this altitude. We're too close to God and too far from the vermin who crawl about this earth."

His intervention restored the good-humour of his party. After a stupendous sunset touching one by one the high peaks of the Bavarian Alps, and flushing the sky with crimson feathers, they came down to a village near Garmisch tired and hungry.

"Who will pay for my meal tonight?" asked the young man, Helder, who had quarrelled with Franz. "Needless to say my wallet is as empty as my belly."

Paul von Arnheim counted out some dirty paper.

"Enough for bread and soup," he said.

"I want a nice juicy steak," said Helder. "I want roast potatoes and sauerkraut, followed by pancakes of the largest size."

This desire seemed to them incredibly amusing as they pushed their way into a beer tavern where they took their places at a bare table. There were three American G.I.s with German girls behaving very respectably. The German girls seemed to understand the American accent. They left after finishing their meal.

The hot soup seemed to go to the right place. One of the young men by name of Nettlenbusch hummed an old Bavarian folk-song beating time with his spoon. The others joined in harmonizing the tune.

Franz watched them with smiling eyes. They were getting back to the spirit of youth, joy-loving, laughter-loving, unconquerable. From Paul he had found out something of their history. Nettlenbusch, who had started the singing, had been in the desert campaign with the Afrika Corps and then in Italy from which he had escaped with Paul von Arnheim though they had parted company. Helder who had turned on him so angrily had lost two brothers at Stalingrad and his mother and father had been buried under their house in Munich. Yet he could laugh and sing and beat time with his leaden spoon. Franz envied them. He could not attain this light-heartedness nor throw off the heavy shadows which darkened his mind.

Later that evening Nettlenbusch spoke to him across the table in a friendly way while the others were discussing an expedition to one of the mountain peaks which few had climbed.

"We jeered at you," said Nettlenbusch, "but I was struck by what you said. You're a thinker, aren't you?"

He spoke the last words with a smile, but not jeeringly.

"Now and again one has to think," answered Franz, smiling back at him. "Doesn't it differentiate one from the beasts of the field?"

"A bit," admitted Nettlenbusch, "but some forms of thinking lead one up the wrong road. We know a man who thought quite a lot and the result? Blood, agony and ruin! They seem to do a hell of a lot of thinking in the Kremlin. Result? Non-co-operation, the siege of Berlin, the Veto in the United Nations, the seizing of able-bodied men for the Siberian mines and timber forests where they die like birds in the snow. How can one be sure that if one thinks one is thinking the right kind of thoughts?"

Franz found this argument difficult to challenge. As a man without high conceit of himself he could not claim that his thoughts were likely to be the purest truth.

"Books help," he said. "I've been reading Aristotle's *Ethics.*"

Nettlenbusch gave a good-natured laugh.

"Must we go back two thousand years to find the right road for Germany? Hasn't the human brain advanced since then?"

"The human brain has gone backwards," said Franz. "The ethics of the *New Testament* haven't been tried out yet. It might be worth while to walk along that road but I'm not a religious man. I belong to no church. I'm just groping for a little light."

He had no light at all at that moment. The beer tavern was suddenly plunged in darkness except for the tiny light of torches flashing round the room.

"Hands up!" shouted a harsh voice in bad German. "The first man to move will be shot."

The girl who had been serving gave a shriek of terror and her mother cried out to the Mother of God.

A shot rang out. Three men had gone towards the till where the old woman kept her filthy marks.

Franz was the first to move. With his unwounded arm he grasped his chair and as he rose from it hurled it at a dark figure faintly revealed by one of the flickering torches. The figure went down with a thud. So also did Franz Reber. Two men jumped at him, hurled him to the ground and felt for his throat. He twisted his head sideways and kicked out with his heavy mountain shoes. Somebody turned up the electric light. It was Paul whose one eye shone fiercely. There were fifteen men in the beer tavern. They were small, underfed-looking men, sallow-faced and unshaven. Paul tackled two of them, hitting out with his fists to left and right. They were shouting curses in some Slavonic tongue. Two more shots were fired and plugged holes through the ceiling because a man's arm had been jerked up by Nettlenbusch. The lights went out again. The fingers that were closing round Franz Reber's throat were relaxed. There was a stampede through the narrow door. The invaders had retreated. Only one of them was left. It was the one at whom Franz had hurled his chair.

Up went the light again. Paul was breathing hard but laughed loudly.

"A glorious victory!" he cried exultantly. "They had to run like whipped dogs."

He turned to Franz who was feeling his throat. "Was it you who flung the chair??"

Franz nodded. He was gasping for breath.

"Splendid work!" shouted Paul "My dear fellow we hail you as our champion. *Heil Dir im Siegerkranz.*"

Nettlenbusch saw some joke in this.

"Not quite in accordance perhaps with the New Testament."

Franz was bending over the body of the man he had knocked out. He was only a young fellow, hardly more than a boy, and he had a half-starved look like most of the D.P.s who had been prisoners of war.

"Poor little devil!" said Franz. "I'm sorry I hit him such a whack."

"It will do him a lot of good," said Paul. "It would do him more good if you had smudged him out."

The boy became conscious and Franz put his arm under his shoulders and propped him up.

"*Wie gehts?*"

"*Nicht gut. Ich habe Kopfweh.*"

He had a headache, that young Pole, which was not surprising after contact with a heavy chair.

"For the love of Wotan!" cried Paul. "What's all this tenderness, Franz? Is this young thief your long-lost brother? Chuck him into the stable and lock him up until the police are told. He'll look fine at the end of a rope!"

"He's half-starved," said Franz. "There's no flesh on his bones. A drop of soup wouldn't do him any harm."

Nettlenbusch was staring at Franz with a grin on his face.

"I seem to remember something in an old book. If thine enemy is hungry. . . ."

"*Unfug!*" exclaimed Paul scornfully. He used a word signifying humbug.

"None of my soup for that young wretch!" screamed the woman who kept the tavern. "They might have murdered all of us."

The young Pole seemed conscious of hostility. He staggered to his feet and made a sudden rush for the door, which was still ajar. Like a young rat he scuttled into the darkness of the village street.

Paul laughed good-humouredly.

"Good riddance to one of Satan's grandchildren. Franz Reber, we still owe you a debt for being quick on the mark with that chair."

"The instinct of the cave-man," said Franz.

"Very necessary," said Helder. "Now that the Americans refuse us any firearms, we are at the mercy of this rabble, who seem to get all the arms they want."

They were served with free beer by the woman who owned the tavern. Thanks to these young men the D.P.s had failed to get away with her hoard of paper money.

CHAPTER XXVI

NETTLENBUSCH came round to see Franz after that evening in the beer tavern. Franz had found a tiny room at the top of a stable in Kaulbach, which had been used by a university student who had gone down with tuberculosis, and was now in a clinic. Its furniture was a camp-bed and a deal table and one chair, and to Franz this seemed like a little kingdom to which his star had led him. He heard the clatter of big boots up the wooden staircase, and then heard Nettlenbusch's voice.

"Are you there, Franz?"

"Come in."

Nettlenbusch glanced round the tiny room and laughed.

"Very princely," he said. "A room of your own, eh?"

"Sit down," said Franz, drawing out the chair and sitting on the camp-bed.

Nettlenbusch dumped himself down in the chair. His hair, closely cropped, was so fair that it looked almost white by the light of a little window looking down to the stable-yard.

He had a good head with fine-cut features and deep-set eyes as blue as the Bavarian sky. He was a man about thirty, or looked like that to Franz, though he may have been younger.

"I was rather impressed by what you said yesterday," he began. "We jeered at you when you asked what fellows like us were going to do about the future of Germany, but thinking it over I thought I would come and see you. Most of us haven't got as far as that. We live only in the immediate and distressful present. House-room! Food! Some kind of job!"

"I know," said Franz. "I've been through all that. I'm not out of it yet, though it's better here in Bavaria."

"The point is," said Nettlenbusch, "has Germany a future? The Russians sit down in the Eastern zone. The Americans, British and French sit down in the Western zone. We try to live and do a little business on inflated money. The Allied Powers dismantle our factories, seize the Ruhr, prevent our having steel and timber for reconstruction, and then expect us to love them.

Where's our hope, and where's our future? How can we hope to rebuild the ruins?"

Franz sat on the camp-bed with his hands between his knees, staring at the floor.

"We shall rebuild the ruins one day," he answered. "Our folk will work like beavers. But we've got to build something else, and that's more difficult!"

"What?" asked Nettlenbusch. "German finance!"

"The German soul," said Franz. "The spiritual side of German life."

Nettlenbusch looked sceptical.

"Are you one of these religious fanatics?" he asked. "If so, I can't argue with you."

"Nothing of the kind," said Franz. "But I believe in a spiritual world, beyond this materialistic illusion, which we call life. I know it somehow. There are times when I've almost escaped from my body by way of hunger and exhaustion, and looked at things as a dead man might see them. Does that seem mad to you?"

He raised his head and looked at Nettlenbusch with a faint smile.

He was surprised when Nettlenbusch answered seriously.

"I've had one or two experiences like that. One was when I lay in a trench before the battle of Alamein. I was badly wounded in one lung. My body was numb with cold—you know how it was. But suddenly I seemed to see everything and to understand everything as though looking down from a star. A most peculiar illusion!"

"Exactly," said Franz.

The two young men were silent for some time, thinking back to their experience of war.

"Did war seem to you a kind of lunacy? Did you suddenly despise all its cruelty and false heroism and that stuff about the Nordic Race, the Superman, the German right to *Lebensraum*, the sacrifice of young men on the altars of the new paganism, whose God was Hitler?"

Nettlenbusch nodded and laughed.

"All that dropped out of my mind as though I had cast off old and verminous clothes. Now I've nothing to put in its place. We Germans who believed in the Führer have no more faith in leadership, or in anything else."

"We must find a faith," said Reber. "Something higher than materialism, something more hopeful than Nihilism, something less ant-like than Communism. There are certain aspects of Christianity—if one could believe."

"One can't!" said Nettlenbusch. "One is asked to believe in miracles. One has to swallow a dogma, which is unreasonable and without evidence."

"We believed in Hitler," said Franz with a laugh. "It's easier and more reasonable to believe in Christ."

"Let's leave out religion," said Nettlenbusch. "Let's answer your question, what are men of our age going to do about Germany's future, if anything?"

"We must accept our share of guilt," said Franz. "We must wash ourselves clean of all that was done by those who dishonoured our name."

"That's nonsense!" said Nettlenbusch. "The German people are guiltless."

"There were many guilty," said Franz. "We're suffering now because of them. The innocent are paying."

"I don't take that view," said Nettlenbusch impatiently. "I'm proud of being a German. I'll never stand in a white sheet before the world!"

"That's all right," said Franz. "But each of us in his own soul must plead guilty in having served the powers of Evil."

"Like all the other nations," said Nettlenbusch. "Our enemies aren't angels!"

"No!" said Franz. "They too have to get clean after this filthy war. They too must wipe war out of their souls as the lowest degradation of civilized man."

"They're preparing for another now," said Nettlenbusch, "Germany will be the No Man's Land between their armies."

Franz gave a groan.

"If it happens again we shall all be blotted out. We must prevent it happening again. That seems to me our job as young Germans."

"How—in God's name?" asked Nettlenbusch who did not believe in God.

"By acting as mediators between East and West, or at least by holding the balance between East and West, by refusing to fight on either side, by acting as missionaries of a new faith which renounces war, defends the liberty of the spirit and offers friendship to its former enemies. Something of that sort. The old French watchword, '*Liberté, Egalité, Fraternité*', reaching up to a more spiritual vision of man's Destiny."

He looked at Nettlenbusch again and laughed and shrugged his shoulders.

"Excuse me, my dear Nettlenbusch, I'm talking like a fool. I'm babbling in my dreams."

Nettlenbusch sprang from his chair, the only chair, and thumped his hand on to his friend's shoulder.

"My dear fellow," he answered, "you're either drunk—and it's too early in the morning and German beer has no strength—or you talk as one inspired. You must form a new Party. I'll join it and be your standard-bearer. We shall probably be killed or put into a concentration camp as a dangerous and subversive sect. *Heil Reber!*"

He was half-jesting, but half-serious.

Franz laughed.

"No more standard-bearers. But we who survived the War must dedicate ourselves secretly, or in comradeship, to preventing the Third World War which would be the last of all. Don't you agree? Or do you disagree completely?"

Nettlenbusch tapped him on the chest with a clenched fist.

"Agree or disagree? These ideas have never entered my head before. They want thinking out. They need endless discussion—preferably over mugs of beer. But, my dear fellow, you mustn't shut up those ideas in a little room over a stable. You must meet a group of my comrades—serious fellows groping about for guidance, trying to shape some new philosophy. Come and talk to them."

"No," said Franz. "I won't talk to them, but I'll talk with them. I shall learn something from them."

"I'll make up a party," said Nettlenbusch. "We will talk to the small hours of the morning. We'll talk like men risen from the dead, that is to say very seriously and with truth. In the course of the conversation some of us may desire to kill each other, but I shall be glad to risk it. There's a pleasant tavern in Kaulbach."

He went away in good-humour and intellectually excited.

CHAPTER XXVII

HERR VON ARNHEIM returned looking weak and ill. There was a heavy bruise down one side of his face. About this he shrugged his shoulders and refused to talk about it.

"The American police are not all angels of mercy."

To his family it was appalling that he had been half-starved and had lost six stone during his imprisonment.

"There's no excuse," cried Christel. "The Americans have all the food in the world and they waste masses of it. The English starve their prisoners but excuse themselves by saying they haven't any food to give them. The French starve their prisoners and are brutal as well. But one would expect more from the Americans."

Her father refused to talk about his prison experiences but said something in favour of the Americans, or at least of two Americans.

"I owe my liberty to the work of Captain Welles and Colonel Hoffmann. Without their good offices I should still be in prison under a false charge."

Christel was rebuked by those words and spoke emotionally.

"Captain Welles, of course, is one of the kindest-hearted men on earth."

Her face coloured up and she gave a light self-conscious laugh remembering a certain kiss she had given to a certain American officer as a reward for her father's liberation.

To Franz the home-coming of Herr von Arnheim was an event of importance in the development of his mind. He came in contact for the first time with a man who had read deeply in philosophy and history—an old-fashioned scholar—whose mind was steeped in a Liberalism which once had been strong in Germany but had died under Bismarck and the Prussians.

In his study one day Franz made an apology for having talked so freely to a man of his years and knowledge.

"To you, Sir, it's just old stuff which worked in German minds as far back as 1848."

Herr von Arnheim smiled at him and made a courteous gesture of denial.

"My dear fellow, there's no new idea under the sun. There are only good ideas and bad ideas. Almost every political system and theory has been tried out since the time of Plato and they've all revealed their own imperfections. But Liberalism is more a spirit than a system. It's a way of looking at things and feeling about things. It means a tolerant mind capable of understanding another point of view, being willing at least to listen. It means a belief, deep in the heart down to the very marrow of one's bones, in the liberty of the individual mind and the liberty of people in a civilized State to have their own faith, their own home life, their own property, provided it's not hurtful to their neighbours. Liberalism abhors tyranny. It loathes a police-controlled State. It has faith and hope that one day the human mind in many nations will be civilized enough, Liberal-minded enough, to settle differences without war and ultimately, perhaps, to establish some kind of world government, a European Parliament or a World Parliament to ventilate grievances and to arrange new methods of international co-operation."

He checked himself with a good-natured laugh.

"*Mein Gott!* I'm talking to you like a German professor of the eighteen-forties. Pardon me, my dear young man. I'm one of the have-beens, old and broken and put on the shelf, but you and men of your age have the future destiny of Germany in your hands or at least in your minds. What you think now—good ideas or bad ideas—will decide not only the fate of Germany, but of Europe and civilization. From what you tell me you seem to be thinking on the right lines. I'm convinced that we Germans must first of all regain our moral status among nations and then lead a crusade if necessary to regain the lost faith in international Liberalism. Only by that means shall we defeat the tyranny of Communism on one side and the renaissance of Hitler's type of nationalism on the other."

Franz Reber was deeply impressed. This German baron—Hilde's father, a scholar and thinker, was putting into words and producing historical and philosophical support for ideas which had been moving vaguely and uncertainly in his own mind.

He sprang to his feet excitedly.

"You must give us a lead, sir. You must speak to big crowds of ex-soldiers like myself. We're all so ignorant. We're all so bewildered. We're all so sunk in despair."

"My dear lad," said Herr von Arnheim in his kindly and self-deprecatory way, "I'm no politician and I'm old and battered."

He put his hand to the scar on his face and was silent for a moment as though thinking back to some unpleasant episode.

"It's for a young man like you to raise the torch and inspire his comrades."

"I'm an artist," said Franz. "I have no gifts of leadership. I distrust leadership though I asked you to give us a lead. I mean I'm afraid lest we throw up a new Hitler or a German Stalin."

Herr von Arnheim looked at him gravely and gave a deep drawn sigh.

"That's one of the dangers. If the Allies exasperate the German people too much, if we're given no chance of independence and a decent level of prosperity after we have paid—God knows we have to pay for much—they'll be tempted to follow some loud-mouthed Nationalist of the Hitler type or some ruthless imitation of Lenin and Stalin. You must help to prevent that, my dear fellow."

"I?" asked Franz with an uneasy laugh. "Some of my comrades think I'm daft or a crawling disciple of a weak-kneed creed."

"Talk to them," said Herr von Arnheim, "go on talking to them here in the village of Kaulbach and later perhaps in Munich. Some will listen to you. Some will agree with you. Presently you will form a group of German Liberals. The Apostles were only a small group, but they conquered the soul of the world. A tiny seed may grow into a tall tree. I'll give you some books to read. They were written by noble minds—the old German Liberals—some of whom fought and died for their faith."

"A thousand thanks," said Franz. "I'm deeply ignorant."

He left the study that evening with three old books under his arm. Hilde met him in the hall and made a laughing remark.

"You and my father seem to be conspiring together. Nothing sinister, I hope?"

"I'm his disciple," answered Franz, answering her laugh; "he knows so much and I know so little."

"Time yet!" said Hilde. "The War was very interrupting to

academic studies, but it taught other things which you seem to have learnt."

"What?" he asked.

"Hatred of cruelty. Pity. Love of liberty. The spiritual values."

"You always restore my egoism!" he answered. "You always make me feel a fine fellow, full of virtue instead of a cellar-rat caught in a trap and trying to fight his way out with tooth and claw."

She laughed at that description of himself.

"I won't flatter your vanity by telling you what I really think of you."

"Yes, do!" he pleaded. "I need encouragement. I'm the victim of an inferiority complex. Please flatter my vanity in order to restore my moral balance."

She smiled and hesitated.

"There was a French knight," she said. "His name was Bayard. What they said about him I think about you."

"Heaven help me!" he cried. "I'm an ignorant fellow. I can't remember what they said about him."

"Turn it up in a book," she said teasingly. "Turn it up in an encyclopædia. Meanwhile come and have a game with the children. That one of the tiger in the jungle was very thrilling to them."

Franz laughed at this tribute to his realistic performance of a tiger.

"I'm pretty good at being an elephant," he said.

That afternoon before the children went to bed he was an elephant in the Berlin Zoo using his right arm as a trunk and giving rides to Hans and Trudel. Then when it was their bedtime he stood up rather shame-faced.

"All this is very childish," he said to Hilde. "For some reason it makes me happy and I never expected to be happy again."

"There's something in an old book," said Hilde. "What is it? Unless ye become as little children. . . . Come and help me put these youngsters to bed. I'm going to give them a hot tub."

It was this chance of home life now and then which seemed the most precious thing to Franz and lifted the darkness from his spirit. Hilde's comradeship, her trust in him, her belief in him, was a soothing balm to his tortured soul. There was nothing he could not say to her, knowing that she would be understanding and wise and tender in her sympathy. He told her all about Magda and she wept when he described her death and told her of his agony.

"So many others are dying like that—so many of our German girls. Tuberculosis is a scourge. And the Pied Piper is calling away so many children. I thank God that Hans and Trudel are now getting enough to eat. We owe most of that to Christel and her friendship with the American officers, and especially with Captain Welles who has the kindest heart."

"I thought she hated them all," said Franz.

Hilde fluttered her eyelashes and laughed.

"I rather think she's beginning to love them. But she's still terrified of losing her pride and patriotism."

"I've lost faith in patriotism," said Franz. "Of course I love Germany. I love the villages and mountains of Bavaria. I love German music and art. I worship the paintings of Pacher and Grünewald, but that doesn't make me want to kill the Americans or the French or the English."

"What about the Russians?" asked Hilde, smiling at him and knowing that this question was difficult to answer. But he answered it.

"I don't hate the Russian people. I saw a lot of them in time of war, and the peasants on the collective farms were not much different from ours though more primitive. The only Russians I hate are those who have seized power and hold it by secret police, mass exploitation of conquered peoples, slave labour, torture and cold, deliberate, intellectual cruelty. Those men are devils like our own sadists under Hitler and I should shed no tears over their mass execution."

"Trudel has some soap in her eyes," said Hilde, when this serious conversation was interrupted by a sudden yell.

It was Franz who came to the rescue with a sponge.

Afterwards when the children were in bed he told them a story about Goldilocks and the three bears, very simply and humorously for a man who had helped the German Army to smash their way through Russian cities, who had walked over the bodies of his dead comrades, who had seen the full fury and horror of modern war. When he went away on tiptoes following Hilde's signal he took her hand and raised it to his lips and spoke emotionally.

"This home life and your loveliness with the children make me want to shed tears, though I don't know why."

"It's because you've come back to the real values of life," said Hilde.

He was still holding her hand and suddenly she put her forehead on his shoulder and wept a little.

"My Peter will never come back," she cried. "The children will never know their father."

There were no words of comfort he could give her.

CHAPTER XXVIII

It was through Captain Welles that Franz obtained a number of commissions for water-colour drawings of Bavarian life and scenery which helped him to pay his way and even accumulate some savings for future needs. He owed this of course to Christel who introduced him to the American officer and insisted that he should bring some of his sketches.

"Say, that's fine work!" said Captain Welles after studying a few of these drawings. "They'd look very well on my walls in Kansas City if ever I get back to that burg."

"Would they understand such things in Kansas City?" asked Christel in her provocative way.

Captain Welles took no offence. Christel's scorn, or pretended scorn, of American life continued to amuse him.

"Lady," he said, "you'd be surprised at the high standard of civilization in Kansas City. We have a very fine art gallery. We're devoted to music. Most of the distinguished men and women on earth—I admit some of them give me a pain in the neck—come to lecture to us and dine at our tables, and accept a hospitality for which they're not in the least grateful. In Kansas City where I had the honour of being born, through no fault of my own, we have several poets of considerable genius. The Kansas City *Star* is one of the best newspapers in the United States and our night clubs make those in Paris look like low dives."

"It sounds very, very dreadful!" said Christel.

Captain Welles grinned at her and returned to his study of Franz Reber's drawings.

"After that digression," he said, "I'd like to say that I'm crazy about these drawings."

"That's very nice of you," said Franz, modestly, but with a little secret contempt for other people's praise. He was his own hardest critic.

"Now I'll tell you what I'd like you to do for me," said Captain Welles. "It's an offer which of course you're perfectly free to refuse, if it doesn't appeal to you."

"May I know?" asked Franz.

"I'd like you to make some sketches in this style of this village of Kaulbach—where I seem to be stationed for life—with the character and costumes of the people in the market-place, going to church, gathered round the post-office, and sitting in the beer taverns. They would be marvellous souvenirs for me of life in a Bavarian village to which fate sent me by strange ways all the way from Kansas City. I know I'm asking a favour, Mr. Reber. One doesn't order these things from an artist as one orders shoes or socks from the local store."

Christel was enthusiastic and excited.

"Franz, isn't that a grand idea? Captain Welles is a millionaire in his private life. He's the King of Kansas. If he likes your drawings he'll heap dollars upon you. He won't ask for change."

Captain Welles smiled at her dryly and then at Franz.

"Miss Christel exaggerates—slightly. I'm not actually the King of Kansas but I have a nice little job waiting for me in the Kansas City bank—second cashier behind golden bars. I should be happy to pay fifty dollars for each drawing if that's not too little for such very fine work."

Christel stared at Franz as though she had heard the announcement of a miracle. There was a kind of wonderment in her eyes. Franz's face flushed heavily and he shook his head.

"Far too much," he said. "Ten dollars would be more than enough. It's all I would consent to take."

"Oh, foolish Franz!" cried Christel. "Oh, the imbecility of men! He refuses the wealth of the Indies. He rejects principalities and powers. He is willing to accept the beggarly sum of ten dollars."

So she cried out but in her heart ten dollars was no beggarly sum. It was like a prince's ransom.

Captain Welles laughed loudly.

"Ten dollars won't hurt me so much," he said, "so we'll make it that, and perhaps you'll do more drawings for me. You might go as far afield as Munich. The ruins are very picturesque."

"And when you get back to Kansas City," said Christel, "you can stand in front of Franz's drawing, when you're shaving, and strike your breast and say: 'That was a crime for which there was no excuse. Just wanton destruction of lovely buildings and priceless treasures."

"Maybe," answered Captain Welles calmly. "But I'll adjust the balance on the same wall above my shaving mirror by pictures of the desert round St. Paul's Cathedral, London, and the devastation in Warsaw."

"Nothing comparable!" cried Christel. "And you shelled Dresden at the end of the War when we were ready to surrender."

"We don't see eye to eye on these things," said Captain Welles calmly. "The Germans continue to wallow in their woes, forgetful of all the destruction they inflicted upon innocent folk whose lands they invaded without provocation."

Christel laughed and Franz was astonished to see her go to Captain Welles and thrust her long fingers through his well-brushed hair.

"For the love of Mike! . . ." cried Captain Welles, looking slightly embarrassed. He gave Christel a pat on her behind, still further astonishing Franz Reber.

'These two seem to be on very familiar terms,' he thought.

He took his leave shortly afterwards having promised to do some of the drawings.

CHAPTER XXIX

TIME had long gone by now since the period of no fraternization between the Americans and Germans. It was an inhuman policy which could not be maintained for any length of time. American G.I.s billeted with Germans found them very decent folk, remarkably like their own farming folk or small-town folk in Massachussetts or the Middle West. In villages which had escaped the worst bombing they kept their houses spotless and their pots and pans burnished like silver, even though there was precious little to cook therein. The way of friendship came often through the children who taught the American soldiers bits of German and spoke a little English with a very good American accent. American G.I.s from Texas or Kentucky, Missouri or Wisconsin, Virginia or Georgia could not harden their hearts for any length of time to the small German boys and girls who looked like pictures in an American fairy-tale book.

Even in the days of hostility by Command—one of General Eisenhower's mistakes—some of them slipped candies, chocolates, and a bit of canned food to children whose pallid faces and roving eyes told of semi-starvation or at least severe under-nourishment. If a German girl—pretty or even plain—lugged along a heavy sack or a load of wood for winter fuel it was not within human nature for good-natured young Americans to refuse an offer of aid, "Say, Missy, let's give you a hand. Pretty heavy, ain't it?" There was the same pull between a young man and woman if a German, girl were pumping water out of a well, chopping up logs of wood, milking a cow, or feeding pigs. "Say, Missy, can I give you a hand? *Sprechen Sie Englisch? Nur ein Bischen?* That's O.K. with me, *Fräulein.*"

Presently, because an Army of Occupation must amuse themselves or go mad, there were dances arranged for the entertainment of American soldiers not only with official permission but organized by their officers. At first German girls were reluctant to go. Their fathers and mothers were hostile and apprehensive, but it soon became known that these dances were conducted with perfect decorum, and with the senior officers present with their ladies. The bitterness of war, the arrogance of victors, the humiliation of defeat was gradually passing, or at least being softened by personal contacts of a more human friendly kind.

Even Christel, critical and hostile at first towards all Americans, found herself on friendly terms with a number of American officers in addition to Captain Welles. It was her skill and knowledge in the art of skiing which brought her into touch with them and put her into the position of being their guide and teacher. Some of them were complete novices and their laughter, and hers, rang out across the mountain slopes when they lost control of their legs, became entangled in their skis and raised a maddening whirl of legs and arms deep buried in a snow-drift. American cries of dismay ascended to the steel blue sky above the Bavarian Alps.

"Gee! . . . For the love of Mike! . . . Jeepers Creepers!"

Christel was a good teacher and highly amused by the agonies and physical frustrations of these American young men trying to master the technique of a sport which to her was as simple as walking or breathing. They watched her with astonishment and admiration.

"Look. Here I go! It's a question of balance. A little forward. . . . Goodbye!"

She swooped down the mountain-side deep in new fallen snow as white and smooth as a sheet of Irish linen but gleaming in the sunlight of a Bavarian sky. It was like flying. She felt like a bird. Her eyes tingled and smarted in the cold air rushing against her face. Her lungs were filled with its coldness which she breathed in like the elixir of life. Her body tense and yet not rigid swayed in an easy rhythm obeying her mind, fine and delicate in its balance.

To Christel this was the supreme joy of life, the most perfect happiness of mind and body in complete harmony and conscious of power, skill and control, with every sense alert. Her eyes saw beauty rushing by. Her ears heard the whirr of her skis and the harp of the wind made by her own flight. She breathed in the smell of dry snow, of pine trees, of woodcutter's fires. With the sense of touch she felt the impact of the air in every living cell of her body, the tingle of life in every muscle. It was the joy of flight unknown to the man who manœuvred an engine. Her own body was her engine. She was like an eagle swooping from a mountain erie.

High up on the mountain-side the little group of American officers watched her downward flight and shouted out to each other:

"Say, boy, she's just marvellous!"

"It takes one's breath away to watch her. Gee! If she had not missed that tree! It's spectacular. That girl sure has courage."

"She must have been born on a pair of skis."

"It's a pity there's such a long climb up again."

It certainly was a pity for Christel that there was such a long climb up again. In the old days with Paul she had thought nothing of it but after two years of under-nourishment it was a harder pull. Her heart felt very jumpy now and then several times—it gave a kind of lurch which frightened her—it was after she had had an attack of coughing—a queer hollow-sounding cough. She spoke to her heart as she might have spoken to a restive pony.

"Steady there, my girl! Steady! Don't be silly!"

After one of these attacks she took it more slowly going up and gave a little mock curtsey—though she was dressed as a boy in her skiing outfit—when her reappearance was greeted by a round of applause.

"Lady," said one of the American officers, "we watched you with awe and admiration."

"There would be a lot of gate-money to see you do that in Massachussetts," said another young man.

"It's your poise that's so perfect," said Captain Welles.

Christel could not conceal from herself that she liked this admiration and its generous expression warmed her towards these American officers and through them to their people and country whom theoretically she hated. They were friendly and simple-minded young men. They were ignorant, of course. None of them except Captain Welles had read Goethe's *Faust*. None of them had read a line of Kant or Spinoza or Hegel, though they seemed to know the names of those philosophers. They were startled and astonished when they discovered that she knew the novels of Sinclair Lewis and the best stories of O. Henry.

"Gee!" exclaimed one of them. "How have you found time to read so much, *Fräulein*—all your own literature and so much of ours? How about English? Any of Shakespeare's plays?"

Christel laughed. It was the belief of every German that they knew more of Shakespeare than the English themselves.

"Of course!"

The young officer tried her with a modern writer.

"Galsworthy's *Forsyte Saga*?"

"Of course!"

"It's fantastic!" said the American officer.

These new friendships with his brother officers were not altogether pleasing to Captain Welles and he mentioned this one day to Christel.

"You always have a crowd with you now. When am I going to be alone with you?"

"Do you want to be alone with me?" she asked, avoiding his eyes. "Don't you find that rather boring?"

"I want to be alone with you on the top of a mountain," he told her. "I don't want any of these other guys within ten miles of us. You taught me skiing first, didn't you? Aren't I your best pupil?"

She could not deny that he was her best pupil. He hadn't started at scratch. He knew quite a bit about skiing but she had improved his style and control and rhythm. She had to admit that he was quite good.

"Let's make an expedition on our own tomorrow morning," he said. "Let's give the others the slip. I'll drive you out to the lower slopes of the Wachserstein and I'll provide sandwiches and tea in a thermos flask. How's that?"

"Fine!" said Christel.

So it happened on a glorious morning when the air was like champagne and after the clearing of a thin mist the sun glinted on the brown roofs of Bavarian villages in the valley and touched the snow-clad mountains with a magical light.

Once or twice during the drive Captain Welles slowed down to tuck Christel more warmly in a fur rug.

"That's a nasty cough you've got," he said. "You ought to see a doctor about it."

She jeered at him.

"You treat me as if I were a doll. I'm as hard as nails. I'm what you call a tough guy."

"Tough guys can catch cold," he answered. "I knew a tough

guy who was cut off in early manhood by a cold in the nose which developed into pneumonia. He was the champion middleweight in Kansas City."

Once during the drive he looked at her sideways.

"Apart from that cough, you're looking fine," he told her.

"I'm feeling fine. A bit tired perhaps. I seem to get tired."

"You have the colour of a midsummer rose."

"One can get that out of a bottle. Besides some roses are yellow."

"Yours is natural," he said. "That's why I like you so much. You're natural all through, body and soul."

"How do you know?" she asked. "I don't think you ought to know as much as that."

He grinned over his wheel.

"You've something in common with my Aunt Elizabeth," he said. "She comes from New Bedford where they're plain of speech and very downright. I'll be glad for you to meet her one day. She'll be glad to know you."

"Unless she comes to Germany," said Christel, "that meeting will never happen."

"Uh—huh?"

He made a funny non-committal noise and studied the road again and took a hairpin bend with skill and courage.

Half-way up the mountain-side he took advantage of a plateau on the side of the road which now ended.

"What about these sandwiches?" he asked.

"My only doubt about them is whether you've brought enough," said Christel.

Six each and not enough for Christel though she refused sternly to accept one of his.

"We have a Bavarian saying, 'Good comrades share all'."

Captain Welles nodded and withdrew the offer of his last sandwich.

"I'd like that saying to be my guide through life—if I have the right comrade."

"It's difficult to find the right comrade," said Christel. "I mean for the long journey through life. I've known some who fail one on a two-hours climb. They begin to make excuses, they drop behind, they show the white feather."

"Yes, it's difficult," said Captain Welles. "Have some hot tea out of this flask."

"*Danke schön.*"

"*Bitte schön.*"

"But one knows somehow when one has found the right guy," said Captain Welles after this interruption of thought.

"Not always," said Christel. "One might be let down."

"I don't think so. My experience is that one knows the fellow who's going to be a good scout instantly with one look into his eyes. I've seldom been mistaken. I include women of course."

Captain Welles looked sideways at Christel to see whether she agreed with this. She did not agree altogether.

"Women can judge other women like that but men can't know women or women men by one look at their eyes."

"Why not?"

"They act to one another. Women pretend to be simple when they're very cunning, or charming when they're bad-tempered or innocent when they're vicious. I know them. I've watched them. Tigresses, cats, vampires, furies."

Captain Welles laughed loudly. His laugh was echoed from an opposite slope.

"I dare say one might find some of those even in Kansas City. But I hold to my original remark that I know a good scout man or woman by one look in the eyes."

"Name a woman," said Christel.

It is quite probable that she knew his answer. Her eyes danced before he named the woman.

"Christel von Arnheim."

She laughed and the colour he had liked heightened, proving that it had not come out of a bottle.

"She hated you and she insulted you. She had hard-boiled eyes and a basilisk tongue. You couldn't have seen any comrade there."

Captain Welles looked into her eyes then.

"My dear Christel," he said, "I read you like an open book. That girl, I thought, when I first saw you, has pride and courage and spirit. She won't flatter me because I might give her cigarettes or candies. She hates me because I come as one of the Army of Occupation. Germany is defeated but she holds her head high.

Any word against Germany makes her mad, just as any word against the United States would make me mad. But she loves beautiful things and she would risk death itself to save her family, and one day if I could win her friendship I should be very glad."

"You've won her friendship," said Christel in a low voice. She slipped her hand into his as they sat together in his car. "Did you really think like that about me, or are you making it up now?"

"I really thought so, in the first five minutes."

"It was very generous of you," she told him, drooping her head on to his shoulder.

He put his arm behind her and drew her close.

"Christel," he said, "you say I've won your friendship but I want something more than that. I want your love."

"It's yours," she answered. "You know that. You're such a clever man you know everything!"

She was jeering at him again.

"For ever and ever?" he asked. "For all our lifetime? In whatever place?"

"Any place almost except America," she answered. "Persia, India, France, Italy, even England, but not the United States of America. Peru, Nicaragua, the Argentine Republic . . ."

He kissed her on the lips and prevented her geographical list from going further.

"Now, Christel darling," he said, "I want to tell you about a place called Kansas City."

"I believe you've invented it," she answered. "I don't believe there's any such place."

"Girlie," said Captain Welles, "it's a fine city and my folk live there. It's crowded with beautiful women most of them like goddesses and some of them as ugly as sin. It has magnificent hotels, tall buildings reaching the sky, very good shoe-shine shops, drug stores at every corner, night clubs with almost naked ladies, churches with very fine preachers, avenues, parks, and stores where one may buy every luxury provided by a crazy world. Kansas City, my dear child, is a hell of a place and that's where I'm going to take you one day."

"I should hate it," said Christel. "And I'm not going there."

"Now, child," said Captain Welles. "Don't you quarrel with

Destiny. It's no good trying to thwart old man Destiny. He ain't going to be thwarted. And let me tell you a few other things about Kansas City. You can forget all the others. Just remember these. In Kansas City are my friends, as straight a bunch of guys as you could meet in the whole world, and those friends of mine are going to be your friends. They'll be a kind of bodyguard round you defending you from any objectionable people or less-pleasing aspects of American life. Some of them are artists who appreciate beauty, and musicians who love music. They'll give you a good time. And my father will fall in love with you, and my mother will do her darndest to make you happy. And in Kansas City you'll find good comradeship, unending hospitality and my great love always at your service. Any good to you?"

"I'm a German," said Christel. "I can't leave Germany and my people in their time of suffering. Don't ask me to, Robert. Stay with me here. Love me here."

"I'll love you here," he told her. "But I'm not staying in Germany much longer. I have to get back to my old job in Kansas City."

"Let's forget that!" cried Christel. "Love me now."

He put his arms about her again and she lay with her head on his shoulder. Their skis poked out of the right-hand window of the car but they returned that afternoon without any snow on their boots, which needed some explanation on the part of Captain Welles when questioned by his fellow-officers. There was no snow on his boots but something of the brightness of the Bavarian sky had caught his eyes.

CHAPTER XXX

Captain Welles was greatly pleased by Franz Reber's sketches of Bavarian life and scenery. He did them in charcoal with a touch of colour and they were certainly strong and full of character according to one judge whose opinion Franz valued most of all. That was Hilde Menzel to whom he showed them before handing them to the American.

"*Wunderschön!*" she told him. "Your figure drawing is full of spirit and you've caught the beauty of the mountains. One day you'll be famous, Franz."

He laughed and shrugged his shoulders.

"Fame is mostly nonsense. But I shall be glad to earn a few American dollars."

He earned more than a few. Captain Welles showed the drawings to brother officers who admired them greatly and were willing to pay a good price for others like them.

"I'm becoming embarrassed by my wealth," Franz confided to Hilde one day. "I've a wallet full of dollars. If this goes on I shall become corrupted by money which someone said a long time ago is the root of all evil."

"A certain amount is very useful," said Hilde, laughing at his dismay.

"An artist must keep poor," he told her. "Directly he's successful he's lost. He loses his soul. Besides there's something frightful in the idea of becoming rich in Germany while every day the tide of refugees comes to increase our population or workless and starving folk."

Hilde reassured him laughingly.

"Don't be scared, Franz. You're not a millionaire yet. I don't suppose you earn as much in a month as an expert on the Black Market makes in half an hour. Besides I don't believe you're keeping many of those dollars. Wouldn't it be a good idea to spend a few on yourself instead of making presents to all your friends? What about a new shirt or a new pair of boots? I hesitate to mention a new suit of clothes. You're still wearing your old uniform and it's getting green and threadbare."

"Oh, that will last me a long time yet," he answered carelessly. "I shouldn't know myself in a new suit. I should feel a stranger."

He sent some of his dollars to Baümer in Berlin asking him to give them to the refugees. In Munich he bought some toys for Hans and Trudel and searched the antique shops for something which Hilde might like, finding at last a little wooden statue of the Virgin and Child of the 14th century, exquisitely carved. It cost more dollars than he could really afford. He found himself in the ridiculous situation of having to borrow some marks from Paul von Arnheim to pay for that week's lodging until he had been paid for a few more drawings. It was a financial miscalculation due to the inexperience and carelessness but for some reason it gave him a secret pleasure.

"Thank God I'm not so rich as I thought I was," he said to himself. "Those dollars began to stink. The only thing is to get rid of them as quickly as possible. It's not really difficult. One can always give them away."

Hilde was enchanted with her wooden carving but rebuked him for extravagance.

"I believe it cost a lot of money," she told him.

"A few marks," he said carelessly. "If it pleases you there's no more to be said."

"It pleases me as much as the toys pleased the children," said Hilde, "and that is a joy beyond words as you heard by their screams of delight. But, Franz, my dear, there's no need to give me presents. Your friendship is enough."

"You give me the only joy I know," he told her. "This glimpse of home life, your company now and then, your sympathy and comradeship. Won't you let me pay back something—a tiny gift as a token of my love?"

She put her hand out and touched his.

"If it pleases you," she answered. "I want to make you happy, Franz. I pray a lot for your happiness after so much suffering."

"I'm not unhappy," he told her. "Sometimes when I'm with you I feel strangely happy with all wounds healed. You've the healing touch, Hilde, but I mustn't take advantage of it by coming too often."

"Come always when you can spare the time," she answered. "I need you as much as you need me."

These words brought sudden light into his eyes.

"Hilde!" he cried. "How generous of you to say that! How wonderful if you think so. Perhaps Fate or Destiny. . . ."

He dared say no more but stood there abashed like a man who is fearful of misunderstanding some message of great joy.

"Oh, my dear," cried Hilde. "Why are you so shy of me? Why do you want me to tell you how much I love you?"

"Hilde!" he exclaimed. "Oh, my dear heart, I'm not worthy. . . ."

She held out her arms to him and he strode forward and took her hands and drew her close to his body and kissed her forehead until she clasped his head and drew his face down to hers.

The revelation of Hilde's love for him was a source of joy which transfused the whole mind and spirit of a man who had been battered by tragic experience. He felt now that everything in his past life had led up to this—even the death of Magda. He had fumbled his way through darkness and suddenly had come out into the light. All bitterness was gone, all self-pity, all despair. He could see, newly revealed, the beauty of life. It was like a reincarnation. He felt that he had been born again, with new perceptions, new sensibility, new courage to face whatever might happen. So Franz Reber told himself, uplifted by a mystical ecstasy yet humble because of his reverence of Hilde.

Anyhow he felt inspired by her to carry on, not only with his work as an artist but with his conviction that the ex-soldiers of Germany, that is to say all German youth, should think out some policy and plan for the future based upon a liberal idealism which had been trampled underfoot by a brutal philosophy leading up to Hitler and his ruffians. In his little room above the stable in the village of Kaulbach, Franz sat up late at night studying the books lent to him by Hilde's father and to this room came, one by one, or sometimes two by two, so that there was hardly room, young men of his own age and experience who were attracted by his ideas or followed the same line of thought. Now and then a group of them met in some nearby tavern and talked half through the night. A bigger group of them met once a week in Munich in one of the old eating-houses which before the War had been famous in many lands. No tourists came now and there was little to eat, but the wenches, not so buxom as in pre-war days, were pleased to see a crowd of young men, some without arms and some without legs, taking their places again on the long benches.

"What are you boys talking about?" asked one of them. "You're not trying to bring back the Nazis, I hope."

There was a roar of laughter.

"Nothing like that," said Paul. "It would be more true to say that we're trying to bring back Jesus Christ. At least we believe, most of us, in the Sermon on the Mount. Or am I wrong, comrades?"

"Religion is barred," said one of the men. "Each man has the right to his own faith, but what we want to form is a political philosophy—one day perhaps a political party—which has for its basis a broader comradeship between nations and a Liberal regime in a united Germany. Isn't that our programme?"

"We haven't got as far as a programme," said Franz. "These meetings are for free discussion. We don't want political speeches but friendly conversation. Above all we want to keep our sense of humour and avoid fanaticism. By talking and arguing we clarify our own minds—if we happen to have one."

"Fanaticism," said Nettlenbusch, "is only another name for the other fellow's strong convictions with which we disagree. I have a strong conviction that Russia is resolved to oust the English and Americans from Berlin in order to create a central government, pack it with Communists and create a so-called People's Republic —that is to say a puppet state of the U.S.S.R."

"We all agree with that," shouted Paul von Arnheim. "It's a platitude, my dear fellow!"

"How can we resist it?" asked another man. "How can we resist anything? The English and Americans dismantle our factories in the West rather more slowly than the Russians have already dismantled them in the East. The French cut down our forests and grab all they can. Our miners in the Ruhr are slave workers who produce coal for our enemies and starve us of steel for the rebuilding of Germany. We sit here and talk like chattering monkeys in a zoo while Germany sinks deeper into the mud."

"The English," said Franz, "are helping to feed our people in the West in spite of their own shortages and desperate poverty."

"Not because they love us," said another man, "but because

they're scared of Russia and want us to fight on their side next time. Nothing doing as far as I'm concerned."

Nothing doing in that line as far as most of them were concerned. These young men had had enough of war. Like Franz himself they were in revolt against that method of argument. They had seen too much of its horror. They bore its marks on their bodies. Their minds were groping for some new conception of life, some new order in the world, which would make war unnecessary and obsolete.

"We must all go Communist," said one young man who had lost a leg in Russia, and had hobbled in on crutches. "If we all go Communist—the whole world—there will be peace among nations. Isn't that the only hope? Isn't it the way of commonsense? Communism is the new religion. It's the new pattern of life. It's as inevitable as the incoming tide."

"Shut up!" shouted Paul von Arnheim. "Chuck him out! We don't want Communists at this table."

"There's nothing we can't discuss," said Franz. "But let us hear from our comrade, Ollenhauer, who has just escaped from the Russian zone."

Ollenhauer was a thin, haggard-looking young man with deep-sunk eyes and sharp cheekbones. He spoke slowly in a low-toned voice.

"I was on the Russian side of the line until a week ago," he said. "I was a prisoner of war in Russia for three years. Then I enlisted in the military police force which the Russians are organizing in their zone—500,000 of us. Shall I tell you what will happen if Germany goes Communist?"

"Tell us, Ollenhauer," said Franz.

He answered very quietly but with a kind of burning passion behind his words.

"If Germany goes Communist it will be an acceptance of slavery and human degradation. None of us here would have any rights or any liberty. There would be mass deportation of our young men and boys. There would be bloody purges of those suspected of coldness or hostility to the Soviet State. There would be new concentration camps crowded with political prisoners who would die like flies because of starvation and forced labour. Our farmers would be driven into collective farms as wage slaves for the State. In every village and in every tenement-house there would be a kommissar and police spy to report on the careless word of some young man or woman. There would be schools of torture for police experts. I know all about that. . . ."

He gave a shudder and his hand trembled as it rested on the table in front of him.

"There were horrors in Germany," said Franz. "Our own concentration camps weren't beautiful places. We had our own torturers. What we have to do—what the world has to do—is to thrust these things away—these devilish cruelties, these human apes and degenerates, this uprising of evil and abomination. We must co-operate with the decent peoples. We must take a leap forward to a new order of Christian democracy. Perhaps we Germans may be destined to lead the world back to sanity and spiritual values. But first of all we must find our own soul and our own faith."

"We're all bewildered," said Nettlenbusch. "We're all sceptics. Personally I can't believe in any dogma or so-called revelation. I believe only in comradeship, the glory of old Mother Nature and the love of a pretty girl."

This *credo* of an agnostic was received with a shout of laughter which thrust back the shadow cast over this company by the tale of Ollenhauer from the Russian zone.

All over Germany young men were talking like this, arguing, thinking, brooding and joining new political parties which one day, not far ahead, would crystallize into the Social Democrats and the Christian Democrats and the Bavarian Liberals and other groups to the right or left who would decide the fate of the German people.

These meetings did not interfere with Franz Reber's work as an artist. He was still getting many commissions not only for black-and-white work but for water-colour paintings of Bavarian scenes. He was also doing a portrait in oils of Hilde Menzel as he had longed to do since those evenings with her in Quakenbrück on the flight from Königsberg. It gave him the double joy of sitting with her for an hour or so each day and attempting to reproduce her delicate features and elusive smile on a strip of canvas. Those were his happiest hours talking now and then, building up his portrait—it was coming rather well he thought—exchanging a smile round the corner of his easel. Several times he asked the same question just to get the same answer.

"Do you love me?"

"I've told you so. Don't you believe me?"

"It's incredible. Why do you love a broken fellow like me so clumsy and so ignorant and so commonplace?"

"Now you're fishing for compliments!"

"Not at all. I just want to know why Beauty loves the Beast."

"Didn't the beast change into a fairy prince?"

"I shall never do that. The best I can hope for is to change into a more civilized human being. I'm doing that now. Every hour I spend with you makes me more civilized. Hold that smile for a second. It's just what I want."

She kissed him when he came and when he went, and to hold her in his arms for those few seconds was a kind of ecstasy which he believed was a kind of spiritual experience.

They never spoke about the future or made any plans. It was enough for them to go on loving like this, to be with each other like this, sometimes talking, sometimes silent, not demanding more than that of each other, not losing control of the emotional happiness by any violence of passion. The portrait went on for more than a month and every now and then Hilde came round the back of the easel to look at it.

"Haven't you finished yet?"

"A few more sittings. I don't want to hurry it. How do you like it?"

"No woman knows her own face but I know that you have made me ten times too beautiful."

"It's only the mask of you. I must get more into your eyes. And your mouth is terribly difficult. I'm trying for your smile when you're half serious but with a sense of humour lurking in your kind like a woman who wants to be kissed."

"You make me look like a woman in love."

"That's how I want you to look."

"That's how I feel," said Hilde. "When are you going to kiss me?"

"When I've dealt with this mouth. Just a touch or two."

The portrait was not quite finished when the sittings were interrupted by a miracle as it seemed, which changed everything in the life of these two people. The miracle came by way of the telephone from Berlin into the room where Franz was painting Hilde.

"Excuse me, dear heart," said Hilde going to answer it.

It was from her Aunt Elizabeth who was speaking emotionally and almost breathlessly.

"Is that you, Hilde? This is Aunt Elizabeth."

"Yes, Aunt."

"Something wonderful has happened. I hardly dare tell you. Oh, Hilde, my darling. . . ."

"What is it?" asked Hilde sharply.

Franz saw her face become very white.

"A batch of ex-prisoners from the Russian zone."

Franz saw Hilde sway a little as though she might fall and he strode towards her. But she spoke again.

"Do you mean Peter is with them? My Peter is alive?"

She listened for a moment and then dropped the receiver and turned to Franz and gave a cry. There was a look on her face of one who has seen or heard a miracle.

"My Peter! He's alive. He's come back. Oh, Franz. I thought he was dead. I thought I knew he was dead."

Franz did not answer. He knew that the coming back of Peter was for him the death of happiness.

Hilde came towards him holding out her hands.

"Oh, Franz," she cried again. "Peter comes first."

"Of course," said Franz. "Peter comes first."

He took Peter's wife in his arms for the last time and she clung to him and wept while he kissed her.

Peter Menzel was brought home on a stretcher, a paralysed man and a living skeleton. He was not like the Peter who had gone away, so gay, so debonair, so quick to laugh with Hilde. He was a haggard, bearded man and so weak that he could hardly lift a hand. But there was a look of intense joy in his eyes when Hilde went down on her knees beside him and put her arms about him and cried his name.

"You're still beautiful!" he said, smiling and touching her face.

"You're still my Peter," she answered.

He shook his head.

"No, not the same Peter. Only the broken husk of what I was."

He began to cry but tried to smile again after that weakness.

"I'll be your nurse, Peter," said Hilde. "I'll bring you back. In a little while you'll be the same Peter as when you went away. My love will make you well, dear heart."

The children were longing to see their father but they looked frightened when they stared at this bearded man who lay there so ugly and so ill.

Trudel sent up a loud cry of terror and had to be taken away from him.

In many homes of Germany the returned prisoners of war from Russia were frightening to their wives and children.

CHAPTER XXXI

"CHRISTEL," said Captain Welles one day, "this is the last time I shall ask for an answer to a very important question which so far you've evaded."

They were sitting in Herr von Arnheim's study. Outside the sun was shining but Christel for once shirked the sunshine and pleaded that she was too tired to go out, and her cough was troublesome.

She turned her head sideways and raised her eyebrows.

"What question do I evade? As a rule I have great candour. You must admit that I've been very frank with you, my dear."

"Brutally frank," he admitted with a laugh. "Except on one point. Are you coming with me to Kansas City? I'm going back. This is my last week in Germany."

Christel turned pale.

"Oh, that's tragic," she cried. "I shall miss you terribly."

"You won't miss me if you come with me," he answered. "That's what I want to arrange. We'll be married in Kaulbach. We'll have a Bavarian wedding. Then we'll fly away to a honeymoon in Kansas. Are you going to say yes and come willingly or shall I have to carry you off screaming and struggling?"

It was perhaps the fifteenth time that he had pleaded with her to go with him and always she had put him off in her laughing, teasing way, but this time the question had to be answered. Time was running out. Arrangements would have to be made.

She sat up, clasping her hands round her knees, and spoke seriously for once.

"I can't come with you, Robert. There are so many reasons against it."

"Give me one."

"I'm a German girl."

"No reason at all. I've fallen in love with a German girl. I want to marry her."

Christel put her hand out and held his for a moment.

"Robert," she said, "I'm terribly grateful to you for a thousand things. It's very good of you to love me."

"I just can't help it," he told her with a glint of humour in his eyes.

Christel had no humour in her eyes.

"Shall I tell you what would happen if I came with you to Kansas City?"

"What's your idea about that?" he asked.

"Your father and mother hate the idea of your marrying a German girl. You've already told me that they're not enthusiastic about it. They think it will lead to trouble, and so it would."

"They'll fall in love with you," he answered uneasily.

Christel shook her head.

"They'd be very nice and kind at first, trying to hide their hatred of the Germans. Then one day they'd begin to attack me as though I were responsible for the horrors of the concentration camps. Then I should get mad because being a German girl I defend my own country. There would be a scene I should lose my temper. Your folk would lose theirs. You would try to keep the peace and you'd be very unhappy. Of course secretly you'd take your mother's side. You would have to agree that I had insulted her. Then I should get mad with you. Then you'd get mad with me. You see how utterly impossible it is, dear Robert!"

Captain Welles of the American Army laughed loudly, but not quite easily and mirthfully. This German girl had touched the truth rather closely in her imaginary picture. Already he had had very vexing letters from his father and mother, about his proposal to bring back a German wife. He had kept back most of what they had written but somehow Christel had guessed.

"Now all that is just boloney," he said, "which being translated means *Unfug* or crazy nonsense. America is the Melting Pot. We hold out the glad hand to people of all nations. Our German communities are highly respected. One more German girl in the United States is not going to create a sense of hostility. Far from it. All my friends are going to fall in love with you and I shall be as jealous as hell."

Christel smiled at him.

"There's another reason why I can't come with you," she said.

Captain Welles gave a groan of despair.

"For the love of Mike!" he cried, "you're taking the blue out of the sky and the gold out of the sun."

"I'm a German girl," she said.

"I believe I know that," he admitted.

"As a German girl I'm loyal to my own folk and to my father and mother and to all my friends who have to go through dark days still under-fed, living in the ruins, perhaps having to suffer the horror of a Russian invasion. What they're doing in Berlin—their blockade between the East and West—looks like a challenge of war. We should be the first victims. They would be ruthless against us. I can't run away from all that, leaving my people in the lurch."

"Holy Snakes!" exclaimed Captain Welles in an exasperated way. "That's one of the very reasons why you should come with me. I want to take you away from all this, I want to feed you up on American steaks and ice cream. I want to get some flesh on your bones. I want to take you from the jungle of Europe into a land of Peace and Plenty."

"It doesn't appeal to me," she told him. "I'd rather starve here."

Captain Welles stared at her with a vexed smile. For some little time he was silent and then spoke in quite a different tone.

"Christel, darling, this is serious. It means that we must try to use the right words and say the right things in utter sincerity and truth. My future happiness or unhappiness is at stake on this. That's not so important as your happiness which I believe also hangs on this argument with life. Now I'll be honest and say that you might have difficulty for a time with my parents and perhaps with a few intolerant people in Kansas City, but I believe it would be worth your while to take that risk. I would stand by you and your coming to my home town might be of more than local importance, or at least more than just a family affair. We would stand together for tolerance for the liberal attitude of mind, for friendship between those who were enemies. I've done pretty well in the War. Anything I say will be noticed in the Kansas City *Star*. Anything you said as my wife would get publicity and comment. Together we could do some fine work for educating public opinion. You could be of some little service to Germany. Your character and spirit would not pass unnoticed. Now that's an odd way of making love to you and asking you to be my wife and share my future. It's the darndest queer way of talking to the girl one loves, but I know you feel very deeply about all this and I'm talking to you straight on an intellectual plane above the ordinary love talk. And there's one other thing I want to say in this very long speech. If you'll come with me to Kansas City and take a chance on it I'll promise on my sacred word of honour—so help me God—that if you don't like it—if you find life intolerable—you'll be as free as the wind to come back to Germany and rejoin your people."

"It's very kind of you," said Christel. "I love you very much."

Suddenly she put both her hands to her face and he could see that she was weeping.

"What's the matter?" he cried anxiously. "Say, Christel, my darling, why are you crying like that?"

There was another reason why she could not go with him. She had hidden it from him until now. She had hidden it from her family. She was ill. Only yesterday her doctor had told her how ill she was, though she had guessed it for a long time. Like so many other German girls who had been through the time of hunger she had been attacked by the malignant microbe. "In both lungs, my poor child," said the doctor gravely. She would have to go into a clinic immediately. She would have to stay there perhaps for two years.

"So you see, my dear, I can't come with you," said Christel. "I shall never see Kansas City."

Captain Welles had turned a grey colour like a dead man. He gave a cry of anguish before holding her half-fainting in his arms. That night she was taken away from Kaulbach in an ambulance to the clinic in Munich.

There was a family conference at which the American officer was present. Herr von Arnheim and his wife had been stricken by this news. Their beloved Christel had been a tower of strength to them through the lean and perilous days. Her gay spirit had never faltered. They had been sustained by her courage. Hilde who had come down from Peter's bedside had heard the news with bitter tears.

"Maybe it's not so bad as we think," said Captain Welles. "Lots of people get cured. We mustn't let her stay two years in that clinic. I'll get her out to the Arizona desert. They say it's a sure cure."

He spoke now as one of the family. Herr von Arnheim, who owed his liberation to this American officer, had given his consent to Christel's marriage, though he had hated the idea of her going to the United States.

Every day Captain Welles visited the clinic in Munich and every day he was buoyed up with new hope because Christel looked so well and kept such a cheerful spirit. He had put off his return to the United States and was getting busy about the Arizona idea cabling out to his people. He couldn't understand the gloom of the German doctor and nurses attending Christel. She looked so much better lying there screened off in a long ward with wide open windows. She had lost her pallor and had a beautiful colour like the petals of a June rose as he had told her. He spoke to the doctor privately one day.

"She's doing fine, isn't she?"

The doctor shook his head.

"It's a serious case. I can't hold out much hope."

"But, doctor," said Captain Welles, "she's looking bonny and she keeps up her spirit."

"We shall have to take out some ribs," said the doctor, "if she gets strong enough for the operation. I'm afraid——"

Herr von Arnheim and Hilde had come to sit with Christel. She was talking and laughing with them. This German doctor was a pessimist. In any case she wouldn't be left to languish in this clinic for two dreadful years. If seven miracles were necessary to get her out to Arizona Captain Welles would work them somehow.

He lingered with her one evening after she had been visited by her father and mother and Hilde and the two children. They were all too gloomy about it, thought Captain Welles. They had gone away weeping after some words with the head nurse. It was German emotionalism, he thought. He went back to Christel's bedside.

"How are you feeling, darling?"

She looked up at him and smiled.

"As though I had climbed the Zugspitz. Just a bit tired, you know."

She took his hand and raised it to her lips.

"Kind American!" she said.

She shut her eyes for a time and then opened them to talk about skiing.

"It's like flying," she said. "It's the next best thing to flying."

"You and I will do some skiing in the United States" he said.

She smiled at him and patted his hand.

"Optimist!"

Presently as the sunlight began to fade and the long ward darkened a little she raised herself slightly and gave a little laugh as though her strength had come back and her jesting spirit.

"Robert!" she said.

"Yes, darling? Are you feeling better?"

"I want to send my love to someone. Tell him I'm sorry I was a bit rude to him now and then."

"Who's that?" asked Captain Welles. "The Colonel?"

She laughed again faintly.

"I mean Uncle Sam. He's a tough guy, isn't he, but he has a kind heart. He means well even to the Germans."

"I'll certainly give him your love," said Captain Welles tenderly. "You're looking better, sweetheart. It makes me feel good to hear you laugh again."

"It makes me feel tired," she said. "Put your arms round me. I'll go to sleep in your arms."

She went to sleep in his arms and he held her until a nurse came and laid her down.

"How is she, nurse?" asked Captain Welles.

A sudden terror clutched at his heart.

"She's gone," said the nurse. "Poor child! It's a pity, isn't it? And there are so many of them."

Captain Welles flew back alone to the United States. Christel von Arnheim had flown farther.

CHAPTER XXXII

FRANZ REBER went back to Berlin—a lonely man with a great well of loneliness in his heart. He did not go back to his father's cellar which was now empty. Elsa had married her English sergeant and gone to England. Baümer, his comrade, was working as a schoolmaster and living in the school-house. Franz had his own work to do having been commissioned to illustrate some children's books. He worked and slept in a tiny room cleared for him in Elizabeth von Meissner's house in the Grünewald where sometimes in the evenings he played chess with Hermann, or from which he went out to a political club of Christian Democrats where he met young men who shared his own ideals and hopes—hopes still darkened at times by new disillusionment and disappointment.

He was in Berlin during the time of the Russian blockade which had for its purpose, nakedly revealed, the freezing out of the British and American force and the capitulation of the Berliners to Soviet control by slow starvation and the creeping paralysis of unemployment. That purpose was frustrated, as history tells, by the British and American air lift and by the stoical courage and resistance of the Berliners themselves. The psychological effect of the air lift was to swing them in favour of the Western Powers and to increase their hatred of Russian domination. Day after day, night after night, month after month the traffic in the air never ceased. In fair weather and foul, through fog and snow, the British and American pilots landed their supplies on Gatow airfield. The blockaded city was relieved by a miracle of organization and the courage of youth. There were many crashes and many deaths, but the Berliners were fed. Sitting in their cellars or the basements of ruined houses they heard the ceaseless roar of engines and at dawn when the workers went forth for that day's toil they stared up into the leaden sky and saw the black flocks of birds carrying their loads. Groups of men in the Berlin streets, and girls going to offices and markets, raised their arms and waved to these foreign boys up there who once had been the Enemy flying over Berlin with high explosive bombs and now bringing food for empty stomachs and the insatiable appetite of a hungry city, risking their lives in this work of rescue.

There were cynics among Franz Reber's friends who said, "They don't do it for love of us. It's not for our beautiful blue eyes. Russia is now their enemy. They want us on their side next time."

Winkelnkempler, who once had shared the cellar with Franz, spoke like this one day when they met face to face in the Leipzigerstrasse.

"It makes me laugh," said Winkelnkempler, "when our Berliners cheer the American and English pilots. They just want us as gun-fodder in their next war against Russia. I'll see them in hell first."

Franz looked into the hard passionate eyes of this man of hatred, this man who lived on hatred.

"The enemies of yesterday are the friends of today," he answered quietly. "Our fate as Germans is linked with the Western Powers. Because I'm pro-German and pro-European I'm becoming pro-English and pro-American."

Winkelnkempler's face flushed hotly and his eyes seemed to have fire in them.

"You've been bought!" he said. "What price did they pay? Thirty pieces of silver or a packet of filthy cigarettes?"

Franz answered with a laugh, keeping his temper.

"A bit more than that. The millions spent on the air lift by those who were our enemies and are now our friends. The price of the lives they're going to rescue from starvation."

"You're a collaborator!" shouted Winkelnkempler. "One day you'll be shot like a dog and kicked into the gutter where dead dogs lie."

He turned on his heel and strode away.

It was perhaps friendship with Julian Romilly and through him with other Englishmen—some of those pilots who were flying every day to Berlin and back—which had made Franz Reber lean towards the English as he had told Winkelnkempler.

He had met Romilly one day and would have passed him with a nod or a hand raised in salute but to his surprise Romilly stopped and greeted him warmly.

"My dear Reber! How are you after all this time?"

"I've been in Bavaria," answered Franz. "You are still here?"

Romilly was looking at him with watchful eyes in which perhaps there was a hint of pity, which Franz resented. He knew from the mirror over the basin where he shaved himself that he had a haggard, lean and tragic look. It was the loneliness in his soul.

"Where can we talk?" asked Romilly.

"Why should we talk?" answered Franz, coldly, and yet glad in a way that this young Englishman should be so friendly.

Romilly laughed and ignored the rebuff.

"I want to talk to you. I've missed our conversations in the cellar."

The smile left his lips and he added a few words.

"They had a tragic ending. I was deeply grieved for your sake, believe me, my dear Reber."

Franz knew that he referred to Magda's death though neither of them spoke her name.

"It's kind of you to remember me," he answered.

"Come to my rooms," said Romilly.

It was in Romilly's rooms, not then but on other nights, that Franz met a number of young Englishmen among whom were some of those pilots of the air lift. He found them friendly and frank and very boyish. There was not a trace of enmity in their behaviour to him. They were keen on the job they were doing and many times expressed their admiration for the courage and good-humour of the Berliners.

'These English boys,' thought Franz, 'have no lasting hatred for us. They have the sporting spirit. They don't want to kick a man when he's down. Why can't we be friends with England? What cursed fate has made our roads cross so often?'

He spoke that thought to Romilly one night when they were alone and Romilly answered without that touch of flippancy which sometimes rankled in the mind of Franz.

"Out here most of us see the need of a closer union with your people. The blue print of the future is pretty clearly marked. The Western nations must unite in common defence against the Slav tide. Russia is waiting to thrust her spearheads deeper into Europe wherever there's weakness and disunity. She's very patient in her policy of the cold war and victory by infiltration. If only she could get Germany Sovietized. . . ."

"Never!" exclaimed Franz. "Our prisoners of war who escaped from the Russian zone tell us too much. We know what happens. We shall never walk along that way to hell."

Romilly smiled and raised a delicate hand.

"It's rather a cheerless hell, I agree. But the Russians have been pretty successful in converting a number of Germans to their beautiful ideal of the People's Republic. A great number of your men have joined up in the military police. Isn't that a danger for Western Berlin and Western Europe?"

"Many escape every day," said Franz. "They join up because they're hungry. If any trouble started they would march to our side with arms and ammunition. On their side is a reign of terror and organized starvation for those who dare to resist."

Romilly nodded but seemed to have a doubt.

"The Russians are pretty cunning. They hold out the promise of German unity with Soviet support. Isn't that a temptation to every patriotic German?"

Franz shook his head.

"We shan't walk into that trap," he said. "We've seen its steel jaws."

Among his own friends in Berlin he saw a revival of energy which almost suddenly, like an abrupt transition, replaced the lethargy and hopelessness through which his own soul had passed. The stabilization of German money in the Western zone seemed to work some magic. Men were getting busy again selling and buying. Houses were going up. The Berliners were losing their pallor and there was a new vitality in eyes which had been dull and dead. The Occupying Powers, apart from Russia, were releasing the rigidity of their control. They were encouraging self-government under a Federal State and there was a new generosity of spirit towards the German people. They wanted the good-will of the German people but by a strange inconsistency—turned it to enmity again by dismantling factories and increasing unemployment.

Franz Reber was in a crowd in the Leipzigerplatz watching the results of the election which had given a narrow majority to the Christian Democrats over the Social Democrats and brought into power an old Liberal as Chancellor of the new Federation of German States. Franz was with his friend Baümer who had been his comrade in the darkest days. Baümer, that straw-bearded cynic, held his arm and laughed as Franz stood with the rest of the crowd packed densely in the square.

"You make me laugh," he said. "You look like a man who has seen the clouds open and heard the voice of God."

"I have," said Franz. "The German people have voted overwhelmingly against the enemies of liberty. The new Germany has spoken. Above the heads of the crowds I see the spirit of the Liberal faith. I thank God for that, Baümer."

Baümer laughed again, good-humouredly.

"What you think is the voice of God, my dear friend, is the voice of crafty politicians struggling for power and mouthing Liberal platitudes. The English and Americans talk fine words about German liberty and go on dismantling German factories and turning our hearts sour against them. You see a mirage above the heads of this crowd."

Franz struck his friend a light blow on the shoulder.

"You've no faith," he said. "You're still in the dark tunnel of despair. I've crawled out and see the pale gleam of a new dawn for the German people and for Western civilization."

Baümer put his arm round his friend's shoulders. The pressure of the crowd was heavy upon them. Thousands of young men and women were noisy in the Leipzigerplatz on the night of the election.

"I hope to Christ you're right," said Baümer.

Franz had tears in his eyes for a moment. He felt uplifted and emotional in this crowd.

"We Germans have suffered enough," he said. "We've paid all our debts. We've earned our right to a decent share of human happiness. We've found our soul again."

Baümer turned to look at the face of his friend, the haggard, lean and tragic face of that young man whom he had known first as Sergeant Reber. Now in those sunken eyes of a man who had suffered much, who had been through agony and despair, there was the light of a new vision and a new faith. In this Franz Reber was perhaps alone for in that crowd there were few who shared his hope. They had not yet found a new faith. Their vision of the future was dark and unhappy. Only Sergeant Reber saw that faint gleam ahead.

By his side was a sceptic who saw how much tragic history would be made before the fulfilment of that hope, if it were to be fulfilled.

THE END